MIDNIGHT'S TWINS

Books by Holly Race

Midnight's Twins
A Gathering Midnight
A Midnight Dark and Golden

MIDNIGHT'S TWINS

HOLLY RACE

HOT KEY BOOKS

First published in Great Britain in 2020 by
HOT KEY BOOKS
4th Floor, Victoria House, Bloomsbury Square, London WC1B 4DA
Owned by Bonnier Books
Sveavägen 56, Stockholm, Sweden
www.hotkeybooks.com

A CIP catalogue record for this book is available from the British Library.

ISBN: 978-1-4714-0916-5
Also available as an ebook and in audio

2

This book is typeset using Atomik ePublisher
Printed and bound in Great Britain by Clays Ltd, Elcograf S.p.A.

MIX
Paper from responsible sources
FSC® C018072

Hot Key Books is an imprint of Bonnier Books UK
www.bonnierbooks.co.uk

To Ada

My other heroine

'The youthfull knight could not for ought be
staide,
But forth unto the darksome hole he went,
And looked in. His glistring armor made
A litle glooming light, much like a shade'

– Edmund Spenser, *The Faerie Queene*

PROLOGUE

August 2005

The street was full of dreams and some of them were dangerous. Trolls stepped forth from the concrete undercuts of the Southbank and did battle with packs of wildcats. Cockroaches and rats swarmed towards squeamish dreamers. The flourish of a whale's spout arched up out of the Thames and over the balustrade, spraying Una in lukewarm river water.

What Una feared, though, was not a dream at all. The treitre had tracked her from Trafalgar Square, down to the river and across the flotsam-topped water. She thought she had lost it when she went underground, but now she could feel it nearby. Awareness crawled along her arms and up the back of her neck. Somewhere, it was watching her.

She had been stupid going underground, where she didn't have a clear idea of direction. Now she'd made the final leg of her journey even harder. She had to get back to Tower Hill, which meant that she'd need to cross the river once more and approach her portal from the south instead of the north, as she had planned. Well, there was no point in beating herself up about it now. She had panicked when she spotted the treitre, it was as simple as that, and not one knight would have blamed her.

Una peered around the corner. Above her, a flock of vultures circled a pair of dreamers. Vultures in this world didn't tend to wait for carrion – they made their own.

No, she couldn't help them. She mustn't. She wasn't a knight any more. Her obligation was to her family now. No. Absolutely not. *Don't even think about it, Una.*

Damn it.

Snatching a heavy stone from the ground, she broke cover, running in superhuman strides towards the dreamers. Was that a flash of gold beneath the archway to her left, or was her mind playing tricks on her? The scar on her arm – barely visible in Ithr but still a fault line of skin and flesh in Annwn – prickled with the memory of its making. If it was the treitre she had better make this stupid charge worthwhile. She measured her leaps as she drew closer to the dreamers. The vultures were hovering in the gathered lull that precedes an attack. She adjusted her grip on the stone, drew back her arm . . .

Tap tap, tap tap.

Shit. It was behind her. Bile seeped into her mouth but she did not falter. The stone hit one of the vultures squarely in the chest, and with a firework boom the vulture exploded back into inspyre. Una didn't wait to watch – she was already sprinting down the riverbank, away from the clattering gait of the treitre. A raking screech told her that the other vultures had diverted their attention to her as well. Their shadows made whirlwinds on the pavement around her, growing darker and thicker as they descended. One dived, its claws ripping at her hair. She knocked it off and built up speed. Past bicycles, leaping over dreamers and moving cars – faster, faster, away from the golden treitre and the nightmares that accompanied it.

A human screamed behind her. She glanced back. The treitre was gaining on her, but though she kept moving she couldn't help but see the bundle of clothes and hair heaped on the ground behind it. One of the dreamers she'd saved from the vultures only seconds ago, cut down just for being in the treitre's path. A rivulet of blood was already winding its way from the dying body to the churning life of the Thames.

Una's terror expelled itself as a throaty cry. She turned and ran, faster than she had ever run before, in this world or the other, leaving the vultures behind but unable to shake that relentless *tap tap* of the treitre's claws.

Dawn was already breaking, autumnal fingers turning the river to flame and the skyline to shadow. An arctic wind blowing upstream numbed Una's face. With a crack, part of the river iced over. Dreams formed there: skaters in mufflers; polar bears and penguins. Una seized her chance. Sliding out onto the ice she aimed for the middle of the water. If the treitre followed her surely the ice would break beneath its weight. Beyond the frost, a sailing boat was making good time. With a great effort, Una leaped for the ship's side and swung herself on board. Dreamers and dreams alike craned over the sides and hung from the poles, but Una ignored them all. She shimmied up the tallest mast and looked back towards the shore. The treitre was there; its head, smooth and featureless except for two black pinpricks for eyes, followed her. Woman and monster stared at each other. Then the boat swung to the East and the treitre fell out of view.

Una wouldn't allow herself to acknowledge that she now had one more death on her conscience. There would be time for that when she was back in Ithr, when she had left all of this behind. Instead, she drank in the unimpeded view of the city that had opened up ahead. Gulls as large as helicopters swooped around her, diving for the dolphins that played in the ship's wake. In the distance, the skyscrapers of Canary Wharf sprouted into existence like flowers bursting from the earth, before collapsing away into the old docks that some dreamers could still remember. She never tired of watching the city she loved morph and mirage before her eyes. But this would be the last time she appreciated it as anything other than a common dreamer.

Normal life. No more responsibility for millions of strangers. The only ones she would need to worry about were herself and her little family. Angus, frown lines forming already across his handsome face. Ollie and Fern, hands no bigger than cats' paws. She'd left them in neighbouring cots, gurgling in conversation. Sometimes the love made her want to rip open her stomach and push them back inside, where they'd be safe. She wouldn't be able to protect them forever, but she had a feeling she wouldn't need to. Not Fern, at least. She'd have to wait fifteen years, but then she could tell Fern everything. Maybe she could even join her. What adventures they would have together.

In the distance, a baby's cry echoed through Annwn. Una was sure that it was one of her children calling to her, across the divide of dreams and reality. She was so close. The Tower of London emerged on the shore, and Tower Bridge just beyond. All she had to do was climb up one of the bridge's piers as the ship passed it, skirt the Tower itself, and she'd reach the portal back to her bedroom. Angus would still be sleeping beside her, one arm crooked under her neck, the other resting on her waist.

On the bridge, inspyre morphed into a pack of wolves, mouths open in a parody of smiles. Another shape took its place beside them. Tall, slender, sharp. The rising sun turned the golden monster into one of smoke. The treitre had found her again.

As though spinning a voice from her terror, the wolves opened their mouths and howled, their song reeling in the wind and scuttling up her spine.

Go.

She couldn't take the bridge now. She would have to go through the Tower. Una dived into the water, praying that she wouldn't attract the attention of the sharks, or their larger companions that lurked on the riverbed. There was no splash, no watery reverberation behind her. The treitre had chosen another route.

Una aimed for the bank, wrestling the currents beneath and the waves above. The Tower's foundations reared up through the murk sooner than she'd expected and she hit them hard, pain wrenching up one wrist. She felt her way along until stone became wood. This was Traitor's Gate – the old entryway to the Tower for those sentenced to die. She'd have to wait there until it opened. She counted the seconds, forcing her mind off the tortuous dance of not knowing where the treitre was and her growing desperation to surface for air.

There was a shimmer in the water: the telltale blue light of a birthing dream. The algae-infested hull of a boat split the waves. The gate groaned open to admit the vessel. Una slipped through to the other side and broke the surface with a gasp. She was inside the Tower.

Ignoring the sobbing of the dream in the boat below, Una crawled out of the water and up a curved staircase. She tried to imagine herself dry, but she couldn't concentrate enough. The Tower had always given her chills – twelve years on from her first patrol here, she still hated hearing the screams of the condemned. Even the jewels locked in its belly seemed cold and cursed. She couldn't think about that now, though. She was so close.

From the bridge, the wolves' wails distorted inside the limestone walls into a siren, into a warning.

Una took the stairs five at a time. Arrow slits circled the turret like soldiers. The views flicked, staccato, from river to bridge to courtyard and repeat. A woman in heavy brocade slid across the enclosure below, the scars at her throat glittering like rubies. Round Una went, up, up. Another glance. The woman's face was a breath away from hers.

Una stumbled back, slipped on a step. Wincing at the pain in her shin, she scrambled to her feet, grabbing the window ledge to pull herself forward.

Fern and Ollie, Una thought, pounding their faces into her mind. *Don't lose control.*

The woman in the window broke apart like a dandelion head. Una wished she could do the same. The fear was dragging her down, like a great cloak. Her babies cried out again, through the portal just on the other side of the Tower.

One step up, then two, quicker, quicker. She looked out towards the river.

Instead of water, she saw golden hide. Before she could react, a claw slashed through the window. The skin on her face parted like a zip.

Terror made Una sharp and swift. Dashing the blood from her forehead, she raced onwards. The staircase reverberated with a cacophony of breaking bricks and lead – outside, the treitre was matching her ascent. She erupted onto the roof and flung herself off the ledge. The air shifted against her legs and she knew that the treitre had tried to seize her.

With her focus divided, she struggled to keep her height as she flew above the courtyard. She had to force her mind away from her pursuer and onto the task at hand.

Fern and Ollie called out again.

Nearly there, munchkins.

She was too panicked to clear the Tower wall. She hit it instead, using her shoulder to take the brunt of the impact. Gripping the stones, ignoring the pain lancing through her bruised arm, she pulled herself onto the escarpment.

The roof was empty. The street below was clear. Beyond it she glimpsed the portal just one good leap away. She climbed onto the edge of the battlement, measuring the distance, gathering her strength.

'Una?'

The voice was soft, curious, familiar. It was of someone she loved. But how could that be?

Una turned and smiled. She reached out in wonder. Then with a jolt she realised the awful truth.

Fern's cries, weaving their way through the open portal, echoed around the Tower long after her mother had gone.

1

Fifteen years, two months and thirteen days later

Una Kathleen King
1978–2005
'Was never lady loved dearer'

Cigarette butts are strewn around the grave. The cemetery's a favourite hangout for local kids who can't be bothered to trek into central London for their fun, and boy have they had some fun here. I kick a beer can onto another grave and slump down to the grass, realising too late that it's still damp from the morning's dew. Great. Moisture seeps through my school trousers, but there are other people around and I don't want them to notice me standing up again straight away. Don't want anyone thinking I'm weird. Ha ha. Like they don't think that just from looking at me.

When I was younger I didn't understand why Dad always wanted to bring me here. I didn't realise that a dead mother was something you had to care about, even if you didn't remember her. 'Come for me, Ferny, eh?' he would say roughly, pulling on boots so tattered he may as well have been wearing sandals. 'Your mum'll like to see you.' But the graves frightened me. I hated the thought of walking over corpses. I'm sure it's one of the many reasons Dad and I don't see eye to eye.

I dig my fingers into the carved letters and wonder, for the millionth time, what my mother was like. I once overheard Gran call her a 'gypsy tart'. In photos there's a wildness to her – dark hair, wide mouth and pale skin. Dad rhapsodises about how kind and loving she was, which just makes me angry. I can't help but wonder whether, if she'd lived, I would have been my mum's favourite, like my brother Ollie is Dad's. We could have done all the things we're supposed to, like buying clothes and make-up, or going to see romcoms at the cinema and feeling awkward because we're both ogling the leading man.

But then I wouldn't like that version of my mum much either. I've never been into make-up anyway – I look so weird that a bit of mascara isn't going to make people stare at me in a way that says, 'Wow, she's hot!' instead of, 'What happened to her *face*?'

'What do you want from her, Fern? She's dead,' Ollie once asked me in the middle of a regularly scheduled argument.

The truth is, I don't know. Nothing about my mum makes sense. I've been told so many different things about her that she's like an abstract painting. Fun-loving, secretive, passionate, icy . . . How can one person be all those things? And if I can't work out who she was, how can I work out who I might have been if she'd lived? So many *what if*s, so little info.

The church bell chimes eight, which is my cue to leave. I'll need to be quick to get to school on time.

'Bye, Mum,' I whisper, touching the marble one last time, and hoist my schoolbag over one shoulder. I'm pulling my hoodie over my face when I spot him. Ollie is skulking at a distance, his expression as inscrutable as ever. I am suddenly very aware of the cemetery's silence. He wouldn't do anything to me here, I tell myself. Not even Ollie would stoop so low, would he?

Steeling myself, I skirt the graves instead of joining the path Ollie's on. I don't watch him, but I can sense him moving away too, towards Mum. We are two moons, spinning around the planet of our differences. Smoky hatred fills the space between us, pressing against my back as I walk away.

You'd never think, to look at us like this, that we are twins.

I take the back roads to avoid having to pass Wanstead Flats. My thoughts boomerang to Ollie. When did he start visiting Mum's grave on his own? My popular, handsome brother has never had time for grief, has never before needed to confide in a dead woman.

As I reach the station and pass through the ticket barriers, my phone vibrates with a message inside my bag. I bet it's Dad with another of his attempts at a motivational joke, but then I think of Ollie again and check. Maybe it's an explanation for his behaviour or, more likely, a cutting remark about our dead mother being my only friend.

I'll be thinking of you tonight.

It's from neither Ollie nor Dad. I raise my eyebrows as I reply to the unknown sender. *Wrong number*.

Tonight's Halloween, and it sounds as though someone's got big plans. Good luck to them. Mine involve changing into pyjamas as soon as humanly possible and cramming for a history test.

On the tube I studiously avoid the curious, pitying glances of my fellow commuters and stare at the front cover of *Metro*. The headline reads, *Ratings Soar for Sebastien Medraut*. The photo doesn't do justice to the politician – or at least, not to his eyes. I've seen him in person, outside school. His deep violet irises – somewhere between amethyst and sapphire – made a cyclist crash into a lamppost thanks to an ill-timed double-take. He has always laughingly denied they are lenses, and I've always believed him. I know all too well that eyes do indeed come in all colours.

I can only read a snippet of the article.

In recent years Medraut has made a staggering comeback to once again capture the hearts and minds of a nation . . .

A typical puff piece, then.

The person whose paper I've been reading catches my eye and rustles the pages irritably. I resist the urge to point out that newspapers can – *shock, horror* – be read more than once, and slide my drawing pad out of my bag. The same face, picked out in oils, charcoals, watercolours, whatever I had to hand really, haunts nearly every page – an ageless woman, her fine features crisscrossed with scars and framed with wild, bird's-nest hair. I go to colour in her mane, but I must have left my orange pencil at home. Damn.

When I come up for air at Sloane Square, I reach into my bag to check the time on my phone. The unknown number has messaged again.

Have you never wondered about your mother's death, Fern?

I stop dead in the middle of the pavement and a man glares as he pushes past.

Who is this? I reply, shock making my fingers clumsy.

But they don't respond. They haven't replied by the time I reach Bosco College, or by the time I'm forced to put my phone away at the start of double biology. They haven't replied by first break, when I am interrupted in my toilet haven by Lottie Medraut and her harem, or by the time break ends and I slip into the back of the Latin classroom. Why would I wonder about Mum's death? It was simple – she passed away in her sleep. Sudden Death Syndrome. Rare, tragic, but it happens to all sorts of people. There has never been anything to question.

It is only when I am standing in the lunch queue that my phone vibrates again. My whole body flushes as I spot the words on the screen.

Your mother knew me by another name, but you may call me Archimago.

Then, soon afterwards: *She and I were knights together in Annwn.*

Archimago? Annwn? I may as well still be in Latin for all the sense these words make. I have had time to order my thoughts now, though, and I know what I want to say. I won't be distracted by a strange vocabulary. *What did you mean about my mum's death?*

This time, the reply comes almost immediately.

Una didn't die peacefully at all. She was murdered.

It's as though the mysterious Archimago has reached through the phone screen, through my ribcage and is squeezing my heart, tight tight tight. I place a hand over my mouth to stop myself from showing too much emotion. No one else in the queue seems to have noticed my reaction, though. Half of them are glued to their phone screens too. I look from face to face, wondering whether this is a malicious prank by one of my peers.

How do you know? I reply, and after a moment I deliberately put my phone back into my bag. If Archimago is watching I don't want to give them the satisfaction of seeing how shaken I am. I stare straight forward, my elbow pressed against my bag to feel the vibration should another message arrive. I choose the chicken curry and chocolate sponge, and take my lunch to my usual table where everyone knows not to bother me. Those words – *She was murdered* – ricochet around my skull until they break apart. *She was murdered. Was She Murdered. Murdered She Was.* I can't help it – I place my phone next to my plate. Elsewhere in the hall, Lottie Medraut's ringing laugh carries over the other voices.

Spoonful of curry halfway to my mouth, the screen lights up once more. Archimago has replied. I draw the phone towards me and rice spills in maggoty drips into my lap.

Because I killed her.

2

The lunch in front of me goes cold as I stare at the message from Archimago. This has to be a joke. *It has to be*. Mum died unfairly but naturally. She died in her sleep. Dad woke up to find her cold in his arms. How could she have possibly been murdered?

My phone rattles against the tabletop, and I realise that my hand is shaking. I put the phone down and trap my fingers between my knees. *Think, Fern*.

I get up clumsily and stride out of the hall, sliding my still full lunch tray into the collection trolley. I need some fresh air. Outside, I try to call Archimago but they messaged me from an unknown number. I have to settle for replying to them. *You're lying*, I type. *I'm going to the police*.

Of course I do nothing of the sort. Uncertainty, confusion and anger curl through my body. I consider calling Dad, but that doesn't seem right. Dad and I have never been able to talk about Mum. Mentioning it to Ollie is out of the question. And they're all I have, really.

The clink-clink of cutlery and plates rings out from the lunch hall. Students laugh, gossip, compare homework. Teachers nod at me as they pass.

Because I killed her.

I cannot be here.

Ignoring the startled questions from the receptionist, I fly out of Bosco and onto the street, running south to the Thames. There, I hang over the fence, nursing a stitch and taking great gulps of river air. A solitary gull is being tossed about on the water, wings flapping fruitlessly. It catches my eyes briefly and I nod in sympathy.

She was murdered.

I check my phone again. Archimago hasn't replied to my threat. Maybe they've been frightened off. Maybe they've had their fun for now and will slink away, a perpetual question mark at the back of my mind.

I open a search on my phone and type in *Archimago*. All it brings up are references to a character in an old poem and a load of Internet personas. I try searching for *Annwn* next, checking the spelling against Archimago's text. This time the results are more interesting: *Ah-noon* is the name for the Underworld in Welsh folklore. Where the dead live. Spectral fingers seem to tippety-tap up my neck. I still don't understand, though.

I read Archimago's messages again. *She and I were knights together in Annwn*. Right. I type *knights Annwn*. The Internet returns a handful of results and at the top, a link to a video. It's titled *The Truth About Your Nightmares*. I click on it, ignoring the irritated glares of the people around me as sound blares out.

A young woman – dark hair, dark skin and sharp eyes – stares up at me.

'Do you think you're safe when you sleep?' she asks. 'Well, think again. The knights aren't just –'

Inexplicably, the video cuts out mid-sentence, leaving me with a blank frame and a timebar that ticks on through nothingness.

I refresh the page and even try turning my phone off and on again, but nothing reveals the rest of the video. Baffled, I head down into the Underground and take the next tube back towards Stratford.

'Don't stare at her! You're being so rude,' a woman whispers to her boyfriend on the other side of the carriage. I catch the boyfriend's eye. He's smirking. The stranger opposite me is watching me intently too. I know the type. He wants to get into a staring contest so he can start something. It's been happening a lot lately. I close my eyes to avoid him.

The train rocks gently. Mum's face, dark hair billowing across crinkled eyes, taunts me. *I was murdered, Fern,* she seems to whisper. *Are you going to do nothing about it?* The raging lullaby of the Underground's tunnels pitches me into my mother's smile. I land in a woodland nightmare. Dough-faced Jenny is there, and so is Ollie. It is his face I see most clearly as he slips away guiltily. Then Jenny steps in front of me. '*You're a witch, Fern King, and we all know what they used to do to witches . . .*'

The match is struck. Autumn's leaves, crunchy underfoot, are ready for the flame. I scream, I plead, I humiliate myself, but my bonds are too tight and Jenny is too eager to taste my fear. Except she's not Jenny now; she's my mother, my father, my brother, baying in turn for my burning.

The exquisite, intimate pain of the fire doesn't reach me, though. Not this time. This time a pair of metal-clad arms lifts me away from the sparks. I catch a glimpse of a face, freckled beneath scars and framed with red hair, before she shoves me backwards. I fall as if from a cliff, and jolt awake. I am still in the train carriage. People are still staring at me. But now I have yet another question.

I search through my bag for my sketchpad and fling open the pages. My guardian angel.

My fingers trace over the wild, bird's-nest hair etched onto every page. Over her scarred, ageless face, and the armour that looks as though it once belonged to someone much bigger. She's been haunting my dreams for as long as I can remember. In my nightmares – and I have a lot of nightmares – this warrior woman has always arrived to save me.

A knight. That's what Archimago had said, and the woman online had mentioned *sleep* and *the knights* before her video cut out. Could they be connected to this mysterious armoured guardian?

'But you're just a dream, aren't you?' I whisper. Her impenetrable features stare back up at me, and with a lurch I realise that the only possible answer – *Of course she's just a dream* – doesn't feel certain at all.

3

The house should be empty at this time of day. Dad's on a long night shift again, working on the concierge desk of a posh apartment block a few miles away. I turn the downstairs radiator on and make myself a cup of tea. The only mug not currently sitting in the sink waiting to be washed is one I made for Ollie when we were eight. Untidy letters are stuck around the circumference: *Best Broth*. I had the *er* all ready to go but ran out of room. Still, it works better now that we can all pretend I simply really liked soup as a child.

I'm not allowed solitude for long, though. I've just put the kettle on for my second cup when the front door opens and Clemmie bundles in, hanging her purple monstrosity of a coat on a spare peg. Clemmie has been Dad's girlfriend for five years, and it tells you something about her that she's stuck around this long when it's clear to even socially-oblivious me that he sees her more as a reliable best friend than a potential life partner.

'Fern? What's wrong?' Clemmie says, finally noticing me.

'I'm . . .' I falter. I wasn't prepared for this. I need to tell Clemmie something, or she'll tell Dad that I'm skiving school.

‘What are you doing here anyway?’ That’s me, defaulting to defensive.

‘Your father mentioned he hadn’t had time to leave anything in the fridge for you and Ollie,’ Clemmie replies, ‘so I thought I’d rustle up a lasagne.’

My stomach rumbles my thanks, reminding me that I barely had lunch.

‘Is it Jenny again?’ Clemmie asks.

I shake my head, furious that tears are threatening to block my throat. As Clemmie folds her arms around me, I find myself overwhelmed again, just as I was in the school canteen, and I stumble out the truth about Archimago’s message.

‘They . . . they say they murdered my mum.’

There’s a long silence. The spectre of Mum has always been extra awkward around Clemmie.

‘That’s not possible, sweetie,’ Clemmie eventually says.

‘But you didn’t know Dad back then, did you?’ I look up at her. ‘I mean, did he ever tell you . . .?’

‘It isn’t my place to say, Fern. Now come on, come and sit down.’

As she ushers me to the sofa and presses a glass of squash into my hands, I realise that she’s not meeting my eyes.

‘Did Dad tell you something? Something he hasn’t told me?’

Another pause as she pulls a blanket from the back of the sofa and drapes it around me. Very, very occasionally I wish I could channel Ollie. He always knows exactly what to say to get people to do what he wants.

‘Please, Clemmie,’ I say, ‘I won’t tell Dad you told me. I deserve to know what happened to my mum.’

'It's probably nothing,' she eventually says, sinking down next to me. 'It's just that your father once told me that she had lots of marks all over her. They faded a few hours after he found her, but apparently they were . . . very alarming for him.'

'What kind of marks?'

'I'm not sure, lovely. He just said they were as if she'd been cut all over, except she hadn't, if you see what I mean? "Like an operation gone wrong." That's what he said, if I remember right.'

I think about the scars on my guardian angel's face. Dad's never liked my drawings of her. He's always avoided looking at them. Now I understand why. There's no point in wondering why he didn't just tell me why they upset him. That's not the way we work.

My heartbeat seems to pound off the walls.

'Fern? Do you want to make a complaint against this person?' Clemmie says, squeezing my knee. 'I can walk you through the process. We might be able to find out who's behind it.'

Clemmie is a police sergeant, so this is one area where she might actually be helpful. But I have no interest in going to the police. The last time I had official dealings with them –after the fire, when they promised to prosecute Jenny and Ollie for what they'd done to me – it all came to nothing. All that would happen is Dad and Clemmie would flutter around making all the right noises but actually doing nothing to protect me. Besides, if they find out who Archimago is, I might lose the only chance I have of finding out more about the knights, and about Mum. I can take care of this myself.

'No. Thanks, though,' I tell Clemmie, then feign tiredness to avoid talking further. She faffs about in the kitchen for a little longer, until the house is filled with the smell of melted cheese, then puts the lasagne on the countertop to cool and kisses my forehead on her way out.

I may have mixed feelings about sweet, beige Clemmie, but once she's gone the house feels forbidding in a way it hasn't before. The hallway is covered in my old artwork: stern faces and lonely landscapes. Ollie's bedroom door is locked. My room is freezing because the radiator's broken. I return to the sofa and continue my search on Dad's old laptop.

It takes hours and three servings of lasagne to find anything more – an interview with a gnarled woman who claims to have once been a knight of Annwn. Her mouth is sunken, most of her teeth missing, which makes it difficult to understand her. 'It happens on your fifteenth Samhain,' she says, pointing a finger at the camera, her mouth pursing around the word – *Sow-ane*. 'The lights change, you see. The lights of Annwn. That's when the knights take you. The lights change and you know –'

The video blanks out, just like the one earlier. A crisp picture turned suddenly to black. I can't find anything else. It matches, though, with the mention of Annwn and the knights, and now another new word. I look up Samhain and find out that it's basically another word for Halloween. I glance at the table lamp next to me. It refuses to do anything remarkable. Archimago had mentioned tonight as well. *It happens on your fifteenth Samhain*. I am fifteen. Did Archimago know?

Behind me, the hallway light flickers. A key is thrust through the lock of the front door and soon afterwards Ollie enters. His school uniform's spattered with mud and even from this distance I can smell the cigarette smoke on him.

'Aww, waiting up for me, Ferny? That's sweet of you.'

He finds the remains of Clemmie's lasagne and shoves a bowl in the microwave without further discussion. I don't say anything either. I'm trying to beat my record of not talking to Ollie, which currently stands at eleven days. I'm on day nine, so I'm feeling hopeful. But equally, I desperately want to tell him what I've found out. Out of everyone, he's the only one who might understand what this feels like, and know what to do about it. Yet the words stick in my throat. The spectre of the fire springs up between us. He hasn't been able to meet my gaze since it happened; not since I saw the blazing guilt in his eyes as he slunk away, his part in the prank completed.

As twins go, you couldn't get two more different-looking people than Ollie and I. We should really be identical, and if you look carefully you can see that our chins and eyes and noses are the same shape. Yet Ollie is a heart-breaker and I'm just . . . weird. My brother has golden skin like he's sailed in from Spain, a mop of dark hair and brilliant blue eyes that make him look like an old-school movie star. Whereas I . . . well, let's just say that when Dad describes me as 'startling', he's being kind. My light blonde hair and pale skin is unremarkable, so when I wear sunglasses, you don't see it. But not many people can get away with wearing sunglasses unless it's high summer, so for most of the year my deformity is very apparent. I have scarlet-coloured irises. The doctors told my parents it was simply a genetic abnormality. *One of those things*. Growing up it hadn't mattered much to me because Ollie was always there. My twin and I, facing the world, and if Ollie said I was acceptable then others followed his lead. For ten years we were best friends as well as siblings. Then secondary school happened and everything changed. I may have only added the burn scar to my face last year, but the differences between my brother and I were cemented years before the fire.

'You're being creepy again,' Ollie says, his back to me still.

'What?' Damnit.

'Staring at me like that. No wonder people hate you.'

'I wasn't staring at you. Don't flatter yourself.' I turn away and march up the stairs. Ollie's tired insults have broken any thought I may have had of confiding in him.

Outside, the church bells begin to chime midnight. My mother's grave is somewhere near those bells. Well, if she was murdered I'll simply have to find out more on my own.

Boom, the bells go. *Boom. Boom. Boom.*

The lightbulb on the landing flickers.

Boom.

'Cut it out, Fern!' Ollie shouts from the kitchen.

'I'm not doing anything!'

If there's a power surge then Ollie's closest to the fuse box. He can sort it out. I'm off to bed. The lightbulb above me flickers again. This time it blooms brightly. My shadow looms alarmingly along the wall.

The lights.

I jump back down the stairs. It's as though I'm entering a nightclub – every light is flashing on and off unevenly. The lamp by the sofa makes suns on the pile of homework beneath it. The lights in the kitchen babble in Morse code. This is no power surge. Ollie's shock, seen like a flip book, is almost comical. He doesn't know what this means, but I do.

The lights of Annwn. That's when the knights take you. The lights change and you know.

Samhain. Halloween. Tonight.

It's true. It's all true.

Boom. Boom.

A different kind of noise rattles the floorboards above us. I rush back up the stairs. It's the fan in the bathroom, whirring so fast that little clouds of dust fly out of the grill.

Ollie appears behind me. 'What the hell is happening?'

I laugh. I'm not going to explain it. The knights must be nearby. Maybe they're waiting for me. I've got to find them.

Something catches my eye in the bedroom window and I whirl around. The street lamps are glowing impossibly bright. I push past Ollie and run back down the stairs. I fling open the door. Every imperfection in the tarmac is picked out in the punishing light. I scan the trees, the pavement, the parked cars. The road is empty. Where are they?

'Fern!'

The panic in Ollie's voice carries me back through the hallway. He's standing next to the sofa. It takes a moment for what I'm seeing to sink in.

He is bathed in light. Every bulb in the room is blinding, but none of them match the unsourced blaze that sits behind him, turning him into a shadow. He looks down at his outstretched fingers, and the light plays around them like static.

I can't breathe.

'What is it?' Ollie's voice reaches me as though we are standing on opposite sides of a deep cave. He looks darkly, powerfully beautiful. 'What's happening to me?'

The light around him starts to pulse, as though its power source is failing. Ollie shakes his head, as though he's dizzy.

'It . . . it tickles,' he tells me, his fear turned to sleepy curiosity.

His form shimmers, the light eroding him, as if it's trying to drag him away.

'No!' I shout, closing the distance between us. Why is the light around him and not me? The bulbs shine even more brightly, as though pouring out the last of their energy.

'Wait!'

I reach for Ollie, but I am too late. The bulbs shatter, the lights go out, and I am left in the dark surrounded by broken glass.

4

I hunch on the floor of our sitting room in darkness, flecked with scratches from where the lightbulbs have showered me with tiny shards of glass. My brother is draped like a damsel on the floor before me, seemingly fast asleep.

'Ollie?' I whisper, prodding him gingerly. He doesn't stir.

'Get up!' I say more loudly, but again there's no reaction. Other than the glass cuts that match my own, he seems fine. He's breathing normally, the sound of his peaceful slumber a taunt to my own panic and confusion. I fetch my phone to call for help, but what would I tell them? *My brother was inside a weird light and now he's asleep?* It sounds ridiculous.

I push Ollie a few more times and kick him once, hard, to make very sure that he's not going to wake up. Then I burst into tears. Nothing that's happened today has made sense, but when the lights changed I felt so sure that I was on the brink of getting answers. Now they've been snatched from me.

Still sniffing pathetically, I fetch a sponge from the kitchen and wash the glass fragments from Ollie's arms and face. I wonder what he's dreaming about, but mostly I have the strongest sense that he is being kept asleep by a force beyond any normal understanding.

Ollie still doesn't wake when I heave him onto the sofa. There was no point leaving him on the floor. Dad would only ask questions that have no plausible answers. Ollie dealt with, I traipse upstairs to the shower and wash the glass from my own body. The skin on my left side is still a different shade from the rest of my torso, but the markings aren't as bad as the scar on my face. My clothes protected me a little from the flames that night, but I still don't like looking.

Brush teeth, brush hair, smother my scar in medical-grade moisturiser. The cream dulls my burn the same way my emotions feel dulled. But I can't bring myself to climb into bed. I need answers.

I have to drag a chair from the kitchen up the stairs to reach the handle to the loft hatch. When I pull it, a considerable amount of dust follows the little ladder that drops down. Up in the attic, I clamber over wooden struts to reach a tumble of boxes tucked into one corner, behind the Christmas decorations. It's even colder up here, so I heave the boxes down one by one into my room. I can't have Dad knowing I've been poring over Mum's stuff.

Back in my room, hot squash in hand and duvet on lap to ward off the cold, I open the first box. Inside is a sleek digital recorder. I put fresh batteries in it but the mechanics must be too old, because it doesn't work.

The next box is full of faded photographs, most of them from Mum's childhood. The third box has exactly what I want: a series of neatly labelled journals. 'Your mother never liked to throw anything away,' Dad once told us. 'She liked to look back over them from time to time. To remind her of who she was, she said.'

It takes me a moment to work out what year Mum turned fifteen, and even longer to sift through the mountain of journals to find the one labelled *1993*. I've read most of these entries before, of course, but there's a difference between reading the diaries of a fifteen-year-old when you're only eleven, and then again when you're fifteen yourself. Snippets jump out at me: *Laura was being a bitch again today. I can't help it if we both fancy Toby* . . . Then a few months later: *Toby got me tickets to see Take That! He is the BEST boyfriend!! Going to take Laura!!!*

Yeah. Mum wasn't like me at all, was she?

I hurry on to today's date, 31st October. Her fifteenth Samhain. She's written nothing special, just a list of homework and a reminder to buy a birthday card for her grandfather. I almost close the diary in disappointment, when I notice it. A tiny star in the corner of the page.

I look back over the diary. Mum wasn't a doodler. She'd scribble things out, but other than that star, there are no hearts, no stick people, no decorative borders.

I turn the page. I suppose I was expecting some sort of explosion of text: *WHAT THE HELL HAPPENED LAST NIGHT?* scrawled in red pen and underlined thirty times. Instead there's . . . nothing. The rest of that week is entirely blank.

It's ten days later that Mum starts writing again, but there's a huge change in the kind of things she's noting. Gone is the chat about boyfriends and friendship squabbles. She's factual – more homework lists, more reminders. In December she writes, *Broke up with Toby today. It was hard.*

I pull out the diary for 1994. There's more of the same – boring lists that half make me wish she'd spice it up with a bit of schoolyard gossip again. But then, on the first of February, something interesting happens. She starts writing complete gibberish.

Fall brought lost
With other lost brought
Unto for other from place unto brought lost
Be with lost is
Place unto unto place other!

Clearly my mother was not going to win any poetry competitions. Obviously it's a code or a riddle of some sort, and I wish I wasn't so tired or I might have a chance of cracking it. I pull a spare notebook from my desk and jot down the secret message.

As I open the diary once more, though, I register that this diary has a dust jacket – a handmade envelope of patterned paper held together with tape. I slide the jacket off and stare with bittersweet wonder at the cover beneath. On the plain grey cardboard, in my mother's bold, spiky print, is written, *Una's Knightbook.*

Out of all the mad things that have happened today, this feels the strangest. It's the most concrete proof yet that there was some truth in what Archimago said, and it sends a shock of determination through my bones.

I keep looking.

By the time I hear Dad come in I have worked my way through to 2001, and I have a handful of further garbled poems in my notebook. Mum didn't write in code often, which makes me think that she only did so when something really important happened. I listen to Dad half-heartedly telling Ollie to go to bed, but evidently when Ollie doesn't stir he gives up and climbs the stairs. Too late, I realise he'll be able to see the light beneath my door and I rush to switch off my lamp.

'Fern?' Dad says quietly on the other side of my bedroom door.

I want to fling it open, to hug him and ask him to tell me everything he knows about Mum. To tell him about the messages from Archimago and Mum's diaries. To ask him to help me work this out.

I sit very still. The door between him and me may as well be concrete. Ever since he refused to punish Ollie for his part in the fire, I have known exactly how much Dad loves Ollie, and how little he loves me. Eventually, he moves on to the bathroom, and a few minutes later I hear him close his own bedroom door. I turn on the light once more.

When the sun begins to reach through my curtains and my fingers are aching with cold, I reach for the last of Mum's journals. 2005. The year she died. The poems are more frequent here, her handwriting less contained. I flick to the last entry: 2nd August. No poem, only an appointment for Ollie and I to get our vaccinations. We would have been two months old.

'What was happening to you?' I wonder out loud, wishing

I could reach through the pages of those diaries and probe the mind of the woman who wrote them. The woman who seemed to become more impenetrable as the years wore on.

A sound from downstairs brings me back from my reverie. Ollie must have woken up. I slip down the stairs and watch from the door as he pours himself a glass of milk.

I hesitate. If I'm wrong then I'm going to open myself up to even more ridicule. But I have nothing to lose.

'Was it the knights?' I ask him. He whirls round, his eyes wide, and I no longer need him to answer.

'I have no idea what you're talking about, Fern.'

'Did you know Mum was a knight?' I say. 'Did you know she was murdered?'

Not even Ollie's normal poker face can mask the shock that flits across his features.

'Dad should know,' I say.

Ollie strides across the room and grabs my wrist. 'Don't be a bitch.'

I wrestle away from him. 'Was it them?' I hiss. 'Tell me the truth!'

'Don't upset him. For God's sake, Fern, what makes you even think he'll believe you?'

'*I* believe it. I've got proof too. Messages from her murderer!' I brandish my phone at him, and he stares, bewildered, at Archimago's confession. When he looks back at me, his face is full of contempt. 'So call the police then. What do you think they'll do?'

'Why won't you tell me if it's true?' I whisper as he turns away from me.

'Leave it alone, Fern,' he says, equally quietly. 'Just accept that Mum died in her sleep. She was normal. Like me, like Dad.'

He didn't need to say it.

Not like you.

5

For the first time in years I am craving the distraction of school. I pull a hoodie over my uniform and drag my tattered satchel out into the bracing chill of early morning London. Before last year, I'd never even dreamed of going to Bosco College, a private school in Chelsea where the offspring of politicians and millionaires are sent. Usually the only way people like me would be there is because we were cleaning the toilets or serving lunch.

Given his daughter, Lottie, goes to Bosco, it seems ironic that it was one of Sebastien Medraut's opponents who got me into the school. After the fire, Jenny was let off with something called a referral order and the rest of her gang were allowed to stay at St Stephen's. Dad wrote an angry letter to our local MP. 'How dare they say they can't do anything!' he'd hissed as he wrote. I remember that being the moment when the rage inside me had erupted.

'*You* can do something!' I'd shouted. 'Send Ollie away!'

But Dad just promised punishments that had no meaning to me at all, shaking his head when I tried to tell him how Ollie had led me to the spot and left me there without a backwards glance. 'Your brother was just led astray, love, that's all. He's not like the others, they're bad to the core. He's moving schools and that's that . . .'

I turned away from him in every way after that. Ignored him when he told me that the MP had written back and was coming to visit. 'She'll be able to pull some strings,' he'd said imploringly through my bedroom door. I didn't believe him, but when I did meet the Right Honourable Helena Corday, MP for Newham, I had to grudgingly admit that she wasn't bad. She'd held my hand and her smile hadn't been dripping with pity. 'I'm so frustrated that there's nothing I can do to overturn the judge's decision,' she'd said, addressing me instead of Dad, 'but there might be something I can do for you. My old alma mater has a scholarship scheme.'

'My grades won't be good enough,' I had told her.

'But your drawings might be.' She had gestured at the paintings and sketches that lined the walls of our house. 'I know something about art. I paint in my spare time. I can see that you have an extraordinary talent here, Fern. I feel sure that Bosco would consider it, especially if I put in a good word.'

So I was sent to Bosco on a full art scholarship and Ollie was moved down the road to Upton Academy. Much as I was grateful to Helena Corday, the rage of how unfair it was that my life had suffered this huge upheaval and everyone else's had pretty much stayed the same, remained with me. I might not be bullied at Bosco, but just the fact that I have to trek across the city to get here is a constant reminder of Ollie and Dad's betrayals.

Today, though, instead of dwelling on how different my life is to the fancy, easy lives of my fellow pupils, all I can think about is Mum and what happened to Ollie last night. I ponder Archimago's texts. *Something* strange happened to my twin last night, and he all but confirmed the existence of the knights this morning. I have to find out more. The question is – how on earth am I supposed to do that?

'You'll work it out,' someone says. At first I think they're talking to me, then I realise it's Lottie Medraut, comforting notorious drama llama Beth Goodman. 'My dad always says that you just can't take no for an answer,' she tells her friend.

Someone else in the group raises an eyebrow and says, 'I wish he wouldn't take no for an answer with me.' Lottie pretends to hurl, Beth smiles and the rest of their gaggle dissolves into giggles.

Don't take no for an answer. That's all I need to do – make Ollie tell me what he knows, whatever it takes.

After school, I sneak into Ollie's bedroom. He's late again – probably hanging out with his friends. I'd been counting on that. His aftershave, deep-voiced and whisky sour, lingers. Unlike my room, his is meticulous. The souvenirs on his desk are placed just so. Folders are stacked head to toe, each subject labelled in capitals. There used to be photos of him with Jenny and their gang pinned to the corkboard above the desk, but now it's empty except for a few Post-it notes.

I open his drawers, searching for anything that might tell me what happened to him last night. It's been years since I've been inside Ollie's bedroom, and nothing is where it used to be. Back then it was covered in my artwork and his stories, and stashes of whatever conkers or leaves we'd found in the park. Now the drawers just contain stationery and the folders neatly written notes from class. It's so strange. There's nothing of Ollie here, as though after Dad told him to break off his friendship with Jenny he just . . . erased his personality from his room.

My hand brushes against something at the back of one drawer and I pull out a wrinkled photograph. My heart bloats as I recognise it. Ollie and I in the garden, covered in sand, grinning at the camera. On the back is the date: June 2012. We were seven. Those two happy children had no idea that just a few years later everything would fall apart.

It was only when we went to secondary school that the way we looked started to matter. I felt it immediately. People wanted to hang out with Ollie, but always made excuses for why I couldn't come too – no space, no spare seats, too many girls already and so on and so on. Ollie went along with it. Then, gradually, it became more overt. At first Ollie didn't participate. He'd make himself scarce when his new friends turned on me. Then he would snort with laughter at a well-aimed 'joke'. Then he'd be the one making the jokes. Then . . .

A front-door key jiggles in the lock, wrenching me back to the present. Shit. I dart into the wardrobe just in time. It's smaller than I remember, the space for hanging clothes too narrow for me to close the door completely. I'm going to have to hope that he doesn't look this way. The bedroom door squeaks open.

The gap in the cupboard only lets me see a ribbon of the room so it takes me a moment to parse the strange sound coming from Ollie's bed. It's so quiet it could almost be someone kicking leaves outside. *Shuffle, squeak, shuffle*. Is Ollie doing something I *really* don't want to witness? No, I realise. He's crying.

Edging the door open a little further, Ollie's back slides into view. Turtle-like, it shakes. I don't want to see or hear this at all. It complicates things.

When Ollie straightens, I worry for a moment that he's sensed me, but no. He's pulling something out from underneath his bed. I can't see what it is or move to get a better view without alerting him to my presence, and I kick myself for not thinking to look there. Ollie seems to perform some kind of psyching-up ritual, breathing hard through his nose. He looks ridiculous. If only his mates could see him now. Then the bedside lamp flickers. It's happening again.

Ollie's holding something in his palm, staring into the sun-bright light bursting from it. It's exactly like the light that seemed to consume him last night. I wasn't expecting this – I thought I was going to have to blackmail him, but this is even better. A chance to get to the source of that light. I shove open the door and reach him before he's even looked up.

'What are you –?' he begins as I make a grab for the object in his hand. 'No, you can't!'

He kicks my shin in the struggle, and my nails make crescent moons on his arm.

'I need to understand!' I say, prising his fist open like an oyster. In his palm is a rose gold locket, the one Dad bought Mum for their wedding. I snatch it.

'Give it back!' Ollie grabs my hands as I twist the locket open. We are both holding it, both acutely aware of its fragility, locked in a delicate wrestle. The light spills out of the locket like oil onto my skin.

Something's wrong.

I am being wrenched apart, my head splitting, my heart twisting. I am being stabbed by a million needles. Ollie stares with panicked eyes, but I can tell that he's not in pain like I am. The room melts into darkness, then light, like we're in a train going through tunnel after tunnel. I catch glimpses of a wooden door flanked by Greek pillars, a stone dome, huge birds in the sky. The building is familiar but I can't place it. In my hand the locket grows too hot. Pressure builds inside my chest, like a stuck bubble. It builds, and builds, and builds. It's too much. I scream and the bubble bursts.

I am standing in Ollie's bedroom again. The needles on my skin have gone, the pressure has lifted. It's all replaced by emptiness. My chest is a vacuum and the room is airless. Ollie is lying on the floor, fast asleep. His hand is closed tight around the locket.

There's nothing more to be done. The light that wanted Ollie doesn't want me, that much is clear. I am empty. Dry. Cracked. I go to my room and pull the duvet over my head. A dark calmness spreads over me; the sign that I am slipping into dreams. Then they take me.

I am back on Wanstead Flats, already trussed up like meat for roasting. A tree knot bores into my back. Jenny is there, of course, her twitch of a smile half coy, half cruel. Instead of lighting the match, though, she opens her mouth wide. Wider than a real human would be able to. From her gaping maw she draws a limp form. In shape, it is a baby, but like no baby

I have ever seen. The skin is puckered from its long gestation in Jenny's mouth, and its eyes are bulging white, a hybrid of human and insect. Jenny thrusts it at me and its boneless arms reach for me, its pale eyes bright with malevolence. I scream, throw myself backwards into the tree, and wake up.

Heart racing, I reach for the lamp next to my bed. My room is its usual mess, scattered sketchbooks and coloured pencils littering the floor. A sculpture of my guardian angel's head sits on the desk, seemingly staring out of the window. In the darkness, the memory of the nightmare still fresh, it's quite creepy. If I didn't know I was awake I'd be terrified it was about to move. Funny, I don't even remember making a sculpture.

The head twists to look at me. Backed against the wall next to my bed, I am frozen. The mouth moves. 'The time is here, Fern,' it says, every syllable weighty. 'Now *wake up*.'

I do. My room is dark again, only a sliver of moonlight sliding through the curtains. But I am not alone. Someone is shuffling across the floor. *It's another nightmare,* I tell myself. Shaking, I turn the bedside lamp on again. The intruder whisks around. They are clutching one of my sketches. Red, bird's-nest hair; scars etching her face; poorly fitting armour. The sketch matches the face. The face that told me to wake up just seconds ago is no longer only in my dreams. She is here. My guardian angel has come for me.

6

She is standing in my bedroom, exactly as I've always dreamed her. I reach out to touch her armour. It's cold but my hand doesn't seem to be able to grasp it, as though it's not truly there.

'How . . .?' I begin, and then I feel faint.

In an instant, the woman is by my side and her arm is around my waist. Up close, I see that every detail of her face is picked out by a halo of soft blue light that has no source. The wall feels cool and solid against my palm, but when the woman's hair brushes against my shoulder everything else blurs. It's the strangest feeling – as though my body is trying to sleep even when my mind is alert.

I'm shaking, my heart's pounding, heat is filling my head. It's not fear exactly, but it's a close relation. This doesn't make sense. How can she be here? 'You're the person from my dreams?' I can't say *guardian angel*. It's too childish.

When she speaks her voice is like the end of an echo. 'I have walked through your sleep, yes. Andraste is one of my names.'

'*Ann-drast?*' I ask, struggling to hear her.

'*Ahn-dras-teh*,' she corrects, leaning towards me. Her

breath – a winter breeze – makes my skin tingle. She has a strange accent that I can't place.

'How are you here?' I ask.

'I've come to take you home.'

'This is home.'

'I mean *my* home. Annwn.'

I shiver. Annwn. The Underworld. Andraste notices my reaction. 'You have been there before, Fern King,' she says, 'You walk in Annwn every night, while your body sleeps here in Ithr.'

At first I don't understand her. Then I begin to piece it together. Mum dying in her sleep. Ollie's inability to wake up. Andraste's appearance in so many of my dreams.

'Annwn is like . . . a dreamworld?'

'That is right.' Andraste turns away from me, looking for something.

'So,' I try to stand and follow her but my legs are having none of it, 'are you . . . do the knights live in Annwn as well?'

'The knights work in Annwn, but they are part of this world, like you.'

'They *work*?'

Andraste sighs, as though she doesn't have much time but knows it will be easier to tell me what I want to know.

'The knights protect the people of your world in Annwn.'

I think of the way Andraste always turns up to rescue me when I'm having a nightmare.

'You protect us from our dreams?'

'I am not a knight, Fern King.'

I look pointedly at her armour, at the sword slung from

her hip. She frowns. 'I mean, I am not a knight in the sense you think.'

'Then . . .' My mind races. 'So what are you?' As soon as I've said it, I wonder whether I've made a faux pas. It sounds like such a rude question. Luckily, Andraste only raises an eyebrow.

'I am one of the Fay,' she replies. She pats my arm, seemingly done with answering my questions properly, and starts opening all my cupboards.

As her fingers – dirt embedded deep under the nails – shuffle through my socks and pants, I realise that I'm not at all outraged at the invasion of privacy. This woman has seen my darkest, most frightening nightmares. She has cut through the ropes that tied me to a burning tree and lifted me through flames. She has protected me when Ollie tried to drink my blood. When I killed my father, she threw the knife away and breathed life back into his wounded body. She's my sister-mother-friend. Of course she can look through my private belongings.

'But why do you – why do the knights – need to protect us from our dreams? I mean – they're just dreams, right?'

Andraste looks back at me disapprovingly. '*Just?*'

'That's not what I . . .' I'm not sure why I've offended her.

She starts rifling through the detritus on my desk, and alights on a square box covered in faded black velvet. She opens it. Inside is a golden pocket mirror, plain on the outside except for the letter *U* engraved in cloudy swirls on the front, and a quote from an old poem on the back.

'This is what I sought,' Andraste says, lifting it from its cushion. 'I am pleased it is still whole. If it had been broken, in either world, I could not have helped you.'

The mirror once belonged to Mum. It was the one item she left me in her will. Dad gave it to me with an odd expression and when I pressed him, told me that Mum had been holding it when she died. 'I didn't want to keep it at all, to be honest, love,' he'd said, 'but your mother was so set on it going to you that I had to. Best put it away now, though, don't you think?' I've spent hours smoothing the surface in my palms during lonely evenings, wondering why on earth Mum left this to me.

'This is the portal to Annwn,' Andraste says, pressing the mirror into my hands. 'Open the mirror and come with me.' She smiles again, but this time the smile seems to reach beyond her mouth. The glow that surrounds her becomes more intense.

The mirror is hot but I'm not sure whether that's the metal or the blood thumping through my body. The vertiginous feeling I had when I first saw Andraste in my room is back.

'Is Annwn safe?' I ask.

Andraste smiles, 'Annwn springs from your dreams and your nightmares. It is formed from the imaginations of every creature in this world. Of course it is not safe for mortals.'

She reaches forward and unlocks the clasp. The mirror springs open in my hand. Blue light – the kind that enveloped Ollie – expands like a bellows until it is flooding my bedroom. It has a shining, glittering quality, like the glowing plankton that turn oceans into carpets of light. Maybe it isn't light at all, but tiny, sentient organisms. Strange shapes, like living shadows, dance across the walls and ceiling. Spirits, cats and bears, old propeller aeroplanes and wolfhounds hunting.

I prepare myself for the pinpricks of a thousand needles

and the feeling of being pulled apart, as I'd had with Ollie's locket, but it never arrives. The light flows over my skin like a silk blanket. It creeps up my arm and across my chest, and I realise that if it continues it will suffocate me. I try to struggle against it, but my growing panic is mixed with an irresistible drowsiness. The last thing I see as the light winds its way over my hair and into my mouth is Andraste's impenetrable gaze. Then I am drowning.

7

I thrash through black waters, unable to breathe but not suffocating. If I open my mouth the darkness pours in like tar, choking me. Sounds distort into vibrations that shudder towards me, my hearing the only sense I have left.

Buried alive.

The meaning of those words hits me a few seconds after I think them.

Can't die like this. Swim up.

But I can't tell which way is up.

Just as I begin to wonder if there is no way out, there's a shift in pressure. My ears pop. My body feels weightier, or maybe the darkness is thinning. The sounds become more distinct. A woman screaming; the grating sound of metal on metal; a guttural sob. Then with an effort I didn't know I needed to make, I push through the night and find myself in sunlight.

At first, all I can take in is that I am no longer in my bedroom. The shapes around me come into focus. Oh. I'm in London. An Underground sign perches overhead. Behind it sit the turrets and ranging windows of the Tower. The streets around us are empty save for a few strangers who, in typical city fashion, seem to be unaware of anyone else. Disappointment niggles. It's all too familiar.

Actually, something *is* different. The people aren't dressed in working garb after all, and they're definitely not behaving in the stiff way they would do in the real world. It's not just that they aren't aware of me – they don't seem to be fully in control of their own bodies. One woman is wearing a floor-length chiffon coat and a necklace of bright yellow flowers and nothing else. She's twirling through the street, arms stretched out, laughing raucously at some invisible joke. As she passes me, the ground stirs.

An eddy of blue light slides over the cobbles. As though touched by magic, they transform. Dirty cobbles become thick beds of herbs and flowers. The ground isn't the only thing that's changing. Every piece of concrete and stone that makes this part of London so austere is morphing into a child's idea of a forest. Ivy, purple moss and clematis wind their way up walls. The Underground sign becomes a sunflower, bigger than any in the real world. The hippy woman twirls her way onwards. In her wake everything returns to its normal state and the memory of what was here only seconds ago makes the stone feel even more grey than it did before.

I should come out with something profound and poetic.

'Wow,' I say.

Andraste beckons me to follow her. Only a few minutes ago I couldn't stop staring at her, but now my attention is constantly caught by Annwn. At first glance everything looks like the London I know – there's even graffiti scrawled across some of the walls – but if you look closely you see so much more. Exotic lizards scramble up the buildings. Secluded gardens rustle loudly with plants that erupt with blossom as we pass. Even the buildings shimmer oddly, sometimes solid, sometimes morphing into the old, beamed taverns that must have occupied these streets hundreds of years ago. I glimpse a golden statue down one alleyway, surrounded by ribbons of every colour imaginable.

As we move past other people acting strangely, I ask Andraste if they're all right.

'They are dreamers,' she explains without looking.

I watch a boy about my age climb determinedly up a sheer wall that towers over our heads, the bricks turning to worms beneath his fingers.

'We're walking through dreams?' I ask.

'Dreamers sometimes see us, and sometimes not,' Andraste says, 'and sometimes they remember us when they wake, as you remembered me. And sometimes they forget us in the space between the worlds.'

'Back in my bedroom, you said Annwn wasn't safe.'

'It is not. It can be deadly. For if you die in Annwn, you die in Ithr – in your world – as well.'

What was it Clemmie had said? *She had lots of marks all over her.*

'So my mum might have been killed here?' I ask, 'But just looked like she died in her sleep?'

'Yes,' Andraste says, grasping my hand, 'Yes, I think that is what happened to Una.'

Vertiginous grief sweeps over me. Andraste marches on, but I can feel that she's only staying silent because she knows that any more conversation about Mum's death would make me fall apart.

A little tornado of blue light gathers in the distance. In its wake a pack of pixie-like creatures scatter into the crevices of the neighbouring buildings. That's when I notice that the air, too, is different from the real world. It's visible, like dust caught in a sunbeam.

'It is inspyre,' Andraste says when I ask her about it. She opens her hand and lets some of that blue light pool in her open palm. 'It creates Annwn. It comes from here,' she says, placing a hand on my forehead, 'and from here.' She moves her hand to press against my heart.

'Humans make it?'

'In a way, yes. Your world, Ithr, makes everything in Annwn. We cannot exist without your thoughts and dreams. But you cannot exist without us. Without Annwn feeding your imagination you could not be yourselves. You would lose all sense of who you are. You would have no hopes, no fears, no ambition, no desires – nothing that makes humans different from each other.'

I reach a hand out as we walk, watching the inspyre play with my fingers. It weaves through them like a pet, eager to please. One particularly playful eddy seems to be enjoying rolling up and down my arm. Then it leaps over to my face, like a puppy trying to lick me. I swipe it away. And freeze.

Something is wrong. I stare at my hand, wondering whether the inspyre has done something to it. I touch my face again. Now with both hands. It can't be. Fumbling in my pocket for Mum's mirror I am almost too scared to open it. There must be some mistake. I hold the mirror in front of me. It takes a moment to focus it on the right part of my face. Red irises, blonde hair, white-as-bone skin. It's me. But the skin is smooth. My burn has vanished.

'It's gone,' I say hysterically. 'What's happened to me? What's happening?!' I can't say why I'm so upset. I dreamed about the fire never happening. It's just overwhelming. *This is my world*. A world where I don't look like such a freak. I never, ever want to leave.

'Why is the burn not there?' I ask Andraste.

'Because it is new,' she says.

'I don't understand.'

'It is not a part of you yet. You don't imagine yourself that way.'

'So I only look how I *want* to look?' But no, I think, that can't be right or I wouldn't have my red eyes.

'No,' she says. 'In Annwn, you look how you think you look. The burning is not old – you are not accustomed to it yet. Perhaps you never will be. So you do not see it on yourself when you come here.'

'So I can't change the rest of my appearance?' I ask.

Andraste's eyes twinkle strangely. 'Is it so bad, looking different?'

I look at her scars and unkempt hair.

'No,' I say at last, although I think she knows I don't mean it. 'No, there's nothing wrong with it, I guess.'

She sets off down the street once more. 'We must keep going. We must go on to Tintagel.'

'Tintagel?'

I try to remember where I've heard that name before.

'Wait – isn't Tintagel a castle?'

'Yes. It is the thanes' castle.'

'But . . . isn't that over the other side of the country? In Cornwall?'

'That is not the true Tintagel. The true Tintagel is here, in Annwn.'

We round a corner, and all sense of direction leaves me. We should be passing St Paul's Cathedral, but all I can see is a deep moat brimming with murky water and a wooden wall beyond.

'Tintagel,' Andraste says, pointing above the wall.

I was wrong. There, just where it should be, is St Paul's. But it's not quite the building I know. The shape is the same – the dome perched on a crown of pillars. But it is a Frankenstein's monster of materials. Patches of marble alternate with red brick and hewn rock. The grand columns are part stone, part scaffolding. Four crenellated towers mark the corners of the building. A flag, its emblem a five-pointed star inside a circle, billows from the top of the central dome. Suddenly I realise that I have caught a glimpse of this castle before, when I tried to snatch Ollie's locket. Does this mean he's inside Tintagel? What would the knights want with my brother?

I am so busy gaping at this new version of St Paul's that I almost don't notice the shadows passing overhead. They roll across the dome like storm clouds. It's a huge flock of birds. Then one of them lands on top of the wall, folding its great wings across its back, and with a heart pound I realise it's not a bird at all.

'Oh my God.'

The sky is full of angels. They soar in many-coloured skins around the castle's spires. More of them rest above the porch. Some gaze on me benevolently. Others land on all fours and grin through fanged teeth. A cherub plays amongst them, meaty and merry.

Andraste leaves me gaping and strides towards a gatehouse set into the wooden wall, beside a raised drawbridge. I trot after her.

'Is this where the knights live?' I ask breathlessly.

'Yes.' She stops and frowns at me for the first time. 'They are not expecting you, Fern.'

'What do you mean?'

'It was your mother's greatest wish that you become a knight, like her.'

'Mum wanted . . .?'

'I will do my best to honour her wish, but you must play your part also.'

'How . . .?' But Andraste doesn't answer, merely holds up a hand to the guardians in the gatehouse. I watch the skies unseeingly, questions about Mum and the knights beating through my head like the wings of those angels. They remind me of one of my few friends back when I was at St Stephen's. Lauren's family was obsessively religious. They never let her invite me round because they were scared of what my eyes might signify. Lauren and I drifted apart. It's hard to stay friends with someone whose parents think you need a dose of holy water and an exorcism.

A screech breaks through the air. The angel that was resting on the wall is no longer alone. Dozens of them perch there, every one watching us through cat-like eyes. Andraste throws an arm across my chest.

'Were you remembering something?' she asks me, her eyes not leaving the angels.

'I was just thinking about an old friend.'

'What about her?'

'Just how the angels reminded me of her parents, and how they were scared of . . . Oh.' Given what Andraste has just told me about inspyre, perhaps musing about people who think I'm possessed when in the presence of angels isn't the best idea.

The angels take flight again. In paintings they are graceful creatures, but now these ones are all angles. One dives towards us, hands and clawed feet stretched in front of it like an eagle. I glimpse a set of horns pushing through the angel's curled hair just before Andraste slashes at its chest with her sword. The angel reels away, but its inhuman cries enrage the others.

'You will run now!' Andraste pushes me roughly towards the drawbridge, which is slowly lowering. But there's no way I'm leaving her to take them on all by herself. Inspyre vibrates around me, like it's being charged by my panic. I can hear the angels' wings now, hundreds of them beating like a giant heart. They drop as one. Andraste stands over me, protecting me as she always has. Her sword arcs, slicing through the belly of one. The angel's furious scream is cut off as it disintegrates back into the air, like burning paper. Then the rest are upon her, diverted from me by her attack. I can't see her any more, only a great, pulsing mass of feathers. As I try to prise the wings away I think dimly that a sword might be useful. Or any weapon, really, I'm not fussy.

Thud. A spear punches through three angels with a single swoop. As they burst back into the inspyre of which they were made, the sound of hooves on stone echoes around the square.

Four riders in medieval clothing gallop towards us. The leader has her horse's reins looped over one arm, and she's wielding another spear. She shouts a single word and her companions fan out. Another rider splits from the main group and signals to the leader with his own spear. Together they send their weapons into the melee, taking out a dozen angels as they power through. The riders catch each other's spears perfectly and spin them round in one toss to ready them for the next throw. The angels wheel up into the air, gathering to face this new attack. A fourth rider emerges, galloping straight for Andraste and me.

Arms sweep me onto the moving horse. I find myself riding side-saddle in front of someone. The horse canters across the drawbridge. I have a brief view of a courtyard and, beyond it, lush gardens, then we are clattering up wide stone steps into the castle of Tintagel.

8

As the horse bounces to a halt, I slide off and wobble to the ground, my head thumping with adrenalin. Through dozens of hooves I spot Andraste running through the wide front doors. She and the other riders push them closed and lift a wooden beam into place to fortify them. The angels pummel the other side.

'It's okay,' one of the riders tells me. 'Nothing that means harm to us can get inside these walls without permission from the Head Thane. You're safe.'

The woman whose spear had been our saviour high-fives her friend. 'First time getting three in a throw, baby!' she laughs.

The oddity of entering St Paul's on horseback is completely overshadowed when I see its interior. I'm used to gilded paintings spread across the ceiling and an atmosphere of awe, where everyone walks toes first. In this world, St Paul's is no longer a place of worship. It's unmistakably a castle. Cloisters still run along the walls, but I am standing in an inner courtyard that is open to the elements. Everywhere I look men and women dressed in strange uniforms call to each other, or hurry with arms full of papers through tantalisingly open doors.

'You okay?' the boy who pulled me onto his horse asks,

dismounting rather more elegantly than I did. He has messy brown hair and a cheeky grin. 'Woah,' he says, looking at me properly for the first time. 'Cool eyes.'

No one has ever described my eyes as 'cool' before. Freaky, yes. Crazy, tick. I don't know how to handle this compliment, but it seems as though I don't have to, because he is immediately approached by a man in a green uniform. 'I'm supposed to be informed about aventures visiting, Rafe,' I hear him chastise, before Andraste takes my hand and drags me onwards.

'What's an aventure?' I ask Andraste, looking back at Rafe as he argues with the man in the green uniform.

'It is someone from your world who has come to Annwn through a portal – someone who is not dreaming but conscious here. Come.' The man in the green uniform spots us hurrying away and gives chase.

'Where are we going?' I ask her.

'To the person we must persuade,' she replies.

'Excuse me!' The man in the green uniform trails behind us. 'Excuse me, please. You need to –'

Andraste whirls around and fixes the man with a steely gaze. He wilts before her. 'Apologies, my lady, I did not realise –'

But we don't wait to hear him finish. Andraste ushers me onwards.

People watch us as we pass from the courtyard through an enormous archway that leads beneath the main dome. The floor here is no longer old flagstones but polished marble laid in intricate patterns. A prickling down the back of my neck warns me that I'm being watched. Instinctively, I look up. High above us, a gallery lines the inner walls of the dome. Looking down upon me is a bear of a man. His hands rest wide upon the ledge, as heavy and steady as the roots of a tree. He is tall, I can see that much even from here, and bearded. I get a sense that he is surveying his domain, and having clocked two intruders is calculating what to do next. We pass beneath a lower ceiling, and I lose sight of him, whoever he is.

We skirt what looks like a large antechamber, pass down another corridor, and then Andraste is knocking on an old wooden door at the very back of the castle. There is no response. Andraste knocks again.

'Were you looking for me, my lady?' a deep voice intones behind us.

It's the same man I saw on the gallery just seconds ago. I'm not sure how he got down here so quickly, but he doesn't look like the kind of person who answers questions like that. Close up, he's even taller than I'd thought.

Andraste tugs me forward. 'This is Fern King. She should be a thane,' she tells him. Clearly being a 'lady' or a 'Fay' in Annwn doesn't mean you get taught the niceties of small talk.

The man holds out a hand to me. 'Lord Allenby. Shall we go in?'

He steps between us and opens the door.

The room beyond is so stunning that I almost forget why we're here. Huge windows range around a semi-circular wall. It must be sunset outside because the light streaming through them coats everything with a tired warmth. The wall behind me is covered from floor to ceiling with bookcases. A leather-topped desk takes pride of place in the centre of the room and a globe sits in a wooden case to one side. It's simple, but everything here – from the wooden cornicing to the crystal whisky glasses on a side table – have been crafted with patience and passion.

Lord Allenby gestures to a couple of chairs in front of his desk. I sit. Andraste doesn't.

'Why don't we begin with you telling me how you come to be sitting here even though you're not a thane,' Lord Allenby starts, his gaze impassive.

I don't know what a thane is, but I sense that this is my opportunity to *play my part*, as Andraste put it. I put on my best Bosco College well-raised student voice. That always seems to go down well.

'I'm sorry for turning up like this, but my mother was a knight, and I'd like to be one too, please.'

'I see,' Lord Allenby says. 'And who was your mother?'

'Una King.'

His whole body tenses.

'The only Una I ever knew was Una Gorlois.'

'Yes! That was her name before she married my dad.'

Lord Allenby sighs, a big bear's breath, and rakes a hand through his hair.

'I'm sorry you lost her so young. When I heard that she'd died I thought of you and your brother.'

I'm about to say thank you, which I guess is the standard reply when someone gives you their condolences fifteen years too late, when something he said clicks.

'What do you mean, when you *heard* about her dying? I thought you might know how . . .'

'Your mother retired from the knights shortly after you were born.'

I sink.

'So you don't know how she died?' I ask. 'Is that why you want to join us? To find out what happened to your mother?'

Andraste, standing behind me, squeezes my shoulder. I know what she's trying to say. *Don't blow this*. The trouble is, I don't think that telling the truth is going to get me what I want, because I *do* want to find out what happened to her, but now, having walked through this world, I want so much more. Eventually, I settle for something akin to the truth. 'I want to follow in her footsteps.'

Lord Allenby stares at me in that steady, unnerving way. Then he beckons for me to follow him. He leads me back to that exquisite marble floor under the dome. Four stone columns, one at each corner, reach up to support the roof. From a distance, it looks as though millions of ants are marching across them in neat lines. As I get closer I see that they're not ants, but names – countless names, each with a year next to them, winding their way up and up and up.

'That,' he says, nodding towards the moving words, 'is a list of our dead. A few centuries ago they were just your standard engravings, but when we ran out of room the Fay had to make them move so they'd all fit in.'

I stare at the roster. A roll call of ghosts, their names set next to the year they died.

'Fern,' Lord Allenby says, 'do you know what we do here?'

'You fight nightmares.'

'We protect people from the worst parts of their imaginations – the parts that could kill them. Sometimes that means fighting nightmares, yes. But it's not just knights who work here, Miss King. The knights are just one part of a larger organisation called the thanes. Hundreds of us protecting dreamers in this world.'

I look around at the purpose and bustle of Tintagel. I imagine Mum walking through the cloisters, imagine her standing where I am standing now. The risk of being added to that roster of names seems like a fair price to pay to get to explore Annwn. To find out more about Mum.

'I'd still like to join,' I tell Lord Allenby, but he just shakes his head.

'It doesn't work like that.' He says, 'This isn't the kind of job you walk into because your parents did it. No one here would allow that. We save the lives of people who will never know they needed to be saved. We are chosen for specific traits. Bravery and loyalty and strength of imagination, which I'm sure you have. But the most important quality is that you're willing to die for anyone. *Anyone*. Do you understand me?'

I nod, my throat dry.

'Can you tell me, hand on heart, Fern, that if your worst enemy was in danger, that you'd risk your life for them?'

I think about Jenny, but then Ollie comes to mind. I know deep down that I wouldn't save my brother if he was in trouble. I would watch, I think; I would watch as he died. My truest enemy is probably inside these very walls. But I can't let Lord Allenby know that.

'I can be that person, though,' I tell him. 'If I could just –'

'There's a reason you weren't chosen, Fern.'

He signals to a couple of people in tunics – one green with

a golden quill embroidered upon it, one black with a silver hawk emblem.

'Was my brother chosen?' I say, unable to keep the bitterness from my voice, 'Ollie King? Is he here?'

Lord Allenby catches the eye of the man in the green tunic, who nods awkwardly. I can't help but laugh. So Ollie's deemed to have loyalty and bravery, but I'm not? What an absolute joke.

'Someone's going to come and help you forget, now,' Lord Allenby says. 'You're going to wake up and all of this will be gone. You won't have heard of the knights, and you'll think your mother, God rest her soul, died naturally.'

Forget? I don't want to forget. I can sense Andraste beside me, trembling with energy. But this isn't her fight. It's mine. Even if he is right, I can't let go of this dream, not so soon after catching it.

'Please,' I say, 'let me prove myself to you. I can be just as good as any of them.'

'No, Fern,' he says, kindly but with finality, signalling to the man in the black tunic. 'Take her to the morrigans,' he tells him.

'No,' Andraste says fiercely. She grabs my arm to stop the man from taking me away. 'She must take the Tournament.'

I cleave myself to her.

'My lady,' Lord Allenby says, 'you know that's not how it works.'

He turns away and the man in the black tunic steps forward, but Andraste doesn't loosen her grip on me. 'I have this also,' she says, with the air of someone playing their trump card. She produces a crumpled envelope. There is a messy wax seal, which has been broken, and the letters *LA* are written in a spiky script that I recognise immediately.

Lord Allenby freezes as his eyes rake over what's written inside. I crane my head to read it, and when I see the words, my heart stands still.

Lionel – I am calling in your debt. Make sure my little girl takes the Tournament. Una.

'You left me no choice,' Andraste says.

Lord Allenby nods heavily. 'Well. There it is,' he says. 'All right. Miss King, you can take the Tournament tomorrow night. We'll see whether you do have a place here. I should warn you that it's dangerous. You need to understand that, before you're pushed into something you don't know much about. And if you do pass it, you might not be placed with the knights. Be ready for that too.'

He turns away, but then looks back. 'Oh and Miss King?'

'Yes, sir.'

'You'll need to bring something precious with you tomorrow. Not expensive. Something that's dear to you.'

'Okay, sir. And . . . thank you.'

Emotions roll through me. *My little girl.* Mum. Mum wanted me to be a knight, and she called in some sort of debt to make sure I had the chance. Warmth builds in my stomach and rises through my chest. Is this what it feels like to be loved unconditionally? To have someone totally on your side?

Someone escorts me to a side room that clinks and clanks with copper equipment. There, a woman in a green tunic takes my mirror portal and holds it steady with a vice. She examines it closely, then adjusts some dials. Five nozzles whir into action, turning to point directly at my mirror. As she works, she talks.

'Every authorised portal has a specific entry and exit point from Annwn. The London thanes, for example, always arrive on the platform just outside Tintagel, and you'd need to get back to that platform to leave Annwn.'

'So I can't just open the mirror and go back to the real . . . I mean, Ithr?'

''Fraid not. It helps us to regulate and record aventures coming in and out of Annwn.'

'Aventures. They're people like me and you, right? Who aren't dreaming.'

'That's right. Of course, you can get illegal portals that let you go back to Ithr without an exit point, but they're tricky things to get hold of. Very tricky.'

She finally settles back in her seat. 'It looks to me as though your mirror here has been a portal for a while.'

'What do you mean?'

'This mirror has had two entry points over the years. See?'

She pushes a button and one of the nozzles erupts into life, seemingly galvanising the inspyre around us to stab into the mirror. The mirror begins to glow, then it puts forth a faint image. I strain to see it: the sign for the Underground near Tower Hill, where I arrived what must be just a few hours ago, if this place marks time in hours. Then the image changes, and I see the same lush gardens I glimpsed when I was carried up the steps into Tintagel.

'These are the places your portal has been connected to. This second image is the portal here – I'd say this mirror used to belong to a knight.'

'It did,' I tell her. 'It belonged to my mother.'

'Well . . .' The woman smiles. 'You'd better do her proud.' She pushes another button. This time all five nozzles leap into action, pointing five beams of inspyre at the mirror until it becomes too bright to look at. A high-pitched whine grows, and I realise it's the mirror itself, screaming under the pressure.

'Won't it break?!' I yell over the noise, but the woman is too engrossed in her work to answer; adjusting the nozzles minutely until the pressure on the mirror seems to ease. At last she looks up. 'There. I've just changed its entry point. Next time you come, you'll arrive in Tintagel's grounds!'

Once my mirror has grown cool enough to touch again, Andraste leads me outside. We walk in silence through the castle's gardens. When we stop beside the circular platform that will apparently allow me to wake up back in my room, I finally ask her the questions that have been playing on my mind.

'Why didn't you give Lord Allenby Mum's note straight away?'

'Because a debt is binding in Annwn. If you don't try to fulfil a debt, then you lose your ability to enter this world. For Lord Allenby, who governs the thanes of London, it would be disastrous. It is a very powerful thing, an oath, and not to be called upon lightly.'

'I wonder what he did that meant he owed Mum.'

'I cannot tell you that. Your mother had many secrets.'

She presses Mum's mirror into my hand. I have one more question, even though it makes me feel childish.

'Is what Lord Allenby said true? Is the Tournament dangerous?'

'Yes,' she says, 'it can be very dangerous if you do not belong.'

'But you think I do?'

'I do.'

I don't find her reassurance particularly comforting. I can't shake the feeling that perhaps Andraste and Mum are simply believing in me out of love or obligation rather than knowledge. Lord Allenby's words, that there's something missing in me, make me uncomfortable. But I cannot voice this fear, not even to Andraste, because she has gone to so much trouble to get me this far.

She draws me in close for a hug. It's pretty uncomfortable with her armour digging into my collarbone, but I try not to wince.

'If you become a knight, you will save us, won't you?' she whispers, so quietly I almost don't hear her.

'What?'

'Be courageous, Fern King, like your mother.'

She kisses me roughly on the forehead. The blue light that surrounds her shimmers, and for an instant I have a sense of déjà vu. A memory of other forehead kisses. A deep, melodic voice. *Sweet dreams, munchkins.* Then it's gone.

'What do you mean, *save you*?' But she has opened the mirror. The light inside it pools out around me. Suddenly the platform I'm on is glowing too. Andraste walks heavily away from the castle. As the light tries to close my eyes, I see her falter and clasp her side. I try to fight the pull towards consciousness, to help her, but it's no good.

The last thing I see before I wake up is the dome of the castle standing proud against a high sun. And ranged around its edge are hundreds and hundreds of angels.

9

Sometimes my head gets stuck inside a nightmare, and even after I've woken up it takes ages to remind myself it wasn't real. This morning I have to do the opposite. Whenever I try to absorb that I've just been in a different reality, something in my brain shuts down. I have to consider it from a distance, like a physics theory where the concept's so intangible that I don't feel its weight. If I think of it like that, I'm safe. I touch my cheek. The burn scar is there again, the crumpled skin thick and immobile.

The beginnings of dawn are starting to reach through the window, but I don't move from the spot on the floor where I woke. My whole body feels different, like wearing an old pair of jeans after they've been washed.

'Sleep well, Ferny?' Dad asks when I go downstairs. He's standing over the row of orchids we keep on the windowsill, using a dropper to feed them just the right amount of water.

'In a way.'

That makes Ollie look up from the TV. Satisfyingly, he's still got red marks on his hands from where I dug my nails in last night. I can't wait to see his face when I turn up at Tintagel this evening.

It's my turn to make lunch so I busy myself in the kitchen. The secret, that I've got a chance to be in the knights, is delicious. Even more delicious is that Mum wanted me to follow in her footsteps and went to great lengths to give me that chance.

'Mmm, that smells good, Ferny. Curry's one of Clemmie's favourites.' Dad nabs a spoonful of sauce out of the pot. A few days ago I might not have been feeling so generous, but actually I planned to make curry for Clemmie as a sort of unspoken thanks for the other day, after Archimago's messages. To be honest, I'd probably be nicer to her in general if she wasn't so beige. But today, when Clemmie arrives in a flurry of lavender cashmere, I embrace her like the gracious host that I am. When she remarks that the orchids are doing well, I don't remind her that we only keep them because they were Mum's favourite flower. When she calls me 'Ferny' over lunch I don't snap that Dad has exclusive rights over that nickname.

'Had any more dreams about your guardian angel lately?' she asks me, sharing a knowing smile with Ollie.

'Last night, actually,' I say, unfazed for once by her attempts to pretend she's part of the family. 'She took me to St Paul's Cathedral, of all places.'

'How strange!'

Ollie tries to titter along but I can see I've thrown him.

'Isn't it?' I laugh, getting carried away. 'I mean, what's she going to do with me next? Take me to a tournament?'

Clemmie and Dad are stumped but smile anyway, obviously wondering whether I've finally cracked. Ollie's smirk, however, is frozen. He knows for sure now. Little victories.

After lunch Clemmie corners me. 'Fern, the other day . . .'

'It's okay,' I tell her, 'it was just a prank.'

'You found out who did it?'

'Yeah,' I lie. 'They fessed up. I'm just going to drop it.'

Clemmie frowns. 'I do think –'

'It's fine,' I say firmly. 'Thanks, though.'

I slip upstairs and lock my bedroom door so Clemmie can't follow me. The sound of Ollie washing dishes and chatting to Dad rumbles up through the carpet. A few moments later Clemmie's higher tone joins in and I sigh in relief. I can't be having her trying to investigate Archimago. Not now I have a chance to investigate them myself, from Annwn. I look round my room and clutter looks back. *Something precious*. That's what Lord Allenby had said. *My pride*, I think, moving piles of paper from one part of the floor to another.

I empty my drawers. There, at the bottom of one, is an old jewellery box. Inside are a few tangled chains, a rosary from a distant uncle, and there – a silver pendant. It twists my heart.

When I was eight I spotted it in the window of a pawnbroker's shop and was captivated immediately. Filigree silver woven into a crescent moon surrounded by five diamond stars. It was battered even then, one setting missing its gem. The delicacy of the workmanship was exquisite. I imagined a Victorian jeweller spending days manipulating diamonds and moulding silver with blistered fingers, only for his work to be passed through owners until it arrived at the pawn shop in this sorry state. Most people wouldn't have blinked at the price tag, but it was still out of reach of my pocket money. He never said anything, but I knew instinctively that asking Dad for more was out of the question.

I looked at the pendant through the shop window every day for a fortnight. Apart from the constant desire to look normal, I'd never wanted anything as much as I wanted that necklace. Once I even took the money out of Dad's wallet, but I got an attack of conscience and returned it before he realised.

Then one day Ollie knocked on my bedroom door and thrust a velvet pouch into my hands. Inside it, the necklace.

'It's an early birthday present, okay?' he told me as I stared at it. Close up, I could see how the silver threads in the moon were twisted together like rope.

'How did you get it?'

'How do you think, crazy? I bought it.'

'But it's too expensive.' I had a vision of the police knocking at the door and dragging Ollie away, Dad crying, me crying, and Ollie in prison forever and ever. 'Did you steal it?'

'Don't be stupid.'

'I'm not stupid.'

'Don't say stupid things then. I'm good at saving. Not like you, spendypants.'

I wore that necklace every single day, even after Ollie stopped liking me. Right up to the day of the fire. I was wearing it when they tied me to the tree. If you look closely just below my clavicle, you can see the outline of the pendant where the burning metal seared my chest. The necklace bears the marks of the fire too. The wires holding the stars are so brittle that one of them has broken. Only three diamonds remain. The crescent moon is grey and mottled. I suppose I should have thrown it away, but it is precious to me, even now. Once I loved it for its battered beauty. Now it's irrevocably deformed, like me. Both of us were destroyed by my brother.

As darkness falls, bringing bedtime closer, I push my doubts away: the fact that I might not get into the knights; Lord Allenby's warnings; the danger of the Tournament. I can't let Andraste down. I can't let Mum down. I can't let myself down.

'You just open the mirror,' the woman in the green tunic had said when she returned it, 'and it will bring you to Tintagel. Just keep it safe and be sure you're alone when you open it.'

When I do open the mirror, it takes a moment for the portal to come to life. Then, like a hob switched on, the mirror grows warm to hot to burning. The light pulls me inside and throws me into the black waters that breach Ithr – the real world – and Annwn.

When I reach up out of the waters I am not standing next to Tower Hill, but on the round platform in Tintagel's gardens that had sent me home last night.

'Hi,' someone chirps. 'I don't think we've met, have we? I'm pretty sure I'd remember your face. Red eyes. Wow. Wish I could imagine myself something cool like that, but I suppose we'll learn that later.'

The prattling comes from a boy about my age, with nut-brown skin and a haircut that might have been cool twenty years ago. I know his type immediately. False confidence. Talks too much. Trying and failing with his appearance. He's me if I'd actually cared about being popular.

'I'm Ramesh,' he says, eagerly holding out a hand.

'Um. Fern,' I say, but I put my hands in my pockets. I don't do physical contact unless I can help it.

Before he can say anything else, I turn back to the platform. Motes of inspyre spark. Like corn in a pan, they reach a limit then burst. But instead of popcorn there's a person standing where the dust was. Another spark; another person appears. Soon the platform is full. Some people are in regular clothing like me, some are in the thanes' uniform of a coloured tunic over leggings and boots.

'Shall we head on over?' Ramesh says. 'We might be unfashionably early, but it shows willing, doesn't it? Never know if there's going to be a queue.'

He sets off without waiting for a reply. Great. I'm stuck with a talker.

'What do you make of all this, then?' Ramesh babbles over his shoulder. 'I legit thought I was going insane when that light came. I wonder if they know when we're on our own or if some people are taken when they're having a sleepover or out at the cinema.'

I know that I should probably reply but I worry that would only encourage him.

'The water when you come into this place is really horrible, isn't it? I freaked . . .'

'Are you as scared as I am?' a soft voice says behind me, and I turn to see a plump, rabbit-eyed girl trailing behind Ramesh and me.

'God, yeah.' Ramesh grins, seemingly unbothered by the interruption to his monologue. 'Didn't sleep a wink last night. I had these really weird dreams.'

They laugh the way strangers do when they want to be friends.

'Fern; Rachel.' Ramesh nods between the girl and me. More come up behind her, offering hands to shake and names to remember, and I am forced to reciprocate. Oh no. This wasn't what I'd bargained for at all. It was supposed to be solitary. I'd be on my own, roaming this world like I roam London after school.

'What are *you* doing here?' At last, someone I know how to deal with. Ollie is standing in the midst of the group. There was a time when I envied the way he could arrive and a whole party would gravitate towards him.

'Special invitation.' I give him my best whattaya-going-to-do-about-it-huh smile.

'How do you know each other?' rabbity Rachel asks.

'We're twins,' I say, knowing that it will pain Ollie enormously to admit to being related to me. 'He got all the looks, I got all the morals.'

Ollie's expression sharpens.

'Wow,' I hear Ramesh whisper to someone. 'If I'd wanted to watch messed-up family arguments I'd have told my parents where I hid their whisky.'

'Fern likes to make out she's special,' Ollie tells his harem. 'Everything's about her, you know the type.'

He breezes past me, his followers trotting along in his wake. I offer a sarcastic smile as he passes. I should be used to his barbs by now. As the rest of the group traipses towards the castle doors, casting assessing looks my way, I make a vow. I will become a knight, find out what happened to Mum, and never, under any circumstances, even think about trying to make friends with any of these people.

10

It's going to take me some time to get my head around the fact that St Paul's has become a medieval castle. As we are shepherded into the area beneath the dome, I try to peer through open doorways, or over the shoulders of a group of thanes who are huddled around a circular table. The marble floor beneath me is made of slabs of silver and purple flecked with gold – shades of marble I've never seen in Ithr. They are arranged in a perfect circle that mirrors the dome above us. I wish I was alone so I could get a good look at the full pattern instead of craning around other people's legs.

We are corralled into a semblance of order by people in green tunics. 'It's imperative you stay inside this circle . . .' one of them begins.

I try to stay on the edges of the crowd, but Ramesh has attached himself to me despite Ollie's jibes, and where Ramesh goes, it seems that Rachel goes too.

'So how come you weren't at the initiation?' Ramesh whispers. 'Did you get a free pass or something?'

'Yeah, Fern, how come you weren't there?' Ollie chimes in from a distance.

'You should have come,' Ramesh carries on, oblivious to the sudden tension. 'It was good fun. It's a great group of people here.'

I shrug. I'm not going to tell any of them that I'm only here on sufferance.

'Do you know which lore you want yet?' Ramesh says. 'I mean, obviously the knights are the coolest, but Rachel wants to be a harker.' He mock-grimaces.

'The harkers look amazing,' Rachel says. 'Did you see the view from the balcony? And the Round Table is so beautiful.'

Lore, harkers, Round Table? I'm even more out of my depth than I'd thought.

'I'd hate to be a reeve, like these guys.' Ramesh indicates the people in green tunics, who are clearly getting exasperated by our lack of concentration.

'The administrators of Annwn.' A boy behind Ramesh has been listening in and now rolls his eyes in disdain. 'Sounds like the most boring job ever.'

Ramesh nods. 'But wouldn't it just be the worst to go through the Tournament and find out you can't be a thane at all? I don't think I'd be able to sleep ever again.'

I withdraw at that. They are touching upon my greatest fear but I can tell from their excitement that they don't really believe it will happen to them. It could very well happen to me, though.

Ramesh's conversation is interrupted by a noise like a sonic boom. The tiles encircling us erupt into a wall of light. Rachel isn't the only one who screams. Above our heads is a cylinder of blue light. At its top, there's a landscape. A ying and yang of grass and sky.

'Don't be frightened,' one of the reeves calls. 'You all came here through a portal. Think of this as the same thing – just on a bigger scale.'

'This way, squires,' I hear Lord Allenby growl from amidst the crush. A moment later his silhouette is moving along the tunnel. It looks as though he's walking on a wall. My brain and eyes are at war with each other, trying to resolve the impossible. The spot between my eyebrows pulses with confusion.

'How do we do that?' Ramesh says.

I move closer to the wall of light. It's made up of thousands of fibres, stretched like harp strings that bend and spring back when pushed. I'm not the only one who's trying to figure out how it works, as if anything in this world makes logical sense. Ollie pushes through the crowd to study the wall himself, and I just know that he's planning on being the first person to follow Lord Allenby.

That's enough motivation for any self-respecting twin sister. I place both hands on the wall, as far up as I can reach. *Think of it like bouldering*, I tell myself, *like the kids' ones in the* Olympic Park. As long as the light strings let me dig my fingers in, it's not so different. When I'm satisfied that I've got a good grip, I lift my feet off the ground and balance them against the wall.

The world lurches.

I'm no longer climbing. I'm on my hands and knees, feeling like I'm going to projectile vomit, on a wall that is no longer a wall but a floor. Shakily, I get to my feet, expecting to fall off at any moment. By every law of physics I can remember – and admittedly that's not many – none of this should be possible. But here I am, standing upright on a soft carpet of light, with the rest of the crowd who should be below me to one side instead. It's them who are on a wall, not me. Up ahead I can just make out Lord Allenby's shadow, watching me.

Ramesh and Rachel clap, and before long the whole group is cheering.

'Give us a hand then,' someone says. A stranger is voluntarily asking for my help. This night keeps getting weirder. I pull him up – or over, I can't decide which. He lands unsteadily, but makes the transition from horizontal to vertical – or vertical to horizontal – more gracefully than I did.

To avoid having to interact further, I walk ahead. I like to think I look confident, but the light is like sand, lapping over my feet if I try to move too quickly. Eventually I stumble out of the tunnel into sunlight. Stubby grass spreads out under a sky streaked with the detritus of clouds. A low bank of earth bends gently around me.

'Wowzers.' Ramesh whistles, emerging behind me, and even as I wonder who on earth says that any more, I turn to see what he's looking at.

The bank, I see now, is circular. In the centre, slabs of marble erupt from the grass. They are joined at the top by smaller slabs, creating a series of archways that face into each other like military commanders at a secret meeting. The sharpness of the cut stone is rendered even more forbidding beneath the relentless sunlight.

I've seen it before, of course. In photos, postcards, online. Stonehenge. Except this isn't some crumbling old monument. Every piece gleams white, every corner is a satisfyingly clean angle. Maybe this is what Stonehenge must have looked like when it was first built.

I move away from the groups now pouring from the tunnel, keen to see this miracle more closely. I don't understand how it's so new in Annwn, when it's thousands of years old in our world. As I get closer to the monument, though, I realise that it's not smooth after all. In fact, I'm not even sure it's made of stone. Pebbles, maybe? Shells? I might not be touchy-feely with people, but I'm a hugger when it comes to art. I run a hand over the surface. Then my brain resolves what it's really seeing and I lurch backwards with a cry of shock.

This Stonehenge is made of bones.

They have been placed with such care that you can only see them close up. The ball of a hip bone rests on top of a jaw, and tiny joints – fingers? Toes? – fill in the gaps. Skulls are placed at equal intervals over the archways, supported by tibia. Vertebrae form zigzags around sternums. It's gruesomely beautiful.

'D'you like my handiwork, girl?' a voice drawls in my ear.

The old man has materialised so close to me that I can smell rancid meat on his breath. His shoulders have hunched right round his chest, and his skin is like a withered apple. From the waist down he wears a skirt made of wooden slats. From the waist up he is naked. He grins like a vulture sizing me up.

'Who are you?' I ask.

'My name is Merlin,' he leers in a crumbly voice, 'and this world belongs to me.'

11

He's nothing like the Merlin I've read about in stories. This is no friendly old wizard. His stare makes me want to put on another layer of clothing. He's standing at the head of one of the motliest groups I've ever seen. Andraste is amongst them, standing between two men: one has red hair that matches hers; the other has a permanent smirk and boney spikes running from his forehead right down his back. I am guessing, from what Andraste told me last night, that these people are Fay.

A thane had pulled me away from Merlin before I could answer him and pushed me into a line along the inner circle of Stonehenge with the other squires. We stand opposite five thanes in uniform. I spot a dreadlocked woman dressed in a blue tunic embroidered with a sword. Ramesh has already told me that's the knights' uniform. So she's the one I have to impress.

Rachel points at a woman wearing a tunic that has an eye emblazoned on red fabric. 'That's Maisie. She's the Captain of the harkers.'

'I heard the veneurs are creepy,' Ramesh replies. 'I guess that's why they wear black.' I look across at the man in the black tunic, a white hawk embroidered across velvet. I'm inclined to agree with Ramesh, given Lord Allenby had ordered one of these guys to wipe my memory last night.

'I haven't met the Knight Captain yet,' Ramesh continues. 'Oh, I really, really, really hope he likes me.'

'He?' I ask, glancing over at the dreadlocked woman.

'Oh, Emory there isn't the Captain. Apparently the actual Captain's been off duty for months now.'

'Why?' someone asks, leaning over.

'No one knows,' Ramesh says conspiratorially.

'Or no one wanted to tell us,' Ollie remarks.

I look back at Emory. However interesting the Knight Captain's absence might be, he's not here. Emory is.

'So,' I say, 'I know that the ones in green with the golden quill are reeves, but who are those guys?'

'The ones in white with the snake wound round a rod? They're the apothecaries.'

Rachel starts to say something but Lord Allenby gathers everyone's attention and all of us fall silent.

'Squires,' Lord Allenby booms. 'Welcome to Stonehenge.'

'A little different from the pale replica you know in Ithr,' Merlin sneers. 'That one was only built by men. This was forged by me and my kind.'

Merlin steps forward, and so does a woman who looks like a fairytale princess. Her bodice is stitched with real flowers and a long skirt falls to the ground in layers of silk and chiffon. A white slipper peeks from beneath the fabric. Her rose-gold hair is long and loose, offering the only covering to her arms. The woman opens her hand and inspyre pools inside it. The people around me gasp as the light sparks and dances and finally forms a harp.

'That's incredible,' Ramesh whispers. Then the woman opens her mouth and steals my reply.

Her lilting voice doesn't seem to come only from her, but from the air around us, from the bones behind us, from within my own chest. The words are quiet but they weave into my thoughts.

Here is the story, the voice says, *of the Fay, of the first humans, of the thread that holds us together.*

It's not exactly a song. There's no discernible tune, no chorus or rousing key change. But it's not a normal story either. As the woman speak-sings, images form inside my head, like a daydream.

In the beginning, the woman says, *we lurked in the shadows of your imaginations. We were creatures of inspyre alone, ephemeral in the youthful world of Annwn. Yet as you told your first stories, sat around fires or drawing on cave walls, you made us stronger. You walked in Annwn and we showed ourselves to you, dropped our lives into your minds, and when you woke you took our stories for your own and made us stronger still. Grand tales you told, of the hunt, of royalty, of courtship, love and betrayal. And thus we were made immortal. Part base human, part inspyre. We can never die while our stories are told.*

In the beginning we were five. First was the Father, who you know as Merlin. Yet he has other names also, like Odin, Zeus and Baba Yaga.

Second was the trickster: Puck and Loki, Coyote and Anansi. Third and fourth the warrior twins yonder.

The woman casts a hand towards Andraste and her red-haired companion, who bow their heads in acknowledgement.

They are named Athena and Ares, Bast and Horus, Nirrti and Mangala, Boudicca and Spartacus. I am the fifth. I am muse and madonna and I have many names. You may call me Nimue, though others know me as Mujaji and Isis, Aphrodite and Ophelia. Our names grow as you add us to your stories, and each time you name us afresh, we become ever stronger, ever more immortal.

As I look upon Andraste, I begin to see the different forms that she has taken over thousands of years. I don't understand how it's happening, or whether anyone else can see it, but she seems to morph in front of my eyes, like shadows on a riverbed. I see how she is one single person – a warrior woman of huge skill and intelligence – but how she is also made of layers of other warrior women: a merciless queen but also a slave girl teaching her sister to write in the dust at their chained feet. They are the same woman in their souls, even if their stories are very different. I look at the singing woman the same way, and I see at once a young girl pining for her lost lover and a proud woman, naked and pregnant, looking with scorn upon her devotees.

The song-speech continues.

Over time, we became gods and goddesses to you. You sacrificed yourselves on alters and offered us your souls for a sliver of our favour. It was not enough for you. You wished to break open the walls between this world and Ithr. For centuries, mankind laboured to build such a gateway, but it was not until we, the Fay, used our powers that the barriers could be broken. Many thousands of years later, when those who built these gateways were long returned to dust, a human came who could rule both worlds, and Arthur was his name. He it was who created the thanes, who begged us to pick from the multitude of humanity a handful who could protect mankind from their own imaginations. Though Arthur, the Traitor of Annwn, the Great Betrayer, would try to destroy us, we, the Fay, have remained true. So, every year when the pull of Annwn is at its greatest, we summon the best of your kind And here we are. Now it is your turn to begin your story.

The song-speech ends. At first I don't even register that Nimue is no longer talking because the power of that music is still stirring inside me. The song folds into my body like the memory of a bedtime story, familiar and rich and full of hidden darkness. Ramesh gives himself a little shake and the girl on my other side can't stop blinking. We are all waking up.

'The Tournament is different for everyone,' Lord Allenby is saying. 'It can be a rough ride, but get your bearings quickly, trust your instinct and you'll be fine.'

'Oh God, oh God, oh God,' Rachel whispers.

'One more thing,' Lord Allenby says. 'You won't be able to see us, but we'll be able to see you. Something to bear in mind.'

'PG-rated swearing only then,' Ollie mutters, eliciting a flurry of titters.

'That's right, Mr King,' Lord Allenby continues, 'but you know now that nightmares can kill. You're about to face your worst nightmare. Something to think about while you're making your jokes.'

That wipes out Ollie's cocky smile.

'Ready your weapons,' Lord Allenby says.

Hang on, did I miss something? Was there a pile of muskets

I was supposed to pick from on the way here? Then I see everyone else producing random items and realise he means the necklace. I pull the broken pendant from my pocket, filled with doubt. If I'm about to face a life or death situation, how am I supposed to defend myself with this?

I sneak a glance at Ollie. I bet his is a lot more useful than a necklace. He's clutching a pair of painted wooden circles; my artwork, given as a Christmas present years ago. I'd been learning about Regency history, and had been obsessed with profile portraits. Ollie and Dad had fidgeted all through their sittings. Ollie's holding the results now; his outline in one hand and Dad's – messy beard picked out in excruciating detail – in the other. I can't believe he's chosen something that I've not only touched but actually made. No, I decide, it's because it's Dad and him on those portraits. It's nothing to do with me.

The Fay position themselves around a white altar at the centre of Stonehenge. Andraste smiles at me as she passes.

'Do you know her?' Rachel asks.

'Sure. For as long as I can remember,' I reply, trying to achieve an acceptable level of smugness.

'Let Gorlois's' girl go first,' Merlin sneers. 'The one not chosen.'

'What does he mean?' someone whispers.

'He means my sister,' Ollie smirks.

'Fern?' Lord Allenby asks.

'Sure,' I say.

Merlin waits for me beside the altar. I remember Nimue's words about sacrifices and wonder whether I'm about to be lashed to the stone like a goat ready to have its throat slit. Mortifyingly, I'm shaking, and it only gets worse when Lord Allenby leans towards me. 'It took guts to talk to me the way you did yesterday, Fern. That bodes well, okay?'

Then he steps back, and I am on my own with the creepy old man.

'Weapon, girl?' Merlin asks.

I show him the pendant. I can't help but glance at Ollie. His gaze is fixed on the necklace. Good. If I'm killed in this Tournament because of this stupid present from my stupid brother, I hope he dies of guilt.

Merlin lifts me with surprising strength onto the altar. The ivory surface is covered in streaks of red. *Well, that's blood then*, I think, feeling a hysterical laugh bubbling up in my throat.

The Fay that now surround me stretch out their arms and close their eyes, as though they're entering a trance. It's very pagan. Suddenly, the air feels charged with static.

Merlin grabs my left hand and holds his free one out to the air. The inspyre around us swirls into a long, hiltless blade. I struggle away from him but his grip is unshakeable.

'Never heard of a blood oath, girl?' Merlin pats my fist with the knife to open my hand.

'No way,' I tell him. It's not that I'm averse to pain – let's be honest, I've faced worse – I'm just not stupid enough to volunteer for it.

Lord Allenby steps in. 'If you don't do this then you can't take the Tournament.'

Ah crap. I open my hand wide. Well, it's only a dream at the end of the day. Despite what Lord Allenby said, how much can a dream cut really hurt?

There's a spark of sun on metal as Merlin brings the blade down.

It turns out that it does actually hurt quite a lot. The knife's so sharp that it swipes into my palm like cheesewire. I overcome the urge to clench my hand. I don't want to show any weakness. I examine the gash instead. Underneath the blood, I spot something white and realise that it must be bone. Bile rises.

'That's it, girl,' I hear Merlin's voice distantly. 'Let it flow.'

My ears are thumping. The blood is mesmerising. I tip my palm this way and that, watching scarlet syrup pool at the edges of the wound. Then it overflows, weaving thickly down my hand, winding around my wrist. A hesitation, then the first drop falls onto the altar.

At first, I think I've been struck deaf. I hadn't noticed the background noise – the murmurings of the squires, birdsong, the breeze – until it had gone. Merlin has disappeared too, though. In fact, I am suddenly completely alone. It's as Allenby said it would be: I can't see anyone but, apparently, they can see me. I get an urge to pull a face and flap my arms wildly. Then I cough experimentally and realise that I'm not deaf; the sound has simply been sucked from this temporary arena. It reminds me of that feeling I get when snow falls in London, when a kind of peaceful oppression fills the air.

The blood from my hand drips stickily. It doesn't pool on the altar but spreads out. I should step off, I suppose, but I'm frightened. I don't know what might happen if I do. Then the blood seeps underneath my shoes. An instant later, perfumed smoke begins to billow around my trainers. Images swirl through it. A seven-year-old Ollie giving me the Flake from his ice cream. Clemmie hugging me a little too fiercely on our first meeting. Jenny studying me from across the playground. It is her face, and Ollie's, that come to the fore again and again. Jenny, Ollie, Jenny, Ollie, Jenny– and then she's standing in front of me, hung in midair, eyes close to mine.

'Hello, witch,' she sneers.

12

I fall back off the altar. As my hands hit the ground, I am no longer in bright sunlight on a carpet of grass. I am back in Wanstead Flats and it's nighttime. The old panic rises inside my throat. I know exactly what will happen next. The ropes will pull me back to a tree, and then the fire will start. Frankly I'm furious with myself for coming up with something so predictable. I'm even more furious that I'm still petrified. The memory of the flames is still raw, even a year on.

The ropes arrive. They whip around my arms, round my waist, round my legs, more than there were when this really happened. *It is really happening,* I think. *If you die in this world you die in the real world too*. And this time there's no Andraste to help me.

I can only move my hands, and they are trembling too much to be useful. The pendant slips through my grip. I almost lose it, hooking the chain onto a finger at the last minute. It's supposed to be my weapon. How the hell am I going to wield a necklace against a bloody fire?

Right on cue, Jenny flicks the match at my feet. Leaves appear around me from thin air only to be consumed by the flames. The heat presses against my shoes, probing for weak spots. I won't scream. I won't. Dozens of people are watching me endure this. I'm not going to give them the satisfaction of knowing how frightened I am.

Think, Fern. The only chance I have of surviving this is by working out how to use the necklace. The fire keeps tearing at my concentration. It's working its way through my trainers and up my legs. Somewhere nearby, someone is groaning in pain. A low *uhhhhhh*. Then I realise that it's me. I wind the chain around my fingers until the silver moon cuts into my palm. That prickle helps me to focus. I think of the blade that Merlin conjured, and wonder whether I could do the same. I picture a sharp edge and a sturdy hilt. Something seems to slide in the back of my mind. An ache, a twinge in my brain that slips from my head, across my shoulder and down my arm. My fingers spasm, and once again I almost lose hold of the pendant. Sparks leap from skin to metal.

The chain erupts into scalding heat, worse than the fire consuming my legs. It jerks inside my fingers, like a cricket trying to escape. It grows and grows until instead of the pendant there is something soft in my hands. A bag. Not quite the handy knife I'd been hoping for. But it's too heavy to be empty.

The flame is up to my hips now. I can't feel my legs any more. Whatever's in the bag chimes like crystal. I have to move carefully, because I can't afford to let the bag slip. Balancing the fabric in my palm and struggling against the stifling smoke, I reach one finger inside. It feels like marbles. I edge one gently up the side of the bag.

There's a shout from beyond the smoke, and I lose

concentration. One of the marbles slips out of the bag, out of my grasp, and drops to the ground.

A deadening boom, like a huge bass drum, flattens all other sound. The smoke around me thickens, but the heat crush eases. As it clears, I see that the fire has gone out. The dissipating smoke smells like newly cut grass. Whatever dropped out of that bag must have extinguished the flames.

Before I can celebrate, the scorching heat bursts in my hand again. Something else is forming there, solid and cool. A hilt. It has to be the knife I asked for, formed at the perfect moment. With an awkward flick of my wrist, I manage to cut through the ropes that bind me. A few more swipes and I am free. I step out of the night and into bold sunlight. Wanstead Flats has disappeared and I am standing once more in a grass-covered circle, the altar sitting innocently a few metres away.

I've passed the test. Instead of relying on Andraste, I've rescued myself. No more damsel in distress. This new, improved Fern's got a blade and a fire-repelling marble, and she's not afraid to use them.

The rush is incredible. I might be in a dream world but I feel more awake than ever before. The tremble in my arms isn't fear any more – it's excitement. I want to do that again. Feel the power of my thoughts flowing through my body and changing the things around me.

I turn my attention to my new weapons. The blade is a curved sword made of dull, mottled silver. The leather handle is inlaid with faded gold wire. It looks like something that should have been found at an ancient burial site. The bag contains just two marbles. Embedded in the centre of each one is a diamond. They remind me of the tiny stars on my necklace. Wait . . . they *are* the stars on my necklace. The silver chain that pulls the bag shut looks exactly like the chain that held the pendant. Which means . . . the curved sword is the shape of the crescent moon. A weapon indeed.

Tucking the bag into a pocket and hefting the scimitar, I wait for the illusion that I'm alone to fade. Another feeling is creeping in underneath the adrenalin. Disappointment. Fire is my worst fear, yes, but with hindsight that all seemed a bit . . . easy.

'That's a pretty sword,' Jenny's voice whispers in my ear. 'How does it feel, knowing I'm going to kill you with it?'

I swing round. Jenny is grinning at me, and she's not alone. I get the briefest glimpse of his face before I realise what he's doing and duck. Something whizzes over my head and embeds into the altar. A serrated disc. It's not just Jenny trying to kill me. Ollie is too. Thanks, subconscious. Always got my back.

I scramble to my feet. Behind Jenny, Ollie grips another serrated disc.

'You might beat me at home, but you're not going to here,' I tell the visions, buoyed by the weight of the sword. Ollie's mouthing a reply but I'm not listening. I am impenetrable to words and I am armed against their weapons. Bring. It. On. My first swipe knocks Jenny out of the way, and my second catches Ollie's arm.

'Bitch!' he shouts, clutching the wound.

Yeah, have a taste of your own medicine.

He dodges my next attempt. The sword might have been created just for me, but I use it clumsily. My hands are used to drawing, not swinging a blade at someone's chest.

'Not a good fighter are you, witch?' Jenny croons. 'Anyone ever told you that you don't belong here?'

She sways towards me. As she advances, her nails grow and grow, each one becoming a spike. I drive at her, trying to sense the natural movement of the scimitar, letting it guide my hand to the correct angles. She ducks and weaves, her claws pricking at me. We are in a dance, the three of us, pirouetting and bowing, promenading and pivoting from one partner to another until the movement of my scimitar takes over my body and I lose sight of who I'm fighting altogether. I am in the moment. I am graceful. I am –

Jenny's claws rake across my jaw and I trip over, throwing my scimitar out of the way so I don't fall on it. I try to scramble to my feet, but the scimitar has landed just out of reach. 'It's bedtime now.' Jenny grins. She bares her teeth and leaps towards me. Without thinking, I roll over to retrieve the blade and thrust it upwards, into her stomach. There's a second of resistance, then it sinks in like she's made of jelly.

'Witch,' she spits, and crumbles into inspyre. The hiss of her last word hangs before me.

I can't consider the fact that I have just murdered someone, even if they weren't real. Not yet. Ollie is still here, clutching his wounded arm over the other side of the arena. I wonder what the actual Ollie feels watching this.

We circle each other, unreal Ollie and real Fern, testing each other's resolve. His hand closes, almost imperceptibly, around the grip on his disc. I don't wait for him to throw it. Running towards him, I lift my sword. I might not be an expert in wielding it, but if I keep slashing it in the right direction I'm bound to score a few points. Ollie blocks my first blow, then my second, my third.

'Fern –' he begins, but I'm not listening to his jibes. This isn't home, where I can't do anything to shut him up. I slash wildly, determined not to let him go on the offensive. I am rabid, and I love it. Being beyond fear is the purest freedom. But in the back of my mind I sense that something is wrong. He's not even trying to attack me.

'Why aren't you fighting back?' I shout.

I catch him on the leg this time. He gives a great roar and swipes his disc at me. Sharp pain across my chest. I press my hand against the spot and feel blood. There we are, now all's right with the world.

We go to work.

The air is a whirl of sharp metal and heavy breath. I lose all sense of thought, of right or wrong, of strategy. I allow my scimitar to lead me through the fight. I'm winning, there's no doubt about that, and actually that's bothering me. I know what the real Ollie is capable of, so why is my imagination making this version pull his punches? And why is nightmare Ollie so hampered by his wounds?

When Ollie trips backwards over the altar that brought me here, I know I cannot show mercy. I've got him. I should bring the scimitar down. Now. Do it now.

We stare at each other. He with his disc half-heartedly raised in protection, his chest heaving with effort and pain. Me, sword gripped but not raised. The truth comes to me like a light through fog.

'You're real.'

'Well done, genius.'

Questions flash through my head. A tantalising possibility. I could kill him now. Dad would never know it was me; he would just find Ollie cold in his bed. The image holds for a second, then bursts. I step back, suddenly exhausted.

'Must be nice,' Ollie says, 'to feel righteous about killing someone.'

'At least I had a reason. What did you have except feeling embarrassed by me?'

As Ollie scrambles to his feet, his clothes covered in muck and blood, sound from outside the arena soaks back into the stone circle. Shouting. Frantic conversations. Then I see them: Merlin, Lord Allenby, the other squires.

'I thought it was my Tournament,' I say stupidly as Merlin and Lord Allenby approach. 'What is he even doing here?'

'That's a good question,' Lord Allenby says, striding over. 'Your brother managed to force his way in.'

'Making sure the nightmares finished the job?' I ask Ollie.

He shrugs. 'Something like that.'

Merlin prods my stomach and then Ollie's. 'Yes, of course,' Merlin mutters. 'They're hatched from the same egg.'

'Excuse me?' I say.

'Twins. It follows that they would need to face the Tournament together. I've seen it once before. In that case they fought alongside each other but you two,' he fixes Ollie and I with sharp eyes, 'you are each other's test. Yes. I see it now. It makes perfect sense.'

'It does?' says Ollie, looking as repulsed as I feel at the thought of us sharing anything.

'It really doesn't,' I add.

'You fear the same thing,' Merlin says, 'and you fear each other. But one fear you must defeat together, and the other you must conquer. You passed both tests.'

Before I can begin to process Merlin's riddle, Lord Allenby steps forward. 'However it came about I think we have our answer, don't you, my lord?'

'Yes. Yes, I think you do.'

'Your weapons have spoken,' Lord Allenby says. 'A scimitar and a pair of chakrams. You will both be joining the knights.'

I want to jump up and down, to squeal improperly and, for the first time in my life, I quite like the idea of hugging someone. I look across at Andraste but she and the rest of the Fay are still deep in their trances. I have to settle with sharing a look with Ollie. Lord Allenby shakes our hands and directs us out of the circle. I follow Ollie to Emory. The other squires are clapping. Ramesh shouts, 'Brilliant, Ollie! Well done, Fern!' and I have to resist rolling my eyes. What a sweet, utterly desperate boy.

Emory grasps my hand and offers a guarded smile. 'Glad to have you,' she says. 'I've never worked with twins before. That was some fight. Brotherly love, eh?'

'Yeah.' I'm not sure what she's getting at, because she doesn't sound sarcastic. 'Don't worry, I'm used to Ollie trying to kill me.'

'What?' Emory looks confused. 'Kill you? From where I was standing, it looked a lot like your brother was trying to save you.'

13

I don't have time to consider Emory's words, nor do I want to. She's wrong about Ollie. He's duped all of them into thinking he has honour, the same way he's pulled the wool over Dad's eyes. I push the niggling thought that she might be right to the back of my head. Right now there's a whole new world to learn about, and I need to focus on that.

On our first night, we are given a whirlwind tour of the castle. We pass the long line of harker desks in the cloisters where Rachel is now stationed, and move out into the gardens where apothecaries tend to herbs. Up on the terraces that surround the dome, we meet more harkers who stand sentinel, watching over Annwn and relaying nightmare activity to their colleagues on the floors below. Then we plummet down to the lower levels. The basement of the castle is divided into two halves, separated by a small courtyard where reeves tend to the under-workings of the huge portal that took us to Stonehenge. On one side are the dungeons and on the other side are the archives, where a hidden door in the wood panelling opens to reveal endless rows of bookcases. 'We keep everything here,' our reeve guide tells us. 'A true history of the thanes from their conception to the present day.'

After the tour, we are sent to the garderobe to get our uniforms. From the outside, looking at what seems to be a humble wooden door squeezed into a dingy corner of the south wing, you'd be forgiven for thinking that 'garderobe' is entirely too grand a word for whatever lies beyond. The wonderful thing about Annwn, though, is that the usual rules of physics don't apply, for the garderobe is the lushest walk-in wardrobe you could imagine. It may be windowless but the triple-height ceilings stop it from feeling claustrophobic. Every wall is covered in shelves and railings, each one laden with rich fabrics that beg to be stroked. The red silks of the harkers; black velvet for the veneurs; fine white linen for the apothecaries; and soft, green wool for the reeves. From the vaulted ceilings hang helmets of every kind and shape, jangling like wind chimes.

A harried-looking reeve passes me a bundle of clothes and directs me to the changing rooms. I sequester one in a corner and pull the curtains together. The material is mirrored on the inside, and although the mirror follows the curve of the fabric, my reflection isn't distorted. One wall offers shelves of accessories like pouches and headscarves. A chaise longue sits against the other wall.

Avoiding the mirror, I take off my regular clothes and lay out my knight's uniform on the chaise longue.

A pair of leather leggings go on first. Luckily they're not the uncomfortably tight kind, but soft, worn leather that's like a cross between favourite jeans and silky tights. They're followed by a long-sleeved chainmail top so light I barely feel its weight. It's padded with a thin layer of fleece that, apparently, is spun from Annwn's snow fields and is designed to regulate my temperature. Thick boots go over the leggings, the low heels supposed to help with riding. The cotton, royal-blue tunic of the knights, with its embroidered emblem of a sword lifted against a circular background, finishes off the outfit.

I stare at myself. For the first time in my life, I like what I see. The belt that holds my scimitar and the marble-filled pouch sits heavily on my hips. I'm a straight-up-and-down sort of girl, but the belt gives me the illusion of a waist. A leather strap binds my hair in a low bun to keep it away from my face, a practical move I'd never have considered in real life, where I use my hair as a cloak to hide my eyes and burn scar. In Ithr, all my clothes have been chosen based on comfort, affordability and whether they will offer a quick disguise if I want to fade into the background. Clothes that make you look good as well as feel good are for other people. Not here, though. In Annwn, I might not be pretty, but I am striking. Here I look confident, strident. And because I look it, I almost feel it too.

A warrior woman indeed, I think, remembering what Andraste said. I ache to show her what I look like, to see her smile proudly. Andraste is the one person I will allow as a friend, but the night she brought me to Annwn she implied that I wouldn't be seeing much of her. Suddenly, I feel very lonely.

As I leave the safety of my changing room, Ollie emerges from his. The uniform makes him look older than his fifteen years. He doesn't spot me at first, so I have a moment to wonder at his sombre expression before he sees me and erases all emotion.

'That almost makes you look like a human,' he remarks.

'Ditto,' I say.

The uniforms give us the right to enter the knights' chamber: a long, narrow space at the back of the castle's central hall. There are no windows here, but a single, huge skylight drops sunbeams and moonlight into the centre of the room. Cushioned pews and high-backed armchairs line the walls beneath paintings of former knights. We're each assigned a locker where we can stash our belongings. They're not lined up against a wall like the lockers in a gym or school, though. These lockers are found in unlikely places. Ollie is given a hidden compartment inside a grand writing bureau. I get a candle-lit alcove that appears when I press my hand against the left side of the fireplace.

I wonder which was Mum's, I think, watching the other new knights open their own lockers with glee. Did Mum take all of this in her stride, like I'm trying to do? Or did she squeal with excitement like Ramesh?

Tables are scattered around the room, each one decorated with a different map and covered in figurines. Rafe, the rider who helped me to safety a few nights ago, shows us how they can be used to plot battle formations. Some show large open spaces, some busy mazes of streets or complicated multi-storey buildings. Ramesh spends a lot of time entertaining the other squires by flinging the figurines around the tables. At first, Ollie keeps his distance, like me, but then Ramesh asks him to help with a fabricated battle move and before long the two of them are chatting like long-lost brothers. Ramesh and some of the other squires try the same tactics on me, but I am made of stronger stuff and shake my head politely when invited to join in. What they're doing isn't learning, it's bonding, and I've got no interest in doing that.

But we don't have long to relax. That same night, a reeve slips into the room and hangs a blank tapestry on the right of the chamber door. We gather round as he presses his hand against the fabric. From that spot, like dye running through veins, threaded words form.

'This will be your training schedule for the next few months,' the reeve tells us, 'until you graduate on Ostara and begin your first proper patrols.'

'What's Ostara when it's at home?' Ollie asks.

'Spring equinox. Near the end of March.'

'But that's months away!' Ramesh complains.

'You think you can just go out there and take on a nightmare with no training, be my guest.' The reeve shrugs. 'Won't be my funeral.'

After he's left, the grumbling continues.

'I spend enough time keeping to a schedule at school without having to deal with it at night too,' Ramesh says.

A red-headed girl I recognise from the Tournament traces the embroidery. 'Look at this though,' she says in a broad West Country accent. 'Don't tell me that's not way more interesting than school lessons.'

'Nothing called a lesson is ever going to be interesting, Phoebe,' Ollie says, raising agreement from his friends. Phoebe shrugs and suddenly I place her. In her Tournament she garnered smirks when she went into the arena clutching an old toy. Those smirks were wiped off when the toy turned into a real lion. I hear a low growl and turn to see her lion accepting a tummy scratch from Emory at the other end of the chamber. I catch Phoebe's eye and she smiles at me, but I turn away, stifling my own. I'd promised myself that I wouldn't make friends here. That can't change just because some of them seem nicer than I'd anticipated.

And Phoebe's right about the lessons. Each night is divided into two; one part is more traditional, where we sit with the trainees from other lores and learn about things like law, history and psychology, chivalry, mythology and symbology. We learn about the ways the thanes of Tintagel coordinate with the thanes that operate across the rest of the country, in castles scattered as far afield as the Scottish Isles and the furthest reaches of Ireland's west coast. The teachers – semi-retired thanes, all of them – show us the different types of nightmare and the ways dreamers' minds work when they invent them. They take us up to Tintagel's highest dome and point out the packs of nightmares – the giants that dwell amongst the skyscrapers of Canary Wharf and the lions who roam Trafalgar Square, a prowling, roaring embodiment of the statues that sit there in Ithr. They teach us how a trickster nightmare can use a dreamer's anxiety to take the form of a loved one whose skin flakes away to reveal a demon beneath.

The other type of lessons are practical, and only for those of us training to become knights. These are lessons in strategy, weapons, acrobatics and *flying,* for God's sake. I learn how to wield my scimitar properly, although my fire-dampening marbles remain in my locker in the knights' chamber; given they're single use, the teachers thought it best to save the remaining two for when I graduate.

But nearly every lesson in these early weeks comes back to one thing: inspyre. The building block of Annwn.

'The main thing you need to know about inspyre,' our teacher, a moustache-bearing man called Mr Blake tells us as he leads us out into the grounds of Tintagel one night, 'is that it doesn't give a shit about you.'

There's some shocked laughter amongst the group.

'You heard me,' Mr Blake continues. 'Inspyre cares about the people who make it – that's dreamers. You and me, we're conscious here so we can use inspyre to change ourselves in a limited way.' He makes himself shrink to the size of a pumpkin by way of demonstration, 'But we can't use it to alter dreams or nightmares. That's something only dreamers can do.'

A freckled boy next to me frowns as Mr Blake returns to his normal height. 'But what about our Tournaments?'

'Yes, well done, young man.' Mr Blake points at the boy. 'Your Tournaments are the exception. They're a different beast. There's Fay magic behind that. But out in the rest of Annwn? No, no, no – that's much trickier.'

He takes us to a remote part of Tintagel's gardens and separates us into groups. Ollie is placed with Phoebe and a bunch of the squires whose names I haven't bothered to learn. Immediately they seem to congregate around him. I'm put with Ramesh, who insists on high-fiving everyone in our group. I move to the edge, directing my focus towards the teacher and trying to zone out everyone else.

'Now,' Mr Blake says, lifting a hand to gain our attention, 'I want you to think of inspyre like the layers of soil.' He kneels and sifts through the topsoil of a flower bed. 'This stuff here is light and easy to pick up, isn't it? But if you go further down you'll find the soil's more compact. It's harder to dig into. You'll need a spade. Then further down you get to rock that none of us would be able to move without the help of some hefty machinery. You all follow me?'

We nod, wondering where he's going with this.

'Inspyre's like this soil, only it gets harder to move it or change it depending on the number of dreamers imagining it. It's nigh on impossible for us to do anything with the Thames, say, because it's built from the imaginations of millions of dreamers who remember it a certain way. Then at the other end of the spectrum you've got things that dreamers don't remember as well. Details like materials and colours. That's where the inspyre doesn't hold together so strongly, like topsoil.'

He hands out tattered pieces of fabric to each group. I examine ours – an unremarkable piece of faded, moss-coloured wool from a reeve's uniform.

'It'll be harder for you than it is for dreamers because they're unconscious and already tapped into their imaginations,' Mr Blake says, 'but if you concentrate, and concentrate hard, you stand a chance. Try it, all of you. Take it in turns to see if you can change those pieces of material you've got.'

Our group looks at each other uncertainly. The length of wool flops in Ramesh's grip, looking utterly uninspiring.

'I guess I'll go first then?' Ramesh says, his bravado knocked away. I feel the vulnerability of his situation keenly. Scratch Jenny and Ollie and their fire; this is the true stuff of nightmares.

'He said to concentrate really hard,' I remind Ramesh, 'so pretend like we aren't here.'

He nods, closing his eyes and gripping the wool tightly. We all stare at the fabric.

'How's he getting on?' the teacher's voice, close to my ear, makes every one of us jump.

Ramesh exclaims, 'Christ!' in alarm and drops the wool.

'Ah, well done, lad!' the teacher says. 'Not bad at all for a first try.'

We stare down at the wool, which is now less mossy green and more . . . lime. I have to stop myself from saying, 'Is that it?' but Ramesh is delighted. And it turns out that changing the fabric's colour just a little is the most that can be expected from us. Some members of our group can't change the colour at all. Others manage to turn it lighter or darker by a few shades. With every person who tries, my sense of dread grows. I don't want to be doing this in front of them. If I can't do it then it will prove that I don't belong here. At last the fabric comes round to me, now a jewelled, jungle green. And by now, everyone has advice.

'Relax into it.'

'Focus on the colour you want as hard as you can.'

'Yeah, until you look like you're constipated.'

I angle myself away from them, staring at the wool in my hands until it takes over my entire vision. Nothing happens. I close my eyes, trying to block out the stifling presence of my teammates. Then I hear it.

'Hey, guys, watch this. She's going to totally balls it up.'

It's Ollie's voice, quiet enough that he can pass it off as a whisper; loud enough for everyone in the vicinity to hear. It's been a year since I had to deal with him at school, and it's obviously turned me soft because my head immediately saturates with tears. They seem to burst inside my skull. I get a sudden pain in the centre of my forehead, as though someone's punctured it. My eyes still closed, I sense a stir amongst my companions.

'Well, you've got the hang of that, haven't you?' the teacher growls. I open my eyes. The fabric in my hands is still, partly, dark green. But the green is now flushed into a melancholy ombre of teal and royal purple. I stare at it in wonder.

'How did you do that?' Ramesh asks, taking the fabric from me and holding it up to the light.

'I don't know.' I am trying hard not to smile. I didn't disgrace myself. As the rest of the squires gather around me, passing the peacock-coloured wool between them, I sense Ollie slipping to the back. I do not let myself watch him walk away.

14

My talent for changing the colour of random pieces of fabric doesn't, in the end, buy me much street cred. It doesn't take too long for the others to master the art of dying fabric with their minds, and it's only a matter of days before we start to learn far more exciting things. We spend long hours up on the towers with the harkers, watching the knights from afar through special helmets. We watch the different knight patrols – Lancelot, Bedevere, Gawain, Palomides and Dagonet – moving like chess pieces across London. We watch them tackling the nightmares that spring from a single dreamer's imagination and the ones that are built over many decades of shared memories until they have become part of Annwn's landscape.

I inhale all of it. Because I don't care about making friends, I save all my energy for learning. In Annwn I spend my free time curled up in an armchair tucked away next to a bookcase, reading and eavesdropping on the more experienced knights as they talk tactics and compare patrol notes. One night I overhear Rafe, freshly back from his patrol with Bedevere, regaling some of the squires with the story of how the mysteriously absent Knight Captain, Samson, once walked into a house full of vampires on his own and emerged shortly afterwards, scratched and bitten but victorious. Vampires, it turns out, aren't just the kind of pointy-toothed blood-suckers I've been led to believe but come in many forms: vultures, spirits, rats and doppelgangers.

'How did he do it?' Ramesh asks.

'No one knows.' Rafe shrugs. 'He's never shared.'

Back in Ithr, I remember the secret label Mum gave her diary, and start to fill up my own knightbook with everything I've learned. The pages are soon covered with diagrams of battle formations. I write about the different types of *aventure* – people who are able to travel through Annwn consciously: thanes like me, but also scientists and world leaders and, sometimes, criminals. I note how to spot the difference between a portal that will take a dreamer to another part of Annwn, and the type that will throw them back into Ithr. But the most interesting lessons are the ones that cannot be distilled into bullet points. Once a week we get to foray outside Tintagel's walls to shadow the patrols. These quickly become my favourite lessons, not just because they let me see more of Annwn, but because of my companion.

Not a human companion. A horse.

When we're sent to the stables for the first time I have some misgivings. The only time I've ridden before was on a holiday in Cornwall when I was eight, which ended up with me clinging to my runaway steed's neck and Dad cantering behind me, stirrups flying, reins flapping, shouting, 'I'll save you, Ferny!' So the thought of spending most of my patrols on horseback concerns me a bit.

I'm not the only one to be nervous.

'Why can't we have cars?' Ramesh moans. 'This must be the only time I could drive an Aston Martin and instead I get a bloody pony.'

'I'd have a Ferrari,' Ollie sighs, 'or a Lamborghini.'

I snort quietly.

'Some thaneships do have cars,' another knight comments.

'Oooh, where? Maybe I can persuade my parents to move,' Ramesh says.

'America uses cars. If you fancied moving to the Scottish Highlands you get planes and hot air balloons.'

'*So* jealous right now.' Ramesh clenches his hands dramatically.

'I wonder if they'll give me a horse at all,' Phoebe says, 'or if I can just ride Donald.'

'Riding a lion would definitely make you stand out,' Ollie comments.

'That would be annoying,' Phoebe says.

'Why?' Ramesh asks.

'Well, I can't help having Donald, can I? I'd rather stand out because of something I've actually done instead of something I can't control.'

'Me too,' I say impulsively, and find myself returning Phoebe's quiet smile.

The stables sit on the outskirts of the castle grounds, set into the wall. Along one side, big square archways are held aloft by wooden beams. Inside, the stables smell of urine and warm animal, which isn't as unpleasant as it sounds. Over the top of each stable door peeks a curious head, all hair, ears and enormous eyes.

'Get in here then, all of you,' a tall, tanned woman in tweed and jodhpurs calls impatiently from the depths of the building. She introduces herself as Elaine Dacre – 'But you can call me Miss D' – and everything she says is a bark. Like the other teachers, Miss D is a retired thane and by all accounts is something of a Tintagel institution.

A dark-haired slip of a knight follows us in and Miss D homes in on her.

'Natasha, you're late. Get Domino and get out of my way. You're setting a bad example for the squires.'

Natasha grins. 'Right away, Miss D.' She has a hint of an American accent. Natasha turns her smile on us as she leads a stocky, Dalmatian-coloured horse out of his stable. 'You're in for the best time, guys.'

'Not to look too keen or anything, but which ones are ours?' Ramesh asks.

'The first thing you have to get in your heads is that these horses aren't *yours*,' Miss D says disapprovingly. 'They're dreams – and someone else's dreams at that. They're just letting you borrow them for a while.'

'But if they're made of inspyre couldn't they change or disappear at any moment?' Phoebe asks. Her lion, Donald, is standing on the side furthest away from the horses, but I can feel him purring. I briefly think about pointing out to Phoebe that she's brought him to the lion's equivalent of an all-you-can-eat buffet.

'Not these ones,' Miss D says. 'They're held in this shape by the imagination of the dreamers who own them – or used to own them – in Ithr. Take Natasha there. While her friends and teachers in Ithr remember her horse and how much she loved him, her boy Domino will always be here waiting for her, even if he's gone in Ithr.'

We all turn round and catch Natasha planting a big, squishy kiss on Domino's muzzle. Eww.

'Domino was hers in real life too?' Phoebe says.

'For fourteen years, I believe. It's one of the great things about Annwn. If we can remember someone, we never lose them in here, even if they've gone in Ithr.'

Ramesh makes fists of his hands and opens them dramatically on either side of his head, as if to say *Mind. Blown*. But I am thinking of Mum, wondering whether she is still alive, in a way, somewhere in this place. A shiver runs through me; whether of anticipation or excitement or fear, I can't tell.

A few minutes later we're lined up outside the stalls. Miss D opens the doors one by one, and the horses inside clop out to examine us. It's basically the world's weirdest dating show. It doesn't take long before a proud creature with freckles covering his white coat shows an interest in Ollie. He explores his chest and arms with his muzzle, then finally lifts his head to touch noses with my brother.

'Very good,' Miss D says. 'Balius, meet Ollie. Off you go, Ollie, take Balius back to his stall.'

'Just how friendly is she expecting us to get?' Ramesh murmurs as Ollie awkwardly leads Balius away. Ramesh gets picked by a big, black monster of a horse and declares that he got 'first prize'. Phoebe's reddish-brown horse tentatively touches noses with her lion. 'No eating, Donald,' she says.

I smile at each horse as it passes, unsure whether I'm

supposed to be offering bribes of sugar cubes or carrots. Several magnificent creatures sniff me briefly, then move on to someone who probably doesn't reek of desperation. 'Not to worry,' Miss D says to those of us yet to be chosen, 'you'll all find your match. The bond between a horse and its rider is unique. Your personalities need to complement each other.'

Something whickers softly behind me. I spin round. The creature staring at me through beautiful doe-like eyes is smaller than any of the other horses. Her whole coat is chestnut apart from one black front leg that makes it look as though she left a sock on by mistake. Her ears are donkey-sized, and she doesn't have much control over them.

'Well, look at that,' Miss D says. 'Llamrei has been here for years, but it's been more than a decade since she had a rider. I was starting to think she was just coming here to get some fresh hay.' Miss D observes me beadily. 'I have a soft spot for Llamrei. Fern, is it? You treat her well, understand?'

I look at Llamrei, such a complicated name for such a sweet little horse. Impulsively, I kiss her nose like I saw Natasha do earlier. It's not disgusting after all. Her muzzle is like a velvet cushion.

'Hi, Llamrei,' I say softly, tentatively stroking her neck. Llamrei wiggles her ears at me, and I melt.

We spend time with our horses every night, learning to tack them up and, more importantly, learning how not to fall off. It isn't long before I give Llamrei a nickname that feels more suited to her thick fur and docile face – Lamb. At the beginning, Ollie liked to poke fun at Lamb's size. 'At least you won't have far to fall.' I get the last laugh, though, because this is something Ollie's rubbish at. While he can barely kick Balius into a lazy trot, Lamb and I whizz around the gardens, circling the other horses and leaping over fences with ease. When Miss D tells us to jump over a wall three times as tall as Lamb, we succeed on the second try. 'Unprecedented,' Miss D exclaims. 'Your bond with Lamb is outstanding already, Fern. It takes most knights months to establish the right connection with their horse and develop the strength of imagination to lift them over the wall.' My satisfaction only intensifies when Ollie and the rest don't even manage it after multiple tries. The memory of Ollie being so determined to beat me that he threw himself over his horse's head and crumpled right into the wall will forever hold a special place in my heart.

When I'm riding Lamb I feel as though we're one being. We rely on each other. I need Lamb to give me speed and height; she needs me for reassurance and direction. But Lamb's uncomplicated friendship comes with a bittersweet aftertaste – it makes me acutely aware of my loneliness. I watch my brother bonding with the other squires, knotting nets of companionship, and try to take comfort in having Lamb. I have learned that I'm too awkward to knot my own – I would only get tangled in them. It's safer not to try.

Then, one night in the break between strategy and law, I spot Ollie standing with Ramesh, looking up at the columns where the names of the dead scroll endlessly. I sidle closer. '. . . was a knight way back,' I hear Ollie saying. 'I think she died in the line of duty . . .'

Rage bubbles up. How dare he trade off her death? Of all the despicable things he's done, this has to be in the top five.

'You won't see her name up there,' I say, making both boys start.

'Why not?' Ollie says, taken aback.

'She died after she retired from the knights. Lord Allenby told me.'

Ollie gapes, the wind taken out of his sails. Ramesh looks back at the columns. 'Still . . . it seems a shame that the people who survived, or who just happened to die later, don't get commemorated anywhere, doesn't it? I mean, they still risked their lives. Why do we only appreciate stuff when it's gone?'

I look at those names too, thinking over what Ramesh said. I wonder, briefly, whether Dad was as smitten with Mum when she was alive as he is now she's dead. Then something catches my eye. 'Oh,' I breathe.

'What?' Ollie says, following my gaze.

'Look,' I say, pointing at one section of the names.

'We *are* looking, Fern. *What is it?*' Ollie snaps.

'Look at the dates.'

Ollie does so, and suddenly he understands too.

'Let me in on the secret here, guys?' Ramesh says.

'Our mother died in 2005,' I tell him. We all stare at the years etched next to what seems like hundreds and hundreds of names. Every single one of them died the same year as Una King.

15

The news that hundreds of thanes died in 2005, the same year as my mother, doesn't spread around Tintagel like I thought it would. I expected Ollie to use it to increase his mystique but he stays quiet, and Ramesh follows suit. His silence is supremely irritating. I don't understand how he can come across this huge mystery and not do anything about it. He's already friends with experienced knights like Emory and Rafe; people who must be able to shed some light on what happened fifteen years ago, and if they don't know he could easily charm someone who does. Sometimes I find myself on the verge of asking Natasha, who seems to like me because my connection with Lamb is almost as strong as hers is with Domino, but the words always die in my throat. Ollie won't share; I can't.

So I watch, I listen and I learn. This is easy to do because, as Phoebe predicted, our lessons are so interesting. Once you understand that Annwn is powered by imagination, formed entirely by different types of inspyre, you can grasp the limits – or the lack of limits – to this world. In Ithr, I've taken to poring over the notes in my knightbook when I should be focusing on my schoolwork.

Today, as Bosco's history teacher drones on about the French Revolution, I flick through, looking for any clues that might help me to crack Mum's coded diary messages. I suddenly become aware of Lottie Medraut and her friends whispering to each other at the desks behind me. It takes me a moment to recognise why their conversation has penetrated. It's because they mentioned a name I recognise: Helena Corday – the politician who was so kind to me after the fire and who secured my place at Bosco.

'Dad's debating her tonight,' Lottie is saying, 'and he wants me to be in the audience.'

'Sounds like a bore,' Victoria von Gellert says. '*Free tickets*, Lot, to *The Minxes*.'

'Sorry, Vix, can't get out of it.'

'You can't run from us, Lottie Medraut. We will find you and we *will* drag you to this concert.'

Oh, to have friends who want to spend time with you that badly. Still, on the whole, my fellow squires aren't as objectionable as I'd thought they would be. That night, as Lottie watches her dad's debate and her friends bounce up and down to The Minxes, I am waiting outside an Annwn classroom with my fellow squires. A reeve slides to a halt beside us, brandishing a sheaf of papers. 'Don't suppose one of you could pop this down to the archives?' he asks us. 'Gawain have just caught some PR guy who's been causing havoc and I need to organise all the checks and identifications.'

One of the facets of the knights' job is to find aventures who've come into Annwn through illegal portals – black market items in Ithr that only the richest can afford.

Ollie pipes up. 'Fern will do it. She's a los— I mean, a loner.'

I wait for the sniggering. So does Ollie. It doesn't come.

'Give it a rest,' Ramesh mutters, and Phoebe glances at Ollie with disapproval. I don't understand what's happening. This isn't the natural order. Ollie makes a joke at my expense, everyone laughs, I remind myself that people are jerks. This new turn of events is too confusing.

'It's okay, I don't mind doing it.' I pluck the papers from the reeve's hand. As I head towards the staircase down to the lower levels, I look back. Ollie is quiet, separated from the others. At St Stephen's he had Jenny and her lot to back him up. I'd just assumed that no matter how welcoming they are to me at the moment, eventually Ramesh and Phoebe would follow Ollie's example and turn on me as well. Maybe I was wrong about them. It's an uncomfortable realisation.

The archives are exactly as I remember them: cosy and not a little claustrophobic, like a cocoon.

The paper I'm holding – *An Investigation into the Inherent Properties of Morrigan Abilities* – is already starting to flicker from new to faded. At some point the inspyre that forms writing in Annwn will probably change the font too.

I turn my attention to the plaques labelling each shelf. Each of the bookcases is on wheels so that they can be compressed and separated, like an accordion.

Personnel records, maps, London reports, national reports 2001–2010, national reports 2011–2020 . . . I heave on the handle and slip inside the gap that opens up. I stuff the report into its appropriate stack and head for the door, keen to get back to class.

That's when the thought occurs to me. *Mum*

I check the door. I know I don't have long before someone starts questioning where I've got to.

I turn around and head deeper into the archives, running my hands over the plaques, looking for the right one.

Personnel records.

Such an innocuous title for something that holds so much potential. I glance round once more before pulling on the handle to the bookcase.

There are more records than I'd imagined. They're sorted by century, then by decade, then by name. I give in to curiosity and pick up the very first folder which, anachronistically, is printed in modern Comic Sans. There, right at the top, is the name *King Arthur Pendragon*. I run a finger over the ink. It's hard to conceive of records so old. I remember Nimue's words at the Tournament. She had said that Arthur had betrayed them; tried to destroy them, in fact. Whenever I've tried to find out what that means, the teachers avoid answering. None of the books in the knights' chamber mention much about Arthur after he set up the thanes, skipping quickly instead to the years after his death.

The folder in my hands contains parchment so ancient and thin that the slightest touch of my fingers tears it. I have to rest the pages on my palm to read them.

King Arthur Pendragon
Herewith founded the Knights of the Round Table in
the Castle of Tintagel in the country of Annwn
On this day 24th January in the year of Our Lord 456.

Through the blessing of the Lord Merlin and Lady Guinevere and all the other Fay of Annwn.
Through Arthur, the once and future king, he of the far-seeing gaze, the wielder of Immral, the power and glory of the Otherworld shall be visited upon the Earthly Realm.

A shiver crawls up my spine. Out of everything that has happened in the last month, this is, somehow, the strangest. I still have books Dad read to me as a child about King Arthur and his knights. Seeing his name here, diluted into a dry entry in a file of records, makes me feel odd. I am living inside the legacy of a mythical king.

Something rumbles in the ceiling, as though someone's dragging a heavy object across the floor above. *Stop messing around, Fern.* I slide the parchment back inside its folder and move down the stacks. I've lost sight of the passageway that leads out of the archives before I reach the 1990s, which must have been when Mum became a knight. I rifle through the Ks, looking for *King, Una*. I find *Kindrick, Scott* followed by *Kingsberry, Cadwyn*, but nothing where my mother's record should be. Then I remember that Lord Allenby called Mum by her maiden name. She joined before she married Dad. How could I have been so thick? I run back up the passageway to G. There. *Gorlois, Una*.

My hand is shaking in time with my heartbeat. The folder has a dusty red cover and is pregnant with paper. My whole life I've wanted to know more about my mother. This is an Important Moment. There should be fireworks, or at least a drum roll.

When I open the folder, I'm expecting a sheaf of typed papers. I'm totally unprepared for the painting that sits on top. Oils are daubed in confident strokes. There's no room for sky or a backdrop in this picture. The artist devoted every centimetre of their canvas to a single face. Wild black hair and pale skin frame dark eyes.

'Mum,' I breathe.

I kneel. *This* is my mother, as no photo of her has ever captured. Warmth and mischief bubble across the dimples in her cheeks. There's unassailable confidence – the kind I see in Ollie – in the toss of her hair. A signature rests in the corner: *E*C.

There's something secret, illicit, about this likeness. It was not created for this folder or these dusty archives – it was intended to be a shared gift, between artist and subject.

Eventually I put the portrait to one side and read the papers beneath. Information I know – name, birthday, residence – flicker in and out of focus through the sudden blurriness in my eyes. Further pages yield facts I didn't know about her. *Lancelot regiment. Horse: Aethon (black Arab)*. I wonder if she was as close to Aethon as I am to Lamb. These snippets aren't enough. She's still out of reach.

The next page I find is apparently a notice of disciplinary action. *15th December 2000. Admitted to negligence while out on patrol. Suspended from active duties for six months.*

Six months. Negligence? This isn't the Mum I wanted. What did she do? *Maybe she took a detour to look into something she shouldn't have . . . like I'm doing now,* I think. That must be it. A big punishment for a small transgression. I push that particular piece of paper to the bottom of the pile.

An ink stamp on the next page prints the word *Resigned*. A date is scribbled underneath it – 2nd July 2005. A month after Ollie and I were born. A month before she died.

I hurry up a few shelves to those marked *Lancelot regiment*, pulling down the one marked *2004–2005*. I flick through until I find a list of the regiment's members that year. There's *Una Gorlois*, near the top. *Ellen Cassell* is just above it. Perhaps this is the EC who painted Mum's portrait.

There's something else: a red scrawl next to many of the names, faded unlike the rest of the ink, as though it doesn't want to be deciphered. *Died in the line of duty*. It's next to Ellen Cassell's name. I scan down the list. There it is again, and again, and again. Next to nearly every single name, right down to the final one: *Clement Rigby. Died in the line of duty*. That tallies with the death call of names on the columns a floor above me. There are only two people who don't have that tragic footnote next to their record. One is my mother. The other name is at the top of the list: *Lionel Allenby*. So he and my mum were the only survivors – at first, anyway. No wonder he said they were friends; they were the only people left in their regiment by the end.

What *did* happen in 2005? This kind of massacre wasn't normal. I'd studied the names and years on the columns at length. Before 2005 there wasn't a death in Tintagel since 1998, and there's only been a handful since.

I run back out into the aisle. My absence is going to be noticed soon but I have to make the most of this opportunity.

Tintagel Records, 2001–2010.

I rush along, pulling out the files for 2005 and flicking

through them randomly until I realise that I'm not actually reading anything. I have to take deep breaths and deliberately slow down. It's no use looking without seeing.

So I look, and I see. One name stands out on the pages, repeated in ever more panicked handwriting.

Sebastien Medraut.

Lottie's father. Up and coming politician. Irrelevant to me before now except as the handsome dad to one of my peers and the opponent to one of the only people to show me genuine kindness.

5th April 2005

Medraut struck again today. As with his other victims, he left his mark. None of the Gawain regiment returned from their patrol, but their weapons were left behind, with his trademark verse. We are working towards uncovering how he is orchestrating the deaths, given that he must be too weak to commit them himself.

'Fern? Fern King?'

The voice of the reeve makes me jump.

'Are you still down here? I've got Mr Blake asking after you.'

'Coming! Sorry, I got lost!' I shout, taking one final look at the papers. On the next page, a single line reads, *He has a treitre. God help us.*

I stuff the papers untidily back into the folder, but before I push my mother's folder back into its place, I slip EC's portrait into my pocket. It drums my hip as the reeve ushers me up the stairs towards the classroom. I don't learn anything else that night. My mind is focused on a man with violet eyes, whose daughter goes to my school. A man who, despite apparently orchestrating the deaths of knights fifteen years ago, is still at large. I want to cry, and I want to scream. *Why is no one hunting him down?*

16

By the morning, my heart has that deep, sinking feeling I always get when I can't process something terrible. For the first time since moving to Bosco, school once again feels like crossing enemy lines. I am on edge as I approach the entrance: will Medraut be dropping off his daughter this morning? Will I bump into him in the corridors as he's on his way to a meeting with the headmaster?

'You're skittish today, Fern,' my English teacher remarks. 'Are you quite all right?'

I shrug her off, inadvertently catching Lottie Medraut's eye. Is it just paranoia, or is she paying more attention to me? It had never occurred to me before that I might already know people in Ithr, other than Ollie, who are also aware of Annwn. Is Lottie one of them? How much does she know about her father? For that matter, how much do *I* know about him?

At lunchtime I head over to the computer room and search for Sebastien Medraut online. I disregard the recent articles and try to find out what he was doing in Ithr at the time of my birth – at the time of Lottie's birth too, I guess. Medraut was apparently engineering the deaths of hundreds of knights while expecting the arrival of his child. The Internet throws up some articles mentioning Lottie's birth a few months before Ollie and I were born. Then, at the start of 2005, I find what I've been looking for.

> ***Rising Star of Politics Steps Down***
> *Last night, in a move that has shocked thousands of his loyal followers, Sebastien Medraut, founder of the One Voice party, announced that he would be stepping down from his role as leader of the party, effective immediately. Looking emotional and visibly shaking, Medraut apologised to the members of his party, which has grown to encompass an impressive 113,000 members since its inception in 2003.*

The article goes on, but I'm already looking up a video of his resignation speech. On the film, it's obvious that Medraut is ill. He's hunched over the podium, his fists clenching and unclenching robotically. He's frowning as though he's having difficulty reading the autocue and his voice, which is usually so measured, has an uneven timbre, occasionally veering into a shout, sometimes becoming too quiet for the microphones to pick up. But the most striking part of the video is his eyes. I can't be certain, but it looks as though they are . . . less violet. As though something's sucked the colour from them and left them bleak and grey.

I pull out my knightbook and scribble, *What happened to Medraut in January 2005?* Then, underlined, *EYES*.

By the end of lunch I am steadier. Research has allowed me

to regain some control, to find a beacon in the sea of chaos and questions that has been pulling me under since last night.

When I get home I turn the telly on straight away, barely greeting Dad.

'Hey, homework first, Ferny,' he objects from the kitchen.

'It's the news,' I tell him, switching channels. I land, finally, on something that looks promising.

'Last night MP for Newham, Helena Corday, debated newly elected MP for Kensington and Chelsea, Sebastien Medraut,' a newsreader says. 'Medraut recently replaced disgraced Shadow Secretary John Lawrence in a snap by-election, storming to a landslide victory with his newly reinvigorated One Voice party.'

The TV displays a clip of the two politicians standing behind podiums. 'We must be unified,' Medraut is saying. 'One voice, across the nation.'

Helena Corday grimaces and rolls her eyes, but anyone watching can see she's the one who's looking weak.

'Not you as well.' Dad nudges me over and hands me a bacon sandwich dripping with ketchup. He tucks into his own.

'What do you mean?'

'Your mother was obsessed with him.'

My blood goes hot. 'Mum?'

'I teased her something rotten about it.'

'Did you ever ask her why?' I ask Dad.

'She said she didn't trust him. That was all. He was only just starting to make a name for himself, then he dropped out of politics altogether. Your mum never stopped checking up on him though. But . . .'

He trails off, distracted by the sound of Ollie getting back from school. My brother barges into the room, his hair messed and his uniform dirty. He bats away Dad's questions and goes to make himself another bacon sarnie with the leftover rashers.

'But what?' I prompt, trying to get the conversation back on track.

'Oh, it doesn't matter,' Dad sighs.

'I want to know,' I say.

'Well . . . your mother was in a funny place, that last year.'

'What do you mean?' I say. Ollie has stopped assembling his sandwich, his eyes darting between Dad and I.

'Oh, you know, little things. She was just a bit . . . a bit down, you might say.'

'About what?'

Dad shrugs.

'Come on, Dad,' Ollie says, 'you can tell us.'

Dad pauses. 'Well, she . . . she was having dreadful nightmares.'

Ollie and I share a glance.

'What kind of nightmares?' he asks.

But Dad shakes his head. 'Your mother wouldn't want you thinking about her like this.'

'We want to know everything about her,' I say, but Dad won't be drawn, even when Ollie turns on his charm.

That night we leave Tintagel again. Natasha accompanies us on Domino, along with a retinue of retired knights acting as bodyguards. I would feel patronised by it if I had the spare brainpower to care.

'Fiver for your thoughts?' Ramesh interrupts.

'What?'

'Compound interest on a penny,' he explains, then blushes. 'Sorry, I'm a geek, in case it wasn't obvious.'

Natasha listens to something through her helmet – the one piece of uniform we only get when we become proper knights at Ostara – the spring equinox. It allows us to communicate with the harkers back in the castle. She nods and steers our group north towards the canals and markets of Camden.

'Have you heard anything about Sebastien Medraut?' I ask Ramesh impulsively.

'The politician guy? My friend in Ithr fancies him like crazy,' Ramesh replies. 'She's part of his youth movement.'

'But . . . you haven't heard anything about him in Annwn?'

Ramesh shakes his head. 'Why?'

I look at Ramesh's open, inquisitive face and wonder . . . Can I trust him with this? Will he use it against me? Is it worth the risk?

'I think he might have something to do with my mum's death,' I say quickly.

Natasha holds up a hand, signalling us to stop and pull our horses to one side of the road.

'God, that's awful,' Ramesh whispers and reaches a hand out, as if to comfort me. At the last minute though he seems to remember who he's dealing with and pats Lamb's neck instead. The gesture makes me smile.

'What about treitres?' I ask him, remembering the strange word that had seemed to inspire such fear in the writer of those records.

'Treitres?' Ramesh frowns. 'I have heard that somewhere, yeah. Where *did* I hear it?'

Natasha silences us with a look and points towards a dreamer who's half walking, half jogging through the streets. This is usually one of my favourite parts of training – when we're shown nightmares and dreams in action. There's always a split second when you can tell that a dreamer is about to enter a nightmare. You can see it in their eyes, as though something has twisted in their head and altered the way they see the world.

'Anyone spot what she's running from?' Natasha asks us.

We all peer down the street. Apart from a few other dreamers there's no one there. Then I see it.

'The inspyre.'

'Yes!' Natasha says, pointing at me. 'Do the rest of you see it, behind the dreamer?'

A swirl of blue light dances after the woman. It doesn't seem threatening, but it is definitely following her. Then the woman glances at it.

'Oh my God,' Phoebe startles. In the split second that the woman turned, the inspyre transformed into a shadowy figure. It doesn't have any features – it barely has limbs – but it's loosely human in shape and shrouded in grey cloud. As the woman speeds up, the figure morphs back into inspyre. Suddenly that dancing light has a sinister feel.

'That's a stalker, guys. It can take any shape or none at all. Dreamers can't see inspyre in its purest form, but with a stalker they can *feel* it, like a lurking sense of dread.'

'Shouldn't you be killing it?' Ramesh says.

'Not yet. Stalkers aren't necessarily dangerous. The harkers have decided this one's safe for now.'

'But what happens if it catches her?'

‘Stalkers tend to match a dreamer’s pace instead of actually aiming to catch them. They feed off their fear, you see. The only time it might get dangerous is if the dreamer decides to give up. The harkers will tell us if anything changes.’

We leave the woman and her stalking inspyre behind and move on down the street.

Ramesh leans over. ‘I’ll see what I can find out, but at some point I want to hear why you think Medraut has anything to do with Annwn.’

I nod curtly and glance back. The dreamer has begun to run. I always hated those kinds of nightmares – my stalkers never took a form. I’d just have a sense that someone was following me, and I couldn’t shake them off. When I woke up it would take me ages to calm the hammering of my heart. That’s how I feel at the moment, I realise. Like a shadowy figure is lurking behind me, waiting to take me out. A shadowy figure that takes the shape of Sebastien Medraut.

17

Ollie joins me as I'm leaving for school the next morning. Neither of us says anything, and I keep waiting for him to peel off, but he sticks beside me like an irritating shadow.

'Are you lost?' I eventually snap.

'Why are you suddenly hung up on Sebastien Medraut?' he asks.

'I'm not.'

'You are. Dad said you were asking him more questions.'

I shrug in what I hope is a disdainful manner. 'Just because I'm developing an interest in politics –'

Ollie's cough of laughter interrupts me. It's fair enough, to be honest.

'Do you think Medraut had something to do with Mum's death?' he asks.

'What? What makes you think that?'

He's about to answer when he spots something up ahead and tenses.

'The plaque next to the herb garden,' he says shortly, then turns on his heel and takes a side street that goes nowhere near his school. I look up and stop dead. Because there, lounging against a wall, surrounded by a cohort I last saw at nighttime on Wanstead Flats, is Jenny. She is looking straight at me.

I hover in place for what feels like hours, wondering what to do. I have been frightened many times in my life, but the only time that fear has paralysed me is around Jenny. I can almost feel the fire licking against my legs; the sudden spark that leaped towards my face that has marked me permanently. She's not allowed to come near me. It's the law. But what use is the law when there's no one to enforce it? Ollie's left me on my own again. For all I know, he purposely steered me this way to help her finish off the job.

Jenny gets up. Her gang follows her and spreads out across the road.

Nah. I turn round and take the long route to the Underground station. Humiliation pumps through me. On the tube, all through school, all the way home, I burn with it. I can't help but feel that people are staring at me more than usual. I am more aware of my strange appearance than I have been for months. I prickle with the certainty that Jenny is going to pounce on me and no one will do anything to stop her.

Ollie was probably just winding me up, but that night I run round to the herb garden before I go to the stables. Sure enough, there is a stone plaque fixed to the wall behind a rosemary hedge. On it are carved the names of every Head Thane Tintagel has seen, starting with *Arthur Pendragon*. I scan the rest, occasionally landing with a jolt of familiarity on a name I recognise from my history lessons. At the bottom I find three entries:

1981–2001: Lady Bethany Caradoc
2001–2005:
2005–2008: Lord David Richards
2008–   : Lord Lionel Allenby

I peer closer at the space between *Bethany Caradoc* and *David Richards*. One name seems to be missing – or rather, erased. Whatever name used to be carved beside the years *2001–2005* has been covered up with some sort of putty. I trace over it with my fingers, desperate to have my suspicion confirmed. My fingers seem to spark; an electric shock that travels along my arm and right into my skull. I snatch my hand away.

'Knight? Shouldn't you be saddling up?' an apothecary says, making me jolt. She kneels down to dig at some saplings.

'Yeah. I'm going now,' I say, casting one last look back at the plaque. I'm sure something's different, but I don't get a chance to look more closely because at that moment Miss D's impatient voice summons me from across the gardens.

We've been invited to shadow Bedevere on a mission to watch them tackle a poisoner – a type of nightmare we haven't been allowed to see until now because it's so dangerous. As we ride out over Tintagel's drawbridge and into Annwn, I glance at Ollie, wondering why he wanted me to look at the plaque. It's an odd thing to do if it was just a prank. To top off my confusion, I'm starting to get a headache.

'Fern?' Ramesh says, breaking into my reverie. 'Are you okay?'

I nod.

'Thinking about your mum again?'

I look around, worried someone will overhear him. It still feels strange to have shared this with someone else.

'It's okay, no one's listening,' Ramesh says, then when I don't reply, adds, 'I did ask around about Medraut, but it's difficult, being a squire and, well, I don't really know what I'm asking . . .' He trails off, clearly hoping I'll give him all the gossip about my dead mother.

'*One Voice*.'

'What?' Ramesh says.

'I didn't say anything,' I reply. 'Did you . . . did you hear that too?'

'*One Voice, One Voice, One Voice*.'

The whole group is now looking round, trying to find the source of the sound. One Voice – the name of Sebastien Medraut's political party.

'It's coming from the air,' Phoebe says in wonder.

'From the inspyre, actually,' Rafe calls back. 'Medraut's been gaining power lately, hasn't he? If you see loads about him in Ithr, it stands to reason you'll come across his slogans and ideas in Annwn. Don't take any notice of it for now.' But I don't think I'm the only one who spots Rafe exchange a look with the other experienced knights. They're hiding something.

We ride to a little square north of King's Cross: a set of Georgian townhouses that stand around a walled garden like gossiping friends. A crowd of thanes is already gathered on the steps leading into one of the houses. There's a solitary reeve and an assortment of veneurs in their black tunics. They move around the house like police at a crime scene.

On paper, the veneurs sound harmless enough. They are supposed to look after the animals in the castle – the horses that carry us knights into battle; the cats that have slipped through cracks in Tintagel's defences to hunt smaller nightmares; the dogs that sometimes attach themselves to a thane.

They also look after the morrigans.

This will be my first time meeting a morrigan. They are kept in the eyrie, at the very top of one of Tintagel's towers.

'They're a bit . . . unusual,' Rafe told us as we rode. 'Technically they're vampires, but don't let that put you off. They feed off your imagination and memories, so they can be really useful to us in certain circumstances, but you should never be left alone with a morrigan unless you're trained.'

Now I see the things, I am even more creeped out by them than I was by Rafe's description. At first they just look like large crows perched on the leather-clad wrists of the veneurs. Each one is hooded like a bird of prey. Then one stretches its wings to reveal ragged grey skin instead of feathers, like a cross between bird and bat.

'What's that on its wing?' Ramesh asks, pointing to a tag attached to the morrigan.

'They all have one,' the Veneur explains. 'A few years back some morrigans went missing from the eyrie so they all have to wear these trackers now.'

Rafe ushers us all in close before we enter the house. 'Poisoners don't kill in Annwn, but they're the most dangerous of all nightmares, and the most difficult ones to deal with. There's no point in killing a poisoner. It will just come back. The key is to find the root of what makes a dreamer create a poisoner and use the morrigans to remove it. It's a very delicate process. Morrigans are tricky creatures to control, so I don't want anyone to utter a sound, okay? It's crucial that they aren't distracted.'

We all nod silently, keen to show off our ability to follow rules like good little squires. As we tiptoe up the steps and into a sitting room, my curiosity grows. What can this nightmare be? I imagine all kinds of monsters – horned, fire breathing, spines galore . . . So when the group spreads out to reveal two men, I am flummoxed.

They sit on a raggedy sofa. One man looks as though he hasn't slept in weeks. He stares straight ahead with dulled eyes. As I get closer, I realise he probably hasn't showered in weeks either. His hands and clothing are grubby and he stinks. The person beside him could be his more successful twin. He's dressed in a tailored suit, his nails are manicured and his hair slicked back. His face is less lined, too, but instead of the lifeless look in the other man's eyes, his are full of malice. He is bent over his companion, whispering in his ear. Then I notice the telltale blue outline around the malicious man's form, and realise that this must be the poisoner.

I crane to hear what he's saying.

'*Pathetic excuse of a man . . . Do you realise how disgusting you are? You stink. You're worthless. No wonder you've got no friends . . . You see those people staring at you in the street? It's because they're revolted by you. What do you bring to the world? You're such a burden. Mum and Dad are ashamed of you, they'd be happier without you . . .*'

And I understand, with heart-wrenching clarity, exactly why

poisoners are the most dangerous nightmares of all. I can see what will happen when this dreamer wakes up. Maybe not today, maybe not tomorrow, but at some point the poisoner will achieve its goal. Suddenly the smell of the man doesn't matter any more because I have been him. Except my poisoner was not in my own image – it was Ollie, or Dad, or sometimes even Mum – telling me in my nightmares, in my daydreams, in the lonely moments between distractions, that everyone would be better off if I were dead.

I glance at Ollie, suddenly furious. How dare he bear witness to this man's most vulnerable moment? But Ollie's expression is a mirror of mine. He is gulping heavily and his eyes are fixed on the poisoner with . . . is that fear? Recognition, at least. But I don't understand – I can't imagine that Ollie has ever had the kind of thoughts that make chains around your heart.

The veneurs surround the dreamer and his nightmare and, as one, remove the hoods of their morrigans. The creatures' eyes are red, like mine. Most of them home in immediately on the dreamer, but one or two peer round at the assembled group. I try to edge closer, slipping around Phoebe to get to the front.

Someone grabs my wrist and I stifle a cry of shock. I am sparking with energy. An arc of inspyre leaps from the ceiling towards me. I look to see who it was who grabbed me – Ollie. He looks just as shocked as me.

I may as well have shouted out because every single morrigan in the room is suddenly fixated on us.

'Get them out,' a veneur snaps. Rafe pushes us from the room and shoves us out onto the street.

'What was that?' Rafe hisses.

'I've got no idea,' I say.

'Me neither,' says Ollie.

'Whatever, you'd both better stay outside now.'

He goes back inside, and I round on Ollie.

'What did you do?'

'I was *trying* to stop you from distracting them.'

'Well, that worked out well, didn't it?'

We shove each other as we peer through the window to see what's happening.

The morrigans are perched strategically on the dreamer's shoulders and head, with their beaks dipped into his flesh as though it's a flower brimming with pollen. I can't hear anything, but the motion of the creatures' throats as they guzzle the dreamer's memories is revolting. It's working, though: the poisoner is fading. At first he goes fuzzy at the edges, then translucent. What is most fascinating, though, is the transformation in the dreamer. Something lifts and sparks behind his eyes. His face, too, seems younger. It's hope, I realise, my heart blooming. He is rediscovering hope.

18

Despite my coldness towards him, Ramesh is taking my queries about Medraut and treitres as a personal quest. One chilly night, as I hurry back from the stables, watching my breath turn inspyre into snowflakes, Ramesh runs out of Tintagel to find me.

'I've got it,' he tells me, pulling me up the steps and through Tintagel's doors, now studded with icicles, 'or at least I think I have. Or it's common knowledge but we haven't been taught it yet. I'm not completely sure.'

'Ramesh, what are you on about?'

We speed walk to the castle's hospital. Instead of the sprawling buildings we have in Ithr, Tintagel's hospital occupies just one of the towers. Platforms are embedded into the stone, spiralling all the way to the top. Each one houses a bed, so the apothecaries can fly between their patients. It's an ethereal place; the open space both disguises and amplifies sounds so that the whole tower echoes with reassuring murmurs, like waves lapping a shore.

Ramesh doesn't make me fly, though. He takes me over to the collection of medical books that lie on lecterns on the ground floor, next to the little pantry where herbs hang to dry. He shuffles through the pages of one of them.

'Here.' He points to an entry. I don't immediately read it, because I am drawn to an illustration of the most extraordinary creature I've ever seen. It's lithe, with slender, hyena legs, a long, pointed tail and a face that tapers elegantly into a featureless muzzle. It stands on two legs like a human, though. Its eyes stare at me from the page, following me when I move.

Treitre, the heading says. My heart quickens. The description follows.

You will find no telltale blue light surrounding these creatures, for they are not nightmares at all, but humans. Few people will ever face a treitre; they are rare beings. A study taken in 1999 identified around thirty treitres operating across Annwn.

Becoming a treitre is an onerous and painful process for any aventure brave enough to attempt it. Only those who lack fear may succeed. They must embrace their boldness to the detriment of all other parts of themselves, suppressing emotion and empathy until their human form merges with inspyre to take on the shape of their innermost soul – hard, cold and deadly. For those who succeed, the rewards are great: treitres are the most effective assassins in either Ithr or Annwn and so may charge a high price for their services.

Established treitres tired of bloodshed themselves can glean further riches by training others in the transformation process, and thus cabals of assassins are formed, with apprentices turning to masters as the years go by.

No one has yet found a way to forcibly uncover the human lying beneath a treitre's shell. They are above the law, for unless they are caught and persuaded to reveal themselves, they shall remain anonymous. If they are killed in their treitre form, then their human identity shall forever be shrouded in mystery. Many kings and queens, dictators and rebels have been brought low by the feared treitre, but the most recent recorded sighting of such a creature was in 2005 in the thaneship of London, where a single treitre laid low some hundreds of knights over the course of several months.

'You see?' Ramesh says. 'All those names on the columns, all from 2005 . . .'

As if she'd been cut all over.

That's what Clemmie had said, wasn't it? I look at the illustration once more. This time I see that the creature's hands have blades in place of fingers.

'Thank you,' I say.

Ramesh puts a hand on my shoulder, and with that tiny gesture of support my throat swells with forbidden tears.

'Let's get some air,' Ramesh whispers, steering me out of the castle and into the gardens. Outside, he watches the paper-clear sky while I try to get control of myself. It's overwhelming: not just the knowledge of what must have killed Mum, but Ramesh's kindness. He's usually so pushy that I hadn't expected him to instinctively understand that his unobtrusive presence is so much more comforting to me right now than a grand display of concern.

A huddle of apothecaries, swaddled in scarves and carrying baskets of herbs, brush past us. Suddenly, I am running.

'Fern? You all right?' Ramesh crashes after me as I vault

the hedgerows that divide Tintagel's gardens from the grazing pastures next to the stables. Round one last curve of a turret and I am there – the herb garden Ollie sent me to just the other day. Everything that had happened with the poisoner had driven from my mind the nagging sense that something about the plaque had changed as I walked away.

'What's the matter?' Ramesh pants, but I simply point. The missing Head Thane between Lady Bethany Caradoc and Lord David Richards is no longer missing. The putty that was once there has melted away, revealing a familiar name: *Lord Sebastien Medraut*.

I reel backwards, unable to take in Ramesh's exclamations. I am not surprised though. Maybe part of me had suspected all along that his name was the one that had been erased from the plaque. No, I'm not surprised. I am in shock. And that shock is rippling its way into anger as I start to piece together the events of the year of my mother's murder.

Medraut was Head Thane for four years before he had some sort of breakdown at the start of 2005. A few months later, he started using a treitre – a half-human, half-monster assassin – to kill knights. What I don't know is why he stopped being Head Thane, and what on earth drove him to kill the people he once led?

'That is mad news about Medraut,' Ramesh is saying. 'Do you think he had something to do with that treitre attack then? I wonder why we haven't been taught about him. Or about treitres, now I come to think of it.'

I shake my head, confused. Is this some sort of cover-up? Why else would they have tried to conceal Medraut's name on that plaque, if they weren't trying to protect him? I can't make sense of it.

'Cool Eyes has turned into Sulky Eyes tonight,' Rafe quips later that night as everyone relaxes in the knights' chamber after lessons.

'You would too if your teachers were putting you in massive danger every time you left this castle!' I snap back.

'What are you talking about?'

'I'm talking about the fact that fifteen years ago a treitre killed a load of knights and instead of teaching us how to deal with them you're teaching us how to cope with stalkers and stupid trickster nightmares that aren't even that dangerous!'

I am on my feet now, anger pounding through my veins. I can barely hear the gasps and whispers of my fellow squires through the thunderous beat inside me. Rafe has turned pale and still.

'The reason,' he says, his voice taut, 'you haven't been taught about treitres yet, is because you aren't ready. You might think you're invincible with your massive *two months* of training under your belt, but if you came up against a treitre right now it wouldn't end well for you, I guarantee that. So until you've mastered the nightmares we've deemed you capable of tackling, me and Emory and the other *actual* knights will continue to risk our own lives to protect you.'

The heat burning through me has morphed from righteous anger to cannibalistic humiliation. Rafe doesn't wait for me to reply but stalks off, joined by Emory and a few of the other more experienced knights.

'Well, *you're* not getting a teacher's pet award any time soon,' Ollie sneers.

'He didn't need to jump down your throat like that,' Phoebe says.

'He was telling her how it is,' Ollie says. 'Nothing wrong with that.'

'Stop it, just . . . please, stop it,' I tell my brother, suddenly exhausted. How can he still be so horrible to me, even when we now have so many bigger, more important things to worry about? How can he want to humiliate me even more when I've never done anything to warrant it? It's baffling, and right now I don't have the energy to parry his strikes.

Ollie opens his mouth to say something, but a meaningful look from Ramesh silences him. Later, Ramesh corners me again.

'Why didn't you say anything about Medraut?' he asks.

I shrug. Even when shaking with rage, something had stopped me from mentioning the former Head Thane. Maybe it's because the book about the treitres had been readily available, while Medraut's name had, before it inexplicably appeared again, been hidden behind putty on a plaque tucked away at the back of the gardens. Someone really doesn't want us to know about Medraut, which makes me think that my best chance of finding out more is by keeping quiet about what I already know. I try to explain this to Ramesh.

'I don't like keeping secrets,' he replies.

'We're not keeping secrets. We're just not spreading gossip.'

And this seems to satisfy him. My first successful manipulation. I have obviously picked up some tips from Ollie.

* * *

As Christmas approaches and more dreamers turn their thoughts to the holiday season, Annwn's landscape changes. Tintagel is festooned with ivy and mistletoe; not the factory-farmed sprigs we get in Ithr but actual vines of the stuff that spread over the walls. Sprigs of holly peep from crevices. A thick layer of snow covers the gardens. Outside the castle walls, clouds of inspyre form miniature snowstorms. Fat little snowmen and Father Christmases wobble around, by turns scaring and enchanting dreamers.

In Ithr, though, things are not quite so happy. I notice it on the way back from school. An almost imperceptible difference that no one but people like me would detect. I sense it first on the tube. The carriage is packed, as usual, but it's a few stops before I realise that there's a gap between me and the other commuters. I catch the looks that people are throwing my way. Curiosity I can cope with, but not this. This is disgust, and something far more dangerous – fear. I try to make myself physically smaller. Being overtly bullied is one thing, but this feels like a level up. When I get off the tube I run all the way home, those accusing eyes boring into my memory.

Annwn, always a welcome escape from real life, becomes even more of a sanctuary for me. Even if Ollie is there, at least I don't get strangers staring at me in hostile silence. In any case, in Annwn I have Ramesh, who has kept my confidence against all my expectations, and Phoebe, whose warmth and laid-back nature soothes the entire chamber, stretching even to the quiet corner where I sit each night. Rafe seems to have forgotten my accusation, and Natasha, who is fond of me because of my riding prowess, finds me one night to say that she heard about my outburst. 'Be patient,' she tells me. 'There's a reason for the way we teach you.'

'*When*, Lamb, *when*?!' I rant at my horse on a semi-regular basis. It's all very well for Natasha to tell me to be patient, but there's a difference between waiting for something you know is going to happen and waiting indefinitely on a promise. Lamb whickers in response and pulls another mouthful of hay from the manger. Sometimes I get the impression that she views me as a neurotic creature to be nuzzled into good humour.

Tonight we're shadowing Lancelot on their patrol of the tidal circuit – a loop of the Thames stretching from Tintagel's turf down to the old brick factories south of the river, all the way along the shore to Kew Gardens, where honeysuckle flowers as big as trumpets turn bumblebees plump.

Emory signals us to drop into single file to cross the river, leading us down into a narrow tunnel that serves as a footpath beneath the Thames in Ithr. In Annwn the echoes of our horses' hooves are joined by the percussion of the nocturnal creatures that lurk in the crevices between the tiles.

When we come up for air, Ollie reins in his horse Balius to match Lamb's pace. He's been unusually quiet since the day in the knights' chamber when I refused to argue with him, and not just with me, but with the other squires who didn't back him up. He doesn't have it in him to be nasty to me unless he has the support of others.

'I found something else,' he tells me quietly, 'about Medraut.'

'What?' I yank on Lamb's bit in my shock and she bucks in rebuke.

'Smooth,' Ollie says.

'You mean the plaque?' I ask, resettling myself in the saddle.

'Something else. Not in Annwn. In Ithr. In Mum's old notes.'

'*I've* got Mum's notes,' I say. 'They're in my bedroom.'

Ollie smirks. 'Yes, they are.'

'You broke into my room? You absolute w—'

'Relax,' Ollie says. 'I only looked at Mum's stuff, not anything of yours. Not like you have anything interesting in there anyway.'

I am rendered temporarily speechless by the fact that Ollie genuinely seems to think it's okay to enter my room without permission as long as he doesn't go through my drawers.

'Mum has a recording of Medraut, did you know that?' Ollie continues.

'The voice recorder? How did you make it work?'

'I got a mate to transfer the data onto my laptop. I'll play it for you at home, if you like,' Ollie says.

I nod, unsettled. I'm in uncharted territory, with this new, mostly civil way of talking to my brother. Part of me wants to embrace it. The other part of me is wondering when I'm going to find the catch; the trick; the betrayal. The idea that he could be helping me just because, is totally alien.

'Did you crack Mum's code too?' I ask, trying hard to sound casual.

'What code?'

Aha. So I know something he doesn't. I have managed to claw back some power.

'In her diaries.' I hesitate, then take the plunge. 'I'll show you back in Ithr, if you like.'

Ollie nods, his wariness mirroring my own.

And Ollie spurs Balius on to rejoin Ramesh. We have reached our conversational limit. I breathe deeply, my heart pumping with nerves. I don't know how to navigate this change between Ollie and I. My guard against him has been so strong and now I've started to dismantle it. I just have to pray that I'm tough enough to cope if – when – he breaks my trust yet again.

Emory has been leading us through the old maze of narrow, cobbled streets that lazily follow the river. Through passageways I glimpse dreams of lives lived long ago: bears being baited, wooden ships painted in garish colours being made ready for adventure. I am just about to see whether I can, after all, inject myself into Ramesh and Ollie's discussion about battle formations when I become aware of a crawling sensation deep within my stomach. It's as though someone is trying to manoeuvre my organs out of me without cutting me open.

We round a corner and see the cosy splendour of the Globe Theatre, its thatched roof a neat hat. But as we approach, an uncomfortable muttering rises from the front of the group. My innards lurch. For the first time since arriving in Annwn I want, desperately, to turn around and head back to Ithr. Ollie drops back once more, but this time he is clutching his stomach.

'What on earth?' says Phoebe, and against my instincts I force myself to look.

At the entrance to the Globe, between the wattle and daub and beneath the blond thatch, is solid darkness. Instead of the raucous laughter of an audience and the sound of Shakespearean players hamming it up, the darkness emits silence. I'd never realised that the absence of sound could be aggressive until

I witnessed this. Emory is talking with urgent tones into her helmet. Ramesh kicks his horse forward to take a better look.

'Get back!' Emory shouts at him. 'Can't you see it's dangerous?'

Even as I double over, even as I hear Ollie retching into a bush behind me, I too nudge Lamb forward. But I don't want to get closer to that hellish doorway. I want to hear what Emory is saying. I close my eyes against the nausea and focus.

'Organise a rota of knights to guard this place day and night,' Emory says. 'We can't risk any dreamers coming near. And tell Lord Allenby to get here now. I don't care who he's in a meeting with. Tell him he was right. Tell him it's started again.'

19

In the short time it takes for Lord Allenby to reach us, I have to be lifted from Lamb's back. I curl, snail-like, on a stretch of beach, trying to keep my insides from becoming my outsides. Ollie is next to me in a similar state. Phoebe and Ramesh hover over us. Ramesh goes to pat Ollie's back but Ollie swats him away, retching.

'How do you not feel it too?' I gasp at them. 'It's coming from that doorway.'

'I don't know,' Phoebe says, stroking my back. 'I mean, it makes me feel really weird but I don't feel ill. I think it's only you two.'

'Lucky me,' Ollie spits, in between heaving out the contents of his stomach.

The distant pounding of hooves marks Allenby's arrival, along with a retinue of harkers, reeves, apothecaries and a single veneur. Lord Allenby barely glances at us, swinging from his charger's back and marching alongside Emory to inspect the doorway. The veneur tries to approach the doorway with his morrigan, but no sooner does it sense the vortex through its hood than it takes off, screeching in alarm.

Two apothecaries descend on Ollie and I, pressing cold compresses on our foreheads. 'It must be an allergic reaction,' says my apothecary – a tall, greying man who introduces himself as Drew. 'It happens more than people realise, although I've never seen anything of this severity.'

'We're allergic to that black hole?' Ollie asks.

He shakes his head. 'It's probably one of these vines.' He points to the neon tendrils currently weaving their way around the wall that separates road from river. I nod, although secretly I'm with Ollie – I feel sure that my sickness is linked to that doorway. I watch, the compress helping a little with my nausea, as Lord Allenby orders Emory's knights to guard the entrance. She whispers something to him, nodding back at the squires. Eventually, Allenby remounts his charger and gallops back towards Tintagel.

'Are we going to get an explanation then or . . .?' Ramesh trails off.

Emory addresses us. 'You're all to go back to the castle immediately. Wait in the hall.'

'Are you coming too?' Phoebe asks.

'No, I'm staying here. We have to make sure no one goes near the Globe.'

She stops the 'Why?' on several dozen lips with a well-aimed stare. 'Get back on your horses and get back to Tintagel.'

We do as we're told. The apothecaries help Ollie and I back into our saddles, and as we canter away from the Globe, the sickness in my stomach lifts. By the time we're thundering over the drawbridge into the castle grounds, it's as if I've dreamed the sudden, devastating nausea entirely. A different energy flows through Tintagel's halls though. It's quieter, the air bloated with unanswered questions. The more senior thanes flurry through the cloisters and offices, their faces tense, while the rest of us are untethered.

I am one of the first to see Lord Allenby emerge from his office. With a glance, Allenby summons the captains of the different lores and murmurs instructions to them. When he's done, he addresses the rest of the castle in a voice that reaches to the highest tower. 'Squires, with me. The rest of you, go to your chambers. You'll be briefed there by your captains.'

Rachel catches my eye and trots over with a few of her harker friends. The buzz of intrigue hangs over the squires as we follow Lord Allenby out of the castle, through the grounds and once more across the drawbridge. Only the knight and apothecary squires have been outside Tintagel's walls yet, and the others – the reeves, harkers and veneurs – pull into the nucleus of the group, nervous of the dreams and nightmares that are now so familiar to me. I ignore their conversations, watching where Lord Allenby is leading us. Emory's words – *it's started again* – fill me with a bubbling anticipation.

We wend our way east, retracing the path that Andraste and I trod on my first night in Annwn. But before we get to Tower Hill, Lord Allenby veers down an alleyway. In the distance I spot a statue, and realise that it's the same one I glimpsed from the main road on that first night. As we draw closer, the alleyway opens out into a courtyard garden. The statue is actually a monument – an obelisk topped by a sphere and engraved with the emblem of the thanes. It's not made of gold, as I'd thought on that first night, but of amber that spins the sun's rays into a blanket that drapes across the garden. Set inside the resin is a bizarre collection: hundreds of seemingly random items – a toy soldier, a silver cup, even a pair of gloves. I had thought that the ribbons I'd spotted all those months ago were attached to the obelisk, but they are festooned from the trees and flowers that border the space.

The others crowd around the obelisk but my eye has been caught by the ribbons of paper hanging from a branch above my head. They are not merely decorations: they are covered in messages.

Dream easy, Rosalind. We miss you.

Charlie – comrade and best friend. I don't know how to be without you.

For Clement and Ellen. I'm so sorry, for everything.

Clement and Ellen – they were listed in Mum's regiment in those archive records. Then Lord Allenby speaks, and the names are driven from my thoughts.

'It's time for you to learn some home truths about our past.'

He pauses, and I'm almost certain that he glances towards Ollie and I, as though measuring how ready we are for what he's about to say. I lift my chin, returning his gaze as steadily as I can.

'You all know about inspyre. You know we can only change it in a limited fashion, and even that's difficult. Well, that's not true for everyone.'

The squires stir, caught between wondering what this has to

do with what happened at the Globe and with the monument before us, and the fact that the fundamental rules we've been taught are, apparently, untrue.

'Once in a while, someone comes along who can manipulate inspyre all they like. And if you can control inspyre, you can control imagination. These people, they can read and control the minds of every person in Annwn.'

'*So cool,*' Ramesh whispers. I imagine being able to read someone's mind – to be able to tell what they're thinking about me. Then to control that; to stop them from picking on me. To make them like me, even. My chest fills with longing. Yes, that would be something.

'This power crops up once or twice in a lifetime, but when it does, you know about it. The first person we know who had this power was King Arthur. That's why it's sometimes called the King's Power.'

'Original,' Ollie remarks.

'It's proper name is Immral,' Lord Allenby says.

That word was mentioned in the archives too, in King Arthur's file.

'People with Immral have used it for great good and great evil. Boudicca, Genghis Khan, even Moses. You see, people with Immral can make dreams and nightmares. Think about what you could do to a dreamer, if you had that power.'

I was thinking too literally, too small, when I imagined making people like me. I could make them love me. I could make them turn on Ollie, the way he got them to turn on me. I recoil from the thought, given my earlier conversation with Ollie, but maybe I need to give him a taste of what he put me through.

Lord Allenby is speaking again.

'About thirty years ago, when I was a young knight, along came a squire who had Immral. We could tell immediately, because all Immrals have one thing in common beyond their power: they all have violet eyes.'

The gathered squires exclaim and whisper around me, as Sebastien Medraut's name is passed from mouth to mouth. Ollie, Ramesh and I exchange glances.

'Yes, yes,' Lord Allenby growls, 'it's very exciting to learn that someone famous in Ithr was once one of you. Everyone was very excited about it back in the day too. Sebastien Medraut became the youngest Head Thane in Tintagel's history. But I said that Immrals have used their power for good and evil. Well, Medraut wasn't one of the good ones. It took a while for us to find out, but he started to run experiments on dreamers. Seeing how far he could push their minds until they turned mad. Working out which nightmares were best at controlling their imaginations. And he started to drain the inspyre from Annwn.'

'Sorry, sir, but what do you mean?' a reeve blurts out. 'How can you drain inspyre? Isn't Annwn *made* of inspyre?'

'It is, Miss Atkinson.' Lord Allenby nods. 'And only an Immral could even think of being able to do such a thing. But Medraut is one of the strongest Immrals we've ever heard of. And when he drained inspyre from Annwn, he made pockets where no inspyre, no imagination, could exist. Our whole sense of self rests on our imaginations. If that's taken from us, well . . .'

He leaves us to imagine the suicidal insanity of not understanding who we are. Not as in 'I can't remember that

I'm a fifteen-year-old girl' but not knowing myself in my very core.

'You saw one of those pockets earlier tonight at the Globe. They're called kalends, and they're one of the most dangerous things you can come across in Annwn. We found them all over the place, twenty years ago,' Lord Allenby says. 'Eventually we linked them back to Medraut. He'd been using his Immral and his position as Head Thane to cover his tracks, but with the help of our morrigans we managed to throw him out of the thanes.'

I think of the articles I'd read, and about what Dad told me – that Medraut had some kind of breakdown and retired from public life for a while.

'But we made a mistake,' Lord Allenby continues. 'We'd meant for the morrigans to take his whole imagination, so he could never come back to Annwn. But he escaped before they could finish the job. A few months later, an assassin – a treitre – started to kill our knights. It was hired by Medraut. Who knows why he did it. Some people think it was revenge or for power. Myself, I think it was a way for him to claw back some pride. Whatever his reason, that one treitre managed to kill nearly two hundred knights inside three months.'

Silence descends. I look up at the monument and the hundreds of items it holds. Each one, I now understand, was the weapon of a fallen knight while they were alive. I catch sight of a pair of headphones, crudely broken in half, and can almost hear the despair and terror of that knight's final seconds. The ribbons rustle in a river breeze, whispering of loss and regret.

'We've been hunting Medraut in Annwn for years,' Lord

Allenby says. 'We never really doubted he'd recover. We have some idea of what he's doing and where he's going in Annwn, and we know where he's set up his base, but his Immral makes it too dangerous for us to face him without gathering more information. That kalend you just found confirms what we'd feared, given his rise in Ithr – that his strength has returned in full. And with Medraut seeking power again, all of us need to be prepared for him to try to finish the job he started all those years ago.'

The whispering resumes; alarmed squires wondering what on earth they've signed up for in joining the thanes. I edge around the garden, my heart hammering with this new knowledge. Then I see what I was looking for. A bright red ribbon with familiar handwriting on one side – my mum's handwriting.

Ellen, dearling, it says, *come back to me.*

20

March 2005

The grief had sunk into a deep well inside Una. Sometimes she thought she would go mad unless she could puncture her ankle and let it all drain out. It was her fault. If she'd never investigated Medraut, none of this would have happened. Maybe he had been working for the good of the dreamers. After all, who was she to judge the morality of conducting secret experiments in Annwn?

With Ellen and Clement gone, Lord Richards had reassigned her to Palomides. So here she was, following Jeffrey Green through Camden, trying to tamp down on her terror. The stalls and bars offered too many places for Medraut to hide. *How* had he done it? He shouldn't have been strong enough to kill her friends, not any more.

She nearly didn't hear the gurgle of the knight behind her above the hubbub of the dreamers. She turned in her saddle, and suddenly realised exactly what had happened to Ellen and Clement. So this is what Medraut had been doing.

The creature that towered over her was beautiful, not because it was gold, but because of its grace. The fearless confidence that it was the most powerful being in this city. For an instant, Una was pleased that her friends hadn't succumbed to any ordinary nightmare.

The creature leaped in one huge bound over Una's head, and landed on one of her companions, ripping his horse's head off with a single tug.

'Urgent backup requested!' Una said into her helmet as Jeffrey marshalled his regiment as best he could. 'He's got a treitre. It's a treitre!' She couldn't hear the harker's reply.

'Una, get back to Tintagel!' Jeffrey shouted at her, shooting uselessly as the creature danced around him. Ros Evans, Jeffrey's second-in-command, loyal and brave to the last, flung herself in front of it even though she must have known the fight was fruitless. The treitre swept her away then threw its head back in a mockery of laughter, before pouncing on Jeffrey.

'Una, I'm ordering you: get back to Tintagel. Tell them, tell them –'

The monster ripped Jeffrey's gun away, taking his hand with it. It landed not far from Una. She stared at the fingers still clutched around the trigger.

'That's a . . . command . . .' Jeffrey spluttered. The monster was playing with him. Stabbing him experimentally with one claw at a time. That was when Una knew that there was still humanity inside the treitre. Only a human could be that cruel.

She leaped from Aethon's back and urged the mare to flee. She dropped to the ground, imagining herself smaller and smaller, so that by the time she was level with the treitre she was the size of a cat. She would never have been able to outrun it if she had fled instantly, but now she might be able to hobble it so that she stood a chance of getting back to the castle.

She was so close to it now, just within reach of the hinged joint that clasped the back leg together. Ignoring Jeffrey's death rattle, she raised her knife, searching for the most vulnerable point in the joint. When she had it, she stabbed quickly and often.

The monster had no mouth, so it could not scream, but it flailed backwards, its skin scraping on the road. Una flickered back to her normal size and ran to Jeffrey. He was still breathing. Una hauled him up and called to his horse, who had loitered as close to his master as he dared. Una threw Jeffrey onto the saddle and wound the reins around his waist, sending the horse leaping down the road, back towards Tintagel.

Now Una had to flee, too.

But.

The treitre.

If she was able to kill this one, then surely Medraut would be defeated once more? This could be her repentance for the suffering she had caused. Revenge for Ellen and Clement and the rest.

The monster flailed in pain from the wound she'd inflicted.

'You killed my dearest friends,' she told it.

It stilled.

'You can't be happy as you are,' she continued. She showed it her knife.

It didn't move. If she could have prescribed an emotion to that smooth head she would have thought it was sad. She dared to take one step closer.

Foolish Una.

The creature leaped up and whipped a claw through the flesh that joined her arm to her shoulder. With a scream of shock and agony, Una fell back, scrabbling at her limp arm, trying to hold it on. She glimpsed nerves and bone. The only thing keeping her from passing out was the sharp awareness of her need to survive.

The treitre inched towards her, only a slight hobble in its injured leg. It had tricked her. It had tortured Jeffrey simply for fun. How much worse would it be with the person who hurt it first?

When Una's back hit a wall, she closed her eyes. This was a path that everyone had to travel eventually. She was just doing it sooner than most. She wished she'd said goodbye to Angus. Most of all, she wished she'd been able to bring her babies into the world. She refused to sob, absolutely refused, but the tears came anyway.

'Please,' she said, opening her eyes and cradling her belly, 'just please don't hurt me here. Kill me any other way you like. Make it as long as you like. Just please don't hurt me here.'

The creature froze. It didn't look at her stomach, but she knew that it understood. Her pregnancy wasn't showing in Annwn like it was in Ithr, but there was a universal attitude of pregnant women and she had invoked it with the way she held herself. The creature bowed its head.

'Thank you,' she said.

Maybe there would be a chance for the twins. Maybe they could be saved in Ithr. She pushed away the knowledge that it didn't work like that. There is only so much despair one person can face. She closed her eyes once more.

One moment she could feel the monster's presence a hairsbreadth from her face. The next, cool air stroked her cheek. She opened her eyes. The treitre had gone.

21

Our training takes on a new urgency with the discovery of the kalend at the Globe. Reeves and veneurs busy themselves fortifying Tintagel. Morrigans are stationed at the guardhouse in the hope that they might be able to finish what they started fifteen years ago.

In Ithr, Medraut seems to be everywhere I look. Maybe he has been for a while, but I'm only really noticing it now. His party's logo – a V sitting on top of a circle – adorns stickers on lampposts, is carved into the back of toilet doors, is worn proudly on badges by teenagers and adults alike. It's impossible to turn on the TV without his face appearing on the news, seemingly ready to give his opinion on any issue. Maybe I'm being paranoid, but I'm sure that every time he's mentioned in Ithr, people cast malignant glances my way.

The confirmation that he was behind all of those deaths is exactly what I needed. It lifts me out of uncertainty and helps me concentrate on our training in how to deal with treitres. 'You want my honest opinion?' Miss D tells us at the end of explaining a complicated counter-attack move. 'If you come up against one of these things, run away as fast as you can or play dead. It's the only reason I'm still here.'

Despite the feeling of impending doom, though, it's hard not to be sucked into the merriment of the Christmas period. As if the garlands of mistletoe and ivy and the drifts of snow aren't enough, it's becoming impossible to ride down a street without being hugged by the smell of cinnamon. When we practise our flying, we're now joined not only by angels, but by reindeer too.

In only a few months it will be Ostara, the day we become fully-fledged knights. We're doing more advanced moves now, like combining flying and parkour so that we can twirl through the air, bouncing off buildings like balletic warriors. We spend more time practising with our weapons. Phoebe has taken to doing impressive leaps between her horse and her lion, using them to distract and confuse nightmares. The heads of each of the five regiments start coming to every session. Rafe takes the absent Samson's place at the head of Bedevere, sitting alongside Natasha and Emory, Arnold from Dagonet and Flora from Palomides. They watch us from the sidelines, making notes and conferring.

'They're working out who will fit best into which regiment,' one of Bedevere's knights, Amina, tells us. 'Natasha probably won't take you, Ramesh, because she's already got two riders with spears in Gawain. No use in having any more.'

Training starts to get competitive, with different groups of friends working together to prove they should be put in the same regiment. Ramesh and Ollie develop a move that involves swapping weapons mid-gallop. For the most part, I keep myself to myself, despite Phoebe's attempts to get me to use Donald the lion as a landing mattress.

People from the other lores start coming to watch our training sessions too. 'Apparently one of the apothecaries runs a castle-wide sweepstake on who gets assigned to each regiment,' Ramesh tells us excitedly. I can't help the thrill that runs through me. It's pretty amazing to be part of Annwn's answer to fantasy football. That's dented somewhat when Rachel later tells Phoebe and I that she's the only one who's picked me so far. 'No one else knows where to put you, Fern.' She shrugs. 'But I took a punt. I've got you and Ollie together in Gawain.' I don't bother telling her that Ollie and I are about as likely to be placed together as Lord Allenby is about to break into a tap dance. Ollie and I haven't crossed paths much in Ithr since the night we came across Medraut's work at the Globe. But one afternoon I get back from school to find a note on my bedroom desk.

Bring Mum's messages to my room tonight and I'll play you the recording. O.

He's only bloody broken into my bedroom again. I have got to see if I can change the lock without Dad noticing. But I'd totally forgotten about Mum's recordings. I do as I'm told for once and knock on Ollie's door with my knightbook in hand.

'Here.' I open my book at the first page of Mum's coded messages and hand it over. 'If you think you can break it, be my guest.'

Ollie stares down at the gibberish. The first poem looks

even more outlandish now I'm not staring at it through sleep-deprived eyes.

Fall brought lost
With other lost brought
Unto for other from place unto brought lost
Be with lost is
Place unto unto place other!

'What on earth?' Ollie says.

'I know, right? Where's the Medraut recording?'

Ollie presses play on a track on his phone, then hands it to me while he pores over Mum's messages. I listen as the recorder crackles into life. A woman's voice whispers, '*Testing, testing, one, two, three*.' Goosebumps prickle across my back and shoulders.

'Is that Mum?'

'Weird, isn't it?' Ollie replies, frowning at the knightbook.

It's more than weird. It's crazy. I've thought about my mother every day since I understood that she ought to be in my life. Now, fifteen years later, I'm hearing her voice for the first time since I was too young to remember it.

'*Recording on the twenty-eighth of December 2004*,' Mum whispers. Her voice is lower than I'd imagined; balsamic. There's a scratching, rustling noise.

'What's she doing?' I say. Ollie flicks his head in irritation, then throws me the digital voice recorder from Mum's belongings.

'I found it on this,' he says. 'It's a spy recorder. Supposed to be able to pick up voices through walls. My guess is she's pressing it against a building. Now be quiet or you'll miss it.'

I bite back a retort and bring Ollie's phone closer to my ear. There are voices, but it's almost impossible to hear what they're saying.

'. . . *Imperative . . . demand they move . . . Sebastien . . . must be the first of May . . .*'

Suddenly, the voices cut out. The timbre of the static on the tape shifts, as though an unknown force is messing with it. The next voice is unmistakably Medraut's, even though it's so muted. 'Too loud,' he says, the 'd' a stab of the tongue. 'Far too loud.'

The voices dip in volume even further, and I cannot hear anything more.

'Is that it?' I say, pissed off that I've given Ollie my knightbook for a few meaningless words.

'Yep.'

I'm about to snatch the book away from him when I realise the importance of something on the recording.

'The first of May is Beltane,' I think out loud.

'That's what I thought too.'

Beltane, like Samhain and Ostara, are important dates in the thanes' calendar. We don't celebrate Beltane like we celebrate the others, but it's important because it's one of the days when the fabric that divides Annwn and Ithr is at its thinnest. All that inspyre pressing against the doors between the worlds means that Beltane is one of the nights when dreamers are more imaginative and the knights are at their busiest. I peer over Ollie's shoulder at my knightbook.

'Have you worked it out?'

He shakes his head. 'No, but . . . these seem really familiar somehow.'

'Well, that's helpful. We still have no clue what they say, but at least you think they're familiar.'

Ollie shoots me a look. 'If you're just going to be a bitch then you can go.'

I'm about to snap a reply, then realise that actually he's been pretty decent to me this evening, or as decent as Ollie ever gets. It's not as if I was getting anywhere with cracking Mum's code on my own. I can't quite bring myself to apologise, though.

'Hopefully you'll remember why it's familiar soon.' I take the knightbook from his lap, holding it like a hot-water bottle.

'Yeah.' His mouth twists into a smile. 'Maybe it'll come to me in a dream.'

'Saddle up quickly tonight, squires. We've got a Christmas Eve treat for you,' Miss D barks as we arrive at the stables.

'The way she says treat makes it sound more like a test,' Ramesh remarks.

'A torture,' Ollie says.

'Bring it on, I say,' Phoebe calls over her shoulder as she shoos Donald the lion away from the horses.

Soon we're all lined up on horseback in gently drifting snow. Miss D is joined by a few other teachers. I welcome the chill on my skin. I've been spending more time lurking around the castle in my downtime instead of practising on Lamb like I used to. But I don't know where to start finding more clues to Mum's life. Perhaps some fresh air and a different kind of challenge will give me new ideas.

'Think of this as an agility course,' Miss D says.

'A race,' another teacher adds. 'We've put the thanes' flag on one of the parapets in the Tower of London. Whoever gets to the flag first, wins.'

'Under *no* circumstances are you to engage with dreamers, dreams or nightmares,' Miss D says. 'You can save the heroics for after Ostara, thank you very much. We'll be stationed along the route, ready to help if you get into any sticky situations.'

'The harker squires will be testing their mettle tonight as well. Pop these on and you'll find out who you've been paired with.'

They hand out helmets to each of us. Slipping the steel cap on feels like a coming of age. A familiar voice speaks in my left ear – Rachel.

'Hi, Fern, how exciting is this? I'll be there with you in spirit, or should I say, in voice!'

'Hi,' I attempt to chirp back, even as I inwardly groan.

'Let's win this, right? Dream team.'

Lamb stamps her hooves and tosses her head. Miss D and all but one of the other teachers disappear across the drawbridge, heading for their stations.

Ollie's murmuring something in his horse's ear. Probably a pep talk. His eyes are scanning the castle walls, looking for the best place to jump over. My feelings towards my brother have mellowed somewhat. Less red-hot hatred, more just-about-boiling wariness. But the desire to prove myself better than him is still very much alive.

'Yeah,' I say, more to myself than Rachel. 'I've got this.'

The remaining teacher stands in front of us, holding up his hand.

'Ready!'

I know Lamb and I can do this. The others might have mastered jumping the walls now, but Lamb and I are still the best at it. What better way to prove that I've earned my place here than by winning this race? Ollie looks over. I meet the sparking challenge in his eyes.

'Steady!'

I plan my route. Over the wall at its highest point then down towards the river, past Monument, and come up to the Tower from the south. I'll bet my scimitar everyone else is going to head for the straight, wide street. It means an easier jump and at first glance it looks as though it would be more direct.

'Go!'

Lamb doesn't need kicking. She springs off like a gazelle. I fixate on the wall, nearly four times our height. I don't hesitate. *Up!* I think, lifting Lamb with my mind at the very moment her front legs take off. We sail over easily. I glance back. Ollie and the others have done exactly what I expected, going for the lowest part of the wall. This is why it pays to enjoy your own company – years of roaming London's streets, instead of going to parties, is going to win me this challenge.

I steer Lamb down an alleyway. Up ahead something is flickering in the sky, like fireworks in daytime. I mustn't let it distract me. The Tower's just beyond the next wall. I can't see the others, but I can feel that I'm ahead of them.

The inspyre feels heavier and more visible here, like a

billowing veil. The Tower's castellated tops rise into view. I spot the thanes' flag on the near corner. A circle enclosing a five-pointed star, signifying the five lores of the thanes sitting within the Round Table.

Then I hear it. The unmistakable sound of fire. How could I have forgotten – the monument marking the source of the Great Fire of London, prone to bursting into flame. I had believed I was being so clever coming this way. My thoughts coagulate. I can see the road ahead of me, hear the pounding of Lamb's hooves, but all I can think is that it is too close, too close, feel its heat before it's touched me.

Concentrate, Fern.

Already burning.

Don't think about it, don't think about how big the fire must be to make that noise.

The fat beneath my skin rippling.

Then I turn a corner and the fire is there. It twists around a stone column, reaching upwards as though it wants to consume the very sun. Everything slows. My head is nothing but a scream. Then I notice the figure approaching it. An old man, confused wonder on his wrinkled face, stares up at the tip of the fire. I want to scream, 'Run!' but my body isn't mine to command. Lamb is whisking me away from the danger even as the man approaches it.

'Fern, are you okay?' Rachel says in my ear. 'You should be able to skirt the fire at Monument, just don't get too close.'

Rachel's voice separates me from the panic. I rein in Lamb.

'There's a dreamer,' I tell her. 'He's in danger.'

A split-second pause where I feel alone and frozen again,

then Rachel's voice reappears. 'We know. Someone's on their way. Don't engage, Fern, you're not ready.' She sounds urgent, excited.

'How far away are they?'

'Palomides is coming. They won't be long.'

But the man is within reach of the flames. He stretches out a hand. The regiment won't make it in time, but there's no way I can go closer to that fire. It would be easier to make me breathe in space. There must be something I can do. If only I had my diamond marbles I might be able to quell the flames, but they're back in my locker.

The man's face is open and trusting. I know what will happen next. When the flame takes hold he'll start to crinkle, the smoke will seep behind his eyes so that he can't see where the fire will strike next. It will take his fingers first, then run up his arms . . .

'Don't, Fern!' Rachel shouts.

But I launch myself off Lamb's back and charge towards the dreamer. I try to pretend the fire isn't there, to ignore the furnace pushing me back.

'Get back!' I shout at the man. 'Move away!' But he doesn't see or hear me, too immersed in his dream to notice something he's not expecting.

The flame catches the old man's sleeve and skips along it until his whole jumper is ablaze. I'm too late. His face crumples in childlike shock, but he doesn't truly understand what's happening. He doesn't know he's about to die. All I can think about is his family finding him in bed in the morning, like Dad found Mum. Maybe his skin will be pinker than usual, or maybe there will be nothing out of the ordinary, no clue as to why he was taken from them. They'll chalk it up to old age, say it was a natural death, when there's nothing natural about this at all.

The man's scream is shrill and I am helpless. Frustration, anger, fear, desperation course through me. I can feel them rushing through my arms. They crackle inside my bones.

'Fern? Fern! Are you okay?' Rachel sounds tinny and distant.

There's a sound like the bursting of a dam. My ears pop. My brain erupts. Something cool rushes over me, but it can't stop the red hot heat spreading across my head, sticking knives inside my eyes. I turn, and am almost thrown off my feet by the curve of water that arches above. The river. The Thames has risen from its channel and is battering the column of fire. *Brilliant*, I think, as the pain becomes too much and darkness takes over. *Whoever thought of that is brilliant*.

22

The first thing I'm aware of is that I'm lying in a puddle. How undignified. I attempt to open my eyes, even though someone is ringing church bells against my skull. I try to ask what's going on, but all that comes out is an incomprehensible groan.

'I think she's coming round. Fern?' Someone tries to lift me up by my shoulders, which sends another shockwave through my head. I must cry out in pain because they quickly put me down.

'Is that *blood* in her *ears*?'

'Shut up, Ramesh.' That's my brother. There's something odd about Ollie's voice, like his throat is too tight.

'Get her up, Drew,' Miss D says. 'Lord Allenby will want to hear about this.' Drew – that's the name of the Apothecary Captain. What's he doing here?

'Lord Allenby will need to wait. She's in no fit state to be interrogated.'

Interrogated? I open my eyes, only to be assaulted by sunlight. I was only trying to save an old man's life!

'This can't wait. Didn't you see what she did? It's all the harkers can talk about.'

I'm bewildered. What did I do? There was the fire, and then the water, but I didn't do anything except stand there like a lemon. 'Is the dreamer okay?'

'He's fine,' Drew says. 'We woke him up. He'll barely have a mark on him, thanks to you.'

'What?' They're not making any sense.

Miss D kneels beside me. 'I'm sorry, Fern,' she says, her voice the tenderest I've ever heard it. Her arms slide beneath my knees and my back, and the next thing I know I'm being lifted onto Lamb.

'She needs proper rest, Elaine, as soon as possible,' Drew calls as she leads Lamb away.

The journey back to Tintagel is excruciating. Lamb is trying her best to move gently, but every clop of her hooves sends painful waves right into my brain. By the time Miss D slides me into one of the chairs in front of Lord Allenby's desk, all I can focus on is the globe, spinning slowly in its stand. She and Allenby talk in low voices, then she leaves. Lord Allenby kneels in front of me.

'Fern? I've been told that you have a rare gift.' It's difficult to process what he's saying. My head is mostly agony, and words are too complicated for it right now.

'It's a mistake,' I say thickly. 'I didn't do anything. There was a dreamer. I was waiting for help and then someone made the wave.'

'That was you, Fern. You brought the wave, because Palomides wasn't going to make it in time.'

I think about the rushing sound, the pop in my ears and the crackle that ran through my bones. Is it inconceivable that it was me after all?

'Oh. Well, you're welcome then. Can I go to bed now?'

Lord Allenby smiles.

'Don't you realise what you've done?'

'Yes. I brought the wave.' That sounds funny. *Brought the wave*. I start to giggle until a fresh bout of pain rolls through my head.

'Yes. You brought the wave. You controlled the inspyre that makes up the Thames – some of the most established inspyre in the world. Think, Fern. Think about everything you've learned.'

I'm struggling to think about anything beyond 'Ouch'. There are two black dots in the centre of my eyes, like that swirling darkness at the Globe. I controlled inspyre, apparently. But that's impossible. Impossible for anyone other than . . .

No. Never. Big, huge nope. I must be a narcissist to even think it.

'Fern.' Lord Allenby lays a hand gently over mine. 'You have Immral.'

'Nah uh.' I shake my head.

'No one but someone with powerful Immral could do what you just did, Fern.'

I can't be. No matter how much I've imagined having the power over the last few weeks. This is too much.

'It's good that you're frightened, Fern,' Lord Allenby is saying. 'A power like Immral can be seductive. Look at Sebastien Medraut.'

I remember something else that they told us about Immral, that night beside the monument to the fallen, and my heart plummets once more.

'I don't . . .' I slur through the growing migraine.

'You'll need to train yourself to manage it, of course –'

'Stop,' I say. My headache is nothing compared to this feeling of total inadequacy. 'I don't have Immral. I should be able to control inspyre *and* read minds, right? Well, I can't read minds. So I can't have it. And I don't have violet eyes, do I? That's how you know someone's got Immral, right?'

To my surprise, a smile breaks out on Lord Allenby's face. 'Wait here.'

He strides out of the room and I can hear him calling for someone. I wish he'd shout more quietly. When he returns, he pours me a tumbler of an alarmingly neon drink that tastes like chilli.

'Fermented lotus,' Lord Allenby explains as I splutter it down. 'Ah, come in.'

I look round. My brother is standing, pale and wide-eyed, in the doorway.

'Why don't you take a seat next to your sister?' Lord Allenby says.

I shuffle my chair over as best I can.

'Now, Ollie,' Lord Allenby says, 'I want you to do something for me, and I want you to answer me honestly.'

'Okay, sir,' Ollie says uncertainly.

Lord Allenby offers Ollie his hand. After a pause, Ollie takes it. And goes even whiter. He gasps, struggling against Lord Allenby's grip. A trickle of blood meanders out of Ollie's nostril, aiming for his mouth. When Lord Allenby releases Ollie's hand, my brother virtually throws himself back in his chair.

'You saw?' Lord Allenby says.

Ollie nods, his expression rigid, although I can't tell if he's dazed or in shock.

'What just happened?' I ask.

Lord Allenby ignores my question. 'Fern, do you remember what Merlin said when you and Ollie took the Tournament together? He said, *Hatched from the same egg*. Do you follow me?'

My red eyes meet Ollie's blue eyes, and with maddening clarity I suddenly understand. I always used to joke that Ollie got the looks and I got the morals, but I was closer to the truth than I'd realised. We are twins. Red and blue make violet.

I can control minds, and Ollie can read them.

We went halves.

23

'Your Christmas feast is ready!' Dad's voice booms up the stairs. I haven't even showered yet. My head feels as though a trickster nightmare is racing round inside it causing havoc.

Usually I help Dad out on Christmas morning – peeling parsnips and rolling stuffing mix into balls. This morning I pleaded sick. There's no way I could face playing nice with Ollie after what we learned last night. Anyway, Dad has Clemmie to help. This is the first time in the five years they've been going out that she's come over for Christmas lunch. I can hear her high-pitched rendition of 'All I Want for Christmas is You' through a flight of stairs and my closed door.

The news of my power had spread throughout Tintagel before I even left Lord Allenby's office. The harkers up in the tower had seen what I could do, and they'd been vocal about sharing the information. That bothers me the most. Not because I'm ashamed of it or out of some misplaced consideration for other people's jealousy, but because I'm going to be the freak again. I'd been starting to feel as though – dare I say it? – I fitted in with the other knights, even if we're not friends. They seemed to like me. Without the burn, they've taken my eye colour in their stride. Now that everyone thinks I've got Immral I'll be different again. It's already started: when I left Lord Allenby's office last night I was greeted by a mixture of staring, muttering and scattered applause. Even Phoebe, who's usually so level-headed, rushed out of the knights' chamber to wave at me as though signposting that she knows the girl with Immral. Ollie had it easy. No one knew about his half of the Immral yet so he was able to slink out of Lord Allenby's office behind me. He was immediately swallowed into the fold of squires waiting there, avoiding any questions by slipping away with Ramesh.

But what scares me even more than being the centre of attention is something that wasn't mentioned last night at all. Lord Allenby may not have said it outright, but it didn't take a genius to work out that he was expecting a lot from us. He'd talked about helping us to train our power. Then there was the sharp, assessing glances he kept sending my way. The glances that I couldn't fully meet. The glances that wondered what a girl like me had done to deserve such power, and whether I'd be up to wielding it.

'Come on, Ferny, food will do you good!' Dad calls again. He might be right. The smell of turkey and chestnuts and cinnamon and all that is good about Christmas has reached my room. Peeling off my pyjamas and climbing into jeans and a moth-eaten festive jumper, I try to shake off the existential dread that has fallen over me along with the headache.

'Oh my word!' Clemmie exclaims in horror when I appear downstairs.

'You've seen me a few times, Clemmie,' I say, miffed, 'you probably should've got used to my appearance by now.'

'No, love,' she says, simpering towards me. 'It's your ears, you've got some blood –'

I step away before she can touch me. She's right though, I can feel something rough coating the bottom of my ears.

'What happened, love?' Dad asks, carrying in a little pot of bread sauce that smells of cloves. 'Do you want me to make up a tray for you to have in bed?'

'It's just a headache.' Ollie comes in after Dad, holding the cranberry sauce in one hand and a bowl of parsnips in the other. 'She'll live. Or are you really at death's door again, Ferny love?'

'Stop it,' Dad says loudly, before I can retaliate.

He puts the pot down hard on our little dining table and stomps back into the kitchen. It seems like his offer has been retracted. There's nothing I'd like more than to enjoy Christmas lunch without the awkward small talk, but there's no escaping now. I pull a face at Ollie, which is exactly what I would always have done in this situation, but it feels odd when I do it now. The revelations of last night hang between us, charging every interaction. Dad and Clemmie talk enough to make up for the silence between Ollie and I, though. They talk about work and the weather, about family traditions. And then they talk about politics.

'You know what, I'm warming to Medraut,' Dad says around a mouthful of honeyed parsnip. 'He had a rough few years.'

'Oh, me too,' Clemmie agrees.

'You didn't used to like him,' I say.

'A man can change his mind, can't he?'

'Mum didn't like him either. You said she didn't trust him, remember?'

'Maybe she didn't. Maybe she'd change her mind, seeing how he's picked himself up.'

'I doubt that,' Ollie mutters. I can't help but catch his eye. My own disappointment is mirrored there. So Medraut's brainwashing is starting to take effect on Dad. I should have known that he was too weak-willed to resist it.

'Helena Corday doesn't like him,' I point out. Perhaps a reminder about the one person of power who tried to help me after the fire will be enough to sway Dad. He's not listening, though; that or he doesn't have a comeback.

'Oh, can anyone hear that?' Dad cranes his ear towards the door in an exaggerated fashion.

Ollie and I groan in unison. Dad has been doing this for as long as I can remember. He pretends that Father Christmas forgot about us and we'll just have to make do with the enormous lunch he's prepared instead. Then, after we've eaten, he pretends to hear a knock at the door and goes to answer it.

'Who is it, darling?' Clemmie calls, genuinely confused. It's almost adorable.

'Look what I found!' Dad returns from the hallway with three presents. Clemmie squeals delightedly.

Ollie gets a new watch strap and I get some clay glazes – expensive colours that I've wanted for a while. I hug my thanks. ('Don't thank me, thank the elves for remembering us!')

Clemmie gets a little chain link bracelet. I've got to give Dad some credit, it's quite pretty. At least it's not covered in hearts or anything cringe like that.

I hand my present to Dad, feeling nervous. It's been a routine between us for years that I draw or make something for him, and it always gets hung on the wall or popped on a mantelpiece. This year, though, I've given him something slightly different. As he pulls off the wrapping, his expression changes from one of false gratitude to one of shock.

'Oh, Fern.' Dad's voice is tight and low. 'That's her. You've got her.'

Ollie cranes to see what I've drawn, and his expression changes too, although I can't read it.

'Mum.'

It hasn't been easy to translate every detail from the portrait of her stashed in my locker in Tintagel onto paper in Ithr. I chose charcoals instead of the oils the original artist had used. I like the way it highlights her cheekbones and her dark hair.

Clemmie's eyes dart between Dad and the sketch. Something squirms in my stomach. I hadn't really thought about how this might make her feel.

'How did you capture her so perfectly?' Dad asks, his voice thick.

'I – I made it up in my head, from photos.'

'Thank you, darling.' Dad throws a burly arm around me, the smells of Christmas cooking still in his shirt. I smile up at him, relishing the fact that today I've made him happy even if I'm a puzzle to him the rest of the time.

Dad looks to Clemmie. 'I'll need to find somewhere special to put her. You'll help me find the right place, won't you? You've got such an eye for these things, love.'

Clemmie stiffly gets to her feet. As they take the frame into the hallway, Ollie turns on me.

'Why did you do that? Did you do it to upset Clemmie? Do you want them to split up? You want Dad to be lonely again?'

'He's not lonely, he's got us!' I say. 'He liked it more than he liked your stupid book.'

His line of questioning has really rattled me, though. I really did just want to give Dad a happy memory . . . didn't I? Now I'm questioning my own motivations. This is why I hate Ollie.

'See what you think!' Dad's voice calls from the hallway. Ollie and I don't look at each other as we squeeze our way through the door and crowd around the little frame.

'It looks great, Dad.' Ollie rests a hand on his shoulder and guides him back to the sofa.

'She's got her just right,' I hear Dad say brokenly from the other room. 'How does she do that?'

'I know, it's creepy, isn't it?'

'You're a very talented artist, Fern,' Clemmie tells me, her eyes shiny and her voice extra chirpy. She goes back into the sitting room without waiting for an answer.

I stay in the hallway. A woman called Una Gorlois stares inscrutably at me, her eyes bright and her smile knowing. She would become Una King, mother of Fern and Ollie, but at the moment that picture was captured she was free of her family, and I can tell that she loved that freedom.

Later that night, as Dad makes himself a BLT to keep him awake on his night shift, Ollie and I bid him a final 'Happy Christmas' and head towards our bedrooms. I'm already in my pyjamas when there's a knock on my door.

'Clemmie?' I say. I really hope she's not here for 'girl talk'.

I should probably try, though, especially after what I put her through.

'It's Ollie.' He opens the door a fraction.

'What do you want?'

'I wanted to check you're okay after . . . after last night?'

'I'm fine,' I lie.

Ollie teeters at the door for a moment, then steps inside and closes it behind him.

'You know the nose bleeds and the ear bleeds are because you're using your power, right?' he says.

'Of course – I'm not stupid,' I sneer, but actually he's caught me out, because I hadn't connected the two at all. Last night Lord Allenby had made me go through all the times when I used my Immral without realising it, like when I lifted Lamb over a huge wall on my first try, and the way I changed the inspyre on the piece of wool. And of course there's the reaction Ollie and I had to Medraut's kalend at the Globe. My instinct had been right: we weren't allergic to the vine, we were allergic to the total absence of inspyre.

'I haven't noticed you getting nosebleeds, other than last night,' I say. 'Maybe it's because your Immral isn't as strong as mine.'

'Or maybe I'm just not stupid enough to overuse mine,' he says. 'Anyway, the bleeding thing is messed up. I had to sit next to those crusty ears all through lunch.'

'That was of course the main reason I didn't wash them,' I say sweetly.

Ollie pulls a face at me and we lapse into silence. The sound of Dad crooning along to 'Let It Snow' wafts up the stairs.

'When did you know? About your power, I mean?' I ask, speaking a little louder to drown out the sound of Clemmie joining in.

'I didn't know what it was called until the other night, at the monument. But I've been feeling other people's memories and emotions in Annwn ever since the light took me. That was how I found out about Medraut being Head Thane. That plaque in the gardens? Well, when I touched the blank space I saw Medraut in Lord Allenby's chair.'

'And you never told anyone?'

Ollie shrugs.

'Thought you'd get a sneak peek into their minds without them knowing, huh?'

'It wasn't like that,' Ollie snarls. 'I . . . I tried not to do it. I pretended it wasn't happening, okay? I tried not to touch anyone, and if I did accidentally I just tried to ignore all the images and feelings that came into my head.'

'Because you didn't want to seem like a freak.'

He shrugs again. 'Can you blame me?'

'No, I can't,' I say truthfully. 'I just think it's funny, considering you made my life hell for ages because you thought I was a freak.'

Ollie's eyes spark with anger. 'Look –' he begins.

'Let's just not?' I cut him off. I don't want to be angry today, and I didn't say what I said to start an argument. If Ollie's part of the Immral has granted him the ability to actually consider other people's feelings then that can only be a good thing.

'I suppose Lord Allenby's going to make us work together now,' I say, trying to change track.

Ollie snorts derisively.

'Exactly.'

The song downstairs ends, and Ollie makes to leave. As he reaches the door, I remember one more thing. 'What did you see? When Lord Allenby took your hand?'

Ollie turns. 'A lot of different things. None of it made much sense. I think I saw his family in Ithr. And there was a morrigan in a garden, feeding from a woman, then the same woman crouched over a dreamer. It all happened so quickly I couldn't make sense of it.'

'Why did you look so weirded out afterwards then?'

Ollie considers this. 'I suppose it was because of the emotions attached to his memories. There was nothing happy in them. Nothing happy in him. Nothing happy at all.'

24

Christmas night in Annwn is supposed to be one of the quietest nights of the year for the thanes, but there is nothing quiet about the reaction Ollie and I get when we arrive at Tintagel. There are shouts from the galleries as reeves beckon to their friends to gawp at us, and the harkers cheer from their desks as we pass. And that's nothing compared to the noise that greets us when we enter the knights' chamber.

Phoebe runs towards us and begs, 'Show me how you do it!'

An older knight comments, 'I bet I could've used that power for so much good if *I* had it.'

'You were keeping that one quiet, weren't you?' Ramesh grins.

'Hey, it's her with the power, not me,' Ollie protests. He'd made it very clear last night that he'd prefer to keep his mind-reading abilities secret, but it turns out that horse has bolted.

'I remembered you getting sick at the Globe,' Ramesh pipes up, 'and none of us could imagine Fern having mind-reading abilities – sorry, Fern – so we figured Ollie must have Immral too.'

'Then we got to talking about your eyes,' Rafe explains. 'It was Natasha who worked out the red-blue-violet thing and how you being twins must mean it got split.'

'Yeah, appreciate you telling us next time you do a spot of mind-reading, eh?' Emory says, lightly punching Ollie's shoulder. She's smiling, but there's an edge to her voice that tells us no one is thrilled about his part of the Immral.

I find myself trailing Ollie to his locker, since 'time alone with fellow super-powered brother' seems to be the one thing that gets the others to stop following me around. As he opens it I study the look of misery on his features.

'You get used to it,' I say eventually, 'being the odd one out.'

'How?'

'You make yourself smaller. Don't say as much. You think about every movement you make and work out how to make it less noticeable.'

Ollie doesn't look at me. 'That sounds horrible.'

'It's not the most fun.'

'And it doesn't always work anyway.'

His hands are shaking. Fleetingly, sympathy makes me lean a little closer and say very softly, 'There are no Jennys here.'

For a moment, Ollie looks at me with such raw vulnerability that I feel sure he's about to apologise for the first time for his part in the fire. Then Ramesh's bellowing laugh blows through the room and Ollie looks away. That's when I see it. A poem, carved into the wood of his locker.

For whatsoever from one place doth fall,
Is with the tide unto an other brought:
For there is nothing lost, that may be found, if sought.

'What's that?' I ask.

Ollie shrugs. 'No idea. It's been there for ages apparently.'

I study the poem for a moment longer, certain that I've seen it somewhere before. Then we're called to training and I forget about the verse. For now.

Luckily the focus on Ollie and me is lifted in the New Year, partly because everyone's pre-occupied with the looming regiment placement, and partly because Lord Allenby removes my brother and I from most of our regular lessons to train in private. We practise our Immral with whichever teachers can be spared. It's a great idea in theory, and it works for Ollie. He's been aware of his Immral for longer and has already learned how to control it on a basic level, after months spent trying to stop himself from reading minds. All he needs are some willing subjects to help him refine his ability to sift through memories and emotions.

It's virtually useless when it comes to *my* Immral, though. The trouble is, they can't really tell me how to access my power, and now that I know I *can* manipulate inspyre, I . . . can't. Whenever I've done it in the past, it's been an instinctive reaction born from panic. I can't recreate the same urgency. That limits the teachers to making suggestions as to how I might kickstart my power, none of which work a jot. It's all very well Miss D informing me that at the height of his powers Medraut walked around Tintagel with a sphinx of his own creation at his side, but when it comes down to it I haven't got the foggiest clue how I'm supposed to create a slug, let alone a complex mythical creature.

I resort to studying my knightbook in Ithr, desperate for

any clue that might help me unlock my power. That's when I make the connection, and barge down the stairs and into Ollie's room without knocking.

'Who owned your locker before you did?' I ask him before he's had a chance to look up from his homework.

'What are you on about now?'

I throw the knightbook down in front of him, the page open at my mum's first poem.

Fall brought lost
With other lost brought
Unto for other from place unto brought lost
Be with lost is
Place unto unto place other!

'See?' I say. 'Doesn't it remind you of that poem in your locker?'

Ollie takes a moment to get my meaning, but then he scribbles the locker poem next to Mum's riddles.

For whatsoever from one place doth fall,
Is with the tide unto an other brought:
For there is nothing lost, that may be found, if sought.

'It's the same style,' he says.

'It's more than that,' I say, running a finger between the verses. 'Mum's messages are written with the same words as the poem in your locker.'

'There are twenty-six words in the verse,' Ollie says.

'And there are twenty-six letters in the alphabet,' I finish.

He points at the first message I found in Mum's diaries.

'If "fall" is the seventh word in the original poem, then . . .'

'G.'

'Well done, you know the alphabet.'

'Piss off.'

Ollie scribbles out the translation. It works perfectly. Each line of Mum's gibberish poem translates to a single word. And suddenly her message makes sense: *Got into Lancelot with Ellen!*

'Mum wrote a message to someone called Ellen in that memorial,' I tell Ollie, marvelling that such an incomprehensible poem can turn with one code into the sort of message fifteen-year-old Una Gorlois would write in her diary.

'Let's do the other ones,' he says.

We each take a handful of poems, writing them out alongside the dates they were entered in the diaries. Mum's life in Annwn blooms before me like a sun-starved flower seeing daylight.

5th December 2000: A murderer as well as a thief. Or I may as well be.
3rd May 2001: Too much fear turns us to stone, but not enough and we are no longer human. It's all going wrong.
4th October 2002: Met the man I'm going to marry.
25th January 2005: Found a way to make it up to E. King Arthur isn't the only legend that's real.
20th February 2005: My best friend died last night.
28th March 2005: The golden treitre came for me today.

As we stand back to study the translations, I latch on to one line in particular. '*A murderer as well as a thief*,' I repeat.

'Looks pretty bad, doesn't it?' says Ollie.

But Ollie doesn't know the half of it. Because something I learned from my visit to the archives rises within my memory. I can't remember the exact date, but Mum was disciplined for negligence while on patrol. What if it hadn't been a minor indiscretion at all? *A murderer . . . or I may as well be*. My heart sinks.

'Well, there's nothing here that gives us anything on Medraut or your Immral,' Ollie sighs, shutting my knightbook and pushing it towards me. 'I guess Lord Allenby knows everything Mum could have known anyway. Well, it was worth a try.'

I gape at him. 'Don't you care about what Mum wrote here?'

Ollie shrugs. 'It doesn't make any difference to us, does it? We didn't steal anything or . . . the other thing.'

As I gather up my knightbook and stalk out of Ollie's bedroom I realise that of course Ollie isn't going to care about anything beyond the immediate concerns of our power and the threat of Medraut. Of course he doesn't care about learning about Mum. He hasn't spent most of his life pinning his hopes on Mum's love, on how things might have been different if she'd lived. His world view isn't going to be irrevocably altered by the fact that Mum might have got someone killed. But I know that unless I find the truth, my mother's memory, and everything I've pinned on it, will be tainted forever.

25

I don't raise Mum's messages with Ollie again, other than to ask him to find out who owned his locker when she was alive. I am expecting him to discover that it was Mum's but apparently it belonged to someone from her regiment – Clement Rigby.

Even though I know there's no point trying to make Ollie care about Mum's time in the thanes, I can't shake the sinking anxiety that maybe she wasn't the brilliant knight I'd imagined. None of this, of course, helps me with my Immral. My training sessions are getting more and more frustrating for everyone involved.

Then, one night, Lord Allenby himself comes to watch me train. And he is not alone.

'Andraste!' I exclaim in a most un-Fern-like manner.

'Lord Allenby tells me that you are in difficulty.'

'Understatement of the century,' Ollie remarks.

'I thought,' Lord Allenby says, 'that since we can't supply you with a teacher with Immral, Fern, that we could at least find a Fay who could help you. Ollie, why don't you rejoin lessons for tonight and leave your sister to it?'

As soon as we're alone, I turn to Andraste with a grin.

I hadn't fully realised until he'd gone how much pressure Ollie's presence was putting on me. She rests a gloved hand against my cheek, studying me warmly.

'Let us walk in the gardens,' she says, looking around at the dreary room that's been my prison for the last fortnight.

When we're outside I expect her to launch into an explanation of how to use my Immral. As a Fay, she can't manipulate people's minds to the same extent as I should be able to, but she has a limited ability to change inspyre. Instead, she talks about her memories of Tintagel's birth; how King Arthur pulled blocks from ancient rocks across the land and cemented them with the sap of the World Tree. She talks about the forge that once lay deep beneath Tintagel, where the Fay made the sword Excalibur to help King Arthur focus and strengthen his Immral. Then, at last, she stops me beside a fountain whose bubbling laughter masks our conversation from the prying ears of the apothecaries tending to the herb gardens nearby. It's only when she turns to me that I notice some of the scars on her face have split open. Pearls of blood ooze from the wounds.

'Why do you think you cannot use your Immral? Are you afraid?'

I shake my head. 'I think it's because I'm under so much pressure . . .'

Andraste cuts me off with a laugh. 'Are you a knight, Fern King? Of course there is pressure on you. Any human who chooses the life of the thanes must endure emotions that would lay low any normal creature. You must embrace this pressure. Lord Allenby told me that you used your Immral to save a man's life. If that is not pressure, what is?'

'But I didn't know –'

'And now you do know. I thought better of you, Fern. You have taken knowledge and used it as an excuse to do nothing.'

'Not on purpose!'

'Then make me a dragon to slay.'

Andraste seems to grow taller as she takes hold of me and with one swing throws me over Tintagel's wall into the streets that run alongside it. The shouts of the apothecaries and knights back in the castle's grounds reach me as I flip midair to land on my shoulder and roll to a halt. I stumble to my feet and pat dust from grazed hands and knees. Andraste leaps the wall and lands beside me. 'What are you doing?' she says imperiously. 'That is not dust, that is inspyre. It is your clay, your watercolour, your unhewn marble.'

I look down. Sure enough, the dust has turned back into blue light.

'You see it, don't you? Now feel it.'

I reach out one hand and the inspyre seems to vibrate against my palm, as though waiting eagerly for me to do something. I allow it to rest there, partly because I have no idea what to do next and partly because the vibration feels both calming and energising, like waking from a long sleep.

'I feel it on my hand,' I tell Andraste.

'Now feel it here,' she says, touching my forehead and my heart. 'You are an artist, are you not? Think how you feel when you draw me.'

It's been so long since I have immersed myself in an art project that I had almost forgotten the concentrated excitement, the sense of building something beautiful, layer upon layer, that would keep me up and working long into the night.

I push myself to sink into the soft, dark landing between awareness and raw inspiration. The inspyre in my hand flutters, and at the same moment I feel a twinge in my forehead. It's working. The inspyre begins to move. It crawls like a centipede up my arm. No, not *up* my arm. *In* my arm. I can feel it crackling its way through tendons and muscles. Then it's in my shoulder and reaching for my neck and . . .

Crack.

My brain is filled with inspyre. I can feel it exploring my imagination, skimming the surface dreams then swinging down into the recesses where the nightmares hide. The inspyre is bloating my brain and my skull cannot contain it. Beyond thought, I bash my hands against my head. I need to get it out – how do I get it out?

'Open your eyes, Fern. Fern, open your eyes,' Andraste is saying.

I open them.

The caged inspyre leaps forth from my skull, back down my neck, across my shoulder, through my arm and arcs from my fingers like lightning. It pools on the cobbles, taking form from my mind, taking the shape that most pleases it.

A baby, wrinkled and limp, flops towards us. Bulbous white eyes stare up at me. I have seen this creature once before, the night Andraste came for me.

'Now make it go away,' Andraste says. A keening noise rises from the baby's lipless mouth. It flops onto its back and begins clawing at its eyes. I have to stop it. Panic paralyses me for a moment, then I remember what I have to do. I keep looking at the baby this time, my arm reached out towards it, sensing the inspyre that makes up the creature as though it is clay to be moulded. I can feel the motes of inspyre that pulse beneath the skin. They don't just speak of muscle and bone; they speak of the baby's soul. Malice, fury and stagnant vulnerability. I sense, too, as the baby continues to claw at its white eyes, what lies beneath those pale fruits. I draw back in horror, losing the connection between us.

'I can't,' I tell Andraste. 'Can't I just leave it? Won't it turn into something else when a dreamer comes along?'

'You are a knight,' is her only response.

Tentatively, I find the connection again, picking it up more readily this time, as though I had simply dropped the end of a thread. I push my mind inside the limp body and take hold of the hands, forcing them to stop clawing at its eyes. The keening ceases. The baby now watches me silently, its shrunken belly inflating and deflating with each laboured breath.

'You need to go now,' I tell it, reaching for the little body's heart with my thoughts. Sadness washes over me, running back from the baby towards me. I had intended to press into the core of the inspyre, to pop it back into light, but at the last moment I twist my wrist instead. The inspyre convulses, spun and disorientated by my silent command. The baby seems to melt, its eyes rolling away like lychees. But the baby itself is reforming, heaving and frothing and unravelling. I can feel it all, at once audience and conductor, every movement reverberating up my arm and into my head. When the vibrations stop, the creature unfurls to reveal its new shape. A little red-haired girl stares at me with unbridled curiosity. Her eyes – one red, one blue – swirl hypnotically with the inspyre inside her. I smile at her. She smiles back. Then she turns and runs down the street, a threat no longer.

Someone sighs in relief, and I realise that it wasn't me – it was Andraste. She looks at me warmly. 'You did well,' she said.

I wipe away the blood trickling from my nose and, trying to ignore my headache, walk back with her into the castle. Lord Allenby is standing on Tintagel's steps, waiting for us. As Andraste hugs me goodbye, I think I spot her nodding at Lord Allenby, but the next moment I am sure I'm mistaken. It doesn't matter anyway. Now I know how to use my Immral, we can all get to work.

26

It's not long afterwards that we are assigned to our regiments. As Lord Allenby reads out our names, it's obvious he's listened to Emory, Rafe, Natasha and the other leaders about which people work best together. Ramesh, Phoebe and Ollie are assigned in quick succession to Bedevere. I wonder whether Bedevere's real leader, the absent Samson, will approve of Rafe's choices.

And then –

'Fern King – Bedevere,' Lord Allenby reads.

Oh. Phoebe squeezes my hand as I join her.

'We got the Immrals, we got the Immrals,' Ramesh sings as we all tack up.

'Ramesh?' Ollie calls from the other side of the stables.

'Ols?'

'If you call me "Immral" one more time I'm going to punch you.'

There's a subtle difference in the mood between this excursion and the many other times we've shadowed a regiment. It's as though we've been given permission to bond properly. Instead of practising formations or investigating suspicious inspyre activity, we're taken on a tour.

'We've got three hours tonight,' Rafe tells us, 'while the other regiments cover our patrol. Let's make the most of it.'

We ride all the way across the city to Richmond Park, where unicorns graze alongside deer, then wind our way along the streams that cross the park. 'Look!' Ollie shouts at one point, his voice free of its usual sharpness. 'Look at the water!' And we follow his outstretched arm and see a huge pod of dolphins, their backs making archways in the shallows, keeping up with us, playing with us, telling us, *This is your world too.*

We stop in front of a magnificent Georgian lodge in the very heart of the park and let the horses graze on wild flowers. It's there, as I watch Phoebe's lion Donald trying to shepherd a pack of grumpy stegosauruses, that Lord Allenby appears on his horse.

'It's a fine day for your first outing as a regiment, isn't it?' he calls cheerily as one of the knights hurries to hold his charger. He dismounts and shakes Rafe's hand.

'What's he doing here?' Phoebe asks.

Ramesh rolls his eyes towards Ollie and I, but another knight, Amina, spots this and shakes her head. 'He always joins the regiments for a bit when the new knights are assigned. It's nothing to do with you two.'

But I'm not so sure that's altogether true, because when it's time to head back to Tintagel, Lord Allenby decides to ride next to me instead of at the front with Rafe. I am happily drained, grateful to be able to have a day off from the intensity of our Immral training and the headaches that inevitably accompany it, so I say nothing, hoping he'll leave me in peace.

'I still remember my first day out with Lancelot,' he says after a while. 'It was a brilliant feeling.'

'Were you in the same regiment as my mum?' I ask lightly. I know what the answer will be, but I want him to tell me about it.

'I was. When I was given command of Lancelot there were just four of us.'

'That's quite small, right?'

'It was unusual, to be sure. But I didn't think we needed anyone else. We were an excellent team. Medraut had been leader of Gawain for a few years by that point, and he had a huge regiment, so it balanced out.'

'Dad said that Mum never trusted Medraut.'

'She didn't. Nor did I, for that matter. But a lot of the thanes were taken in by him. There's no shame in it. He's a charismatic man, and he knew how to use his Immral to bring people round to his way of thinking.'

I think I know where Lord Allenby is going with this conversation, so I try to divert him.

'At the monument to the knights killed by the treitre, I saw Mum had written a note to someone called Ellen. Was she in Lancelot with you as well?'

Lord Allenby darts a glance at me that I can't decipher. 'Yes,' he says. 'Ellen Cassell. Why do you ask?'

I've been reticent to tell anyone about Mum's secret notes because I suspect that even coded messages about Annwn wouldn't go down well with the thanes. I weigh it up, then I tell Lord Allenby about Mum's messages in Ithr and the code Ollie found in his locker.

'Ah yes,' he says. 'So your mother used that code in Ithr as well, did she? She invented it for our regiment, so we could leave secret messages to each other all over Annwn. All inconsequential, of course.'

Is it me, or did he sound nervous when he said that? We ride on in silence, crossing the Thames at a bridge festooned with lights, like a spider's web covered in dew.

'What did your mother's messages say?' Lord Allenby asks.

'Oh, all inconsequential,' I counter. 'She talked about Ellen a lot.'

'They were very close,' he says. 'Very different personalities, but they were well matched as friends.'

'How do you mean?'

'Well, Una was very brave, very stubborn. Always got what she wanted. Ellen was more circumspect. She struggled in the knights to begin with. We tried to help her, your mother most of all. But . . . towards the end she was the most fearless of all of us. I know she would have put up a fight when the treitre came for her.'

'You weren't there?'

Lord Allenby shakes his head. I notice that one hand is bunched into a fist that he strikes against his leg as he talks. 'She had taken another knight from Lancelot – Clement Rigby – to look into reports of a poisoner up in Whitechapel. It wasn't supposed to be a dangerous mission. But neither of them returned.'

It occurs to me that there is one point where Lord Allenby might be able to set my mind at rest. The trouble is that if he and Mum were as tightly knit as he claims, then I might be accusing him as well. 'We did find something in Mum's messages,' I tell him warily. 'She said that she was a thief and a murderer – or that she might as well be. Do you know why she'd say that, sir?'

Lord Allenby's face clouds over.

'She wasn't a murderer. None of us were.'

'I didn't mean –'

'A dreamer died on our patrol,' he continues. 'It was dreadful, but it was an accident. Una was disciplined for it afterwards but that wasn't fair in my opinion. These things happen sometimes, and we all have to live with the guilt.'

I notice he hasn't explained the part about being a thief, but his tone makes it clear that follow-up questions will not be tolerated. We are nearly back at the castle now, and my former lightness has been thoroughly stamped on. As Tintagel's towers come into view, Lord Allenby excuses himself and trots forward to join Rafe at the head of the patrol.

I don't have much time to consider my conversation with Lord Allenby over the next few weeks because, with Ostara only a few months away, my nights are packed. Ollie and I are now asked to go to Annwn early so that we can practise our Immral before lessons begin. We have to excuse ourselves for bed just a few hours after getting home from school. Dad starts talking about taking us to a doctor for exhaustion and is baffled when my brother and I, speaking as one, insist that we're absolutely fine. Those few hours each night are essential, because even though I now know how to use my Immral, my progress is slow. My excursions with Bedevere bring home how speedy I will need to be to defeat nightmares, but it still takes ages for me to sink into the right state of mind. I know everyone's hoping that Ollie and I will be able to help the thanes hold off any attack from Medraut better than they were able to fifteen years ago. The extra fortifications installed in the wake of the discovery at the Globe now seem normal to me, and while other kalends have been discovered all over the country in Annwn, they have simply been assigned guards and nothing more has been said. The professionalism behind it all has muted the fact that Medraut's power is clearly back to full strength – as far as we know he's the only person alive who has the ability to make so many kalends.

Then, one night, we pause while training in the gardens, listening to the harkers shouting from the guardhouse. A straggle of knights from Dagonet is running, hunch-backed, across the drawbridge. Each one of them carries a bundle. Ramesh and I glance at each other before following the rest of our regiment to see what's happening. As I get closer I realise that the bundles are actually dreamers. Some of them are so young they look as though they're barely toddling in Ithr. The oldest clings to a walking stick.

'What's happened to them?' Ramesh asks. I crane to see what their injuries are. On rare occasions dreamers are tended to in Tintagel after particularly horrible nightmares, to ensure that their wounds aren't so bad that they'll have an effect on them in Ithr, but I've never seen so many brought in at once. Then I catch sight of one of the dreamer's faces and recoil. For where his mouth should be, there is only skin.

Apothecaries run down the steps to greet Dagonet, removing the dreamers from their arms and hurrying them into the hospital wing. Then one of the youngest, one of the few who still has her mouth, begins to scream. An arc of blood shoots from her open jaws.

'He cut out her tongue,' Phoebe says, turning away, her skin sheet white.

'Who?'

'Medraut,' she whispers. 'I overheard one of the knights telling the apothecaries.'

'But . . . why would he do that?' Ramesh says, looking as untethered as I feel.

'To take away their voices,' Ollie says from behind us. 'That's what he does, isn't it? When you really watch him in Ithr? He silences everyone else so that he can speak.'

No one who isn't badly injured is permitted inside the hospital that night, as the apothecaries work to restore the dreamers' tongues and mouths. A retinue of thanes lurks outside, eager to help, more eager for news. At one point the veneurs are called in to use the morrigans to remove the dreamers' memories of Medraut's torture. By the time the dreamers wake up, only a few have been cured. I am not one of those waiting outside, but I do pass by on my way to the stables and, when the door opens, spot the old woman with the walking stick. Her lips have been fixed, but they may as well have been painted on, for she is unable to move them at all.

'It won't look like anything's changed in Ithr,' Natasha tells us later, trying to comfort a distressed Phoebe. 'It's all in the mind, isn't it?'

'But something will have changed, won't it?' Phoebe says. 'We know what he does. He's taking away their voices.'

I can't help but feel attacked. It's my power that can do this to people – that can turn them mute in Ithr, or incapable of forming their own opinions. I want to tell her that not every Immral is like that – I'm not like that – but I don't know how to say it in a way that doesn't make all of this about me.

Where many thanes become timid and fearful with the reminder of Medraut's threat, I am galvanised. I take to staying in Tintagel long after the thanes on the daytime shift have arrived, and return to Ithr with barely enough time to shower, grab my bag and run to the station. At the weekends, some of my fellow knights offer to stay and help me train too. It is Phoebe who laughingly cajoles me into morphing her so that she's as tall as a tree. Rafe bowls cricket balls at my head that I must snap back into inspyre before they give me concussion. Ramesh chatters encouragement at me as I use my Immral to pull an old oak tree from the ground and then replant it, the soil crackling with inspyre as the roots reach for their usual resting place.

Something stops me from telling anyone what using my power costs me. It would be admitting a weakness, and proving Ollie right, neither of which I will do unless I have no other option. And anyway, what does a little pain matter when Medraut is inflicting all kinds of horrors on people? So I put up with the headaches, the nosebleeds and the occasional ear bleed, and ignore Ollie's silent glances when he spots me wiping away blood or rubbing my forehead.

Eventually, he cracks. He storms into my room one Sunday, just after we've both woken up from a training session. I can barely focus on him through the migraine ravaging my head.

'For God's sake, Fern, you're going to seriously hurt yourself!' he hisses. Both of us are aware of Dad getting ready for his shift in the bathroom next door.

'I'm fine,' I say, my tongue struggling to move.

'Really? So you won't mind me doing this.' He swipes a pile of books from my desk. They land on the floorboards with a thump that ricochets around my skull. I can't help but wail.

'What do you care anyway?' I spit, already regretting what I'm about to say but unable to stop myself. 'You didn't care when I was being burned alive.'

Ollie laughs wildly. 'You're never going to let that go, are you?'

'Why should I?' I stand unsteadily. 'You nearly got me killed and you've never been punished.'

'You really think that?' he says, his eyes bright and hard. 'If you really think I haven't been punished then you're even more blind than I thought.'

Dad's face appears in the doorway, his beard still flecked with toothpaste. 'What's going on?'

Ollie pushes past him.

'I don't know,' I say truthfully.

A few days later I find out. The answer lies on a quiet road near my house, in a bundle surrounded by bullies.

27

It happens when I am walking home after school. I'm mulling over my day at school. I had entered Bosco to find that nearly every girl there was wearing exactly the same accessories: the same nail polish, earrings and elaborate plaits. The boys, too, had subscribed to an unofficial uniform – each wearing grey chequered shirts with the sleeves rolled to the same length. I had asked someone if I'd missed a school memo, but he only laughed at me. The effect was subtle but distinctly creepy, making me feel as though I was still in Annwn, inside someone else's vision of a school.

As I round a corner, still wondering whether something as simple as clothing could have anything to do with Medraut, I spot Jenny and her gang, and freeze. It's a scrum. They are pushing someone backwards and forwards. I try to shout at them, but like the last time I saw Jenny in the flesh, I am frozen in fear. Then they vomit out their victim. With a lurch, I recognise him. Ollie. He lands in a crumpled heap in the middle of the road, moving feebly. Jenny bounces out of the group to wrestle his schoolbag off him. My first instinct is to run. But I can't leave Ollie in the road like that.

'Oi!' A woman has her phone out in one hand and is wrangling her child with the other. 'Oi! I'm calling the police!'

Jenny and her harem look up and scarper. I duck my head, hoping they won't recognise me.

'Are you okay, dear?' The woman pulls her little boy along as she approaches Ollie.

'Mmm,' Ollie mumbles as he struggles to get to his feet.

'I'll call the police, all right?'

I run up behind her. 'There's no need,' I say. 'He's my brother. I'll take care of him.'

I grab Ollie and his schoolbag, and half carry him down the street, ignoring the woman's objections. I don't ask him any questions, and he doesn't offer any explanations. But I am intrigued as to why my good-looking, popular brother has become like me – an untouchable.

At home, with an icepack on his head and antiseptic cream on his grazed hands, Ollie starts to come back to himself.

'Don't say anything to Dad.'

'Obviously.'

He hobbles towards his bedroom. I'm not having that. 'Why has Jenny got it in for you?'

Ollie scowls. 'Do you want the actual truth, or something that's going to fit in with your cosy little view that I'm the devil incarnate?'

'I do not –'

'It's because I rescued you,' Ollie snaps.

This is such a ridiculous statement that I laugh. 'When? When did you "rescue" me? When you called me a witch?' My voice rises. 'When you led me to the Flats to be burned alive?'

'It wasn't meant to go that far!'

'I was tied up there for hours, and you just walked away!' The sense of betrayal wells up inside me, every bit as raw as it had been that day.

'I was the one who called the police,' he spits.

I stare at him. 'They said it was a neighbour who saw the flames.'

'It was me. I made an anonymous call. Jenny worked it out over the summer.'

I reach for something that makes sense. 'So you got scared you'd be expelled and wanted to save your own skin, big deal. You never do anything unless there's something in it for you.'

Ollie laughs hollowly. 'What, unlike Saint Fern? You're the most selfish person I know. You convince yourself that everyone around you is awful so you don't ever have do to anything for them.'

'I helped you today, didn't I? I didn't have to do that!'

'Yeah, and I bet you're going to hold that over me for the rest of my life as well.'

'So this is the big punishment you got?' I can feel tears coming now and I don't want them because I am not upset, I am furious. 'You get the same treatment you dealt me for five years? Big deal! You've still got all your friends in Annwn. You're still Dad's favourite. In a few years you get to walk out of school and begin again. I'm *always* going to have this,' I point to my burn, 'reminding everyone what happened to me.'

'Why do you think I haven't told anyone that Jenny waits for me literally every day after school? Because I *know* I deserve it, okay?'

Ollie moves away, running a shaky hand through his hair. Then, suddenly, he turns back with a surge of energy and manhandles me out of his room.

'*You* pushed *me* away, Fern. Not the other way around. You *love* looking like you do. If you wanted to you could've got contacts, but you didn't. That burn scar just gives you another excuse to behave the way you do. I bet it was the best thing that ever happened to you. You wanted me to bully you, because it gave you a better excuse to hate me than the real reason – I just fit in. I belong and you don't, you never have, you never will, and you've never forgiven me for it.'

The door slams shut in my face.

I spend the evening torturing myself over Ollie's accusations. I rack my brains to remember whether Ollie ganged up on me first, or whether the distance between us predated that. I was always aware of the differences between us – I knew that people were frightened by my looks and even though he tried to hide it, Dad just seemed to click with Ollie – but I didn't hold it against my brother, I'm sure I didn't. The neighbourhood kids never made me feel like an outcast exactly, but in all of our games in the park, I'd be the villain. The wicked witch. The snow queen. The mad albino. It had been fun at first, but after a while I started to get annoyed. One time, Dad told Ollie to get the others to give me a go as the hero. The other kids agreed – they'd do anything Ollie told them, frankly, the lemmings. But the role didn't fit me at all. My attempt at a rousing speech fell flat. When I led the attack on Freddie Burroughs's' evil fortress of doom my group fell into chaos and we ended up losing. It was just easier for me to be the bad guy after that. I looked the part.

On our first day at secondary school, Ollie and I held hands tightly as we entered. I remember it because Dad still has the photo on the wall in the hallway – my face is turned away from the camera, my sky-blue coat flapping behind me. Ollie is grinning cheekily back at Dad, as if to say, 'We're going to have a ball.' That was the last day I was truly happy.

That night, alone in my room, I let myself admit what I've been denying for years.

I miss him.

What's more bittersweet is that I start to realise that the distance between us maybe isn't, after all, solely Ollie's doing. He did draw away from me, but for every step back he took, I leaped in the opposite direction. I was protecting myself, but maybe the wall I built was too high, too wide. Maybe I should have given Ollie a chance.

When I enter Tintagel and see my brother for the first time after the argument, I can tell immediately that things have shifted between us. In the stables, he silently holds Lamb's reins for me while I swing into the saddle. If he's busy chatting when we're being taught something important, I tap him on the leg with my scimitar instead of enjoying his floundering when the teacher asks him a question.

Long-held resentments have been aired. We understand . . . No, *I* understand better what has really been happening this last year. All the times where Ollie came home late, dirty and bitter, weren't because he was enjoying himself with Jenny and her pack, but because they were tormenting him. I was flippant with him before, but the truth is that no one can know better than I how it feels to have your closest friends turn against you. I begin to see that Annwn is just as much of an escape from Ithr for Ollie as it is for me. We have both been protective of it in our own ways, jealous of the part each other has to play in it because we want all of its pureness for ourselves.

But understanding cannot rewind time. We cannot go back to being friends the way we once were, a long time ago. But we can build something new; something formal rather than friendly. He can be a peer if not a compadre. So when Miss D tells us to follow her one night, we nod at each other like colleagues heading into an important meeting.

'Lord Allenby wants to see you,' Miss D says, herding us through the herb gardens and past the stables. Lamb's grazing outside and she trots over to me.

'Sorry, girl,' I say. 'Can't stop.'

She looks most put out that her attention is not being rewarded with carrots or at the very least a head scratch. Miss D leads us on, until we're standing beneath the window of Lord Allenby's office, and knocks on the wall. I don't know why I'm surprised when the stone parts to reveal a concealed door. Tintagel wouldn't be a proper castle without a few hidden entrances.

'Go on, then,' Miss D says, pushing Ollie and I through impatiently. She doesn't follow. Before I can say anything the door swings shut and we're plunged into darkness. Around us, little lamps of inspyre burst into life, illuminating a short staircase and another door at the top. Ollie jumps up the staircase and places his ear against the door for a moment.

'Hear anything?'

Ollie shakes his head, and knocks. A few seconds later Lord Allenby opens the door and steps back to allow us into his office.

'Thank you for coming,' Lord Allenby says, gesturing to us to sit in the chairs in front of his desk. He waits for us to settle before he speaks again. 'A few weeks ago, Dagonet escorted a group of dreamers into this castle. You'll know, I suspect, that those dreamers had been experimented upon by Sebastien Medraut.'

I nod. It's common knowledge now that the dreamers who had their tongues cut out were Medraut's work.

'What I am about to tell you is privileged information,' Lord Allenby continues. 'Only my most trusted lieutenants know this, but Dagonet didn't come across those dreamers by chance. They were released, from Medraut's fortress, by someone who has been working undercover there for some time. The Knight Captain, Samson. He got them out at great risk to himself, and it's now been several days since I've heard from him.'

My heart quickens. Samson, the person who walked into a house full of vampires on his own and lived to tell the tale. Samson, who has been mysteriously missing ever since I first set foot in Tintagel.

'I need someone to help find him,' Lord Allenby says. 'I'm not forcing either of you. I'm asking you to enter the stronghold of someone who has one of the most twisted, powerful minds the worlds have ever seen. I'm asking you to do this on your own to avoid attention. I'll understand if you refuse. But Samson has risked a lot already, and I want to get him out alive if I can. You two are my best hope of doing that.'

His eyes and voice remain steady, but this is as close to pleading as Lord Allenby will ever get. I think about what he's asking; about what I've seen Medraut do; about that amber monument just a little ride from where I sit, filled with the weapons of Medraut's victims. But I also know that I'm not ready. I need more training. I need more time.

I look towards Ollie and see the same panic in his face. Then I remember the toddler with its tongue cut out; the old woman whose mind will never be the same; my mother.

'Of course we'll do it, sir.'

Although God knows how.

28

It looks like my first mission will be my last mission, if what Lord Allenby tells us is anything to go by.

'We learned that Medraut had taken one of the buildings in Royal Arsenal for his own ends about a year ago,' Lord Allenby says, 'and I decided that it would be better to gather intelligence instead of launching some kind of kamikaze offensive.'

Royal Arsenal was once a grid of military warehouses that sit, squat and stately, on the south of the Thames, east of the Royal Parks of Greenwich. In Ithr the warehouses have been turned into apartments, but in Annwn they've mostly stayed true to their history, until Medraut came along.

Ollie and I have been excused from training for as long as it takes to retrieve Samson. We go straight to the stables to tack up and ride out of the castle without being stopped. The harkers open the drawbridge without questioning us. They must have been briefed.

I thought it would be liberating to be out here in regular clothing, but somewhere in the past few months the knights' uniform has become a precious token of affirmation. Ollie rides next to me in silence. When it becomes too much, I fish my helmet out of my saddle bag and slip it over my ears.

'Hello?' I say like a numpty.

'Fern?' Rachel replies. 'I was wondering when you were going to get in touch. What's it like out there with just the two of you?'

'Weird.'

'I bet.'

'Is the road looking clear?' I ask.

'Don't cross the river at Millennium Bridge – it keeps forgetting it exists,' she says. 'Otherwise it's pretty clear, yeah.'

I slip the helmet off again and relay Rachel's message to Ollie.

'Do you reckon it's worth it?' he replies.

'Getting Samson?'

He grunts.

'Lord Allenby thinks so.'

'You're going to be using your power a lot. It's going to be dangerous. I don't like that we're not going in together.'

'It's part of the plan.'

'Yeah, I get that I'm needed on the outside to keep a lookout for Medraut, sense if anything's changing, blah blah blah. Doesn't mean I have to like it.'

'I don't either. I'd . . . I'd rather you were going in with me.' That's true. Ollie is now so sure of his Immral that even if my half is more useful when it comes to fighting, I think his confidence would reassure me by osmosis.

Ollie snorts. 'Now you decide to get sappy.'

'Well, if I die, don't tell anyone. It'd ruin my image.'

I catch his eye and we smirk at each other. The next moment, anxiety settles on me again like a vulture. Lord Allenby's plan was as foolproof as a plan can be, given what we know about Medraut's stronghold.

'I can't give you a map,' he had said. 'Medraut shifts the layout of the buildings all the time, unpredictably. I'm afraid that's where you're going to need to use your intuition.'

As if the job wasn't hard enough.

When we reach the cover of Canary Wharf's skyscrapers, I look at Ollie. 'Time to split up?'

He nods. 'See you there.'

I don my helmet and check the route with Rachel once more. The plan was for us to approach Royal Arsenal separately, so that if anyone is watching at least one of us stands a chance of not being seen. I urge Lamb into a gallop as we skate alongside the river and allow myself to forget about my quest, to forget about Ollie, to just enjoy the freedom. I reach out a hand and feel the inspyre gathering at my fingertips. A bitter wind blows grit and sleet into my face.

'Fern?' Rachel's voice says into my helmet. 'Looks like there might be some trouble on your route. Probably not related to Medraut but best avoid it just in case.'

'Heard,' I say. I glance at the river, then at the streets that I would need to take – ones that lead me away from my destination. I clutch a handful of inspyre and bring it down against Lamb's shoulder. Pressing it there, I imagine it sinking into her muscles, strengthening her legs and hooves. There's a tug at the back of my brain that travels through my neck and along my arm, down into the fur beneath my fingers.

'Now fly,' I whisper into Lamb's mane. Her whole body gathers itself, the muscles tensing at once, then she stretches her front legs, kicks her back legs and takes off into the wind.

'Fern!' Rachel shouts. 'Oh my God, Fern!'

I let the harsh air cleanse my worries. Beneath me, the city turns to dollhouses. An enormous gull swoops down alongside me and squawks in greeting. Its flock joins in, and soon Lamb and I are flying amongst them as they head to richer hunting grounds.

When the birds tire of us and decide to wheel away, I call to them with a mind-tug, and they rejoin us, compelled by my imagination. They'll be good camouflage as I approach my destination. We turn a bend in the river and I spot it. Royal Arsenal is as grand as its name suggests, the complex of stone buildings laid out around courtyards that face the river. I steer Lamb towards the edge of the warehouses, releasing the part of my imagination that had been keeping her in the air. My head is already throbbing from the effort.

'Careful,' Rachel says in my ear. 'Keep the birds with you until the last minute if you can. There are dreamers in the area, but the harkers are finding it difficult to tell if there are aventures hiding amongst them.'

Lamb lands softly in a park a short walk away from Royal Arsenal. As quickly as I can, I untack her and stash her saddle and bridle in a nearby bush. I touch the leaves, twining the inspyre in my hands, letting it feed from my power. It grows quickly, folding itself around the tack until it's almost impossible to see it hidden there. A final touch, and from the bush grows a single, purple flower. That will tell me where to look if I forget when I come back. A goodbye to Rachel, and I take the helmet off too. Finally, I return to Lamb, who's already made a start on the lush grass.

'Wait for me, okay?' I say. She whickers and nuzzles me, then returns to her grazing, evidently more concerned that someone else is going to find the good grass than by the prospect of my imminent death.

'Well, love you too,' I tell her, and walk away.

'Fern!'

Ollie jumps off Balius, whose sides are heaving from cantering the long way round. Ollie skids up to me. 'Be careful,' he says.

'Don't come in after me unless you're sure . . .' I begin, handing him the helmet so that he can keep in touch with Rachel back in Tintagel.

'I know,' he says. 'I won't cramp your style unless I'm pretty certain you're dead, okay?'

'You're the best.'

There are only a few roads to cross before the high walls of the Arsenal come into view. I spend the time gathering inspyre, arranging it around me in an attempt to make me look like a dream. The trouble is, my efforts so far are already resulting in a mild headache that is growing in strength by the second. The knowledge that Lord Allenby has overestimated my abilities taunts me.

The gate to the Arsenal is guarded by armed aventures, undoubtedly in Medraut's employ. But I'm not sure they're needed – they're certainly not there to guard it from dreams, because any time a dream or nightmare approaches the walls, it either diverts its course as though repelled by something inside, or breaks down into inspyre. Then I feel it – the same stomach-churning emptiness that came over me at the Globe. The inspyre surrounding me clings to me momentarily, before being blown away before the force of whatever power is inside those walls. I am exposed, no longer appearing as a dream, but maybe they won't have seen me.

'Halt!'

Ah, crap.

29

It's okay, Fern. We planned for this. I take a deep breath, tell my heart to pipe the hell down, and approach the guards.

'Thank God you can see me,' I say.

'You're a bit young to be an aventure,' one of the guards says.

'Look,' I say, 'I opened my mum's mirror and there was this white light, then I ended up here. I am freaked, okay? So, is this a virtual reality game or something?'

The guards glance at each other.

'It's probably best that you come with me.' One of the guards grips my arm and pulls me beyond the gates.

'Get off me!' I try to sound appalled. 'I haven't done anything. Look, if you can just show me how to get out of here I'll go, okay?'

'You should be quiet,' the guard says softly. 'No one's allowed to shout in here. He doesn't like it.'

He. Medraut. Just as he took away those dreamers' mouths, he's taking away his own servants' voices. I carry on protesting – albeit more quietly – as the guard leads me down wide pedestrian streets. Cannons and military flags stand sentinel along our route. I look at the flags in closer detail. A white background, a simple black circle and a V-shape slicing into it. It reminds me a little of the thanes' emblem, except Medraut's flag has only a single point, instead of a five-pointed star.

'Here.' The guard pushes me through a wooden door, down a blank corridor and finally into a brick-lined cell that contains nothing but a wooden chair. 'Hands against the wall,' he says. He pats me down, searching for anything that might incriminate me or endanger him. He's thorough, but of course he doesn't find anything, and soon enough he's left me on my own, to begin my task in earnest.

At first, I just move around the cell, feeling for any inspyre that might be lurking in the vestiges of this prison. The dreadful, empty feeling has only intensified the further I was dragged into this place, but I try to ignore it.

Lord Allenby told us that the very walls and rooms of the place would alter according to Medraut's whim, but I hadn't expected it to feel so alien. The emptiness scrapes at my bones. The building has been so strongly manipulated that the ability to change has almost been crushed out of it, like wood pressed into charcoal. But there, deep within the brick, I can just about sense the inspyre. I run my hand over the wooden door. There's no lock on this side, but there is one on the outside. I try to reach the mechanisms, but the wood is too dense. I need something else.

The chair. It's been popped there as an afterthought – a shadow of courtesy – and I can tell. The inspyre that holds it together is less set than the walls or door. One of the legs should do. I tap into that other sense, the one that usually springs from my fingertips or the back of my head. I pull at the inspyre, encouraging it to let go of its form. Gradually, it responds and the shape falls away until I have just a handful of inspyre and a chair teetering on three legs. I gently tip the chair onto its side so it doesn't fall and give me away, then go to the door. Pressing my inspyre through the wood, I urge it to find the spaces between the compressed lattices of Medraut's imagination. It wends its way into the wards, moulding itself into a key. The levers are reluctant to move, sensing the trick, but gradually they slip away, and at last I hear the gentle click of the door unlocking.

The corridor is empty, although I can hear movement not far away. Clearly the guard didn't think I'd be able to leave my cell – and why would he? As far as he's aware, I'm just an odd-looking teenage girl.

Lord Allenby said I'd need to navigate by intuition. Well, at the moment my intuition is telling me to run, as fast as I can, away from the corridor to my right. The feeling of impending doom is strongest from that direction, so I should probably go that way. As fortification, I clutch the remaining inspyre against my stomach, which helps to quell the nausea a little. The corridor splits into two, and I take the left turn, always pushing towards the direction my gut is screaming at me to avoid.

The sickness peaks as I pass one particular door, then begins to lessen. I force myself to turn back and allow myself a retch or two before using some of my precious inspyre to force the lock again. This time it's harder. The ache that's been growing in the back of my head is matched by the strength of the lock inside this door. I'm also terribly aware that someone could catch me at any moment. At last, the door clicks open.

Nausea hits me with such force as I step inside that I can't help it – I vomit over the concrete floor. Bile sour on my tongue, I look at what caused that reaction. At first I am sure it is another kalend like the one at the Globe. This time, though, the kalend has a shape. It's human in form. No – it's clothing. Armour, to be precise, draped over a mannequin. From a distance it looks as though someone has meshed iron with black silk; smooth, flexible but impenetrable. It is made of the same stuff on all sides, although I can't think why anyone would want to create something so terrible, especially if they have Immral themselves. Perhaps it's a torture device, designed to send the wearer insane. The remaining inspyre that was in my hand gathers at my stomach as though hiding there in terror. I cannot be near it any longer and I flee the room.

Further down the corridor, the space opens up into an echoey hall. A group of men and women surround a table, talking in low voices. I press myself to the wall, wishing that there was a door between us. As quietly as I can, I peer around the corner, trying to hear what they're saying.

'Almost ready . . .'

'He's going to be here soon . . .'

'When did someone last check on the prisoner?'

The prisoner. Could that be Samson? Lord Allenby didn't know whether Samson had been captured or was simply unable to communicate. He had feared the former, and it sounds as though he was right yet again. Now all I need to do is find out where Samson's being held.

I follow my path back towards the corridor of cells, the twisty feeling in my stomach lightening with every step. I hadn't paid attention to the other doors on my way past them before, but now I do I can just about tell whether they're occupied or not. Just a few cells away from the one I'd been imprisoned in, I feel movement beyond the wood and brick.

'Hello?' I whisper, trying to send my voice through the web of inspyre between myself and the prisoner.

There's a pause, then, 'Hello?' It's a thin, nervy voice.

'Samson?' I say.

'Who?'

I step back. Not Samson. The person I want must be in another cell. I turn and walk straight into the chest of a guard. I look up at him. He is dark skinned and strong jawed.

'I think you're looking for me,' Samson says.

30

'I'm here to rescue you,' I say dumbly.

Samson smiles. 'If Lord Allenby thinks that the Knight Captain needs rescuing by a squire then I must've gone down in his estimation.'

'I'm not *just* a squire,' I retort. Ignoring the pounding headache that tells me not to use my power unless absolutely necessary, I send a shot of inspyre into the lock of the door containing the weedy-voiced boy and with a further twist turn it into a key.

Samson's smile vanishes immediately. He looks at me sharply.

'Who are you?' he says.

'Lord Allenby sent me. My name's Fern. I'm a squire in your regiment. Dagonet got the dreamers you rescued, but when Lord Allenby didn't hear from you again he got worried that you'd been caught.'

Samson doesn't seem to register what I've just said. 'You've got Immral too?'

'Well . . . yes.' There's no time to tell him about Ollie.

That'll have to be a surprise if we manage to get out of here. 'Look, what do I have to gain from being here if I'm not who I say I am?'

After some thought Samson seems to accept this, but instead of heading for the exit, he puts a hand on my arm. 'There's something I want to try doing.'

Oh, God. He's going to suggest something stupidly brave, isn't he?

The door beside us opens and a young, pale face peers out. I'd forgotten that I'd unlocked it. I look at Samson. 'Is he dangerous?'

'He was brought here last night. Medraut's decided to experiment on aventures this time, instead of dreamers.'

'Can we let him go?' I ask.

'Please do,' says the boy, wide-eyed.

'He might blow our cover,' says Samson.

'I won't.' The boy tries to push the door open further. 'Please.'

Samson and I look at each other. The spectre of the dreamers he rescued, with their mutilated faces, hangs between us. 'Of course we won't leave you,' Samson tells the boy, 'but you need to wait in here for a little while. I promise I'll come back for you. Okay?'

The boy looks doubtful, but retreats back into his room. As Samson closes the door, I see the boy sit on his own chair.

'Wait.' I dart in and turn the chair into inspyre, keeping some for myself and turning the rest into a little, silent bird that hops and flits around the room, making the boy smile.

As I lock the door on boy and bird, I catch Samson watching me. 'Sorry,' he says. 'I've spent the last ten months in this place.

I never thought I'd say this about someone with Immral but . . . you're really a breath of fresh air.'

'Yeah, well . . . thanks.' His sincerity wrong-foots me. 'I've heard a lot about you,' I tell him. 'The story about the vampires is legendary.'

But Samson barely smiles at my compliment, as though the knowledge of his fame doesn't please him.

'We'd better be quick if we're going to pull off what I want to do,' he tells me, setting off. 'If they weren't on to me before they definitely will be after this.'

'So you weren't in danger? *More* danger than normal, I mean?'

'They found the helmet I'd been using to get word back to Tintagel and I couldn't risk trying to get it back. I just had to hope that Lord Allenby would find a way to get me out or get another helmet in. But he sent you, and much as I'm ready to get out of here I'm not going to pass up this chance.'

He peers round a corner and nods an all clear.

'Medraut keeps something locked away, in a place I can't reach. I don't know for sure what it is, but he's the only one who ever touches it so I'm guessing it's important. I've been dying to get my hands on it but without Immral I didn't stand a chance. You'll see.'

We break out into the open air and dart across a manicured lawn towards a cannon.

'Here,' Samson says, and lifts me into the cannon's mouth. Inside is a tunnel. I worm my way through until I fall, head first, onto soft earth. Samson lands, cat-like, next to me. We move deeper down the tunnel, my inspyre the only thing lighting our way.

'How did you find this place?' I whisper.

'I've had a lot of time to explore,' he replies, 'but I haven't managed to see everything. It's much bigger than what's up there.'

When we spot light I fold my hand over my inspyre to extinguish it. I had assumed that we'd emerge into the harsh light of a laboratory. But instead I clamber out of the tunnel into grey. We're not inside, but we're not exactly outside, either. Everything is the kind of grey you get just after sunset, that flattens a landscape. I think I am walking on stone, although it's so dull I can't be sure it exists at all.

'I reckon Medraut made this place,' Samson says. 'It's just like the warehouse up above, isn't it?'

'Yes, I see what you mean.'

Being inside Medraut's fortress makes me realise what I love about Annwn. The whimsy and joy brought by millions of imaginations clashing together. This place has been created by someone so focused that he has lost sight of what imagination should be. This is imagination turned into single-minded purpose.

'This way.' Samson pulls me to one side.

As we jog through the grey, I sense walls rearing up on either side, although much like the floor I can't be certain they are really there. How Samson knows where he's going is a mystery to me, but he leads me left and right, down and up, without hesitation.

'Here,' he says at last. 'It's behind there.'

We have reached a dead end in the dullness. I press my fingers against the wall and nod. I can feel the difference between this wall and the ones on either side. This one is supposed to be a door, although it has no handle and, as far as I can tell, no lock. My inspyre-into-key trick isn't going to work here.

'Do you think you can get through it?' Samson asks.

'I don't know. I think . . .' I call to the inspyre lurking beyond the door, but it doesn't want to respond to me. This time is different from when I simply wasn't using my Immral in the right way. It's as though the inspyre is actively turning away from me; as though it's been cowed into listening to one person alone. 'I can't. It . . . I think it only answers to Medraut.'

Samson frowns. 'I might be way off here, but could you maybe do what you did up there, for the boy?'

'Why?'

'Just try it?'

I take some of my little store of inspyre and mould it into a bird again. The sparrow flits to the wall and taps against it, looking for seeds. At first, nothing happens. Then –

'There!' Samson whispers. 'Did you see it?'

The door doesn't give way, but it shimmers like mother of pearl, as though the inspyre inside is responding to the bird.

'Try something else.'

I make a butterfly, a squirrel and, just because, a small dragon that breathes hundreds and thousands instead of fire. The door shimmer intensifies as it responds to the dreams I've created. Then, like chocolate melting beneath warm sauce, it breaks back into the inspyre it came from.

'How did you know?' I ask.

'I figured the inspyre here needed reminding of what it could be.'

The room beyond is more of a cupboard, so despite his efforts to give me as much space as possible, I find my face uncomfortably close to Samson's chest. He smells of cinnamon and chilli. The warmth from his body in this cold chamber makes me shiver.

There's another shimmer, then a shape forms in midair.

It's the most beautiful piece of woodwork I've ever seen. A mahogany cube, inlaid on all sides with black resin that weaves over it like lava.

'A puzzle box,' Samson says, running his hands over it. 'The lid stays hidden unless you press the right sequence of levers. I've never managed to get close enough to see it.'

I turn it over, but try as I might, I can't find a button or a lever anywhere. Samson tries next, with the same success.

The inspyre that has been drifting freely starts to vibrate. Samson feels it too. 'He's changing the layout,' he says. 'Shit. We've got to go.'

Samson stows the box inside his guard's uniform. We pass back through the grey space, but already the walls are rippling.

We dart between them, but the route we came down no longer exists. Samson tries leading us in the right direction but the sameness of the surroundings makes it impossible to keep track of our path.

'Samson, stop!' I pant.

'Can't,' he says, and for the first time I hear a note of panic. 'I can't be stuck down here. I can't.'

I put a hand on his back and Samson turns and grips my arm, steadying both of us.

'Okay,' he says. 'I've no idea where we are. Let's go for a process of elimination. I see three openings up ahead.'

I nod. 'Let's take the left one first.'

So we do, but quickly meet another dead end – an actual one, this time.

We retrace our steps and take the central opening.

'I can hear something,' Samson says. We press ourselves against the walls. I nearly trip over a step but Samson pulls me back before I fall. It's a good thing he does, too, because we have stumbled across a vast room that is packed full of beings.

The steps lead down into a vaulted hall where hundreds of people stand in rows. They are still, and if it weren't for the quiet murmur of their shifting movements they could be mistaken for mannequins. A familiar energy pulses around the hall: the same energy I feel when I sink into my mind to access my Immral.

A gong sounds from the far end of the space. The bass note hugs the walls.

The energy emanating from the rows of people changes. I can feel them absorbing the inspyre around them like sponges, and as they do so they begin to change as well. Some of them expand, some of them stretch, but every one grows bigger. Their human skin cracks like a nut de-shelled, and is consumed by the underbelly of the creature beneath. Wings spread where there were once human shoulder blades; tails whip out from spines. Nothing remains of the human face. Instead, there are only smooth, domed heads with deep-set, pinprick eyes. Every one shines with metallic skin.

I have seen creatures like this once before, in a book laid out on a lectern in the hospital. That book spoke of assassins, souls and murder. This is what treitres look like.

31

The writer of that book in the hospital had said there were no more than thirty treitres in the whole of Annwn – but there must be three hundred of them here at least.

'How can that be possible?' Samson says, horrified.

'It's an army,' I say.

'We have to go.' Samson tries to pull me back, but I am transfixed. I had always wondered how treitres could go unnoticed by the harkers, but now I understand. The transformation only took seconds, and until that point every monster here looked like a regular human. It would have been impossible to pick these people out of a pack of dreamers right up until the moment they transformed. A patrol wouldn't have stood a chance.

At the far end of the hall one of the treitres is pacing in long strides. While the other treitres are copper or silver or brass, this one is cold, bright gold. It doesn't have great, dribbling jaws like some – in fact it doesn't look as though it has a mouth at all. It may not even be the largest treitre down there, but it moves with such precision and grace that it is easy to see why it's in charge. Something Mum wrote in her diaries pours ice down my back. *The golden treitre came for me today.* Is this the creature that killed all those knights fifteen years ago? Is this the one that killed Mum?

'Come on, Fern.'

I allow myself to be dragged up the corridor. Samson pushes me down the right-hand path. At last the end of the tunnel comes into view. I wriggle into it and pull myself along the earthen floor, glad to feel a familiar substance, even if it is just dirt. When we land on the lawn outside the cannon, I set off for the pathway that will lead us back to where Lamb and Ollie are waiting, though every muscle and thought is focused on the golden treitre.

'Wait!' Samson says. 'The boy, remember?'

Of course. I can't let what I've just seen throw me off balance, not while there's still work to do here.

We slip back inside the warehouse, passing through now-unfamiliar corridors until we spot the one with cell doors. With the final piece of my inspyre, I unlock the door and summon the boy with a finger to my lips. He leaps from the floor and the bird hops onto his shoulder as he skips towards us.

He stops, his face contorting in horror. Then I feel it. The door is moving, moulding itself around me, trying to trap me inside the room.

'It's him!' Samson hisses. 'Get out!'

He pulls at me and I reach for the boy, who grabs my arm. The bird hops up and down on his shoulder in alarm. The wood is trying to force its way through me, and for a terrifying instant it begins to prise open my chest.

'Focus, Fern,' Samson says, and I shut my eyes, concentrating on the inspyre within the door, forcing it back. Something bursts inside my forehead and a gush of hot liquid rushes from my nose, but the door retreats, allowing me to slip out. The boy isn't so lucky. I am still holding his arm, but he is now stuck inside the door as the molten wood flows around him. His head and shoulders protrude, but from the torso down he is imprisoned. Tendrils pierce his skin and he screams in pain and fear.

Samson and I hurl ourselves against the door. Samson pulls at the boy's disappearing arms, while I try to focus all of my remaining energy on the inspyre within the wood, commanding it to retreat. But Medraut is near and his command is far more powerful.

'Fern, please!' Samson says, his muscles straining to free the boy.

'I can't!' I sob. 'The inspyre won't listen!'

The boy can't scream any more – the wood has forced open his mouth and is reaching down his throat, absorbing him from the inside out. The bird, though, is still on his shoulder. It looks at him, and it looks at me. Then it very deliberately pecks the boy on his ear; a kiss goodbye. It takes off, hovering in front of me, trying to tell me something. I understand. I reach out a shaking hand, and with a little flutter the bird bursts itself back into inspyre, and with all my remaining strength I slam it inside the flowing wood.

For a second the door simply freezes. Then, like a video on rewind, the little-bird inspyre begins its work and the wood flows backwards, out of the boy's mouth, out of his shoulders, away from his body, until he collapses into Samson's arms. I fall to the ground too, completely spent, my head pounding, black spots growing in my vision.

'Right, let's get out of here,' I hear Samson growl. He pulls me to my feet, the boy a wilted flower in his arms. I stumble after him. The walls are still moving, a living maze trying to trap us inside, but Samson remains calm this time, and that gives me strength.

'This way, I think,' I say, feeling a weight lifting as we reach an impasse. Samson heads down the path I'd indicated and soon we see a point of light – grey daylight, not the manufactured grey of Medraut's mind. Suddenly, the walls ripple more urgently.

'He knows we're here,' Samson says, and sure enough the opening begins to close. At the same moment something tips inside my stomach.

'*He's* here,' I say, my voice grating. It feels like something is trying to rip out my vocal cords – a power so much greater than mine that it is trying to suck my Immral from me. I topple over, my organs rebelling against my body. I convulse. Samson doesn't kneel next to me, doesn't ask what's wrong. He simply shifts the boy to one arm and lifts me in the other. With a roar of strength he powers towards the closing opening. We aren't going to make it. We aren't going to make it. We –

We are through. A river breeze bathes my aching head.

I look up, over Samson's shoulder as he runs for the wall and leaps it in a single, great burst of imagination. I'm not certain, but I think I see Medraut's figure at the opening we escaped through. I think he sees me too.

32

April 2001

The applause that followed the announcement shook the bones of Tintagel. It was official: Lady Caradoc was handing the reins to Sebastien Medraut. She had led the London thaneship for twenty years, and she wore every one of them in the lines of her face and the weariness in her posture. There had been rumours for months that she was going to step down and that Medraut would take her place. The longest-serving Head Thane giving way to the youngest-ever Head Thane. So fitting. So poetic.

Una was one of only a handful, all stationed at the back of the hall, who were not clapping. Lionel wore a rueful smile. Not that he had expected the position; he was a few years older than Medraut but always seemed to be a few years behind him. Ellen's face was clouded with concern too.

Yet as Medraut ascended to the podium to shake Lady Caradoc's hand, Una realised that most of the applause was coming from Medraut's old regiment. The rest was polite, even resentful.

Medraut had made it known that if he was given the position, he would make some changes, and a lot of the thanes didn't like the sound of that. The reeves tended to be set in their ways and were wary of what Medraut would alter. He had never been a friend to the veneurs either, and many of them were concerned about what would happen to their morrigans with him in charge. He had never liked the creatures.

Medraut stepped forward to give his acceptance speech. He was trying to act humble, but he wasn't yet skilled enough to suppress the inspyre that shimmered around his body, telling of his glee and triumph. Una prepared herself for an onslaught of Immral-powered words, girding her mind with scepticism.

Sure enough, as Medraut began to speak, the atmosphere in the hall took on a new energy. From uncertainty stepped determination. Doubt metamorphosed into enthusiasm. Medraut's words picked up his audience and buoyed them along on his ideas: ideas of unity, betterment and ancient traditions. When he had finished, even the veneurs were cheering heartily. Even Una couldn't help but whoop.

It was only afterwards that Una was able to see that she had been taken in. But others didn't want to hear it. She'd never know whether their ignorance was genuine or whether they knew that they'd been duped but didn't want to admit to the weakness. The knights' chamber was full of chatter about what an incredible speech he had given. They droned on about how everyone was going to pull together behind Medraut in a way they hadn't done with Caradoc. Yet when Una challenged them to tell her what Medraut was going to do to bring about this change, none of them could give her a straight answer.

In the end, she wedged herself in an armchair in the corner

of the room with Ellen, Lionel and Clement, listening morosely to the chatter of those around them.

'Maybe it's not as bad as you think,' Clement said. Then, in response to her glare, he added, 'You're not always right, Una. Honestly? I think he might be exactly what we need.'

'How can you say that?' Una hissed.

'I joined the same year as Medraut and he's never been anything but nice to me.'

'Oh, well, as long as he's *nice* to you –'

'Stop arguing,' Lionel said. 'I hope you're right, Clement. I really do. But – sorry to pull rank here – I've been in the knights longer than all of you and I can't see this ending anywhere good. King Arthur –'

Clement rolled his eyes. 'Not your King Arthur schtick again.'

'He had good intentions at the start as well,' Lionel said doggedly, 'but look how that ended up. No one likes to talk about it, but the man tried to take away our freedom.'

'Exactly,' Una chimed in. 'That's where this leads.'

'Not always.'

'Not always,' Lionel agreed, 'but if you really think about it, Clement, has Medraut ever done anything that didn't boost his status? That's what worries me. He always thinks he's right, and for what it's worth I think it's pretty dangerous to hand power to someone who won't be told when he's made a mistake.'

Clement shook his head but didn't respond.

'What do you think?' Una said to Ellen, who had been listening to their argument impassively.

Ellen frowned. 'I think you should be careful.'

'You think he's already dangerous?' Una said.

'No. Maybe not. But you're going to try to investigate him, aren't you?'

Clement looked up, startled.

Una smiled. 'You know me too well.'

'Keep your distance from him then,' Ellen said, not returning the smile. 'You don't want him to read your mind and see how much you distrust him. If he's as dangerous as you think he is then nothing good will come of him finding out.'

Una nodded and clasped her friend's hand in thanks.

'The rest of us should congratulate him, though,' Lionel said. 'We'd better keep up the pretence that we're happy for him. Help cover for our Una.'

'Yes. That's a good idea,' Ellen said.

'Do you remember when you hissed . . .' Una started, but looking at the woman Ellen had become, the memory died on her lips. That was another Ellen and a simpler time.

Then Medraut entered the room and everyone bustled towards him.

'Come on then,' Lionel said.

As Ellen rose from the sofa, Una caught her arm.

'You shouldn't go either,' she whispered, 'or at least don't shake his hand. Remember . . .'

Ellen disentangled herself gently and sighed. 'I remember, dearling. I remember.' And as Una watched, her friends joined the throng jostling to greet their new lord.

33

By the time we reach Lamb and Ollie I have just about regained use of my legs. Brother and horse rush over with gratifying speed. While Lamb nuzzles the little boy, Samson shakes Ollie's hand and fills him in on what happened.

'We should get moving,' Ollie says, hefting the little boy onto Balius's back. Samson helps me onto Lamb and then he and Ollie run next to us as we make our way back to Tintagel.

It must be the end of the night shift by the time we ride through the gates, and some of the regiments have only just returned themselves. Natasha sees us as she swings off Domino, and throws herself into Samson's arms as though they're long lost siblings. Rafe punches the air and leaps towards his regiment commander, while Emory comes in over the drawbridge behind us, rides up to Samson and gets him in a headlock by way of greeting. From the centre of the commotion, Samson smiles at me, his relief and exhaustion mirroring my own.

I ride onwards. I don't belong to this joyful reunion of friends. I place the boy in the care of the apothecaries, and slip up the steps into the castle. Luckily we got him out before he could suffer the same fate as the tongueless, mouthless dreamers who occupied those prison cells before him.

What I really want, more than anything, is some dreamless sleep, but since that's not going to happen I permit myself a bit of downtime in the knights' chamber before I am inevitably asked to report to Lord Allenby.

When I open the door, Phoebe and Ramesh look up from their usual positions by the fire. Without a word, they lead me to the sofa. Ollie joins us shortly afterwards.

'So I hear Samson's back,' Ramesh says, and for some reason I find that immensely funny. My hysterical laughter bounces around the room, into the mouths of the others and out again.

'Can you tell us what happened?' Phoebe asks.

I glance at Ollie. 'I don't think so,' I say. 'Sorry.'

Phoebe throws herself back on the sofa with a sigh. 'So bloody cool.'

Ollie disappears for a while and returns with a sweet smelling muslin and a pot of water for my bloodied nose and ears. The chamber is relatively empty, with everyone else outside celebrating Samson's return, so Phoebe and Ramesh take advantage of the fact by putting an old record on the player that sits in the corner and we all listen to it in companionable silence until the rest of the knights crowd into the room, jubilant at the return of their captain.

Mercifully, I am saved from too many back pats and hand shakes by the arrival of a reeve. He doesn't need to say why he's here. I am exhausted. I am in pain. All I want is a rest and maybe a foot rub, but Lord Allenby needs Ollie and me.

'Come on,' Ollie says, and I limp out of the chamber after him.

When we arrive, Lord Allenby props me up in his large leather chair with another glass of that hot, spicy drink. Samson lays a blanket over my lap with a tired smile.

'I know you need rest, Fern,' Lord Allenby says, 'but with this treitre army Samson tells me about I'm worried we don't have much time.'

'They had a leader or a sort of general,' I tell Lord Allenby. 'A golden treitre. Do you think it could be the one . . .?'

Lord Allenby tenses.

'Perhaps,' he says. 'Perhaps it's still doing Medraut's bidding, after all this time.'

'Sir, the box,' Samson says.

'Yes, yes. If this box is as important to Medraut as Samson thinks, we won't have much time before he tries to retrieve it. Samson and I have tried to find a way of opening it, without luck. Do you think you might be able to take another look?'

Lord Allenby holds out the puzzle box. I take it, running my hands over the black resin that adorns it, then turning it over, tapping into the part of my head that hurts the most, testing different parts of the mahogany for hints of the inspyre that must lurk within.

'What are you hoping to find?' Ollie says.

'Some hint at what he's going to do next,' Lord Allenby says. 'Something that will help me and the other lords formulate a plan for stopping him.'

I shake my head. 'I'm sorry, I don't know if it's because I'm tired, but I can't find a way of opening it. I can't sense any locks inside. I don't think this is a puzzle box at all.' I meet Samson's eyes, knowing how much this is going to confuse and upset him, to have gone through everything we did for nothing. 'I think it's just solid wood.'

'But he was so protective of it,' Samson says.

Ollie moves forward, an odd expression on his face. 'Can I try?'

Lord Allenby takes it from me and passes it to my brother.

The effect is instant. Ollie cries out as the box is placed in his hands, but he doesn't seem to be able to let go of it. He falls to the ground and convulses.

'Get it off him!' I shout. Samson and Lord Allenby try to prise the box from Ollie's grasp, but they're being too gentle. I throw myself off the chair and wrestle with it. A lightning bolt of inspyre shoots out from the place where our hands touch. The pain in my head spikes, then seems to rush down my arm, fusing my hand to my brother's. My vision goes black, then is replaced by something else entirely. A new world. A future already set in motion. Blank expressions; grey buildings; and blood, blood everywhere. I tear the box – and myself – away from Ollie, and the vision dissipates. Ollie sits up shakily. Blood is trickling from his ears.

'What did you see?' Lord Allenby says.

Ollie looks up at him from the floor, tears in his eyes. 'Everything. Everything that Medraut wants to do to us, to Annwn and Ithr.'

I sink back into the chair. That vision – was it what Ollie was seeing? Does our Immral allow me access to Ollie's thoughts when we're touching? I feel numb.

'Tell me then,' Lord Allenby says.

'I don't think I have the words. I wish there was a way I could show you,' Ollie says.

'Maybe there is,' I say, although I feel exhausted just thinking about it. I offer Ollie my hand. 'Just trust me for once,' I tell him.

I tuck one hand inside the crook of his elbow, steeling myself for another bolt of lightning. On my command, Ollie takes a deep breath, then grasps the box. I only get a fraction of the pain he's experiencing, but that's enough. I don't dwell on the images I'm seeing. I channel them instead, out through my shoulder and my arm, out through my fingertips, into ghosts that march across the wood-panelled walls of Lord Allenby's office.

We see millions of people dressed in identical uniforms, marching beneath Medraut's banner. Sound is banished across the country, and then the world. The only noise permitted is that which cannot be avoided. Why do people need voices when Medraut tells them what to think?

The shapes on the walls take on new forms as the puzzle box tells Ollie and me of its master's intentions. They form magnificent structures – Buckingham Palace, Edinburgh Castle, the Angel of the North – and tear them down, replacing them with huge factories where workers march mindlessly to the only job they know how to do. The inspyre forms children, then rips them away from their parents, whisking them into training camps where they learn only the job they have been assigned to do for life. Then the inspyre shows rows upon rows of laboratory jars, each one growing a baby. Love is outlawed in Medraut's world. It is not needed. It is not efficient.

We see anyone who looks or acts unusually dragged from their homes. Some of them are forced to change, their souls warped into Medraut's idea of normality. If they cannot be made to conform, they are put to death. The streets run scarlet with the blood of outsiders.

Huge bonfires erupt on the walls. Books, paintings, musical scores are thrown upon them. The only art needed in Medraut's world is sculptures of himself, sitting in austere, soulless temples and shrines. This is all that humanity knows.

The inspyre changes colour, from reds and coppers to cool blues and aquamarines, and somehow we all understand that it is now showing us Annwn. Here the colourful and joyous world we know has been transformed into a desert landscape. The little inspyre that remains drifts mournfully, unable to find any dreamer with the imagination left to use it. The Fay – Andraste, Merlin, Nimue, all of them – lie broken and breathless, before disintegrating into the inspyre they came from long, long ago. Then, as one, the dreamers in that blank landscape come into focus. In Annwn none of them have mouths, simply smooth skin where a mouth once was. In Ithr they are not allowed to speak; in Annwn they cannot.

The inspyre on the walls splits now, between Annwn and Ithr. An image of Medraut fills both parts – in Ithr as statues and paintings, in Annwn as an immortal Fay. The only Fay. In Ithr, the real Medraut lies in opulence – an old, dying man. Yet as he takes his final breath, life in Ithr continues as he decreed it. A mortal leader is no longer needed, when the only leader, the only thought, anyone now knows is Medraut. He alone is the controller of Annwn, and so he no longer needs a body in Ithr. This is now human existence; subjected to the rule of a man who has made himself into the one true God.

Ollie lets go of the box, and we both stagger back. The inspyre on the walls disintegrates.

The four of us sit in silence. My heart aches at the vision of Medraut's empty majesty. I cannot understand how anyone could wish for a future so grey, so single-minded. I think of this world that I love, that is my only solace and source of joy, reduced to the same soulless vessel as that underground lair beneath Royal Arsenal. I think of Andraste, my guardian angel. Her scars were cracking open when I saw her last, and when I first met her she was in pain. I cannot bear the thought of both my mothers being eradicated by that man; the man who sees the torture of innocents as his right.

Eventually, Ollie speaks. 'We've found this early, though, haven't we? Early enough to stop it? I mean, it hasn't started in Ithr yet, has it?'

'You're lucky if you think that,' Samson says 'Haven't you noticed what's happening? I know I have.'

Lord Allenby nods. 'Fear. That's how these things always start. Making people fear others. It's already begun.'

My journeys to school – the commuters who take steps to avoid being near me – take on a new significance. I am *other* and therefore must be feared. How long until they drag me from my home and put me to death in the streets, brainwashed by the new master of their minds?

'Why is he doing this?' I burst out. 'I just don't understand why . . .'

I feel so, so useless.

'You were in the knights with him, weren't you, sir?' Samson says. 'Do you think he was always like this?'

Lord Allenby considers this sombrely. 'I can't answer that. He was always a quiet man, but confident with it. I think . . . I think it must be intoxicating to know that you can control someone's mind. I think he started small – testing the limits of his power, so to speak. Then when that worked he thought, *What's the harm?* and tried a little more.'

'Small steps,' Samson says.

'That's right. Until before you know it you believe you have a God-given right to control anyone you want to.'

I shift uncomfortably. Before I knew that I had Immral, I had daydreamed about making people hate Ollie.

'And can you really blame him?' Lord Allenby says with a grim smile. 'I can't tell you the number of times I have argued with the other lords and ladies over protocol or what we should be teaching our squires. It's exhausting, defending your opinion over and over again. Sometimes you just want people to accept that you know what you're talking about.'

'But you'd never *make* them do what you wanted if you did have Immral, sir,' Ollie says.

'Maybe not, Mr King,' Lord Allenby replies, 'but I thought I knew what was best for someone once before, and I was proven wrong. Perhaps if that hadn't happened when I was a young man, I might take a different view now.'

I gesture to the puzzle box sitting innocently on Lord Allenby's desk. 'What do you think he needs this for?'

Lord Allenby frowns. 'It's hard to say. Maybe it's no more

than a way for him to refine his vision. But I'd be surprised if he didn't have some other use for it.'

'So what do we do now?' Samson says.

'First I tell the other thaneships,' Lord Allenby says, 'then we prepare for the backlash. Medraut will be furious that you've stolen this. You've got past defences that he thought only he could manage. He might not realise that you two have Immral yet, but it won't be long before he works it out.'

Lord Allenby leaves the next part unsaid, but I feel it with a dread that runs from my toes up to the nape of my neck. The box didn't just tell us what Medraut wants for the future of Ithr and Annwn, it told us what kind of man he is and what kind of man he isn't. He isn't a man who shares. He is a man who wants to be all-powerful. He won't take kindly to Ollie and I existing at all, and I can imagine exactly what he'll do about that.

34

When I wake up, the headache from the events of last night is worse than ever before; even worse than the night I raised the Thames. I can't really remember getting to school. The first thing I register is sitting at my desk in biology, when Lottie Medraut taps me on the shoulder and tells me in a sing-song-sorry voice that I've got congealed blood protruding from my nose like a giant, red slug.

That's the nicest thing anyone does for me all day. For months people have been giving me a wide berth on the tube, but now there's a sea change. In Annwn, the mythical monsters that usually haunt London's streets are being rapidly replaced by nightmares not so different from me: people who don't follow the crowd, who don't fit in. In Annwn, dreamers run from them, but in Ithr they cover their fear with hate. They stare at me with open hostility instead of avoiding my gaze. I'm used to people moving away from me as I pass them, but now some of them deliberately walk close to me, knowing that encroaching on my personal space will intimidate me. Knowing that if I confront them they can start something more physical.

By the time the bell rings at the end of the day, I am more on edge than I ever was at St Stephen's. Jenny's bullying was overt. This is more insidious. Desperate for some air, I decide to walk home, so at least I can escape anyone who might start a fight. As I stand on Bosco's front porch, pulling my hoodie over my face, Lottie and her friends push past me on their way home.

'Guys, please don't,' Lottie's saying.

'We just want to support our friend's dad,' one of them teases.

'It's just a speech. It'll be really boring . . .'

The thought of Medraut merrily garnering support for his cause, fawned over by the likes of Lottie's friends, induces the kind of rage I haven't felt for a long time. I look him up when I get home and see that he's speaking at an event in Trafalgar Square next week. I mention it to Samson that night, and he nods. 'We'd better be on the lookout for a spike in nightmares then.'

Samson has taken back his mantle of Knight Captain and Commander of Bedevere without breaking his stride. I thought Emory and Rafe might be rattled by their demotions, but they are both genuinely happy to have him back. He smiles with his friends, he gives orders to his regiment, he encourages his squires. He is everything that the Knight Captain should be. Sometimes, though, I catch him gazing into the fire in the knights' chamber, and I know that he must be thinking about what he saw in Medraut's fortress and in that puzzle box. I want to be able to say something comforting to him at those times, but despite what we went through together it doesn't feel like my place. Now that we're back in Tintagel, I'm just a squire and he is my leader.

Thaneships around the country have thrown their efforts into the hunt for Medraut too. It's a delegation from Cardiff who discover that he's moved his stronghold from Royal Arsenal to a more central location, inside Madame Tussaud's. A waxwork museum might seem like a strange choice for a military base until you remember who's chosen it. A huge warehouse full of empty human vessels? Row upon row of silent mannequins, waiting for his command to give them life? Yeah, that actually sounds right up Medraut's street. I hear rumours that knights from Yorkshire and Belfast have tried to infiltrate the new fortress, but were all returned to their castles within days, their tongues, eyes and ears hacked off, the words *Try harder* carved so deep into their chests that the apothecaries could do little to heal them. Medraut won't allow another spy to infiltrate his ranks.

Maybe my sense of powerlessness is why I make the leap; because I have to do *something*. A reeve has asked me to drop off a parchment at the guardhouse on my way to the stables. I'm knocking on the guardhouse door when I notice the wax seal holding the paper in its tight roll. The impression on the stamp is the thanes' emblem.

I hand the paper to the harker manning the guardhouse without a word, then turn and run back into the castle, along the cloisters and past the entrance to the knights' chamber. I knock on Lord Allenby's door and barely wait for him to call out, 'Enter!'

'Sir,' I begin, then have to catch my breath, 'the note from my mum – the one that made you accept me into the thanes.'

'Ah, yes.' He smiles ruefully. 'I often think about where I'd be if Lady Andraste hadn't given me that note.'

‘Sir, the seal on it. Was it the thanes’ seal?’

Lord Allenby frowns, then opens the top drawer of his desk and picks out the note. He examines the broken wax, his eyes widening in understanding.

‘No,’ he says. ‘She didn’t use a seal. But look – there’s something set into the wax.’

He hands me the paper and I stop myself from lingering on my mother’s handwriting. At first the seal looks blank, but then I spot it. A tiny piece of fabric pressed deep in the wax, barely visible. I prise away the fabric with a nail.

‘Do you think Una left it there for us?’ Lord Allenby says.

‘For me,’ I reply, lifting the fabric up to the light of the window.

‘Why do you say that?’

‘Because this is from the curtains in my bedroom when I was born.’

‘You’re certain?’

‘There’s a photo at home of Dad holding me and Ollie when we were babies. He was holding us in front of the window and it had this exact pattern.’

‘Well,’ Lord Allenby says, ‘what are you waiting for? Go. Take Ollie, and go home.’

The ride to our house in Annwn has a different flavour to the last time we left Tintagel with only each other for company. Then we thought we were on a kamikaze mission to rescue Samson. This time we have the promise of our mother’s secrets.

As we ride I fill Ollie in on the note Mum left Lord Allenby.

Make sure my little girl takes the Tournament. The strangest emotions flit across Ollie's face. Disbelief, confusion, hurt and . . . yes, it's jealousy, but not the kind that makes me feel smug. With a jolt, I realise that this is the kind of jealousy I've been feeling towards Ollie for the longest time. It isn't some petty grudge; it's the kind that takes root in the foundations of your soul and, like ivy, creeps up until it becomes difficult to see who you really are underneath. It's only in the last few weeks that I've started trying to tear mine down – to find the Fern who doesn't automatically assume the worst of others, who doesn't always leap to be a victim.

'I'm sure she had a note for you too,' I tell Ollie, 'except Andraste didn't need to use it, did she? You were always meant to be a knight.'

'It doesn't matter.' Ollie shrugs, but he doesn't meet my eyes. 'Let's hope she left you something juicy.'

A quick ride across a park or two and a swoop through Stratford later, and we're standing outside our own front door. Much to my disappointment, it's exactly the same as in Ithr. When we open the door, everything's as I remember it, right down to the half-eaten toast I left next to the sink this morning. We go straight up to my bedroom – the room we shared when we were younger. But it's identical to my bedroom now, the carpet covered in piles of abandoned clothes and art supplies.

'Where do we start looking then?' Ollie says, flicking one of my drawings off the desk.

I shrug. 'Well, the fabric was from the curtains, so . . .' I look at the curtains, hoping they might be embroidered with a message. Something like *A Comprehensive Guide to Destroying*

Sebastien Medraut would be handy. But the curtains here are the ones I chose eight years ago, when Ollie moved downstairs and this became my bedroom.

'Do you think we need to match the fabric somehow?' Ollie says. 'Can you change them into the curtains that were here before?'

'Maybe.' But as soon as I take hold of the material I can tell that I'm onto a losing battle. The inspyre doesn't want to shift at all, just like it didn't in Medraut's stronghold. It was so in thrall to his Immral that it couldn't see any other way of being. Suddenly, I realise why.

'We're idiots.'

'Speak for yourself,' Ollie says.

'The inspyre's reacting to our Immral. It means everything here is the way we remember it. We've got the strongest power over inspyre here, so any leftover memories of Mum or Dad's aren't going to stand a chance.'

'So you think Mum's version is underneath ours?'

'Yeah, but we need to find a way of overriding our own power.'

Ollie presses his hands against the wall, trying to get a sense of whether the inspyre is hiding other memories beneath it. He frowns, pressing the wallpaper in different places, working his way out of my bedroom and onto the landing. Then, without opening his eyes, he reaches one hand out to me and says, 'See what you can do with this.'

I take his hand and am immediately assaulted, not by Mum's memories, but by things the inspyre here has witnessed. Dad running through every room in the house, calling for Mum.

Dad kissing a dream version of Mum, before she disintegrates into ashes in his arms. Again and again, Dad sitting up in bed and finding Mum dead – shaking her, pleading with her, clinging to her body. So this is what Dad dreams about. I feel a stab of pity. He really did adore her.

Then the visions change. These aren't Dad's dreams any more. Mum runs up the stairs and into my bedroom. She pins things to the walls in the hallway and peers out of the windows as though paranoid that someone is following her. Yes, these are what I need. I place my own free hand against the wall and try to push away everything I know about the house. In fact, I try to bypass my brain altogether. I channel the inspyre flowing from Ollie's hand across my chest, across my heart, and out the other side, pulsing it into the drab wallpaper. I can feel it sparking and changing. The whole house creaks and sighs as it morphs into another version of itself, one that hasn't been seen for fifteen years.

When I open my eyes, the house is transformed. The wallpaper is a deep teal decorated with blush-pink hummingbirds. We stand on oak floorboards, not carpet. Every piece of furniture is covered in trinkets. The walls are a collage of drawings and notes.

'Was Mum a hoarder, do you think?' I whisper. Something about the place – the feeling of stepping into a stranger's territory – makes me lower my voice.

'If she was she had good taste,' Ollie says, picking up one of the trinkets. 'Look.'

He passes me an antique box. Inside is a set of silver spoons, each one with a tiny mermaid carved into the handle. I turn the spoons over. There's writing carved into the back too.

But Artegall pursued him still so near
With bright Chrysaor in his cruel hand

'What does it mean?' I say.

'No idea,' says Ollie.

The drawings and notes pinned to the walls make more sense. Some of them are maps of Annwn. Tintagel is marked there. Other places are circled in red, the Globe amongst them.

'She knew where Medraut was going to make kalends,' I say, pointing to the circles.

'That makes sense,' Ollie says. 'There's the Royal Albert Hall, the Science Museum, a load of university buildings. They're all places that make imagination grow, aren't they?'

We follow the pinned notes through to my bedroom. It's strange not to have a bed in here, or to see the clutter of my clothes, art supplies and sketches. A basic desk stands against one wall instead of beneath the window. Perched on it are an assortment of bowls and vases, each one growing an orchid – my mother's favourite flower. I move the vases to one side to examine the curtains – the same ones that decorated the room when Ollie and I were born. Sure enough, one corner has been ripped. I dig out the fabric from the wax seal and press it against its match.

'Look,' Ollie says, and shows me a stick of red wax, a box of matches, some pens and a pad of paper in one of the drawers.

'Why would she put everything in the hallway but leave it so bare in here?' I say.

'There *is* something here,' Ollie says. 'I can feel it, I just can't see it.'

'That means it's behind something,' I say. 'You take the walls, I'll take the ceiling and floor?'

We move methodically around the room. Ollie knocks on the walls at intervals, while I move up and down the room on my knees, testing the floorboards. *Come on, Mum. We need you.*

'Yes!' Ollie says, at exactly the same time as I exclaim, 'Aha!'

While Ollie peels back the wallpaper at his spot, I prise up a loose floorboard.

'Anything?' I call over.

I continue to work at the board while I wait for an answer. When none is forthcoming, I look up. Ollie is peering into an opening in the wall – a hidden shelf that is far deeper than the thickness of the plaster should allow. He turns back to me. 'Empty. What about yours?'

I finally wrestle off the floorboard.

'I'm not just a pretty face after all.' I grin.

Ollie joins me, and we both look down into the gap between floors, where two boxes sit, each one overflowing with papers covered in Mum's neat, spiky script.

35

The journey back to Tintagel feels as though it takes forever. I am intensely aware of Mum's papers stored in the saddlebags hanging on either side of Lamb, gently rubbing against my calves. Lord Allenby beams at us when he sees everything, and rifles eagerly through the papers himself, before handing them back to us.

Over the next few nights we work our way systematically through Mum's notes in between our training sessions. A handful of reeves sometimes join us, under orders from Lord Allenby, and Phoebe and Ramesh often stay late to help Ollie, Samson and I read through it all – even though they haven't been asked to. Their presence irritated me as much as the reeves' at first. I felt sure that Mum wouldn't like total strangers reading her work. This was a family affair. But Phoebe's thoughtfulness and Ramesh's energy quickly become invaluable to our morale, because it becomes clear pretty quickly that Mum wasn't spilling much about Medraut that she hadn't already shared with the thanes fifteen years ago.

That's not to say that what she wrote isn't still fascinating.

There's reams of research on King Arthur, all far more

detailed than the basics we've been taught in our history lessons. I get lost in stories about legendary swords and how Guinevere and Lancelot worked together to overthrow Arthur when he was trying to destroy Annwn, just like Medraut is doing now. Less helpfully, she didn't find much about the practicalities of how they brought him down. She just goes off on a tangent about a grail quest.

Samson finds a whole sheaf of papers about morrigans and stays well beyond his shift to finish reading it. 'Your mum was shockingly clever, you know that, right?' he says when he's finished. He holds up a page covered in diagrams. 'I'm not exactly stupid but I've been researching morrigan use for years and she's just debunked one of my best theories in a single paragraph.'

'What was your theory?' asks Phoebe, looking up from her own set of papers.

'Oh, I always wondered whether morrigans could be used to extract more than just bad memories.'

'What do you mean?' Ramesh asks.

'Well, we use morrigans to take away specific memories and emotions that give poisoners power. If we can do that, couldn't we just remove the whole emotion of self-hatred?'

'That's a really good idea,' Ollie says quietly.

'It's not, though,' Samson says, rustling Mum's notes. 'Right here, it says that she's investigated it and it's way too dangerous. *My research can only conclude that fear is a core ingredient of any normal creature, not just necessary but beneficial to a balanced mind.*'

Samson looks up. 'See? I should have thought of it myself but, well, sometimes an easy fix just looks so appealing, doesn't it?'

'Too much fear turns us to stone, but not enough and we are no longer human,' I say.

Ollie looks at me sharply.

'Did you just come up with that?' Samson asks admiringly.

'No,' I say, squirming, 'it's something Mum wrote.'

'Like I said, shockingly clever.'

Still, clever or not, I can't help but wish that Mum had focused her efforts less on morrigan research and more on whoever was killing her friends. Especially a few days later, when I'm leaving school and overhear Lottie once more telling her mates in no uncertain terms not to go to her dad's speech tonight. They reluctantly agree, but I am not so easily persuaded. I want to see Medraut in the flesh. I want to be able to take his followers by the shoulders and shake them into seeing what he's doing to them.

As I near Trafalgar Square, I fall in with a steady stream of people pushing to find a decent position. The event is titled *Your Future Leaders: Live, Honest and in the Flesh!* but there's clearly absolutely nothing honest about the first few politicians who bore the crowd with talk about education and balancing the budget and how because they once set foot in a supermarket they're *totally* one of us. I am on the verge of giving up and heading home when the screen behind the makeshift stage flicks to indicate the next speaker. A black circle on a white background, with a V stabbing into it. The last time I saw that banner was in Sebastien Medraut's stronghold in Annwn.

The crowd shifts. People wearing black and white jostle to get closer to the stage and I am pushed along with them. I try to ease my way back, but all I end up doing is getting forced deeper in, until I am right at the front of the stage. The crowd stirs, but remains silent as Medraut himself steps up onto the dais and moves the microphone to one side.

He's tall, with greying hair that is swept away from a chiselled face. His movements are relaxed but precise. His violet eyes sweep over the crowd and his gaze is like a lighthouse beam. I can feel the ripple as everyone, even me, stands taller in the hope that his eyes will settle on them.

He is not expecting applause and he gets none. Instead, the people around me raise a clenched fist over their mouth, nails facing outwards. A sign of respect. A sign that they are his people and they will listen to him alone.

Then the strangest thing happens. Medraut begins to talk, and what he says is *fascinating*. But I couldn't say exactly what he's talking about. There's something about the importance of drawing together and the need to present a united front to the world. He uses his hands sparingly but forcefully, punching them outwards at the speech's crescendos. Every time he does it I feel it in my chest, as though with each punch he plants a seed of agreement, and by the end of the speech a forest is growing there, with every branch reaching for Medraut. I find myself nodding along, mouth half open. It is only when he stops talking that some of the power he emitted fades. I feel foolish for having been drawn in. I am alone, though. Every other face, even those who did not come for him, is illuminated with adrenalin, every cheek flushed with a new passion for everything that Medraut believes in, even though I bet not one of them could recall a single sentence he said. His Immral is the kind that has power in Ithr as well as Annwn – true, whole Immral. This is what I could have been if Ollie and I hadn't split ours.

The murmur is indecipherable at first. But as it is taken up by the next person, and the next, I make out the words.

'*One voice*,' the crowd whispers. '*One voice. One voice. One voice.*'

Medraut's voice. They are giving up their own voices, their own thoughts and feelings and opinions, and replacing them with his.

The chant never increases in volume, but with so many people saying the same thing it becomes far more sinister than any noisy rally. The crowd begins to move, as one, out of Trafalgar Square and onto the streets that lead towards Westminster and the Houses of Parliament. Medraut watches them, a small smile playing across his features, but he doesn't follow. I, too, stand firm as the crowd passes. I stare up at him until he becomes aware of me. Slowly, against my better judgement, I lower my hood. I want him to know that he can't manipulate everyone. Not yet.

His expression doesn't change. If anything, he wipes his face clear of all emotion. That's how I know that he saw me the other night in Annwn and recognises me now. He knows that I was one of the people who stole his puzzle box.

We remain looking at each other for a long time. I no longer feel the crowd jostling me. It's only when Medraut's mouth lifts a little – a knowing smile – that I realise why. His silent mob has stopped. I am surrounded by them. A wind shivers through me, and I can't be sure whether it's the weather or the wave of hatred that is directed towards me. I try to see over the top of them, but I'm in the centre of the square, and it is filled on all sides with a crowd loyal to him. There are no cameras to record what is about to happen.

They begin to close in on me. Their gaze roves over my burn scar and my eyes. They don't touch me at first. They're physically repulsed by me. But the fear, the need to eliminate the cuckoo in their midst, is too strong. One hand grabs me, then another and another. My hoodie is pulled off, exposing my school uniform. Through the mass of people, I glimpse Medraut descending the stage. He is no longer watching. He trusts his people.

I shout out, hoping to use the silence of Medraut's followers to my advantage. If I'm loud enough maybe someone outside the square will hear me and send help. I crawl beneath legs, kicking and biting at those who try to stop me. My hands are filthy, my school trousers ruined. Someone pulls off one of my shoes.

'Move away!' a voice shouts.

Stomping footsteps approach. A policeman ploughs through and almost trips over me. He and his colleagues lift me up and push me behind them, forming a shell as they manoeuvre out of the silent crowd. Without me to focus their hatred on, the people renew their chant of *One voice*, and follow their comrades out of the square.

'Get a blanket around her,' a familiar voice says, 'and for God's sake go and arrest someone.'

'It doesn't work like that, ma'am,' one of the officers says, but retreats anyway.

Helena Corday, the MP who came to visit me after the fire, turns me to face her. 'Oh my. It's Fern, isn't it? Fern King? Whatever are you doing caught up in all this?'

I can't answer her. My teeth are chattering. She folds me into a hug.

'You do have some bad luck, young lady, don't you?'

'He's t-turning everyone against people like me,' I stutter. 'He's dangerous. He's so, so dangerous.'

Helena looks me very clearly in the eyes. 'Believe you me, Fern: I know *exactly* what that man is, and what he wants.'

She rubs my arms, the way people do to children when they're chilly. 'Shall I call your father to collect you? Do you feel up to making a statement to the police?'

The nearby officers glance at each other. I see one of them place his fist over his mouth, nails facing outwards. He does it almost unconsciously, but the gesture is so specific that its meaning is clear. These are Medraut's policemen.

'The thing is, ma'am,' one of them says, 'we can take the young lady's statement, but . . . she's all right, isn't she? No harm done.'

Helena Corday virtually hisses with indignation.

'It's okay,' I tell her, 'I'm used to it.' I try not to sound bitter. I want her to think I'm resilient. Eventually, she agrees to let me go, but insists that her driver takes me home. Not wishing to risk bumping into Medraut's people again, I accept. She walks me to the car, parked a few streets down.

'What *were* you doing in there?' she asks me.

'I got caught up in it,' I tell her. 'I don't know. I wanted him to see me.'

She laughs. 'Yes. Sebastien does have that effect on people.' Before I can tell her how very wrong she is, she continues, 'But you know now that he isn't for you, don't you? Be careful, Fern. Your parents wouldn't want anything to happen to you.'

Ah. So she doesn't remember me well enough to recall that it's just Dad now.

'Why were you there, if you don't mind me asking, Ms Corday?'

'One of my colleagues was talking, and when he finished I thought I'd listen to the others. Nothing like getting a gauge on your enemies first-hand, is there?'

Helena's chauffeur opens the car door for me and her assistant climbs in after me, already calling my dad to let him know to expect us. Inside the car is all beige leather; the sticky kind that squeaks embarrassingly. Helena raises a hand as the car reverses into the road. I watch out of the rear window as she turns her attention once more towards Medraut's retreating army, her expression unreadable.

36

The uncontrollable shaking may have receded by the time I get home, but I can't stop thinking about what could have happened if Helena Corday hadn't been there. I have no doubt that those people would have killed me. It's like the fire all over again: two different groups of people wanting to take down the person who stands out.

Ollie's already home when I get in. As I fling myself up the stairs he emerges from the bathroom dabbing a cut lip.

'What happened?' he asks, but I am too incoherent to answer. I know it's unfair of me to ignore him like this – it looks as though he's had troubles of his own on the way home from school – but I can't help it, not today. I retreat into my room and don't come down to dinner. Instead, I relive the terror I felt inside the scrum at Trafalgar Square, nursing it until it ferments into rage. When it's time to go to Annwn I don't head to the knights' chamber for the start of lessons. I go straight to the stables and throw on Lamb's tack. At the drawbridge the harkers and reeves question my going out, but when I just stare at them they lower it. They'll assume I'm being sent out on another mission and Lord Allenby's just forgotten to let them know.

I am out in Annwn. Now I need somewhere to go.

The anger at Medraut and his followers, and at those police officers, fuels me as I head east. What happened today has only underlined what I already knew. That Medraut may be breeding bullies but they existed in plentiful amounts before he started gaining power.

The memory of the fire crackles to life: the pause before the flame caught; the beyond-pain moment when it bloomed up to my face; Jenny's expression – half shock, half hunger – as she realised that she had lost control. All the humiliation that I have worked so hard to overcome this year floods back. There is no justice. None. There wasn't with the fire, there wasn't today and there won't be in the future. I'm supposed to have this incredible power, but I'm still getting ostracised and threatened on a daily basis. What use is my Immral if I can't even protect myself with it?

And suddenly, I know exactly where I'm heading.

I'm going to administer a little justice of my own.

When I arrive outside the white-washed townhouse there's an inevitability to what I'm going to do. My head feels cottony. I've never been inside, only watched Ollie emerge from the hallway. She would always see him off with a coy wave. I glance up the road and then at the park opposite. A large black dog flees from a pack of rabid squirrels, each one a nightmare etched in blue, but otherwise I am alone.

I climb the steps to the front door. The door's locked but that's not a problem – with one flick of my brain the catch slides back and I'm in. Downstairs the house is chilly and empty. Upstairs the air changes. I climb up to the top floor. As

I put my hand on the door into the loft room, I sense someone behind it.

Jenny is lying in her bed, dressed in pyjamas, duvet pulled up to her chest. She stares, unmoving, at the ceiling. I am halfway down the stairs before I can stop myself. Why am I running? She's not dangerous to me here. In Annwn, I am the one with the power.

Slowly, sure that at any moment she'll stir, I return to the bedroom. She doesn't move, even when I wave a hand in front of her face. She sees nothing. She's the kind of person who comes to this incredible world full of possibilities and can only imagine herself in her bed, just as she must be in the real world.

Conjuring the flame is easy. Keeping it alight requires a little more effort. The dull ache at the back of my head grows with the fire. I move closer to my tormentor, holding the flame just above my palm. Her eyes remain fixed on the ceiling, unaware of me. She doesn't realise how vulnerable she is. Right now, I am her puppet-master, her hell, her God.

The flame floats above her chest, just below her exposed collarbone. The next bit's going to be tricky. I've never done it before, or not consciously anyway. Dreamers usually choose what they see and hear and feel in Annwn, even if they do so unconsciously. I have learned from what Medraut did to those dreamers that I should be able to overcome that. The question is how to do it.

Tentatively, I place a hand on each side of Jenny's head and stare down into those stupid, malevolent eyes. Inspyre vibrates through my fingers. A taste seeps into my mouth – the tang of out-of-date milk and unbrushed teeth. This is what Jenny's imagination tastes like. It's oozing up into me through my hands. No, thank you, that can go right back where it came from. Gathering my willpower, focusing it on Jenny's mind, I *push* against it, squeezing Jenny's sour thoughts back into her and following them with my own. The crackle runs from my head, down my arms, pools in my fingers, but it can't make that final leap. Jenny's brain is fighting me, unable to contemplate anything beyond her narrow view of the world. I push again, letting the pain in this time. I think about the flame that I've created, resting it in my imagination as I concentrate on working my way into Jenny's mind. There's a final barrier, then her fight falls away.

The flame drops. It pools out over Jenny's chest, like mercury. At first she doesn't react. Then her eyes flicker, as though she's waking up. She doesn't try to escape the fire. She just opens her mouth and screams. I reel back, away to the other side of the room. The fire laps up her neck and into her hair. It's the scream that frightens me, though. Expressionless, no fear in it, just pure pain. I've never heard anything like it.

The wrongness of what I've done crashes down on me. This isn't justice or divine retribution. I'm not teaching Jenny a lesson, I'm just torturing her.

'I'm sorry! I'm sorry!'

I'm across the room again, my hands either side of her head once more. My panic makes it difficult to order my thoughts enough to pull the nightmare from her. I have to calm my mind, all the while listening to that unwavering scream of pain. Finally, I'm able to block the noise for long enough to extract the nightmare from her, like sucking poison from a sting. The flame dies gradually, then it burns out. The screaming stops immediately.

I drop off the bed and stumble away from Jenny, from the scene of my wrongdoing. In the corner of my eye I see something moving at the dormer window. I start up, adrenalin surging through me once more. Is it a nightmare? A dreamer? Someone is staring in at us, at me. They are looking straight at me and it is neither nightmare nor dreamer. It is far worse – it's a knight.

37

The shock on Ramesh's face tells me that he's seen everything. In an instant I've disappeared the glass and shot out of the window to catch him. Grabbing him by the ankle, I pull him to the ground. We land in a soggy flowerbed. 'I can –' I begin to say, but I can't. How can I begin to explain what I've just done?

'You were burning . . .' Ramesh, too, can't get the words out.

He pulls away and starts running back towards Tintagel.

'Wait!' I shout, but he doesn't stop. He's always been a better runner than me. I'll never catch up. I reach for the ache in the back of my head and throw it out towards him. Ramesh freezes mid-stride.

'Please just let me explain.'

'Let me go,' he says through gritted teeth.

I release him and Ramesh stumbles as he regains control of his limbs. He doesn't meet my eyes, and I realise with a strangely pleasant rush that he's frightened of me. We both know now that I could do anything to him to keep him from telling on me. I could make him forget. I could hurt him until he agreed. I could make him kill himself.

I'm the one to step away from him. It's the headache, it's confusing everything.

'I'm sorry I had to do that to you, Ramesh. But if you understood –'

'She bullied you,' he says. I stare at him.

'How did you know that?'

'It's not exactly hard to work it out. She hurt you, you hurt her. We've all been there. We've all imagined getting revenge. Except *you* can actually do it. That doesn't make it okay.'

'You don't know what she did to me.'

'I don't care!' His face twists and he dashes tears from his cheeks. '*Nothing* she could do would make torturing her okay. It's not what us knights do.'

His words hit me harder than any insult Ollie could throw at me. *Us knights*. He thinks I belong, like him. It's as though all the doubts I've had about myself are standing in front of me, demanding I stop running from them. I've known since the Tournament, deep down, that my inability – no, my *unwillingness* – to forgive is what's holding me back. Ollie had accused me of wanting to be bullied, and in this moment I realise that he is right. The truth is, I've never wanted to let go of that part of me. Without it, who am I except something pitiable and broken?

'Please,' I say. 'I can't be thrown out. I need this.'

Ramesh doesn't answer for an eternity. Then, finally, 'All right.'

That's it. He walks away.

'You – you're not going to tell?' I run to catch up with

him. He doesn't reply, but he doesn't try to avoid me either. He leads me back to Tintagel, where Phoebe and Rachel are waiting anxiously to sneak us back in.

'You okay?' Rachel says, more to Ramesh than me.

'Fine,' he says. 'Fern just needed to get some air.'

Rachel smiles at me. 'One of the harkers at the drawbridge thought you didn't seem yourself and told me. It was Phoebe's idea for Ramesh to follow you.' I nod at Phoebe, praying that she won't be suspicious of Ramesh's unusual quietness and take it upon herself to dig deeper into my antics.

As Ostara approaches and our training ramps up, I sometimes catch Ramesh looking at me and feel certain that he's wondering whether he made the right decision. In Ithr, I daydream that tonight will be the night I am met in Annwn by Lord Allenby, Ramesh lurking behind him. I'll be told I've disgraced the knights, taken to the morrigans and sent back to Ithr an empty shell.

But every night I am proved wrong. Ramesh does not betray my confidence, and I go to great efforts to ensure that he has no more reason to do so.

'Why are you letting me win?' Ramesh asks me one night during our weapons' training.

'I'm not,' I say lightly, turning away from his strike deliberately slowly, so that he'll catch me.

Ramesh smacks the back of my leg with his spear and backs off, frowning.

'It's probably all the Immral training,' I tell him. 'It's making me sloppy on my actual fighting.'

We start again, and I half-heartedly parry his blows with my scimitar until the teacher steps in to guide me.

'Fern, you know you don't need to do this, right?' Ramesh says quietly as the teacher walks away. 'If you're worried about me telling anyone, I won't.'

'I'm not worried,' I lie. It's not that I'm worried about him telling *anyone*, my fear is very specific: I'm worried he's going to tell Lord Allenby or, worse, my brother.

'Good, because you know if you keep fighting me this badly I probably *should* tell them just to get you taken off the knights.'

'What? Why?'

'Well, you're a danger to everyone right now, aren't you?'

I twist my scimitar and Ramesh's spear clatters to the ground. He smiles triumphantly. 'I knew it.'

Panting, I retrieve his spear and hand it back to him. I don't know how to play this at all. I'm not good enough at this kind of thing to balance keeping him onside with not making it obvious that I'm keeping him onside. As if he's borrowed Ollie's power and read my mind, Ramesh punches me lightly on the arm. 'Friends don't lie to friends, Fern. Come on, why are you being so nice to me all of a sudden?'

'I'm always nice.'

He just looks at me.

'Okay, yes, I'm terrified you're going to tell Lord Allenby what I did.'

'Even if I did – which I'm not, by the way – do you seriously think he'd throw you out of the thanes when you've got Immral?'

The idea that Lord Allenby might need me hadn't occurred to me, even though it probably should have. I had been so preoccupied with the fact that he didn't want me in the thanes in the first place that I hadn't considered that my power might change his opinion.

'But . . . he should throw me out,' I say.

Ramesh shrugs. 'Maybe he would, I dunno. I'm just saying that if I was him, I'd probably stretch my principles a bit for you. Come on, let's go again, and fight me properly this time. I want to actually get better.'

We circle each other once more.

'Is that the only reason you didn't tell him?' I ask, spinning into the air to attack him from above.

'So you wouldn't get thrown out? Well, yeah,' Ramesh huffs as he somersaults over my scimitar. 'But not because of your power.'

'What then?' I throw myself forward in the air to thrust at his ankles.

'Because we're friends.'

With a thump, I fall to the ground. He lands next to me a little more gracefully and helps me to my feet.

'But I'm not cool,' I say.

'Neither am I.'

'I'm grumpy all the time. I never sit with you.'

'True. But you want to, don't you?'

I nod. Then the anxiety that has been gnawing up my throat for months finally reaches my mouth. 'But I'm not supposed to be a knight.'

'Who says?'

'I wasn't chosen like the rest of you.'

Ramesh looks genuinely bemused. 'What does that matter? I'm not chosen for a lot of things in Ithr. Doesn't make me any less of a person for doing them anyway.'

I don't have an answer for that. The anxiety retreats into my stomach once more. Not gone but not as ravenous as it was. Ramesh gets me fighting again by punching me in the ribs with his spear handle, and we end up in a melee with the other Bedevere squires, prevailing at the eleventh hour with a move that sees Ollie and Phoebe cornered up a tree like lost cats.

That's the start of it. Ramesh said he was my friend, and in the days that follow I begin to see that the others are too – Phoebe and Rafe, Natasha and Samson. If I arrive at the chamber before them, they will automatically join me. If I enter after them, I now choose to sit with them. When Phoebe finds something interesting in one of the books in the chamber, she will leave it on the arm of my chair with a note. Best of all, they were Ollie's friends first, yet any cutting remark he makes towards me – more out of habit than real malice now – is either met with rolled eyes or ignored entirely. The guilt of what I did to Jenny becomes a second skin, but slowly the terror of what my actions might mean fade. I now know that I am not like her. I may have started to hurt her, but I couldn't continue. I wouldn't have, even if Ramesh hadn't seen me. And with that knowledge, something strong and beautiful opens inside me.

* * *

Spring is firmly in the air in Ithr. Natasha had told us to expect lambs and chicks clogging up the streets back in Annwn, and flowers budding from between stone blocks. She'd warned us that the horses would be friskier. But a gloom has been hanging over Annwn for weeks now. This year no cute baby animals appear, and the stones remain resolutely grey. Lamb seems to move more slowly than before. We all know why. Medraut's kalends are becoming a common sight in Annwn. The fact that the army of treitres hasn't yet been sighted should be a blessing, but all it does is put us more on edge. We know they're coming; we just don't know when.

Ollie and I continue to work our way through Mum's papers each night in the knights' chamber, yawning after long training sessions, knowing that we'll wake up to sore muscles and Dad chastising us for sleeping in yet again. Neither of us have found anything that might help us in the fight against Medraut, but nevertheless we continue. I wonder whether Ollie's reason is the same as mine: because reading Mum's work brings me closer to her.

Like the night when I spot Ollie's face clouding over as he reads.

'Found something?' I ask.

He beckons me over. 'Listen to this,' he says.

'Listen? What . . .?' But Ollie has already grasped my arm. There's the now-familiar arc of inspyre and the stab of pain, then my ears fill with a conversation had long ago. The words crackle as though I'm listening through a bad line, but one voice is unmistakably my mother's.

'*I promised you I would find a way,*' she's saying.

'I don't mind,' says an unknown voice. A woman's, if I'm not mistaken, timid like a rabbit. I can't shake the feeling that I've heard a voice like it before.

'I'm not going to let you down now.'

'Maybe it's for the best, Una. I've never belonged here. I'm not brave, like you.'

The voices fade out. Ollie and I look at each other, puzzled.

'You heard this through the paper?' I ask.

'Weird, right? As soon as I touched it I felt that there was a memory attached to it.'

We both peer down at Mum's writing. It's dated *November 1999* and it seems to be more research into morrigans, the sort of impenetrable essay that would interest Samson.

'What was she up to, do you think?' I whisper as the chamber door opens and the day-shift knights flood in.

'I wish I knew,' Ollie answers. 'I wish I knew who she was talking to as well.'

I touch Mum's lettering, skating over words I only half understand. *Amygdala, trauma, eliminate*. 'I think she was talking to Ellen Cassell.'

'Who?' Ollie asks.

'Lord Allenby said that Mum was friends with someone called Ellen, who struggled in the knights. She was one of the first knights to get killed by Medraut's treitre.'

'Poor girl,' Ollie says. 'Sounds like Mum persuaded her to stay and then she got killed anyway.'

Poor Ellen indeed. Her words – *I've never belonged here* – find a mirror in my soul. Was Mum her Ramesh, encouraging her to stay? Making her believe that she did have a place in this castle? I can't help but feel as though whatever Mum was working on for Ellen holds a key that has a part to play in the oncoming storm. If only I knew what it would unlock.

38

With Ostara imminent, Tintagel pushes aside the threat posed by Medraut to celebrate. The graduation of the squires has traditionally been a time of raucous fun, with a feast and a no-holds-barred party after we return from our first proper patrol. This year the tone isn't going to be quite as hedonistic, which I'm relieved about as wild partying was never really my scene, but there will still be a feast and festivities I let myself be buoyed by the atmosphere, even though I know that it can't last. As our training reaches its end, the reeves flurry around Tintagel to get the castle ready for the ceremony. Long tables line the hall. As Phoebe and I practise complicated battle moves in the castle gardens, apothecaries gather garlands of spring flowers from around us to decorate the archways. One night when we return from a practice patrol, actual trees, pregnant with blossom, are sprouting from the tables themselves, making the most spectacular centrepieces I've ever witnessed.

Then Ostara is here, and the reeves are placing platters filled with exotic fruits and cooked meats along the tables, and everyone's smiling at each other, looking forward to their first patrol and then to the feast that will follow. Everything feels fresh, new, numb. I am hyper-aware of my body as I pull on my uniform, even though I've worn it hundreds of times. When we're dressed, Ramesh pulls Phoebe and Ollie and I to one side and pulls a flask from his tunic.

'Hot chocolate with a dash of lotus juice,' he tells us, passing it round, 'to mark our graduation.'

We each take a sip of the sweet, fiery liquid, quietly relishing each other's company in our final few moments as squires. Then together, hands resting on each other's backs, we wait for Lord Allenby's traditional address.

'You've all shown outstanding commitment and drive,' he tells us. 'I know that you'll do your best to save every dreamer out there. But I want you to do something else for me – take care of yourselves, and take care of each other. As long as you do that, you can't go far wrong.'

'Bedevere, over here!' Samson calls. 'We're on the royal circuit. We'll head as directly west as we can and cover Hyde Park first, okay?'

Everyone nods silently. My mouth is very dry.

'Stay in training formation at first; new knights on the inside. Rafe, you're up front with me. Amina and Nerizan, you protect the rear.'

It's time to go. We file out of the chamber and march through the castle.

'First patrol!' Lord Allenby booms. The rest of the thanes cheer. I spot Rachel beaming from her place at the harkers' desks. Up in the gallery, reeves and veneurs clap and whistle. Then we're out of the castle and crossing the gardens. The concentration that fills the air as the new knights fumble with bridles and girths makes the usually roomy stables feel claustrophobic.

Lead horses outside, mount, form into regiments. One of the harkers at the gatehouse sounds a horn as the great drawbridge lowers. This is the only time of year that the horn will be used, to mark the graduation of another set of squires. The noise rolls like thunder around the gardens.

The other regiments cross first. I pull my back straight, trying to remember everything I've ever been taught about formations and strategy and how to stay upright on a horse. As if channelling my nerves, Lamb's ears point robustly forwards instead of flopping about as usual.

'You'll be okay, girl,' I whisper, smoothing her mane. 'I'll look after you.'

Ollie looks back at me. 'You know it's a sign of madness to talk to your pets, Fern.'

Balius bucks, as if to say, *Who are you calling a pet, matey?*

We cross the drawbridge, dozens of hooves pounding the wood. We round the corner, leaving Tintagel behind, and the spell breaks. We're proper knights, at last.

'Fall out, Bedevere!' Samson shouts. Ollie, Phoebe and Ramesh cheer, and even Samson cracks a smile. I'm back in my body, here, now.

Rachel's voice crackles into life in my left ear.

'Head to your patrol route for now, Bedevere. I'll let you know if we spot any trouble. Your nearest apothecary base is in Harrods.'

'Heard,' Samson replies.

As Samson had planned, we take the most efficient road to

the royal circuit patrol route, passing south of Soho's narrow streets. This patrol covers the poshest parts of London – Buckingham Palace, Westminster, the expensive shopping streets of Belgravia and Kensington, and up to Hyde Park. We won't be far from Bosco. I wonder if I'll spot any of my classmates.

'Couldn't have asked for a better patrol on our first night, could we?' Ramesh says. He's riding next to me, Ollie and Phoebe in front of us. 'When I was little my mum used to take me and my sisters to Hyde Park for picnics. "Let's have a sneak at the prigs in crowns, eh?" she used to say. I thought she meant the tourists in their baseball caps. Course she meant the royals.'

'She wouldn't like my dad then. He's a sucker for the queen. Listens to her speech at Christmas and everything.'

We smile at each other. I wonder if he's also thinking about that night. It feels like an age ago, even though it's actually only been a few weeks since he caught me torturing Jenny. This time I only have the painful shame of what I did. Gone is the fear that Ramesh is going to snitch.

Ahead of us Gawain veers off right to their patrol in the northern hills with silent waves.

Rachel's voice appears again in my ear. 'Bedevere, we've got reports of nightmares coming down Constitution Hill.'

'What kind, harker?' Samson asks.

'A swarm. We think insects – it's hard to tell.'

'On our way.'

The laughs and conversations dissipate like popped bubbles. My first proper mission. Samson spurs his horse to a gallop, and the rest of the regiment follows suit. I glance over and see that Ramesh's jaw is as clenched as mine. This is what we've been training for, but all our previous outings feel inadequate now. Then we'd had time to explore the side streets, to ask questions, to play games. There's no room for any of that now as we careen down the Mall. St James's' Park seems wrongly serene on my left – why is it so quiet when I am such a confusion of responsibility and fear?

I rack my memory for my notes on swarms. *Method of tackling depends on size. Can be deadly if small – e.g. poisonous spiders, locusts, etc. Clear area of dreamers a.s.a.p.; remain mounted at all times.*

The only noise is the sound of hooves on tarmac, the occasional swear word from Rafe as we detour to avoid packs of dreamers, and a few words of encouragement from Rachel through our helmets.

Finally, Samson says, 'Weapons,' and I draw my scimitar. In front of me Ollie clutches one of his chakrams. Samson is holding his bow aloft in one hand and looping his reins around his arms so he can get to his arrows.

'Ready?' he asks over the helmets.

'Ready,' we all whisper back. I can't breathe and I'm breathing too fast all at once. Any moment now we're going to see the swarm. Just one more road to go. The scimitar gives me courage; its solid handle, its reassuring weight. This is the last corner, then we'll meet our first mark.

We skid round. Phoebe shouts out, her voice half fear, half adrenalin.

The road is clear. A couple of dreamers wander aimlessly.

'How small is this swarm, exactly?' Ramesh asks. 'I mean, are we talking parasitic small or . . .?'

'Harker,' Samson says into his helmet, 'there's nothing here. Any update?'

Rachel swears. 'Sorry, Bedevere, looks like it's gone.'

'Be clearer. Gone moved or gone dissolved?'

'Sorry, sorry – dissolved. We can't see them anywhere nearby.'

I'm strangely disappointed. It's good, I suppose, that no one's in danger any more.

'Okay, heard,' Samson replies. One of the other knights, someone a few years older than me, says, 'This happens all the time. You get used to the anticlimax.'

'Dreams are fickle creatures,' Rafe adds.

'At least it wasn't a swarm of rabid corgis,' Amina jokes from the back. 'Remember that? They came running out of Buckingham Palace like a load of furry beetles. I haven't been able to look at a dog the same way since.'

'Let's get back to our route.' We follow Samson as he urges his horse down the road and out of the park.

'Damn,' Ramesh says, 'I got all dressed up and now I've got nowhere to go.'

I turn to him, smile, open my mouth to say something clever. There he is, grinning at me. Then there's just the stone building, behind where his head should be.

39

Something warm splashes across my face. My first impulse isn't to run, or scream, or fight. It's to look for Ramesh's head. It's important to find it and put it back on his neck. His torso is still perfectly balanced on its saddle. Then his horse rears and it topples backwards, and I am in hell.

'Get back, Fern!' someone shouts. I'm too slow to draw up my reins. Luckily Lamb is listening. She bolts forward, swinging around as she reaches the other knights to face Ramesh's killer. I have seen it once before. Back then it was far away, at the end of a vast underground hall. It is even more beautiful up close. Skin like molten gold and a long, elegant body that towers over us. Its hands have no palms, only claws – each one as long as my arm – that extend straight from the wrist. Its tail tapers to a spear-like point. Eyes like black marbles watch us, calculating who to take next. The treitre that has lurked in the corners of my thoughts for months. The treitre that I think killed my mother.

It advances on us slowly. It has no mouth, no facial features at all apart from those jet black eyes. It kicks something out of its path. There's something unsettlingly human about its movement, despite the tail and the featureless face. Or maybe I only think that because I know there's a human beneath the metal hide.

'Everyone in formation. Single attacker. Ollie take Ramesh's place,' Samson orders, only a slight quake in his voice.

The months of training have paid off. I nudge Lamb to one side, slotting into the left flank, trying not to fixate on Ramesh's still-smiling face. I blink tears from my eyes. I cannot cry right now; I need sharp vision if I'm going to survive this. Phoebe's lion pads behind us, its steady growl like a distant engine. I glance over at Ollie, now next to me. His normally tanned face is snowdrop white. His eyes, too, flicker towards Ramesh.

'Hold steady,' Samson says. 'It's only one treitre.'

Only one. I almost laugh.

Rachel's voice comes through. 'Lancelot and Gawain are on their way to you.'

From the nearby streets emerge two more treitres. One copper coloured, one mottled silver. The silver one has a back covered in spines like razors. The other has an unnaturally long neck that snaps, snakelike, from side to side.

Before we can move into a different formation, the golden treitre springs forward in a leap big enough to clear a house. It's amongst us, its claws slicing this way and that, its tail lashing out. Two knights go down quickly, deep gouges across their chests and necks. Phoebe's lion roars. Then the other treitres pounce as well and I'm not registering anything that's happening to anyone else. All I can do is focus on me and Lamb. Wheeling her round the back of the golden treitre I carve at its skin with my scimitar, but it barely makes a dent.

Samson flies overhead, unleashing arrows at the silver treitre's spines. A few pierce its skin but do little more than irritate it. Another knight works with him, sliding beneath it and stabbing at its belly. Amina and Phoebe leap from their horses to land on the copper monster's back, using Amina's wire to try to strangle it.

Rachel's saying something in my ear but I can't hear her properly. Ollie's horse jitters past us, riderless. I can't see him. Where is he where is he? There, crawling along the ground, towards the monster.

Rachel's voice is in my ear again. 'Lancelot are being attacked too! And Gawain. Every regiment. They're everywhere. No one's coming to help you. Fall back! Get back to the castle!'

Amidst the pandemonium I guide Lamb towards the golden treitre.

'Here!' I shout. The monster twists around and every sinew in its metallic skin seems to quiver with concentration as it focuses on me. 'You're short staffed. Three of you aren't enough to take on an Immral.' *Them's fightin' talk, Fern,* I think, delirious with fear. *Now how are you going to back it up?*

I reach out with my mind to the ground beneath the treitre, commanding the tarmac to rise up. The familiar crackle in my skull builds as the tarmac bubbles and melts, falling inwards so that the treitre has to scrabble to find its footing. It's enough for Ollie to reach the monster, grab onto it tightly and smash one of his chakrams down on its tail. His face contorts with pain and something else – shock, I think – before the treitre flicks its broken tail, throwing my brother across the street. He hits the building on the other side and slides to the ground, motionless. The silver monster thrashes once, twice, and Phoebe and Amina are thrown against the opposite wall with a sickening crunch. Donald leaps to protect his mistress but two treitres jump on his back and claw at him like rabid dogs. His roars of pain and confusion tear at my heart.

'Fern.' Samson's voice comes through the helmet. 'We need space to get the injured. Can you do anything to distract them?'

'Yeah, I've got a few ideas that might work,' I say, steeling myself.

Guiding Lamb to a safe distance, I reach out to the damaged buildings. At first nothing happens. Samson's voice is shouting too loudly in my ears. 'Get the injured and fall back, Bedevere. Fall back now.' He's ruining my concentration. I pull off the helmet and push all of my focus into the building. The imaginations of thousands of dreamers resist me. They all remember the structure as it should be. The building wants to be whole.

I imagine it as a clay slab and dig my fingers inside it, tearing at the concrete holding each block in place. Gradually, the wall shifts. As the pressure builds in my head, I inch a huge block of aged marble out of its slot. I have to be careful not to collapse the whole structure, or Phoebe and her lion will be crushed. *Do as I say.* It edges further from the wall.

'Fern!' Samson shouts. 'Get out! Move away!'

As I turn back to the street, ready to hurl the block towards the treitre, I realise why Samson is yelling. Two of the monsters – one gold, one silver – are advancing towards me on all fours, bounding in ugly strides.

'Steady, girl,' I tell Lamb. The loyal creature listens, and holds her ground.

They are only a few leaps away now. The whole building is shaking as I fight all those memories. One leap away. It has to be now.

I throw my power towards the stone. It slides out in one smooth movement and I hurl it towards the treitres. There's no precision, no accuracy, but the block hits true. Both treitres are swiped sideways with a jarring wrench of metal on stone. Further down the street Samson and five other knights are surrounding the copper treitre. Its huge jaws snap this way and that. Two knights fall, but Samson is clinging on. He has snapped his bow, and despite the creature's efforts to throw him off he is steadily wrapping the bowstring around that snake-like neck. Round and round it goes, tighter and tighter. The treitre makes a horrendous burbling sound, black blood gushing up through its throat to join its victims'. A moment later it gives a great, rasping, final breath and falls to the ground.

I rush to Phoebe's side and leap off Lamb. Samson is beside me in an instant, dealing with Amina.

'Well done, Fern,' he mutters. 'That's bought us some time.'

'Ollie . . .'

'Rafe's getting Ollie.'

Phoebe's blood-soaked lion stirs feebly a few metres away, and a second later Phoebe opens her eyes. She mumbles something incoherent.

I hear Rachel's shaken voice crackling through Samson's helmet. 'Apothecaries are on their way –'

'Negative,' Samson snaps. 'We can't guarantee their safety. For God's sake, tell them to stay back.' He bends over Amina again. 'Let's get them out of here.'

But even as we lift the women, I hear stone shifting. The silver treitre is still buried beneath the block, its spines pushed inside its body, but the golden treitre is getting to its feet. It moves slowly. One of its legs is injured and that pristine golden hide is now dented along one side, although I see no blood.

'Go!' Samson urges, and shoves Phoebe onto his horse. Rafe is already halfway up the street, pulling Balius alongside him, my brother's prone body lashed to the saddle.

'Donald . . .'

'If she lives, her lion lives. Get out of here, Fern – that's an order.'

With a surge of Immral I fly Amina onto her horse's back, leap into my own saddle and kick Lamb into a gallop. But I'm not following Samson. There's something else I need to do first. Ignoring Samson's shouts, I steer Lamb in a wheel around the treitre. It watches me, its body shifting to keep me in sight. I cast around for what I'm looking for. I can't fail him.

There's a clatter of claws, and I look back at the treitre. It's scratching the ground in an odd way, as though it would be laughing if it had a mouth. It curls its tail around something. Ramesh's head.

We watch each other, sizing each other up. I am trying, desperately, to fight my migraine. I just need to hold the pain off for long enough to work out how to get Ramesh to safety. The thought of him abandoned in the street like this is inconceivable.

'Archimago,' I say, thinking to buy time. 'So it was you who sent me the message?'

The treitre tilts its head to one side, listening, understanding, even though it cannot reply.

'I always wondered who could be that cruel to taunt someone about killing their mother. But now I see you I'm not surprised. You're made of cruelty, aren't you? That's all you are.'

Lamb is shaking. I won't let it hurt her. It hasn't shown any interest in the horses, only the knights. Right now it seems to be waiting to hear more from me.

'I bet your master doesn't know that you contacted me, does he? Bet he's going to be pretty mad at you when he finds out, since I'm the one with Immral.'

The treitre looks round, and I realise that it is making sure that its companions are dead. It scrapes the ground again. It's trying to say something, but I am not inclined to try to understand.

'I'll be sure to tell him what you did, the next time I see him.'

The great golden head sways a little, the body tenses, ready to pounce. As it does, I leap off Lamb. 'Go!' I tell her, and she bolts. My head pounds even harder as I use all my energy to fly over the treitre's body and crumple to the ground. The monster turns just as I sweep Ramesh's head into my tunic. Can't think about the blood. Can't think about his body, lying like a doll on the other side of the street. I try to move but the pain in my head is too great. It's paralysing my limbs.

I look up, trying to focus. The treitre is upon me. I can't escape.

Something bursts between my eyes, robbing me of my sight, robbing me of any feeling except sheer agony. All I can think is that I won't see my last moments and how furious that makes me. I didn't manage to bring Mum's killer to justice – instead it will kill me too. There's nothing I can do to stop it now.

Just wait for the claw to slice my neck or my chest. The tail to spear my body.

Yet . . . nothing happens. The pain hasn't lessened. If anything it's got worse. But I don't seem to be dead, or having my arm chopped off. Is the monster playing with me?

Every fibre of my body fights the blindness, urging my sight to return. I remember the times when I've had hiccups and worried that they'd never stop. Now, faced with the idea of losing my sight forever – *Will I be blind in Ithr too? Please, no, please, no no no* – I'd gladly exchange eternal hiccups for functioning eyes.

When something touches me I can't help a high-pitched scream. It's not claws, though. It's velvet. Lamb is nuzzling me. I reach out and feel for her neck. She's trembling.

'Where is it, girl?' I ask. 'Is it close by?'

She whinnies, softly enough that I can just hear the footsteps approaching. I thrust out a hand.

'It's me, Fern.' Samson's voice is barely a whisper.

'Has it gone? I can't see –'

'No. It's right next to you. It's not moving.'

'What do you mean? Get out of here then!'

'It's frozen. It hasn't moved for the last few minutes. I thought you'd done that.'

Maybe I did, instinctively, the same way I raised the Thames to save that man. Perhaps my power acted to save my life. Maybe that's what's made me lose my sight – the effort needed to keep this one monster at bay. It shouldn't be this difficult, or cause this much agony, surely? But then, I've never tried to control something with this much rage inside it.

I don't know why, but I reach out one shaking hand, feeling blindly.

'Don't, Fern,' Samson warns, but I have to.

My fingers touch ice and spring back. Hardly daring to breath, trying to push the throbbing agony from my mind, I reach out again. This time when I touch the cold, smooth metal I don't flinch. I run my hand up the treitre's neck and across its frozen head. I cannot read its mind like Ollie, but I sense the edges of its being. I can feel the inspyre that is woven into the fabric of the creature's human soul. I taste the essence of this treitre, as I did with Jenny. The taste of acid is almost overwhelming, but there are other notes beneath it. The homeliness of treacle. Ash from a fire long burned out. And something else, deeper still. Orchids. I withdraw my hand, unsettled. Orchids were my mother's favourite flower.

Samson's arms slide around my waist. Gently, he lifts me onto Lamb's back. He twines her reins around one of my hands and I snake the other around her neck. I suddenly realise that I'm missing something.

'Ramesh –'

'I've got him now. You did right by him. But whatever you're doing to freeze it, Fern, please don't stop. I'm not sure we could outrun it if it got moving again.'

I nod, but I've no idea how I stopped the treitre in the first place, so I'm at a bit of a loss. As Lamb breaks into a jerky trot, I tap into the pain that's coursing through my head. If my power over Mum's killer is linked to my blindness, then so long as I stay blind maybe the treitre will remain frozen. I keep my eyes open so we'll get some warning if my sight starts to return. Sounds and touch become sharp. Every quiet command of Samson's is like a drill next to my ear. Every tiny misstep Lamb makes sends pain coursing through my body. Unable to see and constantly worrying about the monster behind us makes the journey feel ten times longer.

'Nearly there,' Samson whispers. 'Rachel, do we have a clear path?'

I can't hear Rachel's reply because I cast aside my helmet during the fight, but I've got bigger things to worry about. My sight is returning. The pain is as bad as ever, but the darkness is starting to recede. As terrifying as it was being totally blind, getting my sight back has a more frightening implication.

'Hurry, please!'

This limbo of not being able to see clearly is worse than having no sight at all, because my hearing starts to fade as well. I mistake the echoes of hooves with the *tap tap* of golden claws. When the drawbridge finally creaks open, I am ready to pass out from the anxiety.

Noise explodes all around me. Everyone is shouting, a few are crying. Someone is wailing.

'Only one from Dagonet got out alive.'

'Why didn't the harkers spot them?'

'He's waking up. Ollie? Ollie?'

Ollie's voice rings through the courtyard, silencing all others.

'Why is no one looking after my sister?'

'He's in shock,' someone says. 'It's okay, Ollie, calm down –'

'*Look at her!*'

The silence that echoes around the courtyard is like the

numbness that spreads through my body. Why is he saying that? What do I look like?

Then someone else screams. The treitre must be back. What if it's managed to get past the drawbridge? How can I protect everyone when I'm in this state? The pain is worse than it's ever been. I don't know how much longer I can stand it.

'I need help here!' I recognise the voice of Drew the apothecary. Cool hands peel me off Lamb's back and grasp my face.

'My God,' he breathes. 'I've never seen anything like it.'

Dimly, I realise that the scream wasn't about the monster. It was about me. Feeling strangely calm, as though I'm the doctor enquiring about a patient, I ask, 'What's wrong?'

'Her eyes!' another voice says, hysterical.

Slowly, I place my fingers over my eyes. Something warm and gooey is oozing from them. As I remove my hands, my eyesight flashes back and I can see clearly again. My hands are red. Blood. I am bleeding from my eyes.

40

'No signs of epilepsy before?' a voice is saying.

'Never.' That's Dad, sounding hoarse.

'She's coming round,' Ollie says, much closer.

I don't really want to open my eyes but now Ollie's given the game away I don't have much choice. The room's too bright and the smell of chlorine makes me want to throw up. The vomit hits Ollie on its way to the floor.

'Srrree,' I gurgle.

Dad's face swims into focus. 'How are you feeling, Ferny?'

'Grrrrmmmh.'

He stinks of cigarettes, but that can't be right because he gave up years ago. The buzz of voices elsewhere in the hospital is painfully magnified. I reach for my memories. Golden claws. Ramesh's head. Blood across my face, some of it mine, some of it not. The pain in my head is matched by a horrendous ache in my heart. He can't be dead. Last night can't have happened. *A bad dream,* I want to reassure myself, except that knowing what I now know about dreams, that's no consolation at all.

A doctor peers over Dad's shoulder.

'She'll need bedrest for a few days, and we'll need to get her back in for regular tests. It might be a simple eye infection, it might be something else. I don't expect us to get to the bottom of this straight away. We can keep her here, or . . .'

'Nnnmmmm.' The word isn't coming out properly. I can't stay here. My portal must be back in my bedroom, and without it I won't be able to get back into Annwn. Ramesh will be there, I'm sure. It will be a cruel prank. They'll all be in on it. They'll laugh at my shocked face and congratulate each other on a joke well played – Ramesh, Phoebe, Samson, Rafe . . . Please let it just be bad-taste banter. Please.

'We can bring her home, can't we, Dad?' Ollie says. I cast him what I hope he realises is a grateful look.

'Can we, Doctor? I'd rather I could stay with her.'

When we finally make it home, it takes both Dad and Ollie to half walk, half push-pull me up our narrow stairs. I don't know whether that says more about my weight or their fitness.

'Like a pig in a blanket,' Dad says, tucking the duvet under my chin like I'm five again. I'd never admit it, but I like it when he does this. I am filled with the urge to keep him beside me.

'What happened? I don't remember anything apart from the hospital.'

'It was your brother. Woke me up banging on my door, saying something was wrong with you.' He glances at Ollie, who's lurking in the doorway.

Ollie shrugs. 'One of those twin things, I guess.'

'Anyway,' Dad continues, 'I'm afraid I had to break your door down because you'd locked it, love. At first I couldn't see anything wrong, then I turned the light on and . . . well, you've looked better, darling. It was like your whole face was bleeding. I thought you must have scratched yourself or your burn had opened up again. It was only on the way to the hospital that I got a chance to clean you up and saw it was leaking from your eyes. Your nose and ears as well. Do you not remember any of it?'

I remember far too much. 'No, nothing.'

Dad laughs shakily. 'Some nightmare, eh?'

You've no idea.

He pats my duvet again.

'Hot chocolate, the proper stuff?'

'Mmm.'

'Coming up.' He slips out, past Ollie, who doesn't seem inclined to follow. My brother looks uncertainly at the chair next to my desk, but then obviously thinks better of it and makes to leave.

'Wait,' I say. Then, 'Thanks.'

He shrugs. The final moments of last night are coming back to me, and in amidst everything else I remember the panic in Ollie's voice. *Why is no one looking after my sister?* I wasn't in any state to acknowledge it then, but now I allow myself to consider the possibility that perhaps Ollie does care for me after all. It feels disloyal to Ramesh to smile at this, but I can't help it. I have wanted my brother to come back to me for five long, bitter years.

I'm about to tell Ollie that I'm almost sure the golden treitre was the one that killed our mother, but then I remember the look of shock on his face before it threw him into the wall.

'You know, don't you? About the treitre and Mum.'

Ollie nods. 'I saw its memories when I grabbed its tail. You were right.'

'It showed you Mum's death?'

'It was right there, like it had just been remembering it.'

The thought of it bolts through my chest. I want to know exactly what he saw, but I don't. Now it isn't Ramesh's head I envision, but Mum's. Her wild hair matted with blood, her thin neck sliced through, her eyes open but unseeing. Unbidden, I start sobbing.

'Don't,' I hear him say, his own voice wobbly.

'I'm not.'

I try to stem the tears, rubbing my hand across my nose and spreading a snotty, salty mess across my upper lip. I have to say something, to take my mind off the images playing through my head. *Like an operation gone wrong*. That was what Clemmie had said. If that was just the echo of her murder, what was actually done to her in Annwn? I skirt around the idea at first. It's too gruesome. It's too intimate. But the need to know is overwhelming.

I take a deep breath and ask Ollie for a favour for the first time in years. 'Will you show me?'

My brother and I are standing in Annwn, looking over the city from the battlements of the Tower of London. An executioner's block takes pride of place in the grass courtyard below us. As I watch, a man in a smock materialises and steps up to the block. I look away before the act itself, but can't un-hear the thud of axe on wood. On the other side of the wall, I can see the very spot where my portal brought me to Annwn.

It's strange being in Annwn during the daytime. Everything's quieter. The dreamers who sleep during the day don't seem to frequent this part of the city in their dreams. For the most part inspyre drifts aimlessly through the streets, waiting for night to fall in Ithr.

'So?' I ask, reluctant to repeat my request. I hold out my hand, but Ollie doesn't take it.

'No, this is sick, Fern! I don't want to see it again. I don't know why I agreed to this.'

He moves away and I almost slip over as I rush after him. 'You can't just change your mind!' I say, grabbing his arm. As I touch him, my sight is replaced by the treitre's memory. I was prepared for that, and for the arc of inspyre as I grabbed my twin. But I wasn't prepared to see my mother. I've heard her voice, and I've seen photos and paintings of her, but this is different. She is before me, fiercely alive.

Ollie's voice bleeds through. 'Fern, I don't think you should see this.'

'I have to.'

The images come quickly. A look of shock on Mum's face as human becomes treitre and picks her up, hurling her against the wall. The monster goes to her, holds her unconscious body in its arms, laying her down on the ground as a lover might. Then, with a sudden lurch, it launches at her, spurred on by a thought I'm not able to understand. It tears into her, as though it wants to remove everything that made her Una Gorlois.

Raking her face, her chest, stabbing those vicious claws through her legs. She was dead after the first few blows, but each new assault rips through my heart. By the time the monster's satisfied, Mum's clothes are in tatters, and her body is more blood than skin. Her eyes, though. Her eyes are still open, and they are looking straight at the monster. Two claws extend, hovering over the unseeing pupils. As they press down, I pull away from Ollie. I can't watch that final desecration.

For a long time, neither of us speaks. I walk further along the wall, away from the place where it happened. Ollie stays where he was. The executioner's axe in the courtyard below thunks once more. A cold wind sweeps along the river from the distant sea. I tug at my jumper fruitlessly. That's when I notice that my hands are shaking.

I glance back at my brother, staring fixedly at the spot where Mum was butchered. If that scene had been playing through my head for the last twelve hours, I wouldn't want to talk about it either. I'd want to block it out, to march up to the eyrie and demand a morrigan suck it out of my head.

'Did you see anything else when you read its mind?' I ask.

'A lot of the memories were of Mum. There were a few of the other knights it killed. Did you know it carved something on its victims' weapons?'

I shake my head and we lapse into silence again. I look out towards Tower Hill station. Mum's portal was linked to that station. She died so close to it. Had she just arrived, I wonder, or was she on her way back to Ithr when the treitre had caught her?

'Did you notice anything, before it turned into the treitre?' Ollie asks.

I think about those first seconds, where the treitre must have been in its human body, and shake my head. 'We were inside the treitre's mind, weren't we? We'd only see who they were if we could see it from Mum's point of view. Why are you asking that?'

'It's probably nothing,' Ollie says. 'It's just . . . why did it act like that?'

'What do you mean?'

'Well, when the treitre attacked us it was just killing us off as quickly as it could until you got involved. There was no emotion, was there? But with Mum it was different. It was upset when it killed her, I could feel that. Then after she was dead it got angry.'

I see what he means – it *was* acting differently from how it did last night.

'Why, though?'

Ollie shrugs. 'I've been wondering that all day, and I still can't figure it out.'

We look out over the Tower courtyard, towards the Thames, both desperately trying to understand the mysterious human shrouded in the deadly, golden skin of the treitre.

41

I had hoped to spend the day curled up in bed, forgetting the events of last night, but it wasn't meant to be. Eyes open or closed, I can't stop the memories. The blood, those claws, Ramesh smiling, then Ramesh dead. I don't even know how many in my regiment survived. And Mum. Again and again I see the treitre slicing into her in its inexplicable frenzy. Eventually I crawl downstairs, every step bringing a wave of nausea from the headache that's been plaguing me since I woke up.

Dad's watching some old sitcom. Usually I'd turn my nose up at it, but when Dad fetches a blanket I snuggle into it, resting my head on his chest, feeling it rumble as he laughs silently. As I lie there, it occurs to me that my life used to be as simple as those characters'. They have straightforward emotions. I used to be the same: anger, rage, loneliness, nothing in between. I was who I was and that was that. The knights has complicated things. Now there are two Ferns: the scarred loner who's cuddled up to her dad because she's not feeling well, and the knight who has opened her heart to friends only to watch one of them be brutally killed. Here, I'm still an innocent, even if I'd never thought of myself that way before. In Annwn, that innocence has been ripped away.

I fall asleep again, head in Dad's lap, until Ollie gets back from school.

'Have you seen the news?' he asks, casting a significant glance my way. He throws a copy of the *Evening Standard* onto the sofa. While Dad makes a start on dinner, I pick up the paper. The front page is a collage of faces. Most of them are posed school photos. Some of them show teenagers clutching beloved pets, or kissing trophies.

SLEEP OF DEATH, reads the headline.

Ollie is talking quietly to Dad in the kitchen. 'Loads,' I hear him say. 'Hundreds, they reckon.'

Dad doesn't reply. He puts some bread in the toaster, then leans heavily on the countertop. 'Thank God it wasn't Ferny,' he whispers.

I look at the photos again, blinking back tears.

A caption at the bottom of the page says, *Story continued on page* 5. I flick through. Hundreds of dead. That means . . .

This morning many in the UK woke up to a living nightmare as hundreds of people have died, apparently peacefully, in their sleep. It is estimated that over four hundred men, women and children died overnight in what coroners and doctors are calling a 'mysterious mass tragedy'. . .

I skip through the text. Sentences pop out at me.

Sixty-one dead in the Greater London area alone . . .

Some family members reported that their loved ones sported what looked like cuts on their skin, although these later faded . . .

Dad turns the channel to the news, where a reporter lists

some of the dead, their photos appearing in a corner of the screen as she speaks. I have to stifle a cry when I recognise Emory, who it turns out ran a tiny charity in Ithr.

I take the paper with me as I rush out of the room.

'Fern? Love?' my dad calls.

I lean my back against my bedroom door and force myself to return to the newspaper. A few pages on there's a list of London's dead, with photos and captions giving the superficial details of their lives. It goes on for pages and pages. I search for one face in particular. Then I spot him. The forehead's a little larger, the jaw's a little weaker, and he's wearing a brace, but it's unmistakably Ramesh.

Reyansh Haldar, 15. Student at St Mary's Grammar School in Bow. Terrence Smedwick, Headmaster of St Mary's, told the Standard . . .

He didn't live that far from me. When he followed me to Jenny's house he would have been on familiar turf. We could even have passed each other in the street. I wonder why he changed his name to Ramesh Hellier for the knights. I suppose I wouldn't have wanted anyone from my Annwn life to have recognised me in Ithr, and thanks to my burn scar I don't have to worry about that too much. Maybe Ramesh was erecting his own walls between his two lives in the only way he could.

I avoided boys like him in Ithr, knowing they'd only give more fuel to my bullies – *Oh, how sweet, the freak and the geek*. But I cannot bear the thought of an Annwn without him riding by my side, making silly jokes as if my smile is a trophy to be won.

It takes me a long time to pluck up the courage to open my

portal tonight. The image of Ramesh's torso falling from his horse, of the weight of his severed head in my arms, won't go away. When I take my mother's mirror from its place in my drawer, I freeze. All I can picture is the golden treitre waiting at the platform in Tintagel to finish me off. Even when I convince myself I'll be fine, my hands shake so badly it takes me three attempts to open my portal.

I'm not the only one who's late. Everyone is gathering in the hall. I spot Phoebe leaning against a wall. Her forehead is sporting a deep gash and her skin is mottled with bruises.

'I'm giving you an imaginary hug.' She smiles wanly as I rush up to her. 'But if you try to give me a real one I *will* scream in pain.'

Samson and Rafe arrive with a chair for Phoebe to sit on.

'You okay?' Samson asks me. 'I . . . We were all worried about you.'

Before I can reply, the reeve captain directs everyone to shuffle into lines. I look around the hall for the first time. Altogether there can't be more than thirty knights left. Nearly a hundred rode out of the castle last night.

'Is this everyone?'

Rafe shakes his head. 'Some of them haven't turned up for duty. Cowards.'

'Can you really blame them?' Ollie says as he joins us. 'I bet I'm not the only one here who took a while to open my portal tonight.'

No one talks after that.

When Lord Allenby emerges, I can see immediately that he's putting on an act. He still strides out, straight-backed and purposeful, but something has broken in him. This is the second time in his career as a knight that a treitre has committed genocide – then it was his peers and friends he lost; last night it was those who were supposed to be in his care. What does that kind of burden do to a person?

Beside Lord Allenby are two familiar faces. Leering Merlin and, to my delight, Andraste. It's only her gently warning expression that stops me from running into her arms there and then.

Lord Allenby speaks. 'I know you all have questions about last night. There will be time later for answers. Right now we're here to pay our respects.'

I've never liked going to church before, but there is a power in hundreds of people bowing their heads as one; a power stronger than any Immral. Silence falls over us like a blanket. On the other side of Phoebe, Ollie closes his eyes in prayer. Merlin digs his arms into the pillars where the names of the dead scroll. Inspyre crackles around his forearms. With a grinding noise, the words come to a halt, and Merlin pulls his arms out of the pillars. Lord Allenby recites without the need of paper.

'Emory Blair.'

Merlin runs his hands over the stone and Emory's name appears. Then something even stranger happens. The inspyre around us forms a shape. Emory's dreadlocked face stares down at us. Her form shimmers for a moment, then vanishes as Lord Allenby announces the next name. And so the list goes on. It builds like a tower of cards in my chest. The same ritual for each person murdered last night – their name is read, engraved, then their shape forms. The silence beneath the dome is gradually replaced by muffled sobs. Even Samson, who is usually so stalwart, has tears running down his cheeks. I wait for it to hit me but I can't absorb the fact that all of these people are gone.

'Ramesh Hellier.'

The cards topple. Phoebe silently takes my hand, her chest heaving. I thought I had done all my crying earlier today when I found Ramesh's obituary, but I was wrong.

At first my search for *Reyansh Haldar* had only raised sensationalist headlines about the deaths. It took a while to find his social media accounts. On one of them his parents had written a brief message.

Reyansh died peacefully in his sleep last night. We can't believe that our sweet little boy, and Sachi and Kala's big brother, has left us. We'll update here with details of the funeral. We ask you not to contact us in the meantime, and please don't pass our details on to the press.

Underneath the message there was a slurry of comments, nearly all of them only a few words each. *RIP mate. Can't believe you've gone. Always such a joker, RIP.* Then, near the bottom: *I'll miss you so much, Rooster. You saved my life once, wish I could've done the same for you. Xx.* The photo was of a black-haired, black-lipped girl from his school giving the finger to the camera. So he had one real friend, at least. If what she'd written was true, then Ramesh was in the business of helping people in Ithr too.

As I think about that message there's a *pull*, from both my head and my heart, like a thread being drawn from them. Phoebe gasps and I know she's feeling the same thing. Those threads seem to take form – at first just a wisp of blue light, then as it intertwines with other threads, it takes on a shape. Rough, maybe a little more noble-looking than he really was, but it's definitely Ramesh. His form flickers, like all the others, then it dissipates. The power of our joint memories, focused through our grief, made him real and alive again, if only for an instant.

After the last name is added to the pillars, the atmosphere in the hall lifts, as though it's been cleansed.

'It's not right,' Phoebe whispers. 'People should know they didn't just die in their sleep.'

'It's best that no one realises,' Rafe replies. 'Think about the chaos if everyone knew the truth.'

'I know,' Phoebe says fiercely. 'It still doesn't make it right that we're the only people who know that they died fighting. It's not fair.'

There's nothing much we can say to that. She's right. It's not fair at all.

Lord Allenby clears his throat.

'No doubt you all know by now that what happened last night was on the orders of Sebastien Medraut. It might not seem like it, but we got off lightly. I've had reports that Cornwall and Oxford have been completely wiped out. Last night was a declaration of war.'

There's more to it than that, though, I realise. The long tables that were intended to be for the Ostara celebrations have been pushed to one side. The glorious trees have been stripped of their blossoms and the garlands of flowers have been torn down. It may seem like a small thing in the grand scheme of the tragedy, but it is symbolic of what we have lost. Medraut knew. He knew that last night was supposed to be a time of joy for the thanes – a brief moment where we could congratulate each other, since no one in Ithr even knows we exist. He knew all of that, and he chose last night to decimate us anyway.

'You know what we have to do,' Lord Allenby is saying. 'As of right now, destroying Medraut is our priority. It's the priority of every thane in this country. We don't stop, we don't balk, we don't rest until he has been brought to justice. Is that understood?'

The call goes up around the hall. 'Yes, my lord.'

I look at Phoebe, Natasha and Rafe, all red-faced from crying. I look at Samson, who has seen more than any of us what Medraut is capable of. Then I look at Ollie, my enemy, my ally, my other half. I reach out to all of them. One by one, they place their hands over mine.

'We do not rest,' Samson says.

'We do not fear,' I add.

'Let's get the bastard,' Ollie says.

Medraut has fired the opening shot. But we will be the ones to fire the closing one, if it's the very last thing we do. And with my dying breath if needs be, I'll take that golden treitre with me.

42

Andraste finds me after the memorial service. Up close, she looks more tired than before. Her face is riddled with oozing scars. When she talks, her lungs rattle.

'It's Medraut, isn't it? Who's doing that to you?' I say.

She nods. 'His influence in Annwn and Ithr grows, and ours wanes. People tell his story, not ours. We cannot survive if our stories are forgotten.'

'When you first brought me here you asked me to save you. Did you know I had Immral?' I ask.

'No – I spoke in a moment of desperation. I did not mean to put my life on your shoulders. My brothers and sisters are angry that I helped you into Tintagel. They no longer trust any human with the King's Power, but I told them that you are different.'

I think about what I did to Jenny, and squirm.

'I am going to try to save you, you know.'

She smiles at that, but it's a sad smile, as though she doesn't believe me. I watch her walk slowly away, the hint of a limp now plaguing her stride.

We feel the absence of our fallen friends most keenly when

we go out on patrols. Despite our losses, Bedevere fared better than any of the other regiments. 'And that's thanks to you, Fern,' Samson says. 'We all know it, and we won't forget it.'

It means that some of our knights are moved to other regiments to even out the numbers. Amina's promoted to the head of Lancelot. It's a bittersweet pill for her; she and Emory were close.

There is one more ritual to perform to mourn our dead. It doesn't take place in Tintagel, but in the sheltered garden where the amber monument marks the massacre of the knights fifteen years ago. We hang our own ribbons from the branches. No words can fill the space between my anger and my grief, but I try all the same. *For Ramesh*, I write. *You were annoying and you talked too much. You made me your friend against my will. Now you're gone and I want you back.*

I notice Ollie slipping his own ribbon onto a lower branch and surreptitiously read it: *Ramesh – you knew who I really am and you liked me anyway. Thank you.*

A second amber monument has been erected next to the first, containing the weapons of the sixty-one fallen. My comrades spend a long time crying in front of it. At first, I can only stare hopelessly at the jet-black fountain pen engraved with the name *Reyansh Halder*, but after a while I find myself drawn to the original monument. Ollie said that the treitre had carved something onto the once-weapons of its victims. Sure enough, each item has the same verse etched into it. *Hereafter dear thou shalt repent*. I move around the monument, seeing the same words on toy cars and bracelets, cufflinks and dolls. *Hereafter dear thou shalt repent*. The more I read it, the more sinister it becomes. Then I come across a paintbrush – spattered with coloured oils – right at the bottom that bears a different inscription. *I claim this life for Sebastien Medraut.*

'Such an ugly sentence for a very gentle woman,' Lord Allenby says. He's standing on the other side of the monument, watching me examine the brush. 'That weapon belonged to the first knight who was killed. We never did work out why the inscription was different for her.'

Lord Allenby has spoken once before about the first people killed by the golden treitre. The woman who didn't belong, like me. 'This was Ellen Cassell's?'

He nods. 'The cricket bat next to it was Clement Rigby's. We found the weapons, but no trace of their bodies.'

I am about to ask more, but at that moment the harkers and knights standing guard at the garden's entrance signal to Lord Allenby. That's our cue to return to Tintagel. I don't see him alone again for quite some time.

Our first patrol after the treitre attack is a quiet affair; a far cry from our former jubilance. When Samson gets a call over his helmet I can tell that everyone in our regiment is steeling themselves. This is business as usual, when nothing will ever be normal again. The call takes us deep into the narrow streets of Shoreditch, and I can tell that everyone is thinking about how simple it would be for the treitre to ambush us here. It's easy to spot the dreamer. A little girl surrounded by the dreams of her friends: a gaggle of children. Then we get closer and I see that their mouths and noses are distorted into muzzles, although these muzzles are covered in skin instead of fur.

'Look, Donald,' Phoebe says, and her lion growls in acknowledgement. It takes me a moment to understand why, then I spot the stuffed toy clutched in the little girl's arms as she cowers away from the wolf-children.

'Mixed nightmare,' Rafe says over the helmets. 'Poisoners and pack. This is a dangerous one all round, guys.'

We form a circle around the group. Samson places himself near to the dreamer, ready to jump in front of her at the opportune moment. We attack as one, Samson slipping in between the dreamer and her tormentors, and tackling the wolf-children head on, while the rest of us move in from the sides. We're clumsy. We used to instinctively know which one of us was tackling which nightmare. Now we have to think about where the holes are and who is covering them. Still, we find our rhythm. Samson takes out four wolf-children at a time, firing one arrow from his bow and using the next like a rapier. Rafe leaps into the air like a gazelle, bringing his club down in just the right place to tackle a wolf-child that's got Ollie in a bit of a bind. I try to do my bit, but I'm rusty using my scimitar.

When the last wolf-child has been destroyed, we allow ourselves a rare moment of congratulation. After the events of the other night, it's a much needed boost. But our satisfaction is short-lived. The inspyre whirls into motion and reforms into more wolf-children. They chase the little girl as a pack, snapping and jeering.

'This is too quick,' Samson says. 'Poisoners don't normally reform in the same night.'

'It's too strong in her head,' Ollie says. 'I can feel her fear from here.'

‘We’re going to have to see if we can wake her up,’ Rafe says. ‘Harker? Where’s our nearest portal?’ My focus is on Phoebe, though. She is staring at the little girl. One of her hands is curled tightly into Donald’s mane. I look between Phoebe, Donald and the little girl clutching her cuddly bear, and I realise what I need to do.

‘Let me try something,’ I say.

I follow the dreamer with an outstretched hand, testing the inspyre that is creating the toy in her arms. There. I can feel its edges. I can feel how tightly she is holding it. The crackle in my brain travels down my neck, through my shoulders and my arms and leaps from my fingertips towards the girl.

Grow, I command it. *Be real.*

There’s a resistance. The little girl is imagining her toy too strongly, clinging to it for comfort. I give her a little shove with my mind, trying to throw her imagination off kilter for long enough to grant me control over it. She falters and shrinks from the nightmares even further . . . but it’s enough. The toy leaps from her arms. It twists, gathering inspyre like a tornado. It grows and grows and finally, when it has fallen to the ground, it unfurls itself. The bear draws its little girl close, gathering her into the fur of its stomach. It looks down upon the snapping wolf-children. And. It. ROARS.

I will always remember that moment. The moment when the wolf-children cringed away from the bear and popped, one by one, back into inspyre. The way the little girl looked up at her bear, grown huge and alive, with an expression that said she’d found her protector forever and always. These are the candles that live inside the chests of the knights: a flame that tells us that we have done something worthwhile with our existence. My God, it's addictive.

For the rest of the regiment, the victory is a renewal of our vows to be thanes. The treitres haven't broken our spirits. Not yet.

We trot along the Southbank, the Thames rippling with sailing boats on our left.

'Do you remember,' Phoebe says, 'when Ramesh thought he saw a giant turtle and dived in?'

'I can't believe he thought he'd be able to ride it,' Rafe says.

We all laugh. A sad, fond laugh.

Ramesh. Or, as I must come to know him – Rayensh.

The message had come through that afternoon.

Rayensh's funeral will be held on Friday 30th March at 4 p.m., in St Margaret's Church.

There will be a small wake at our home afterwards. All friends are welcome to attend.

Natasha had warned us not to go looking for the fallen in real life. 'It's an unspoken rule,' she'd said. 'I know it might seem like it would give you closure, but it's not fair on the dead.'

'Did you lose someone in Annwn then?' Phoebe had asked.

'Only once, about seven years ago, but he was my best friend. I tracked him down and I wish I hadn't. It turned out his real life friends were quite nasty. He looked nothing like he did in Annwn. Didn't even have the same name. Anyway, it changed my memories of him. Messed with my head.'

Well, I already know that Ramesh doesn't look like he did in Annwn and that he doesn't have the same name. But from what I've read, he wasn't that different from the Ramesh I knew.

Anyway, I can't exactly get high and mighty about someone wanting a fresh start here. Going to Ramesh's funeral feels like the only way I can honour what he did for me. He was loyal and open and he made me think about people differently, and I'm starting to understand that that's what friendship means.

43

March 1996

Una's eyes flitted around the knights' chamber as soon as she arrived, as they had done every night for the last week. Yet again, Ellen hadn't turned up. Una spotted Lionel and Clement deep in conversation, perched on the armchairs in the corner.

'The harkers can't find her,' Lionel told Una as soon as she arrived.

'It's been six days. She can't have been awake for –' Clement tried to do the math, '– that many hours.'

'Which means two things could have happened,' Una said. 'Either she's dead, or she's alive but can't get into Annwn.'

The three knights looked at each other, their worry reflected in each other's faces.

'I looked, you know,' Clement said quietly, glancing around to make sure no one else was listening. 'In Ithr. For her.'

He hung his head, clearly awaiting their judgement.

'So did I,' Lionel said.

'Me too,' Una told him. They started laughing, but not too loudly in case it angered Sebastien Medraut, who was holding court on the other side of the room.

A voice echoed through the gramophone that sat beside the mantelpiece.

'Una Gorlois, can you come to the entrance?'

Una sprang to her feet and was out of the door before the others could even think about following. She jogged past the harkers' tables, running through scenarios in her head. She couldn't be in trouble because, for once, she hadn't done anything wrong – or nothing that the harkers could have seen, anyway. It had to be Ellen, didn't it? A harker was waiting for her near the castle doors. He beckoned her over.

'She's outside.'

Una broke into a sprint. What could have happened? If Ellen was injured she would have been brought straight to the hospital, surely? Out on the porch, Una looked around wildly for her friend. There she was, standing on the platform clasping her portal in one hand. In the other she held her weapon – a great fang – as though she was expecting to be attacked even inside the castle walls.Una ran over and they stood in each other's arms for a long time.

Ellen wasn't injured, or not that Una could see anyway. She felt like a toy that had some of the stuffing ripped out of it.

'Where have you been?' she whispered.

'In Ithr.'

'Awake?'

'I took some drugs that let me sleep without dreaming.'

'Can you come into the castle?'

'No. Please don't make me.'

She could barely hear Ellen's voice, even with their heads so close together.

'I'll never make you do anything,' Una said. She knew she had to tread delicately.

'Shall we walk in the gardens then?' she suggested.

Eventually Ellen nodded. As they'd done so often before, Una tucked Ellen's arm into the crook of her elbow.

In silence, they walked around the back of the castle. The herb garden emerged like a shy child from the corner of Tintagel. A few apothecaries were tending to the plants, but they didn't look up.

'I just . . . It all got too much, here,' Ellen said eventually. 'I wanted to help. I *do* want to help. It's so important, what we do, isn't it?'

'Well, yes. But we're not far off being squires ourselves. We're still learning.'

'But if we miss just one dreamer, if we can't defeat one single nightmare, then someone dies. We may as well be murderers ourselves.'

'In Ithr we don't call police or doctors murderers if they can't save someone.'

'You think I'm catastrophising.'

'I don't even know what that means, dearling.'

'Yes, you do.' Ellen smiled. Una had been protective of her friend since they had first met, but not because she thought that Ellen was a drip. Ellen had proved herself many times over out on patrol. She was a considered warrior, which was exactly what Lancelot needed with hotheads like Una and

Clement on board. Ellen would always be the one to find a different approach to tackling a nightmare, or she'd surprise them all when a fight seemed to be lost, channelling whatever monster her fang came from to clinch a victory.

'If it weren't for the panic attacks . . .' Una began.

'They're getting worse.'

'Do you remember what you did, the first day we met?' she asked Ellen.

'That seems so long ago now.'

'You hissed at Sebastien Medraut. You *hissed* at the most powerful thane Annwn has seen since Arthur. I couldn't have done it.'

Ellen laughed, Una laughed. Their merriment echoed against the castle until it seemed as though Tintagel was laughing with them. Beneath Una's laughter, though, anger brewed. Not with Ellen, but with this whole situation. Ellen was too young to have become a thane when she did. Some people could handle it at fifteen and some couldn't. Why couldn't the Founding Thanes have understood that? Why had no one changed the rules over the centuries? It was barbaric. They were going to lose a talented knight because the system was too rigid.

Una took Ellen's hands in her own.

'I can't stop you from leaving if that's what's best for you, dearling. But if you stay, I promise that I will find a way of helping you. It might take me some time, but I won't stop until I do it.'

'If it was possible, don't you think they'd have managed it by now?' Ellen said.

'*They* are not *me*. Have you ever known me to give up?'

Ellen looked at her with a fierce belief. The kind of belief someone puts in a god or a parent; the kind that never recovers once it's toppled.

'No. No, I know you'll find a way.'

44

When Friday comes round I'm still off school on bedrest. With all morning to kill before I need to leave for the funeral, I decide to do some drawing. That plan's scuppered by Dad coming in with a breakfast treat of eggs Benedict.

'I don't think so, love,' he says, plonking the tray on my desk and plucking the drawings from my hand. 'If you're well enough to be drawing, you're well enough to learn. Might do you good to go back to school.'

I huff and puff, but he's immovable. I'll have to find another way of getting to Ramesh's funeral.

I hatch my plan in the afternoon break. Slipping into the girls' toilets, I fiddle around in my bag for some make-up. I'm applying white powder to my chin when Lottie Medraut walks in. I freeze, revulsion and anger turning my bones to concrete. She hesitates when she sees me, but then joins me at the mirror. I force myself to carry on as if the daughter of a mass murderer isn't standing next to me. I wonder whether Lottie knows what kind of man her father really is.

I can feel her side-eyeing me.

'I'm not trying to look pretty or anything,' I snap.

'Of course not. It's not like that's what make-up's for.'

She steps back and studies me more intently as I dab red eyeshadow under my eyes. Then she says something unexpected. 'You're trying to skive off school. I used to do that when I wanted to go home and train my puppy. You're doing it all wrong. Come here.'

And she turns me round and grabs the brush from my hand. Before I can say anything she's sweeping it across my skin.

'How sick are you wanting to look?'

'Umm. I don't know. Not too much. Just like I have a migraine or something? Maybe a nosebleed?'

'Okay, hang on.' She fumbles in her own bag for some lipliner. My embarrassment at her probably being able to see my nostril hair is matched by bafflement. She doesn't owe me anything. Is she planning on grassing me up as soon as I get permission to leave? Is she in on some elaborate plan of her father's to trick me into getting suspended?

'So have you actually been ill these last few days or were you skiving the whole time?' she asks me.

I want to tell her that the reason I've been off school is because her father ordered the murder of a ton of my friends. 'Actually ill,' I say instead. 'I went to hospital.'

'Damn.' She draws the word out into two syllables: *day-um*.

She smiles, and I find myself warily smiling back. 'There.' She finishes up, and I look in the mirror. She's done it perfectly. I look just ill enough, with a smeared bloody streak beneath my nose to suggest I've tried to clean it.

'You could be a make-up artist on movies,' I tell her.

'I could be a lot of things,' she says primly, returning to her own make-up. I have no idea how to reply to such an assured statement.

As she leaves I blurt out, 'Your dad . . .'

She waits for me to finish, but I have no idea what I was going to say. Your dad's planning on mass-brainwashing the country?

'Ugh, don't tell me you like him as well,' she sighs. 'Look, I'm sure you're fine, Fern, but seriously, this whole deal with people our age fancying him is just gross.'

'I don't . . .' I start indignantly, but she's already gone.

The chemistry teacher takes one look at me and sends me home. 'Get a taxi, won't you? You shouldn't be getting the tube in your state.'

Ah, another demonstration of how little these people know about my family. As if we'd have the money for a taxi across London. As I head for the Underground and scrub Lottie's make-up from my face I only feel a little guilty. Saying goodbye to Ramesh is more important than science.

The church is a Victorian stone affair in the middle of a huge cemetery, not all that far from the one where my mother is buried. As I approach, I watch a familiar figure hugging a woman who can only be Ramesh's mother. The figure pulls away gently, then walks down another path. It takes a moment for me to understand what Helena Corday must be doing. Of course, Ramesh's family are her constituents too. How thoroughly decent, to pay her respects then leave before her presence turns the funeral into a PR exercise.

I approach Ramesh's mother – an ashen woman with his nose. She hands me an order of service. It's got a photo of Ramesh's face on the cover. I can't help but think of the last time I saw that face. 'And how did you know Rayensh?' she asks me.

I take a punt. 'We met online.'

'Ah. Well, he did love his games. Thank you for coming. I suppose you might know him better than some of the friends here from school.' She casts a dark look at a group of teenage girls who are taking sad-face selfies. I want to run away and hug her all at once. It must be awful to know that your child wasn't actually that popular. Maybe that's how Dad would act if I died in Annwn. I imagine Lottie and her gaggle turning up. No, Dad would pretend I was popular at Bosco, turn a blind eye to the fakeness.

I find a pew at the back of the church and look around. Thankfully the hoodie I brought to cover my hair and face isn't as out of place as I feared it might be. The church is filled with a mix of older people I assume are Ramesh's family, people from his school looking for an afternoon off and a handful of fellow hoodie wearers who seem to have been genuine friends.

The organist is playing a reedy version of a tune from a movie soundtrack. It's one of my favourites and it makes me smile and ache at the thought that Ramesh must have loved it as well. I wonder what else we had in common.

Surreptitiously, I look around for anyone else who looks like they're here on their own. The goth girl who said Ramesh saved her life sits near the front. A few others are scattered around, but I don't recognise any of them from the thanes. But just as the service starts, the door opens again and someone I do know slips inside. Ollie. He glances at me before sitting at the other end of my pew. We studiously ignore each other for the next hour. His presence helps me not to cry. Ramesh's dad reads a poem in a dry, wracked voice. Ramesh's middle sister gives a short speech, looking over the congregation with cold fury, as though challenging us to grieve as much as her.

I know I should be focusing on Ramesh, but seeing his family crumble brings home the reality of what I do every night. So far I've been able to keep my two lives separate. It's been easy to think of Phoebe and Samson and the others as being dreams, in a way. Sitting here, watching Ramesh's coffin being carried past me, makes what happens in Annwn so much more real.

I decide not to go to the wake. It's too risky – there are too many questions that could be asked. Ollie, it seems, thinks the same, because we both start down the road towards home instead of veering left like the rest of the congregation.

'You know what I can't get my head around?' Ollie says.

'What?'

'That Medraut thinks he's totally right. In his head, we're stopping him from saving everyone.'

'How do you know?'

'I felt it, in that box of his. To him, anyone who tries to stop him is working against the best interests of humanity. He can't see it any differently. That was the hardest part about touching that box. Getting his feelings in my head. It was like I was being polluted by all his thoughts.'

I don't say anything. Once, a different Fern would have made a snippy remark about my brother's thoughts being polluted already, but I know now that Ollie's vindictiveness had the same roots as my self-pity – fear. If I'm not a lost cause then neither is he.

As we get closer to home, I realise that our quickest route is going to take us past the spot where Jenny and her gang hang out. I can sense Ollie tensing beside me.

'Do you think . . .?' he begins.

'No,' I say. 'I'm done with running from that cow.'

I mean it, too. Jenny is a speck now. If I can't face her, how am I ever supposed to face Medraut?

We continue walking, preparing ourselves for what might happen. When we do see her, swinging her legs against the wall she's sitting on, I can't believe how young she looks. When she spots us, she leaps down onto the pavement. Her friends amass behind her.

I stuff my hands in my pockets. So does Ollie. He looks straight ahead, but I meet Jenny's gaze, and I hold it as we approach. My blood pumps more aggressively; my muscles twitch with awareness. If I were in Annwn right now, I swear I'd have inspyre crackling around me. That's how powerful I feel. Jenny recognises it too, because although she looks like she wants to start something, she never moves towards us. As we pass her, close enough to see the pins on her bag, I finally break eye contact. I know that she won't follow us. The spell she once held over me has been broken, and in turn whatever was broken between Ollie and I is starting to heal.

45

We may have faced down Jenny, but that doesn't mean I can tackle everyone who comes after me. Things are getting worse in Ithr. Medraut's influence is becoming stronger. His nightmares have done more than take root; they have grown into strong, vigorous trees that block out all light. I take to walking to school, even if it does mean leaving the house at six and forgoing my regular visit to Mum's grave, because tube journeys are so uncomfortable for me these days. In any case, I don't feel the same need to sit beside her headstone when I have the portrait of her in my locker in Tintagel.

But it all comes to a head one sweaty April afternoon. It's rush hour and Stratford is a slalom course of shoppers and locals and commuters at the best of times, so it takes me a while to notice the suited man who keeps glancing back at me as I stomp through the shopping centre. When I accidentally catch his eye, he stops dead in his tracks and I almost plough into him.

'What do you want?'

He towers over me, his bulk not hidden by a tailored suit.

'What?'

'You're following me.'

I step back, but he steps forward. This close up, I can see that he's shaking with anger. His fist is gripping his briefcase so tightly it's turned white.

'I'm – I'm just going home,' I stutter.

He snorts and steps forward again, until I am backed up against the glass wall of a shoe shop. Other commuters hurry past us, heads down.

'You want my wallet, is that it?' He pulls his wallet out of his pocket and brandishes it in my face. 'Well, I'm wise to you lot now. In fact . . .'

He pulls out his phone as well, which in any other situation would make me laugh because he has to do a weird juggle to hold his wallet and briefcase in one hand. He dials 999.

'Police. A strange-looking creature is harassing me.'

I don't wait to hear the rest, but dodge past him and leg it. His shouts follow me through crowds of shoppers who look astounded at the girl pushing them out of the way. One woman tries to stop me, obviously assuming I'm a thief.

'I know what you look like, monster!' is the last thing I hear before I turn a corner and pass beyond reach.

I run the final mile home. I push the door shut and lock the chain before I let myself collapse against it. I press the heels of my hands into my eyes, taking deep breaths to stop myself from crying. When Ollie gets home he has to bang on the door for me to let him in.

'What's wrong?' he says as soon as he sees me. 'Did Jenny do something?'

'Medraut.'

I finally give in to the tears that I'd been keeping at bay. Ollie holds my upper arms as though he'd like to hug me but isn't sure it would be welcomed.

'Come on,' he says eventually. 'Dad's left us fish pie.'

Ollie puts the TV on while we eat dinner. I feel inexplicably awkward throughout the whole thing. We are not a family that sits in companionable silence in front of a costume drama. The only silence we've historically understood is the passive-aggressive kind. But I like the charade, so when we're finished I take Ollie's plate and wash it up alongside mine.

'See, we can be normal,' he says, perhaps sharing my unease at this new turn of events.

I smile. 'Speak for yourself.'

The drama ends and the news picks up the gauntlet.

'And rising star of Government, Sebastien Medraut, today issues a warning in the wake of the mysterious phenomenon that saw over four hundred people die in their sleep . . .'

'Turn it off,' Ollie says, but I don't make any move towards the remote control. I want to know what he's up to; I want to know how he's spinning his mass murder into votes. When the segment comes, though, I can barely watch it.

'As the families of those who died in their sleep call for research into the phenomenon, MP for Chelsea, Sebastien Medraut, suggests an alternative cause.'

The footage of the newsreader cuts to a clip of Medraut speaking from a podium. Once again, I notice that he has eschewed the traditional microphone, talking quietly and relying on the power of his charisma to silence his audience. He talks about the dangers of science, about progress for progress's' sake. He subtly suggests, in a way that no one could ever accuse of being unsympathetic to those who died, that perhaps the reason for the deaths lies closer to home. *Look at the people who died,* he says with everything but his actual words. *They were outliers. They were weirdos. Maybe they brought it upon themselves. You have nothing to fear unless you, too, are Different*. And when he's finished speaking, his audience erupts with applause.

As soon as I enter Tintagel, I can feel my own anger join the anger of every other soul in the castle. People whisper and hiss about Medraut's statement. In the knights' chamber, Rafe and Amina are crying. Phoebe is sitting in the armchair that was once Ramesh's, dazedly running her hands through Donald's fur. All the loss that we'd absorbed has been extracted from our still stinging bodies and flung at us once more. Samson hails me from one corner. 'Lord Allenby wants to see us. Come on.' We pick up Ollie on our way out of the chamber.

Lord Allenby is the first truly calm person I've seen since entering Tintagel. The captains of the other lores are there already. He gestures for us to take a spare seat. 'We've had intelligence from our friends in Manchester and Edinburgh that Medraut is likely to be planning another attack soon. They've noticed unauthorised portals appearing in parts of the cities where dreamers commonly congregate. At the moment they don't seem to be connected to anywhere else in Annwn, which is puzzling because that shouldn't be possible. It suggests that it's Medraut's doing.'

'We haven't noticed anything here, sir,' Samson says, 'but that doesn't mean they're not in London too. As you know, we haven't had the numbers to do more than protect dreamers since Ostara.'

'I know, Samson, and I'm not blaming you in the slightest. Maisie, have you seen anything?'

The captain of the harkers shakes her head. 'We've seen a lot of strange things over the last few months, sir, but we'd have noticed any illegal portals.'

'That's what worries me,' Lord Allenby sighs. 'There's been no sign that Medraut has set up fortresses anywhere else in Annwn, and no sign of treitre activity elsewhere either. It makes me think that he's planning on repeating his attack at Ostara, connecting those portals back to London, so he can move his treitres from Madame Tussaud's to the rest of the country. But we need to know who his targets are and when he's going to launch this attack.'

'I can't authorise another infiltration attempt,' says the captain of the apothecaries.

When and who. I desperately wrack my brains for something valuable to contribute to the discussion.

'Isn't he repeating the pattern of what he did fifteen years ago?' Ollie asks. 'Could we figure something out from that?'

Fifteen years ago . . . I feel sure that I do know something helpful – it's hiding in a far corner of my memory . . .

'Beltane!' I blurt out.

Seven faces turn towards me.

'Beltane's only a week away, sir.' I turn to Ollie for backup. 'Do you remember Mum's recording from Ithr? They kept on mentioning the first of May.'

'That's right,' Ollie says. 'He launches his attacks on dates where the walls between Ithr and Annwn are at their thinnest.'

'It must be easier to use his Immral then,' the veneur captain suggests. 'Dreamers' minds are more susceptible, maybe?'

Lord Allenby nods slowly. 'That would make sense. Fern, Ollie, can you think of anything else from Una's notebooks that might be useful?'

Ollie and I shake our heads. 'We're still going through the papers we found in Annwn,' Ollie says, 'but she doesn't really talk about Medraut in those.'

'No, she probably wouldn't have,' Lord Allenby says heavily. 'If she did most of her research when he was Head Thane she would have been worried about them falling into the wrong hands. Still, go back over them tonight. If Medraut's attack is indeed only a week away we've barely got enough time to organise counter-measures. While you do that, I'll consult with the other thaneships.'

Ollie and I fly back to the knights' chamber and pull out Mum's old papers from our lockers, but there are only a few that even mention Medraut. These pages are not neat annotations or research notes; they're laden with emotion. All of them are dated after March 2005, when the golden treitre took Mum's best friend as its first victim. About a month after the first attack, she becomes more philosophical.

We are spending too much time focusing on what makes it a monster. As with everything that is frightening to us, the most important thing is to find out what makes it human.

I scribble it down; it makes me think of my own encounter with the golden treitre, and the way it listened to me so intently.

By the time the others return from their patrols we are tossing the final pages back onto their respective piles.

'Nothing!' Ollie storms. 'She must've written thousands of pages on bloody morrigans and the philosophy of fear, but she can't put an ounce of time into figuring out what Medraut might do next?'

'Well, it was always a long shot,' Samson says. 'What we really need is someone on the inside, but we've tried all the avenues we can with no luck. Medraut's rightly wary now, after the stunt I pulled. Well, at least we have a probable date, Fern, thanks to you.'

But Samson's comment has sparked a plan. 'Oh,' I say. 'Oh, you might have more than that.'

46

It doesn't take long for the harkers to find Lottie at her fancy home in Chelsea. That's our first bit of bad news. Medraut's place has been under surveillance for fifteen years, and not only has he never been sighted there but any knights who've tried to enter haven't come back the same; they are alive, but in name only.

Still, we have to try.

'It's a long shot, and it's going to be every bit as dangerous as retrieving Samson was, I'm afraid, but you're right, Fern,' Lord Allenby tells us as we mount Lamb and Balius. 'You could find a memory in Lottie Medraut that might help us understand what he's got planned. It's got to be worth a shot.'

It makes me nervous, how galvanised he is. If I'm wrong then I've given all of them false hope.

I know the area well from my time at Bosco – I've never been invited back to anyone's home but I hear talk of who lives on which street. All the houses here are terraced Victorian goliaths. Some of them delve deep underground like icebergs, hiding gyms and swimming pools.

Sebastien Medraut's house, though, is on another level

entirely. There aren't many detached houses in this part of London but he owns one of them. An oak-lined drive leads up to a double-fronted mansion. In Annwn, the trees are filled with parrots and monkeys. In one, a leopard lies on a branch, swinging its tail as it observes Ollie and me.

Medraut's house isn't guarded by aventures as his fortress in Royal Arsenal was but it's impossible not to worry that someone might be watching us. We avoid the path and edge along the hedge of the neighbouring garden. We leave the horses grazing there and leap over the foliage, landing on one side of the house. I look up at the windows.

'I can't see anyone.'

We dart to the porch. I look at Ollie. 'We could lose our minds if we go in here.'

'Do it,' he says.

With a crackle of inspyre the lock shunts aside. The door opens noiselessly.

I know immediately that something's not right with this place. At first, everything looks as it should. A few dreams drift across marbled floors and up a carpeted staircase. Butlers and maids etched in blue. A large dog, more fur than animal, bounds up to us and licks my hands enthusiastically. But I cannot bring myself to set foot inside. Ollie feels it as well. It's not exactly the same as the nausea that Medraut's kalends gave us, but it's a distant cousin. Ollie tugs at my arm and gestures upwards. We'll try to find Lottie through the windows, instead of entering the house.

While Ollie creeps around the building on the ground, I fly up and press myself against the wall next to one of the bedroom windows. I peer inside. This must be the master suite. It's an apartment in itself – striped sofas and an antique armchair sit at the end of a king-size bed, while exquisite vases brimming with flowers stand guard on each side table.

I fly on, past a bathroom, another empty bedroom, and another bathroom. Ollie mirrors me from below. We strike lucky with the final window, on the far side of the house overlooking the grounds. Lottie sits on her bed facing away from us, perfectly still. In front of her on the otherwise bare wall is a portrait of her father.

I signal to Ollie to join me, then press my hand gently against the glass. With a twinge in the back of my skull, I silently disappear the glass. I am about to climb in when Ollie stops me and points to something attached to another wall. At first I think it's a camera, but when I crane to get a better view I can see that it's some kind of weapon; half gun, half telescope. It's pointing at the door to Lottie's room. I use the inspyre from the window to create a mirror, and hold it just inside the frame. Sure enough, another weapon sits above the window on the inside, pointing at the floor where I was about to stand. I raise my eyebrows at Ollie in thanks.

I use a little more of the inspyre to create a cat, and let it pad its way through the window and onto the carpet. It steps forward, prepares to leap onto the bed.

One moment it's tensing its back legs, the next a pitch-black beam bursts from the weapon with a deep boom, and the cat is shredded into its component inspyre. Ollie and I cry out, not just from shock but from the instant punch of sickness that hit us when the weapon activated. A sickness that is all too familiar.

'What was that?' Ollie gasps.

'I think,' I answer, still clutching my stomach, 'that was a kalend.'

So this is how Medraut has been keeping people away from his house. This is why he doesn't need guards. He has booby-trapped the one thing of interest – his daughter – with kalends, so that anyone getting too close will lose their mind.

Lottie hasn't moved throughout the chaos going on behind her. I am momentarily reminded of Jenny, who struggled to imagine anything beyond her own bedroom, but this feels different. This feels as though Lottie is being held there against her will. I try to throw my Immral towards her, to sense whether there's anything binding her. Sure enough, there are invisible restraints around her legs and head.

I turn to Ollie. 'I can get her free, but I don't know how to pull her out without putting us in the line of fire.'

'I've got an idea,' he says. 'Give me that mirror.'

I hand it to him and he carefully inches his way just inside the window. He drops the mirror onto the floor, then looks at me.

'Get the restraints off her, then when I say go, pull her out as quickly as you can, okay?'

I nod and get to work, using my mind to prise away the bindings holding Lottie in position. It takes far longer than I'd like, but the rope resists my attempts to simply turn it back into inspyre, and because I can't see it I am having to use my power to sense where it is. At last, though, it's done. I nod at Ollie, taking a firm grip of Lottie's waist with my mind.

Ollie nudges the mirror forward, painstakingly slowly.

'Nearly there,' he says. 'Get ready.'

He nudges the mirror forwards again.

'And . . . *go*!'

I pull Lottie with all my might as Ollie pushes the mirror directly in line with the gun above the window. It activates instantly, but instead of burning up the mirror, its beam bounces up and catches the other gun. The two weapons battle with each other, trying to suck each other into their kalends via the mirror. Then, with a great crack, they shatter, casting fragments of thick steel across Lottie's bedroom.

Lottie herself has landed spread-eagled on the grass beneath her window. For an instant, she just lies there. Then she flops over onto her back, laughing, and rolls down the lawn like a maniac.

Checking that no one has heard the weapons exploding, Ollie and I float to the ground and follow her. I can't help but like Lottie a little more, seeing her like this. She's so carefree, so young, so childish. It's such a contrast to the teenage girl at school who acts as though she's already in her twenties, or the one just now who was sitting uncannily still, staring at her own father's portrait.

'How do you want to do this then?' Ollie asks.

I take Lottie by the arm, leading her to a bench that overlooks a lake. Koi carp gather at the surface of the water, expecting food. Something huge emerges from the depths and snaps a couple up before sinking out of sight.

Ollie sits on Lottie's other side.

'So?' I say. 'Work your magic.'

'Yes, boss,' Ollie snarks, but he closes his eyes and places his hands on Lottie's temples.

'Anything?' I ask.

'Give me a minute, will you?'

I bite my tongue. I hate not knowing what's going on.

'Does this girl have *any* friends?' Ollie says.

'Tons, why?'

'Because literally all her memories are of her dad. It's like she's obsessed with him.'

'Is he saying anything useful in the memories?'

'No, it's all boring.' Ollie adjusts his grip slightly and freezes. 'Wait.'

I wait. He doesn't say anything.

'Hello?' I say at last, prodding his leg.

'There's something here. I don't understand – it's like one of her memories is blocked. Something's stopping me from getting to it.'

'But that's probably the one we want!'

'All right, Captain Obvious.'

'Well, you're a lot of use, aren't you?' I say, and grab his elbow to see for myself. My sight is replaced by Lottie's memories. Ollie was right. All I can see is Medraut's face. No one else features; not her mum, not one of her many friends. Then I see what Ollie means. In my peripheral vision I can see other memories, but straight ahead of me is a void. I press against it. I become aware of a taste in my mouth, like I got with Jenny and with the golden treitre. The blockage, whatever it is, is rancid.

'I think it's an emotion,' I say.

Ollie raises an eyebrow as if to say, *What do you know about other people's feelings?* but when he focuses on Lottie again it's with renewed energy.

'You're right,' he says eventually. 'I think – it's like a wall made of pure fear.'

I consider the void, rolling it around my senses. Ollie's right. It's the kind of fear that only resides in the darkest nightmares – fear of murdering someone and not knowing whether to confess or to try to live with the guilt. Of being taken in the middle of the night and killed slowly, bit by bit, until the mind is screaming for death even as the broken body is holding on to life. Behind that wall, so faint I can barely feel it, is the truth.

I pull away. A trickle of blood is meandering from Ollie's nose to his mouth. He wipes it away and looks at me. 'She does know something, doesn't she? And her dad's blocked it so she can't tell anyone.'

'Looks like it, but I've no idea how to get through that wall.'

Ollie considers for a long time. When he speaks, he's very deliberately not looking at me, as though even he doesn't like what he's about to say.

'You could hurt her.'

'What?'

'It feels to me like that's the only thing that might bring down that wall of fear. If you could . . . overcome the fear with something bigger. Maybe that would reveal the memory.'

I gape at Ollie. 'That's torture.'

'It's nothing you haven't done before, with Jenny.'

'How do you know about that?'

'Oh, think about it, Fern. I can read minds, remember?'

'You had no right –'

'Ramesh said –'

'*Don't* talk to me about Ramesh.' The thought of Ramesh alongside what Ollie's asking me to do is too wrong.

We fall into silence, but now I can't stop thinking about Ramesh, and Emory, and all the knights Medraut has killed. He might do it again if we don't stop him. Hundreds of potential deaths and I'm wavering over hurting one person? The image of Ramesh's headless body toppling from his horse plays in slow motion in my head.

'I don't like it either, Fern,' Ollie says, 'but if she can help us find out what Medraut's going to do, wouldn't it be worth it?'

'We took a vow . . .'

'Do you think she'd treat you any differently if she had Immral?' Ollie continues. 'She's just like Jenny, you know.'

'She's not actually.'

'If she grew up like us she would be. She thinks you're a freak.'

'You don't know that.' I don't know why I'm so hurt by what Ollie said. It's not like I ever wanted to be friends with Lottie.

'Dad always says that if anyone hurt us he'd kill them. That's what you do when you love someone – he'd do it if he knew about Mum and if he had your power.'

'He – he wouldn't. Not this,' I say, uncertain.

'Mum would have done it for us,' Ollie says, leaning forwards. 'How can you know that Medraut was behind her death and not do anything you can to get justice for her?'

Quickly, not letting myself think, I place both hands on either side of Lottie's face. I don't have anything as refined as fire this time, just pure, harsh, nightmare energy lifted from the pool of my soul where all my anger lives, pushed up, out, down, leaping across the divide between my palms and her head, digging into her skull.

Lottie's scream almost dissolves my willpower, but Ollie takes that moment to grab my wrist, keeping it flush against her skin. Ollie starts feeding me memories. Not Lottie's memories but memories of Mum being killed. He's forcing me to relive her murder.

'Remember what we're here for,' Ollie says.

I send the pain deeper into Lottie's mind, hating myself more with every second that passes. I seek that void, pummelling against the darkness. The barrier seems to have a mind of its own, pushing against me then receding, as though we're in a tug of war. We start to catch glimpses of the memory beneath it.

An office, one I recognise from the house behind us – Medraut's office. Lottie is peering through a crack in the door. She's checking the room is empty. She slips inside and closes the door behind her. Medraut's desk is spookily tidy: no pens, no family photos. Just a two-tiered tray – an inbox and an outbox, each holding a small stack of papers, and his laptop lying closed in the centre of the desk.

Lottie pulls at drawers, but they're all locked. Then she opens the laptop and tries a few passwords. At last she finds the right one – *SILENCE* – and the screen reveals itself. Lottie clicks randomly on files and emails, until she comes across a folder marked *Bright Fire*. When she clicks on it, a series of websites and scanned articles appear, all amalgamated into a single presentation. Lottie scrolls through them. The first page is population figures for each part of the country, and the rest is lists. Endless lists of places and names. Why on earth would anyone want to hide something so dull?

Then I come across a list of names that I recognise. Politicians, all of whom oppose Medraut's party. Helena Corday's name is near the top. I think back over the other entries, and realise that there is a connection. Journalists who've written unflattering pieces about Medraut. Scientists at the top of their fields. Actors, writers, musicians and teachers. Further down, the lists become even more sinister. The names become whole addresses: homes for the elderly, schools for people with disabilities.

'Ollie,' I say, my voice distant through Lottie's memories. 'Beltane means "bright fire" in old Celtic, doesn't it?'

I think of the portals around the country, waiting to be activated, and of the vision from the puzzle box. 'Oh my God. He's going to use the treitres on dreamers. It's a purge.'

But Ollie doesn't answer me because in the memory there's a creak, and Lottie looks up from the screen. Medraut is in the doorway, watching her. She slams the laptop shut, terrified.

'Daddy, I'm s-sorry,' she stutters in her honeyed voice. 'I just . . .'

Medraut says nothing as he approaches her.

'Daddy, no, I only wanted – Daddy, please, no!'

Medraut reaches out to her, and everything goes black.

Lottie's screams fade in again. I can't help but push to see more – what did he do to her? I must be able to see that if I just try hard enough . . .

'Fern!' Ollie shouts suddenly. 'Fern, stop it! What are you doing? Stop, for God's sake!'

I pull away from Lottie and watch in horror as she sinks

back against the bench, her eyes wide, her mouth opening and shutting like one of the fish in the lake next to us. I examine her for blood, but can't see any. I feel my own face – I'm fine. I look up at Ollie, wondering why he made me stop when I was so close to getting more answers. But Ollie isn't looking at me. He's looking behind me. I turn, dread pooling in my stomach.

Lord Allenby and Samson stand at the edge of the lawn. Their horrified eyes are fixed on me.

Ollie has betrayed me yet again.

47

Lord Allenby might be the one dragging me by my arm. He might be the one who throws me into his office so hard I land against the wall with a painful crunch. But I am every bit as furious as him; every bit as up for a fight. The lot of them can go to hell as far as I'm concerned. Allenby. Samson. Ollie. Especially Ollie. The way he ducked away the moment Lord Allenby showed up, avoiding my gaze, staying silent when he could have told Lord Allenby that it was his idea. This fresh treachery prickles through my blood like poison.

'Torturing a dreamer, Fern? Is that how you've decided to use your power now?'

'You told me to find a way. We needed that information!'

'Not like that, Fern,' Lord Allenby says desperately. 'I said to look for anything obvious, not to hurt her, for God's sake. Don't you realise that's how it starts? Do you think Medraut was always the man he is now? Don't you think he justified his crimes to himself the same way you're doing?'

'I did it for you!' I say, but I know that's not strictly true. I did it for Mum, for Ramesh, and for me. The pain and terror on

Lottie's face will never leave my conscience, but I tell myself it was worth it.

'He's going to kill thousands of people, and you're worried about one dreamer?'

'I'm worried about every dreamer,' Allenby says. 'I'm worried about all my thanes and all the other thanes. Fern, I'm terrified that Medraut's going to win. But as soon as I stop worrying about one person I may as well stop worrying about all of them. Don't you see?'

He goes to the wall and presses his hands against it. He doesn't speak for a long time. I am very aware of the hardness of the wooden panelling pressing into my back. When he speaks again, he sounds perfectly calm.

'Tell me what to do, Miss King.'

'What to do?'

'You've put me in an impossible position. In normal circumstances I would have you taken to the morrigans for what you've just done. But you're too valuable to me.'

I don't know how to answer him. With his anger turned to resignation, I turn my own inwards, where it ought to be, where it should have been all along.

'Your mother would never have wanted you to do what you just did,' he says. 'If she'd known you'd become this, she would never have held me to that oath.'

'I'm sorry,' I whisper, devastated at the thought of Mum's disappointment.

Lord Allenby turns back to me.

'We'll put it behind us for now, and talk about how to deal with it afterwards.'

'No,' I say.

'Fern?'

'I can't.' Lottie's scream, her agonised face. I had wanted to see what Medraut did to her, but why? He had done exactly what I did to her. Two people who should have been protecting her – one her father, one a sworn guardian – instead tortured her for their own ends. Is this the path I'm on now? To follow in Medraut's footsteps, to let my power take hold of my conscience, to believe I am above right and wrong?

Ramesh thought that I was better than this, but the truth is that I'm not at all. He thought I was meant to be in the knights, but he was mistaken.

'You should never have let me take the Tournament,' I tell Lord Allenby.

The realisation that I've let Ramesh down is too much. I see again the horror on his face when he caught me with Jenny. It would be multiplied tenfold now. Lottie was more than innocent: she was being held in a dream not of her making by her own father. That's the only way I can rationalise what was going on in her bedroom. And I freed her from that nightmare only to tip her into a more painful one.

'I'm not a knight,' I say.

'You are –'

'I resign,' I say, bleakness flooding my body.

'No. Fern, please. I appreciate the gesture but we need you . . .'

'I can't do it,' I tell him. 'I'm sorry. I can't turn into that man. I can't.'

I flee the room, pushing past reeves and harkers as I rush out of the castle.

'Fern?' Rachel calls after me. 'Fern, what's wrong?'

The knights, hearing the commotion, pour out of the chamber. Ollie is nowhere to be seen but I glimpse Phoebe and Rafe looking puzzled. Samson is beside them. His expression is grave. I can see his disappointment and judgement. That, if nothing else, tells me that I am making the right decision.

I burst out of the castle and run down to the platform that will take me back to Ithr. More people call my name from the open doors. I fish for Mum's mirror. As I open it, I glance back. They are there, all of them. Phoebe, Rafe, Samson. Phoebe is shouting something, but the light from mirror and stone meets and drowns her out. As it swallows me, I realise I never said goodbye.

The conviction that I've done the right thing wears off before the sun has risen. This is what losing your first love must feel like. Devastation that comes and goes in waves, leaving a void behind it. The uncontrollable crying adds to my existing headache, brought on by my torture of Lottie. Stomach-heaving sobs wrack through me every time I realise I'll never again walk through the castle, or play in Annwn, or ride my darling Lamb. Will she think I've abandoned her? I'll never again see my friends. Friends. The only ones I had, and they're in another world that I can no longer visit.

When the tears finally stop I'm left with a numbness that spreads like a rash. Just as I'm thinking about dragging myself out of bed to face the day, someone thumps up the stairs and knocks on my door. They don't wait for me to answer. Ollie's face appears in the gap. He doesn't have the guts to come in properly.

'I let you down again,' he says eventually.

'You did a bit more than that. You told me to torture someone, then when we were caught you said nothing. It's kind of impressive, how despicable you are. Or maybe you're just a coward. I can't decide which.'

'I just wanted to find a way to catch Medraut. And when I saw them standing there . . . I was scared, Fern.'

'And your automatic reaction was to let me take all the blame?'

'I don't belong anywhere else either. Everyone here knows what I did to you. Even if they're nice to my face they know I was the guy who got his sister burned. I can't ever be the good guy here, not really. In Annwn . . .'

'You think I don't understand about fresh starts?' I say. 'I will always be the sad little victim here.'

'But I *need* friends, Fern. You've always been good on your own.'

'Because I've had to be!' I rummage through my desk drawers and find a series of old photos. Ones of Ollie and I when we were young, playing with the neighbourhood kids. I throw them at him. 'Five years of having no one, Ollie. *Five years*. And yes, I thought I was fine with it. Until I became a knight, and remembered what it was like to have people who don't treat me like shit.'

'You could have told Lord Allenby the truth. I wouldn't have denied it.'

'*You* could have told him yourself,' I say.

'I . . . I will. If you want me to.'

It's a pathetic offer and we both know it.

'Don't bother. It wouldn't make anything better.'

I don't admit my other truth: that I did not tell Lord Allenby about Ollie's part in torturing Lottie because I have always prided myself on not being a lemming. I know I don't blindly do what other people tell me to do. At the end of the day, Ollie didn't force me. I hurt her all by myself, just as I'd hurt Jenny.

'Are you done?' I ask, pretending I'm busy – not that I'm fooling either of us. My bedroom's such a tip it's impossible to look like I'm doing anything other than trying not to trip over.

'Is it true? That you quit?'

I don't reply.

'Fern, you can't. They need you. It's stupid to –'

I just look at him, and his argument dies on his lips.

At school, I can't focus on anything. I replay our interrogation of Lottie, wondering whether there was another way of reaching that memory. If only we hadn't been so impatient. If only I had said no to Ollie. When I see Lottie in class she doesn't look any different. How can anyone hide the amount of damage that's been done to her?

The nighttimes are the hardest. It would have been easier if I'd asked Lord Allenby to let the morrigans remove my memories of Annwn because sleep is now impossible. I would be unconscious, a dreamer, helpless. I wouldn't be able to protect myself from my nightmares . . . or the other things that stalk me. For there's no doubt that I'll be on Medraut's kill list, when the attack happens. And even if I'm not, I reckon the golden treitre that killed Mum will want to get its hands on the one girl who was able to defeat it.

For a few days at least, I come up with a very simple solution: I just won't sleep.

As I sit against the coldest, hardest wall of my bedroom and try to ignore the heaviness in my eyes, I torture myself over everything I've lost. It helps me stay awake like pinching. As they always have been in times of crisis, art and sugar become my refuges. I draw sketch after sketch of my time in Annwn, a different kind of self-flagellation. I make sure no one hears or sees me raiding the cupboards at night, but when we run out of our second pack of chocolate digestives in as many days Dad goes on strike and refuses to buy any more. It becomes harder and harder to stay awake; even when I make myself drink the awful instant coffee that Dad likes so much. Sometimes I allow myself brief naps, setting my alarm every half hour so I can get some rest but still stand a chance of escaping any nightmares.

Ollie tries to persuade me to rethink my decision.

'They all miss you,' he tells me. 'They've got a plan for taking out the treitres before they can strike. It would be a lot easier with you there, though.'

'I don't want to hear about it,' I say. I know what I have lost without having Ollie passing on sentimental messages. If I pretend hard enough, I can kid myself that Phoebe and Samson and the rest of them never liked me after all.

The one concession I make to my time in Annwn is to try to warn Helena Corday of the impending danger. I call her office several times, but when I finally get through to her, I don't know what to say.

'Is everything okay, Fern?' she says over the phone.

'You need to be careful,' I tell her. 'You're in danger.'

Her voice turns cooler. 'I deal with a lot of threats, Fern.'

'No, not from me! Listen. This is going to sound crazy, but try not to sleep too much this week, okay?'

She's conciliatory, but by the end of the conversation I'm certain she thinks I'm completely bonkers.

By the time Friday rolls around I am catatonic with exhaustion. I sit in front of my homework on the sofa. It's a while before I realise that I've just written the word Beltane over and over on the paper that was supposed to be a French translation. When the key goes in the door I am just staring at the letters. Two days away.

'Your dad said I could pop over to collect – Oh God, Fern, are you all right?'

Clemmie drops her handbag by the door and kneels in front of me.

'I'm fine,' I burble. 'Why do you ask?'

'Sweetheart, you don't look yourself. Are you sick?'

Clemmie makes me go to the bathroom to run some water over my face. Looking in the mirror properly for the first time in ages, I can see why she's concerned. My hair is greasy and matted. My eyes are bloodshot, which combined with my red irises makes me look even more demonic than usual.

'I'm just stressed about homework,' I tell Clemmie when I come back downstairs.

'You must make sure you get your beauty sleep.' This is the

kind of thing Clemmie says that makes it hard to warm to her. Nevertheless, Clemmie insists I climb into bed. She strokes my hair and hums a tune as I fight to keep my eyes open.

'Sleep, Ferny,' she whispers, her voice low and strangely compelling. 'Have a long, long sleep now.' My fight wafts away, along with my consciousness.

In my dreams, I walk up an endless drive lined with perfectly mushroomed trees. A young woman, all wild red hair and scars, matches my pace on one side. On the other side I am shadowed by a headless boy. The stump of his neck oozes blood. I'm sure I've met them both before.

Gradually, I become aware of a metallic sound, like the staccato twinkle of a star, and realise that there is something behind me. I turn.

Dad is tending to the flowers that line the path. He's kneeling, his back towards me.

'Dad?' I say.

He straightens, and I see his face for the first time. His mouth has gone. Below his nose, the skin is smooth. Then he returns to his gardening, and there is worse. Something's wrong with the back of his head. As I get closer I stifle a scream. There is a hole in his skull, and where the brain should be there is only blood, and the hollow interior of his eyes.

'Daddy!' I blurt out.

He turns once more, his mouthless face devoid of emotion. He stands, jerks towards me, and I jolt awake, fully clothed, in my bed.

48

The image of my dad in Annwn, his brain and mouth missing, stays with me. Was the Dad I saw my real father, also dreaming? Or was he a dream, created from my own fearful imagination?

When I come downstairs it's later than I'd thought. I've been asleep all night and most of the morning. Thankfully it's a Saturday, so no school for me. Dad's in the middle of making the kitchen resemble a bomb site.

'I'm taking the afternoon off work, Ferny,' he tells me, flipping a pancake.

Well, he looks and acts like the same Dad I know. Maybe it was just a dream. Then I notice the TV is on and Medraut is speaking in Parliament. Dad never usually watches TV during the day.

'I thought we could have some dad-daughter time,' he says.

'What did Clemmie tell you?' We can't afford for Dad to take time off work, which means he probably thinks I'm dying.

'Nothing.'

'You shouldn't lie to your children. It gives us bad life lessons.'

He adds chopped bananas and chocolate sauce to the pancake, plonks it on the table and holds a chair out for me.

'We're worried about you. I think you need to take some time off.'

'So you're bribing me with sweet things.'

'You're eating it – that means you accept.'

It wasn't quite what I had planned to do today, but Dad's insistent, so half an hour later we're walking towards Stratford in awkward silence. I'm rapidly regretting wearing my favourite jumper because what I'd taken for spring chill when inside, turns out to be the kind of warm sun we get when summer's just around the corner. I can't help but feel a bit miserable as we wander through the Olympic Park. I used to love walking around London, but everything looks bland in Ithr. In Annwn, walking along the canal as Dad and I are doing now, we'd have met a few water gypsies and a kelpie or two, instead of dog walkers and out of control children.

Dad nudges me off the path when we reach Victoria Park. Where we live the pavements are covered in litter and unpicked dog poo, but here, just a few miles away, the streets don't even have a stray chewing-gum mark.

'Chips?' Dad asks, but before I can answer he's striding through the door of a posh chippy. I loiter outside. Conversation between us is already dwindling, and I want to stave off that awful feeling of not knowing how to connect with my own father for as long as possible. When Dad emerges, he doesn't just hand me a greasy box filled with fat chips, but a milkshake too.

'Your mum used to live around here, you know,' he says as I munch on a fat, salty chip. He points at a window above the butcher opposite. 'Shared a flat with some friends just there.'

The windows on the first-floor flat are open in the April heat. Beyond the curtains I glimpse floral wallpaper and antique paintings.

'Don't know what she saw in me.' Dad smiles.

We take the food and milkshake to the park and Dad picks a bench overlooking a football pitch, and carries on telling me about Mum's youth, occasionally stealing a chip from my box. During a lull in the conversation, Dad lays a hand over mine.

'What's going on, Ferny?'

I stare at him. 'Nothing.'

'Is it school? Are you being bullied again?'

How do I tell him that it's not just at school – that it's everywhere I go? How can he not have noticed the glances shot my way as we walked here? He might mean well, but he's all talk, no action.

'I'm fine.'

'You know you can tell me anything.'

I shrug. Then something occurs to me. 'Can I ask you anything?'

'Of course.'

'A few months ago you said that Mum was having nightmares.'

Dad nods, obviously not liking my line of questioning.

'Did she say what they were about?'

'Fern . . .'

'You said I could ask you anything. This is what I want to know.'

Dad shakes his head. 'She never told me. But . . .' Dad rubs his eyes, unwilling to continue.

'But?' I prompt.

'She'd wake up screaming. "Not him," she'd be shouting, over and over again. "Not him."'

I nod. That doesn't give me much to work with. 'Him' could be any number of people: Medraut, her friend Clement who died alongside Ellen, maybe even the dreamer Lord Allenby said died on their patrol.

I hand Dad the last chip and stare determinedly down at the empty box. The grease coating the paper lining makes me feel a little ill. It's got a strange illustration on it, though. A crude drawing of a red eye, and beneath it the words, *Come back, Cool Eyes*.

Cool Eyes. That's Rafe's nickname for me. It must be a bizarre coincidence.

'Shall we go?' Dad asks, and I nod silently. I fold the paper lining into my pocket before he throws the box away. Maybe the tiredness is playing tricks on me.

We head down to the canal that runs along one side of the park and point out the prettier narrowboats, imagining what it would be like to live on one. One of the boats is adorned with flowers. Just off the plank that joins boat to path, several bouquets rest in buckets of water. A woman emerges from the open door.

'How much?' Dad gestures to the flowers.

The woman looks at me. 'Oh, I've just the thing for the young lady. Here.' She takes a note from Dad and offers me a bunch of white peonies and lavender. 'You've got a good father there.' She nods at Dad before disappearing back inside.

I'm not usually a flower person, but these are really lovely.

We're much further down the path when I register that something is attached to the ribbon that binds the flowers together, but I don't have a chance to inspect it, because Dad is leading me back onto the main road that will take us home.

'Note for a note?' a voice utters nearby. A grizzled man playing an accordion nods to an old coffee cup. I dig in my pocket, but Dad hands me a fiver instead. I drop it into the cup and smile at the man.

'Bless you,' he says. 'Take your note then.'

I look between Dad and him. 'Sorry?'

'A note for a note, I said. It's there, in the cup, see?'

I peer into the cup and slide out a folded piece of dirty paper. My name is scribbled on the outside.

'What? Who are you? How do you –' But the man has hurried away.

I round on Dad. 'What's going on? Why did you bring me here?'

Dad holds up his hands. 'We're just on a walk, Fern. I've no idea what your man there was talking about.'

He's lying, I'm sure of it. But Dad is already walking ahead.

I open the paper and immediately recognise the blocky handwriting.

You are a knight, Miss King. I knew it months ago. We all forget what's right from time to time. In Annwn, our mistakes have terrible consequences. You are not Medraut, but you are needed if we're to win the war against him.

I don't need the initials *LA* at the bottom to know that this is from Lord Allenby himself. Choked up, I fold the paper but keep it in my hand. Could he be right? Does he truly not see me as a liability, or is he just saying that to get me back for this one battle?

'Come on,' Dad calls back at me. 'I've got to do an evening shift and I want a bite of dinner before I go.'

Trailing him, I fiddle with my flowers. They now seem like a strange gift to give a tired, ill daughter, especially given what else has happened. I examine the ribbon that binds them. Something's wound into it. I stop to remove it.

It's a plastic toy; the kind you get with kids' meals. A lion. My own little Donald.

I swallow, hard.

'Wow, Fern, come and look at this,' Dad says a little way ahead. I join him, still studying the toy.

'I'm not the expert I admit, and I normally don't hold with graffiti, but that's a masterpiece, isn't it?'

He's staring at the wall of a building – one that's been sanctioned for graffiti. Usually these places are just covered in mindless tags, but this one has been taken over by a single, huge work of art. A grey dragon looms over most of the wall. Its face is strangely human, the hybrid of man and beast rendering it even more monstrous. It towers over a small figure dressed from the neck down in armour. Her hair is pale blonde, and it flies out behind her as if buffeted by a gale. In one hand she holds a scimitar, but it's her other hand that's raised towards the dragon's head. From her outstretched fingertips crackles blue lightning. Then I see that the dragon's head is made of two shapes: a circle for its upper head, and a V for its muzzle. OV. One Voice. In the bottom corner I get the confirmation I need. A tag: S. 'S' for Samson.

'Does it make sense to you, Ferny?' Dad is watching me closely.

I nod dumbly, still staring at the beautiful mural Samson has created for me. When Dad speaks again, I hear worry in his voice.

'Ollie told me it might help you feel better. He gave me the route and told me what to do. He wouldn't explain, and he made me promise not to tell you that he was behind it. Was it – did I do the right thing?'

For the first time, my father has done something that is just for me. For years I thought that the two people I loved the most would have preferred it if I didn't exist. Today, I can see that I was wrong, just as I've been wrong about so many other things. Ollie and Dad have given me a gift greater than Immral.

'Yes, Dad,' I tell him. 'You did okay. You did very okay.'

When we get home, while Dad busies himself in the kitchen, I tap on Ollie's door. He's sitting on his bed, reading a book. From his old speakers comes the sound of a smoky-voiced singer and a guitar. I point to the duvet and he moves his legs so I can sit down.

'You arranged all of that for me?'

'I just made the route and did some organising. The others came up with the flowers and the chips and everything.'

I look down at the plastic lion and the letter still in my hand. '*You* didn't leave a message.'

'Yes, I did.'

For a moment I wonder whether Dad forgot part of the

route, but then I catch Ollie's meaning. The whole thing was his message.

'I want to go back, but I can't.'

'Why not? You read Lord Allenby's note –'

'It's not that.'

'Why then?'

I've had a lot of time to study my memories over the past few days and I can't escape the fact that something in me wants to inflict pain. If I wasn't twisted in some way, I wouldn't have done what I did to Jenny and Lottie.

'When you told me to meet you at Wanstead Flats,' I begin, watching Ollie tense at the reference to the fire, 'did you . . . Were you looking forward to seeing me get hurt?'

I can see that Ollie wants to snap back defensively, so I hold my hands out, a gesture of peace. 'I'm not trying to have a go at you,' I tell him, 'I'm trying to explain.'

Ollie frowns, clearly not understanding where I'm going with this. But when he answers, he answers honestly.

'The thing is, the fire was never really meant to happen. Jenny wanted to scare you, that's all. She's a bitch, obviously, but she didn't actually mean to hurt you. So I just thought I was helping her play a cruel joke on you. And . . . yeah, I guess part of me was looking forward to seeing how you'd react, even though deep down I knew it was a horrible thing to do.'

I nod. 'That's it. I knew what I was doing to Jenny and Lottie was wrong, but I did it anyway. And with Jenny, right up until she started screaming, I . . . I really enjoyed having some power over her.'

Ollie looks at me quizzically. 'Yeah, but as soon as the reality kicked in you stopped hurting her, didn't you?'

'But Lottie –'

'Fern,' Ollie interrupts, standing. 'You know I can read memories *and* emotions, right?'

I nod.

'Well, I've read yours, remember? Believe me, sis, you're not a monster.'

I want, so badly, to believe him.

'They'd never let me turn into Medraut, would they?' I say.

Ollie snorts. 'Delusions of grandeur, much? Fern, you've only got half the power. We'd both need to turn into maniacs for that to happen. *And* we'd need to agree on everything, which doesn't exactly seem likely, does it?'

I hadn't thought of it like that. My greatest fear is, it turns out, nigh on impossible.

'All right,' I say.

'You're in?'

I grin at him, joy and excitement coursing through me. Ironically, I suddenly feel wide awake. 'Yeah. Let's do this.'

49

After Dad's left for work, we both depart to our bedrooms early. Ollie stops me before I go up the stairs. He says nothing, only holds my hand for a second. There is no arc of inspyre to acknowledge our connection, but we understand each other.

For the first time in nearly a week, I sit on my bed with gladness. I rest my portal in my palm for some time. I never thought I'd be able to do this again. I let my heart fill up with gratitude before I open the mirror and almost squeal with delight as the blue light engulfs me.

The sun is only just rising in Annwn when I land on the platform. Ollie is waiting. I speed ahead of him, longing to see everyone, so it takes a while to realise that Tintagel looks different. The doors have been reinforced, and the drawbridge is now held up by metal rods instead of rope. The gatehouse is packed with guards.

'You've all been busy,' I say.

'We've had to be,' Ollie replies, gesturing to the world beyond the castle walls. Perhaps I wouldn't have noticed it if I hadn't been away for a week, but the break makes the slightest change jarring. The ancient oak trees that drape over the castle's walls are dying, their bark flaking off in clumps to reveal a blank space beneath. As I scan the horizon, a great chunk of stone falls from one of the grand buildings opposite the castle, shattering on the pile of rubble already gathered at its feet. Then I realise that something else is missing from this landscape: the sound of wings. I look up. No angels fly above our heads as they used to. A smaller flock of them lie, exhausted and broken, on Tintagel's roof. One of them tries to preen his wings, but ends up pulling out a handful of feathers. One drifts down towards me but evaporates into inspyre before it touches my upturned face.

'Let's go in,' Ollie says sombrely.

Inside, the atmosphere is more hushed than usual. The harkers' stations have been pushed back to make a wider space in the centre of the castle. Those at their desks are scribbling intently. 'No movement yet,' one of them says into her helmet. 'Stand by.' But as we stride deeper into Tintagel, some of them notice me. Reeves and veneurs pause to offer welcome-back smiles. A mutter goes up in my wake; disbelieving, hopeful.

Lord Allenby lets out a bark of laughter when he sees me. 'Ollie's plan worked then?'

'Yes, sir. Your letter –'

'Was the truth. Even at my most disappointed, Fern, I never believed you capable of turning into Medraut.'

'Was that man with the accordian a friend of yours?'

Lord Allenby's eyes twinkle oddly. 'From time to time.' He accompanies me to the door of the knights' chamber. 'You're back not a moment too soon. Are you ready?'

'I think so.'

'Samson will make sure you're up to speed. Now, if you'll excuse me, I have harkers to get into position.'

The knights' chamber is blessedly empty when I enter to retrieve my uniform and weapons from my locker. Running my hands over the knight emblem on my tunic, I realise that this may well be the last time I wear this, if Medraut's successful. Well, at least this time I'll be going out doing the right thing.

'Fern?' Phoebe is standing in the doorway, and behind her some of the other knights who have just arrived for their shift. She squeals and runs over, enveloping me in a hug.

'Thank you,' I tell her.

Rafe enters next, along with the rest of Bedevere. 'Cool Eyes!' he crows, and shouts the news of my return to Natasha.

'I've missed you!' Natasha sweeps over. 'Not as much as Lamb's missed you, of course, but . . .'

After the exclamations of joy, I find myself walking with Samson to the stables, ahead of the rest of the regiment.

'That was really good graffiti,' I tell him.

'It felt good to do it for a purpose,' he says, then looks at me with a brightness in his eyes that I've never seen before. 'Did you really leave because you were worried about what you were becoming?'

I nod. For some reason the idea of Samson thinking badly of me is worse than Lord Allenby's disappointment.

'I wish I was as strong as you.'

I look up in surprise. 'What do you mean?'

'The story everyone tells about me – the one with the house full of vampires.'

I nod.

'There's a reason I've never told anyone how I killed them all. The truth is, there's no way I should have gone in there to start with, and definitely not alone.'

He pauses, but I don't try to encourage him to say more. Before we reach the stables, he pulls me to one side, so that we're hidden a little by the drooping branches of a willow.

'When the harkers sent us to that house, I recognised it. My girlfriend lives there.'

I smile, to cover for the strange weight that has landed in my stomach at the mention of Samson's girlfriend.

'She'd been sick for a while, you see, her and her sisters. So when I heard that there were a load of vampires in there everything made sense. I told my regiment to stay put and I marched in there. I couldn't tell you how I killed them. I don't even remember myself. I was so angry and frightened. When I came to they were all gone.'

'Did your girlfriend and her family get better after that?'

'Yes, but that's not the point. They were never *mine* to save. It should have been my whole regiment going in there. I put myself in needless danger for what? To feel like I'm her knight in shining armour?' Samson snorts, disgusted with himself. 'I should have told Lord Allenby then and there, but I was too frightened of being turfed out. Not like you, taking responsibility for what you did.'

I can't help but smile a little. It's not exactly akin to torturing someone for information. Even at his worst, this man is heroic.

'Well,' I say, stepping away from him, 'I won't tell anyone. You have my word.'

Lamb's greeting outstrips everyone else's. She nearly kicks

her stable door down in an effort to get to me and knocks me over with the force of her nuzzling. I end up in a heap on the ground with half a horse on top of me. It takes twice as long to tack Lamb up because she keeps sniffing me, as if to check I'm still here. When we leave the stables, knights from other thaneships have arrived – nearly three hundred of them from across the country. But what should be a celebratory occasion is starting to feel like what it is: the build-up to battle, forces amassing. Bedevere is joined by knights from the castles stretching across the centre of the country, from Bristol to Peterborough.

When everyone is divided into groups on horseback, Lord Allenby rides to the front. He raises a gloved hand. His crossbow is slung across his back, and a hooded morrigan perches on his shoulder. A small team of veneurs rides behind each regiment.

Lord Allenby turns to address us, and the whole company falls silent. 'Well done, all of you, for the work you've put in to pull this plan together in only a week. You know what happens if we fail. If Medraut is allowed to activate those portals and his treitres go through them, then it won't be a few hundred lives we'll have on our conscience. It will be thousands upon thousands. We must keep the treitres in London at all costs, do you understand?'

'Yes, sir!'

'Mr King?' Lord Allenby nods at Ollie. It is Ollie's job to try to run interference on any mind-manipulating Medraut might attempt, by casting his power like a shield over us all. It's something he's only ever managed a handful of times in training, and then has only been able to protect a few thanes from my Immral. This is on a far wider scale.

'Be careful,' I mutter to him. I know how much doing this is going to hurt him.

And we start to march. If we do our job right, the treitres will be trapped in London. We will be lying in wait for them as they leave Madame Tussaud's. We will have every street in the area blocked off. Nets of fine wire mesh will stretch across the sky, preventing any flying treitres from escaping. Medraut's army will be surrounded by ours, making them far easier to take out. And with them gone, all that remains is for us to unleash the morrigans on Medraut if he shows his face. With my help, hopefully, they'll be able to finish the job they started fifteen years ago.

We cross the drawbridge as a single force, but as soon as we're outside Tintagel we split into separate regiments. A few larger regiments than usual could be overlooked by any passing spies – an army couldn't.

Bedevere, led this time by Lord Allenby, takes the shortest route, while the other regiments approach Medraut's fortress from different directions, some through Regent's Park, some doing a huge loop and cutting back on themselves to avoid notice. The harkers keep up a running commentary as we ride, confirming that there's been no movement sighted from the fortress. Ollie's nose begins to bleed as the strain of the ever-widening mind shield takes its toll.

As we pass through Soho I see that the thanes have been busy here too. Every circle – every place that could become a portal to a different part of Annwn – has metal bars nailed over it. Every Underground sign, every drain, every circular fountain. If Medraut wants to create portals to London, we're not going to make it easy for him.

'Gawain and Palomides are all in position,' the harker captain tells us. 'Lancelot and Dagonet are three minutes away.'

'Understood, Maisie,' Lord Allenby says.

As we ride down Baker Street, past long lines of violin-playing men in odd hats, the low building that houses Madame Tussaud's comes into view. I catch a glimpse of Natasha keeping watch from a nearby roof with the rest of her regiment. We halt our horses at one end of Baker Street. Lancelot block the other end.

We wait for a long time. The horses start to shift. Phoebe jiggles her leg nervously. Only Lord Allenby sits still and upright on his charger, like a man who has waited a very long time for this moment.

At last, when the sun is setting, casting a silken glow over London's rooftops, the main door of Madame Tussaud's opens, and treitres pour out. They lope and prowl and march up the street towards our hiding place.

'Hold it,' Lord Allenby's voice growls through the helmets. 'On my signal.'

The treitres are close enough that I'm able to hear the sickening crunching, drooling sounds those of them with mouths are making. Something's wrong, though. I just can't work out what it is.

'Wait until they're right in the belly of the trap,' Lord Allenby says. 'Dagonet, Palomides, take up your second positions. Let's close in tight.'

What am I missing?

I realise what it is at the exact moment Lord Allenby says, 'Now!' and we urge the horses forward to attack. The golden treitre, the leader of the army, is not there. And if it's not there – where is it?

As we wheel into the pincer movement, the other regiments emerging from their positions to surround the treitres, I call into my helmet. 'Stop! Stop! They know we're here!'

But I'm too late. With a sound like an earthquake, the buildings behind us unfold. Brick and marble join hands, around and above us. So much for our nets. These treitres never intended to fly away. We are all trapped together, inside a giant hangar.

My stomach churns, my organs curl up. I fall from Lamb's back. A figure emerges from between his soldiers. Medraut is amongst us.

50

He does not look like the man who spoke from the stage in Trafalgar Square all those months ago. In Annwn, Sebastien Medraut is even more impressive. His features are sharper here, his eyes brighter, and he is followed wherever he goes by a lightning storm of inspyre. It crackles around him like electricity, and I realise that all my talk of matching him was just bravado. Neither Ollie nor I have ever commanded inspyre in such a way.

He's wearing the armour I saw in his stronghold. The one that seemed to be made of iron and silk, the one that made me vomit when I came close to it. It makes him look like a dark god.

'Now!' Lord Allenby says, removing his morrigan's hood and launching it into the air. The veneurs behind us follow suit and the birds form a raincloud that pelts Medraut with deadly hailstones. But no sooner have the morrigans landed on him than they take off again, screeching in pain.

'That won't work, Lionel,' Medraut tells Lord Allenby.

The veneurs soothe their distressed morrigans. So this is what the armour was for – to protect him from his only weakness. I should have realised when I first saw a morrigan flee from one of the kalends, for the armour is made of the same stuff. An armour made from something that leaches inspyre and turns it inside out. For a morrigan, which feeds off the blue light, that void would be poisonous. What I can't understand is how Medraut is wearing it at all. I can't go near it without it draining my power. How powerful does Medraut have to be to wear something like that and still have the ability to wield his Immral?

Medraut's eyes rove over his captives, until they come to rest on me. When he speaks, his voice is just as soft as it was in Ithr, but the effect is even more disarming. I *want* to do what he asks.

'I am offering you a choice,' he says, and even though he now looks at Lord Allenby, it feels as though his offer extends to all of us. 'Outside your castle, my treitres are holding two groups of people.'

He holds up a hand and inspyre radiates from his palm, forming like puppets into a scene and dancing to his command. Tintagel is held siege, surrounded by hundreds of treitres.

'You know that Tintagel is protected against those who wish its inhabitants harm,' Lord Allenby says. 'Your army will never be able to enter without my permission.'

'I do not wish you harm,' Medraut replies. 'I only wish for a favour.'

He alters the perspective on the scenario he's created. Before Tintagel's gates the golden treitre paces between two frightened flocks of dreamers. On the left side the dreamers are elderly, or wan and thin. 'These people are close to death already,'

Medraut says. On the right side the dreamers are young. Some of them are babies, barely crawling. 'These have their whole lives ahead of them,' Medraut continues. 'If your people lower the drawbridge, surrender to my army and hand us the keys to Tintagel, I shall tell them to only kill the first group in their travels across Annwn. If you fight us or try to stop us in any way, I will tell them to kill the second group.'

'Why, if you mean my people no harm?'

'It was your own doing,' Medraut says, 'when you closed off the portals in the rest of London.'

Medraut has outplayed us, I realise. There's only one portal left in London big enough to allow the treitre army loose on the rest of Annwn: the portal in Tintagel. By trying to protect the dreamers outside London, we have doomed our own people.

'And,' Medraut says, 'I want what you stole returned.'

He must mean the puzzle box. So it does have a use beyond holding his vision for the future. But what could that be?

Maisie's voice comes over the helmets. 'Lord Allenby? Tintagel, it's surrounded . . .'

'I know, Maisie,' Lord Allenby says, and I can tell that he is trying to keep the panic from his voice.

'What should we do?'

Lord Allenby doesn't reply to her. Instead, he addresses Medraut. 'For someone who rabbits on about *One Voice*, Sebastien, you certainly enjoy dividing people, don't you? You know I won't make that decision.'

'You're going to die soon,' Medraut says, 'and then it will be up to your captains.'

'I'm curious,' Lord Allenby says. 'Did you only plan this –' he gestures to the walls that lock us in, 'after you discovered that Fern had read Lottie's mind? Or did you plant that memory in Lottie's mind in order to trap us?'

'Do you really think my daughter would ever go against my orders? Of course it was planted.'

But I'm not listening to Medraut any more. Something about the way Allenby spoke – the way he pointed at the walls, the way he looked so significantly at me . . . Oh God. He wants me to move the walls, doesn't he? Imperceptibly, Samson nudges his horse over to cover me. Phoebe's lion moves to his other side, so that Medraut can't see what I'm up to. I try not to think about the fact that all these people are going to die if I can't find a way out. There may be more of us than the treitres, but we're trapped between them and the walls. They could pick us off easily.

I reach out, trying to sense the corners of the building. It's so, so heavy. Medraut's command to knit the buildings together is too strong. There are raw spots, though, where the joins used to be. Medraut has created a Frankenstein's monster of buildings, and the sutured skin might still be torn. I test those fault lines, pressing against them with my mind.

Medraut is talking again. 'So many people think that *free will* is something to be treasured, but the truth is, very few truly want it. They like the illusion of it, but the reality is exhausting. It is difficult, working out the right path in a sea of facts. So people look to their leaders to tell them what to think. They want to simply agree, to not have to constantly question everything when there is so much else to get done.

If free will is so precious, then why do people throw it away so easily?'

I push harder against the weak spots in the walls, but they hold. It doesn't matter that they're newly formed, because the force holding them there is far stronger than I am. The same rancid taste seeps into my saliva as it did when I tortured Lottie: Medraut.

'And you think that you know what's best for everyone?' Lord Allenby growls.

'Does it matter, as long as *they* believe it's best for them?'

I press with all my mind against the fault lines in the walls. Medraut's willpower pushes back against mine until my head is thumping with the effort.

'Do you truly believe,' Medraut suddenly raises his voice, 'that a little girl with half my power – less than half if what I've seen is anything to go by – can break through my creation?'

I meet his eyes. He's right, of course. This is impossible, but I have to try.

'She may have half your power when she's on her own,' a voice calls from the crowd. Ollie pushes through to stand by my side. I slip off Lamb's back. 'But I have the other half. What's the betting that together we can wipe that patronising smile off your smug face?'

He holds out his hand. Our eyes meet, and already I can feel the inspyre crackling towards us, resisting the pull of Medraut and his armour.

'Try again,' Ollie says. I nod, and take his proffered hand.

The electric shock is instant, but I'm ready for it. I harness it, throw it at the fault lines, and I can feel Ollie's mind channelling into mine, pushing his will through me. Medraut reaches out a hand to steady his creation, but he's too late. My inspyre – *our* inspyre – is at work already. The fault lines crack. They tear. Something rumbles beneath our feet, to match the earthquake in my head. The ground moves. It rolls like a sheet tossed over a bed. Then the wall explodes.

Ollie and I are thrown to the ground in a hailstorm of rubble. I can see nothing through the cloud of inspyre that billows around us. I can hear nothing but a high-pitched ringing, and while my body is bruised from the explosion, that's nothing to the pummelling going on in my brain. There's blood on my face, but I can't tell if it's from a nosebleed or the buildings' collapse. I reach out, frightened for Lamb's safety, but she's on her feet still, and she responds to my touch by nibbling my fingers.

'Everyone out!' Lord Allenby roars. He's already mounted his charger.

I look around for my friends.

Phoebe gets up stiffly. She clambers onto Donald, coughing violently. Rafe follows a little distance away. And then . . . yes, there's Samson. Lord Allenby is shouting commands through our helmets. 'Everyone directly to Tintagel, as fast as you can.'

Beside me, Ollie stirs.

'Are you okay?' I ask him.

'Cracking.'

I pull him onto unsteady feet and swing myself into Lamb's saddle. As I settle there, Lord Allenby's voice comes through my helmet.

'Fern? Ollie? I wonder if I might ask you a favour.'

I know what he is about to say. There's unfinished business here.

'Yes, sir. We'll stay behind. Keep him off your tail for as long as we can.'

'Thank you.'

It feels like a goodbye. I watch my friends ride off. Samson reins his charger in as he passes, uncertainty playing across his face.

'It's okay,' I say. 'Go.'

He reaches across to clasp my hand. 'You can do this, Fern,' he says, his gaze as warm and steady as his grip. 'I know you can.'

And then he's gone, dust billowing in his wake.

Ollie hauls himself onto Balius's back just as Medraut's figure emerges through the dust. As he walks, the dust transforms in little eddies back into inspyre, so that he remains pristine, his armour as soul-suckingly dark as it ever was. He says nothing, but as his eyes meet mine I can see that he is furious. Suddenly my theoretical fear at facing down this man two on one becomes very real. Because even though we managed to break those walls, I have felt the amount of power he can wield, and there's no way Ollie and I together can match it for long. Any small test of our Immral has us bleeding and aching for days. Medraut seems to be wholly unaffected by using his. The best – the only – chance we have is to surprise him, and to do it quickly, before we are totally spent.

Ollie is clearly thinking the same as me because he wheels off to one side and aims his chakrams at Medraut as he goes. I reach out and create four more Ollies, hundreds more chakrams, each one heading in a slightly different direction. Medraut isn't fooled. With a sweep of one hand he dissipates my illusions. With his other hand, he throws a handful of inspyre at my brother. There's an almighty crash, and Ollie and Balius go down.

'Ollie!' I urge Lamb towards the figure of my fallen brother. But as we canter towards him I feel the inspyre around me flocking to Medraut. I glance back – he is gathering another handful. This one's for me. I throw myself from Lamb's back and push her in the other direction, so that the ball of inspyre barrels between us. So. He's not going to let me get to my brother. I suppose that means it's just him and me then.

I manage to slow the next ball of inspyre, but it still leaves me winded. Medraut follows that with a third ball. I try to scramble out of the way but it crashes into my shoulder. Bones crunch against each other inside my arm, every one an agony. I pour what energy I can into stopping the next ball, but I'm too weak against Medraut's onslaught. I only manage to slow it. It rolls into me, toppling me so that I land on my injured shoulder. The ball moves onto my chest and stays there. I can do nothing but lie in pain.

Medraut walks into my vision. He reaches out a hand, and in my delirium I think at first that he means to help me up. It's only when the ball of inspyre flattens and presses down on me that I understand his true intention. Breathing becomes almost impossible.

'Please don't,' I wheeze. He doesn't reply. I stare into his eyes, trying to understand how he can do this to anyone. To someone his daughter's age. There's no particular pleasure in his expression. He's not being vindictive. But he's not bored either. It's as though he's simply extinguishing an upstart rival.

I can feel my chest beginning to collapse. My lungs are burning. I close my eyes and try to reach a level of calm. I'm not accepting what's about to happen, but it's the only way I stand a chance of thinking clearly. I channel inspyre into my bones, strengthening them as much as I can. I open my eyes briefly, and catch Medraut smiling in acknowledgement at what I've done. He twists his hand and the weight increases tenfold. My ribcage cracks and I scream out the last of my breath.

Something glitters in my peripheral vision. I can't see much any more, but that catches my eye. When Medraut moved his arm, he dislodged something that was tucked into his armour. Could it be . . .?

He is so focused on what he's doing to me that he does not notice the twitch in my hand that sends the inspyre out of my bones. He does not notice as the inspyre pulls the object gently from its hiding place.

A golden cylinder emerges. A bullet's shell, burnished until it glows. A perfect, pocket-sized portal. My vision is going again. There's another crack in my ribcage. My organs are failing. But there's a little strength left in my mind, and that's all I need.

'What are you doing?' Medraut says sharply.

'*Work it out yourself,*' I gasp, and with my final strength I force the shell into his hand and activate it with a flick of his wrist.

Medraut's snarl is the last thing I see as he is taken by the light, back to Ithr.

51

The weight on my chest disappears instantly, but my torso is still in agony. Blood seeps through my tunic. When I try to move, the cracked ribs grate against each other. But I have to move. What was it Andraste had said about Mum's mirror, all those months ago? *If it had been broken in either world I could not have helped you*. I grasp a stray rock and smash it with as much force as I can muster onto Medraut's portal, until it is flattened. There. He won't be able to return to Annwn until he's managed to secure another one in Ithr, which won't be easy, even for a man of his influence. He's out for a day, at least. That done, I collapse.

I'm not allowed to pass out because Lamb chooses that moment to trot over and lick my face. A little way away, Balius is on his feet and nudging Ollie's figure. Eventually, my brother stirs. When he finally sits up he spots me and crawls over.

'You okay, sis?'

'So bloody like you to stay out of the way when someone's trying to kill me.'

Ollie's laugh is more like a grimace. He pats me on the shoulder that was crushed, which should send pangs of agony through my body. Instead, the electric shock soothes the pain.

'Medraut gone?'

'For now.'

Ollie nods. 'So it's just the treitres left.'

'Yeah, *just* the treitres.'

Shakily, I roll onto my front and make it to all fours. Ollie is trying, unsuccessfully, to get to his feet. He falls back in a cloud of rubble.

'This is going well,' I remark.

Casting around for something to help, I turn some inspyre into a crutch for Ollie, then I fashion a bandage and wrap it around my chest. Tightly bound, it doesn't remove the pain but it does at least make me feel confident that my ribs aren't about to stab my internal organs. Lamb and Balius evidently recognise how pathetic we are, because they both lie down to allow us to flop onto their backs.

Side by side, the horses trot out of the wreckage of Medraut's prison and into the open air of a London ravaged by treitres.

Dreamers' bodies lie scattered haphazardly across the road. Some have been seized by the flying treitres and hang from lampposts like butchers' carcasses. Each one is now lying dead in their bed in Ithr, maybe alone, maybe next to an unsuspecting loved one. They went to sleep to dream. That's all they wanted – a good dream.

Wordlessly, we urge the horses into a gallop.

'We could get there quicker,' Ollie says. I nod, pushing away the migraine that tells me I've already done too much. I pat Lamb on the neck, mutter, 'See you soon,' and leap off her back into the sky.

Ollie joins me and we fly low over the rooftops, heading as the crow flies for Tintagel.

We hear the battle first. The sound of screams and metal on metal. There's a deep boom of something huge crashing to the ground. Winged treitres, their bodies catching the sunlight, circle the domes of the castle. From this vantage point I can see the full extent of what's happened while I've been fighting Medraut. Ranged around Tintagel are hundreds and hundreds of treitres. Each one is sleek-skinned and metallic, but that's where the similarities end. Their bodies are constructed of a delightful range of terrifying killing devices. Some of them scuttle, spider-like, along the side of buildings, delving long arms inside the windows and pulling out dreamers and knights to toss them to the ground hundreds of metres below. Some have huge jaws with rows of shark-like teeth that crunch through human and stone like they're biscuits. And some are like the treitre that killed my mother – lithe and elegant, with long, whip-like tails.

The knights have killed a few already. The bodies of a copper and a bronze treitre lie in the centre of the battle. I catch brief glimpses of my friends. Samson shooting his bow at the reaching claws of one treitre; Natasha diving off Domino to stab at the underbelly of another. Phoebe leaps between her horse and her lion, using them each to distract the monsters from attacking another knight. In the centre of the fighting is Lord Allenby, still proudly astride his charger, shooting and whipping his crossbow back and forth faster than I thought possible.

There are far more fallen knights than treitres, though. I can barely see them beneath the fighting, but they are there, carpeting the ground. Then my heart catches in my throat. On the outskirts of the battle, one body has been half eaten. His face is the only thing recognisable about him. Rafe. The Rafe who rescued me from the angels on that first night, the first person to give me a nickname. I gulp the wind, needing it to fill the cave in my stomach.

'Ready?' Ollie says, his voice catching with emotion.

'God, yes,' I reply. Let's turn this devastation into rage.

I force the image of all those bodies out of my head. Mustn't think about them. Must. Not. Think. That becomes a mantra as Ollie and I dive down into the fray. I can't dwell on the dead, but have to do what I can to keep the living safe. One treitre grabs Natasha by the waist and is about to feast on her when I pick it up and throw it against a building with such force that its metal skin cracks. There are too many to tackle at once though. Everywhere I look, knights are being killed. A boy only a year older than me has his ribcage sliced open and his organs torn out. They spread like ribbons across the road. His vacant eyes stare up at me accusingly.

In the distance, I hear a whinny. Lamb gallops into the square, dodging between treitres, searching for me. I leap towards her, landing in the saddle and snatching up the reins. A silver treitre clatters towards me. I push from beneath it with my mind and lift it into the air, before throwing it towards another one that's tearing dreamers from the rooftops. With a flick of satisfaction, I use the first treitre's rapier claws to stab its fellow, pinning both of them to the ground where they fall, one immobile, one dying.

Then I spot Samson. He's fighting off a treitre four times his height. I steer Lamb towards him, drawing my scimitar from its sheath. 'Duck!' I shout. He throws himself to the ground as I slash at the monster. It doesn't move, confident that a simple sword won't do it any harm. But this is not a simple sword – not in my hands. I push some inspyre into it through the handle. A glorious blue flame ignites along the blade. When I slash at the creature, its hide parts beneath the inspyre inferno and it falls to the ground, writhing as the light works its way deep inside the skin. On my way back, I pull Samson up behind me.

'We're too few, and too small,' Samson shouts above the din.

'I'm trying my best!'

He clings on to me as Lamb swerves to one side to avoid a fallen knight. Pain courses through my ribs and shoulder.

'I just wish we could match their size,' Samson says. 'It might take away some of their advantage.'

Of course. I curse inwardly at not thinking of it myself. As Samson leaps onto his horse, I slip off Lamb's back and roll away, finding cover. I'm going to need stillness to do this, and most of all I need to be able to see everyone. I realise I'm leaning against the platform that leads out of Annwn. All I need to do is pull out my mirror and I could be safe at home. The thought crosses my mind for a second and no more.

A few of the knights are still on horseback, and it's them that I focus on. Holding them all in my mind is difficult when I keep hearing the sounds of slicing, and metal on metal, and death, but I try my best to block all of that out.

Bigger, I think. *Stronger*.

My already ragged brain is stretching, wrung out like a wet sheet. The pain is almost unbearable, but underneath that is something else. I can feel every one of my fellow knights growing in stature, their horses too.

When I open my eyes, the knights match the assassins, head to head. Samson leaps on one treitre's back and, now too heavy for it to throw off, yanks its slender throat back and stabs an arrow through its jugular. Ollie's horse leaps like a stag into the air, giving him an opening to bring one of his chakrams down on another treitre's head. Lord Allenby holds his horse still as he corners two monsters and peppers them with a stream of super-sized arrows.

I wade out into the fray again, keeping half my concentration on holding my comrades in their new forms and half on the scimitar in my hand. Now my comparatively small height is an advantage. The treitres are so focused on the larger knights that they don't notice me. Swiping at back legs, I hobble a few of them, before darting underneath their bellies and stabbing upwards.

In amidst them all I can just spot Ollie and Phoebe, fighting back to back. Phoebe's lion, snapping its powerful jaws left and right, pushes the assassins back. Arrows rain down on us from above, and I look up to see reeves and harkers firing makeshift bows from the parapets. A raincloud emerges from the highest tower of Tintagel to divebomb the fray. The morrigans flit from treitre to treitre, pecking at their eyes. They are no match for the monsters, though – the treitres gobble them up, ten to a mouthful.

'No!' I hear Ollie shout, and twist round to see Phoebe's lion with its claws dug deep into the flank of one of the assassins. Then I spot why he's so distressed. Instead of fighting off the lion, three more treitres have pounced on Phoebe. They hold her down. I run towards them, dodging the spiked tail of one treitre and leaping over the open maw of another. Phoebe screams incoherently. Between them, her figure looks tiny. Ollie bats at the assassins helplessly. Phoebe thrashes against their grip. For a split second her eyes meet mine. Two different kinds of desperation punch together: the desperation of knowing I cannot save her; the desperation of knowing that she cannot be saved. I throw my power towards her, but it's too late. One of the treitres rakes its claws across Phoebe's chest, blood blooms in neat lines, and her lion falls to the ground beside her still body, a stuffed toy once more.

For an instant the other knights return to their usual size, like a lightbulb flickering, before I kick myself back into focus. I can't go to pieces yet, or everyone else will die, just like Phoebe, just like Ramesh and Rafe. Their deaths are already on me, I can't bear any more.

'Fall back!' Allenby shouts in the distance. Some of the knights try to obey him, but more treitres block their way, leaping easily in front of the castle steps.

Ollie tugs at me, and I jump up behind him. He rides away from Phoebe's body as though he's haunted.

'It's too much,' Ollie gasps. 'It's too hard, Fern.'

'I know. We can't . . . We're not enough.'

The castle doors open and people stream through them. Thanes in tunics of every colour, clad in ill-fitting armour, charge, seeing us faltering and refusing to let us fight alone. None of them are trained warriors, though. Drew the apothecary is tossed high into the air. A flying treitre swoops down to catch him. I don't see him again.

I'm forced to cling on to Ollie as Balius dodges wildly to avoid a treitre. We come so close to it that we brush its flank as we pass. For a split second, I am jolted by a vision. A little red-headed girl, clutching a red-haired man's leg. Ollie gasps in pain, and I am back in Annwn.

'Did you see that too?' I say in his ear.

'Of course I did. That was his sister.'

Something Mum wrote springs to my mind. *As with everything that is frightening to us, the most important thing is to find out what makes it human.*

'I have an idea,' I breathe. Maybe it's not much of an idea, but it might just do the trick. It relies on these creatures having some humanity left in them, and I don't know if they do. Who knows if it can be done at all? The image of Rafe, what was left of him, discarded on a pile of corpses, flashes before me. *Deep breaths, Fern.* Phoebe, trapped, those claws in her chest, her scream, her scream, her scream.

Focus. I have to do this. For all of them.

I fixate on the treitre we just brushed past. Inspyre gathers in front of me, ready to do my bidding. I imagine the little red-haired girl – the treitre's sister – and there she is, hovering in midair. With a flick of my mind, I conjure a knife and hold it to her throat. She calls out to her brother in fear. Instantly, the treitre twists round and transforms into a burly teenager, a scar stretching from cheek to cheek. The nearby knights don't wait to ask what's going on. They pounce on the man as he runs towards his sister, his human form now no match for the knights' swords and arrows.

'*Yes!*' Ollie hisses. Something splatters onto the hand that's holding his waist. Blood. I feel my own nosebleed coming on. We have to be quick.

We move on through the battle, a group of knights shadowing us as they start to realise what we're doing. One assassin is felled by the sight of his former comrade, dressed in khakis, his head split wide open. Another rises into the air as a winged treitre, but falls to the ground as a pale woman, sobbing at the sight of her lover, his face bloody and his limbs mangled.

We are winning. Some treitres flee, choosing to abandon their job rather than risk death or, worse, coming face to face with their greatest fear. My head feels as though it's being crushed beneath Medraut's inspyre again. I can feel the blood seeping from my ears now as well as my nose. But I'm not done yet.

'Just . . . one . . . left,' I say, right before it crashes into my shoulder.

My hip explodes in pain as I am thrown from Ollie's horse and smashed against the cobbles. I curl into a foetus.

Everything is seething darkness. Then something beautiful appears through that night. The treitre that killed my mother has cornered me at last. I try to push the monster away with my power, but that rips through my head so badly that I can't help but wail.

I can feel the other knights wink back to their normal size. The treitre walks towards me slowly, like a hunter not wanting to startle its wounded prey. It slips a long claw beneath my body and scoops me up as though I weigh no more than a sparrow.

It has no breath, but its skin is hot.

I struggle, but my strength is utterly spent. Dimly, I hear Samson's roar as he throws himself uselessly at the monster.

The treitre's claws tinkle prettily, like crystal.

'Fern!' Ollie shouts. 'Think of Mum!'

Mum? She isn't here. How will she help?

'Mum is the key, Fern! Mum is the key!'

The puzzle starts to slot together.

A woman called Una Gorlois swims into focus before me. Her dark hair undulates as though she is underwater. 'My darling,' she says in her balsamic voice, and every syllable jabs through my head because I am making her say it. 'Darling, I'm so proud of you.'

The treitre pauses to study the image of my mother. Still in its grip, I watch its eyes, deep and black, and to me they seem sad. But not enough to rip through its golden skin to the human beneath.

'Fern.' Ollie is beside me. He doesn't step in front of the treitre, but he's here, with me, and that's what matters. 'Fern, do you understand?'

All that I have learned about my mother spins together at last. Morrigans, fear, regret and long-dead friends.

I claim this life for Sebastien Medraut.

This life, not this death.

Yes, I understand. I reach out, and Ollie grabs my hand. Now we know exactly what to do.

Summoning up the last vestiges of my power, I make my mother turn away from me, towards the monster.

'You've betrayed my little girl,' Mum says.

The treitre drops me and dips its head, as though it's trying not to meet Mum's eyes.

'You betrayed me,' Mum says, 'after everything I did for you.'

The treitre bows down, clawing at the floor as if desperate to burrow into the ground.

'How could you? How could you, Ellen?'

And with those words, the treitre falls to all fours and convulses. It writhes as the golden hide shrivels, as the claws recede. The skin falls off it in great, ragged flakes. As the human face emerges from beneath that deformed head, I see someone I recognise. Not a stranger called Ellen at all, but one of the few people I ever respected. Before I lose myself to the oblivion of pain, I give her a name.

Helena Corday.

52

'Hey, sis,' a sleepy voice says close by. I crack open an eye.

The bland Ithr ceilings of our local hospital are becoming a little too recognisable these days. Ollie isn't sitting beside me this time, though. He's lying in the bed next to me with his head swathed in bandages. Something thick is pressing on my forehead. My head must be bandaged too.

'What happened?' I ask groggily.

'The usual.'

'Bleeding noses and ears?'

'And eyes. Don't forget the eyes.'

'Of course.'

I try to sit up, but the back of my head pounds and I think better of it.

'How long have we been out for?'

'Most of the day.'

The events of last night come flooding back to me. Rafe, only his head recognisable. Drew, who knows how he died? And Phoebe's body, the stripes of blood on her chest, her young eyes wearily accepting. I turn my face to the wall and let the tears flow. Ollie sniffs, and I turn to see him pressing his hands into his eyes to stem his own sobs.

When my grief has hollowed me out, I reach across to my brother.

'Helena, Ollie, it was Helena,' I say.

'Ellen. Ellen Cassell.'

'She's our MP. She came to visit after . . . after the fire.'

'What?'

'She seemed . . . good,' I say, more to myself than Ollie. It doesn't make sense. She was supposed to be fighting Medraut.

'She must have changed her name,' Ollie says, 'or maybe she always had different names in Ithr and Annwn, like Ramesh.'

'How did you realise?' I say.

'I wasn't certain,' Ollie admits, 'but the feeling I had when I was inside her memory of killing Mum was so weird. It was like she hated her and loved her all at the same time. I know something about that.'

He looks at me guiltily.

'Then last night I remembered you talking to Lord Allenby about how close Mum was to Ellen.'

I nod. 'I remembered that no one saw Ellen being killed, and she was the first one. She must have faked her own death.'

Ollie nods, but before we can unpick the mystery further, the door opens and my dad enters bearing two cardboard cups. Clemmie is right behind him, clutching a barrage of *Get Well Soon* balloons.

'Ols, I got us hot chocolates –' Dad sees that I'm awake and breaks into a grin. 'Ferny! Here, have mine.'

'It's okay, Dad. Fern and I can share.'

I look across at Ollie. He smirks back. Bastard. He knows

that sharing and chocolate don't go together in my vocabulary.

'Sure.'

Dad looks from Ollie to me and back again. Then he sets the cups down on the table between us and goes to the window, where he rubs his eyes vigorously.

'Let me get the doctor,' Clemmie says and potters out of the room.

I don't think I've ever felt such a mix of emotions in one day. When he finally gets us signed out of hospital, Dad seems so overjoyed that his children are speaking to each other that he infects Ollie and I with a manic happiness. Even Clemmie is only mildly annoying.

Once Dad's forced some food into us, we persuade him to turn on the news. Of course, we already know what's going to be the leading story.

The anchor looks sombre. 'More devastation swept the nation this morning as hundreds were found dead in their beds. Nearly four hundred lives were lost in similar circumstances just a few months ago in March. The latest deaths, which current estimates suggest are close to a thousand, could indicate a trend that scientists are calling a "tragic phenomenon".'

Nearly a thousand dead. All for the sake of Sebastien Medraut's lust for power.

It's with some relief that Ollie and I bid Dad goodnight.

'Sleep well.' Ollie smiles up at me, then grimaces and puts a hand to his head. Dad follows him into his room, and Clemmie helps me up the stairs to my bed. She tucks me in and squeezes my hand before she turns the light out.

Ollie and I land in Annwn at the same time. It feels so strange to be back here, when only yesterday we were surrounded by the carnage and noise and the smell of battle. I go to the place where Phoebe died and kneel. This time I forbid the memory of her final seconds, and force myself to remember her alive instead – quiet but confident, warm but strong. The kind of woman I wish I could have been.

'Fern? Let's go.' Ollie is still on edge, perhaps not quite believing that the treitres have truly gone.

The castle is silent. Thanes approach us to squeeze our shoulders or shake our hands. Rachel folds me into a hug and we just stand there, in the middle of the courtyard, quietly crying into each other's necks.

Samson finds me before long. He holds me at arm's length and smiles sadly. He lost more friends last night than I did. It's only now that I realise that Rafe was always by his side – his absence is a sort of kalend. 'You really are extraordinary, Fern King,' Samson tells me, but I ignore the compliment. If I were that extraordinary, Tintagel wouldn't feel so unbearably empty.

'Did you get her?' I ask him.

'Who?'

'Helena – Ellen.'

'Oh yes,' Samson says darkly. 'Lord Allenby wants you and Ollie to be with him when he talks to her.'

We follow Samson down to the lower levels. The barred door to the dungeons is unlocked. Inside, a damp, bleak space is lit only by candles. Lord Allenby sits in silence on a wooden bench at the entrance. When he gets up to greet us he looks more tired than ever.

'I'm glad you're feeling well enough to join me for this,

Fern, Ollie.' We pass a series of thick, anonymous doors that line each side of the corridor. I catch glimpses of other treitres inside each one, most of them in their human forms. One or two stare at me curiously, or with anger. Others look utterly defeated. Allenby unlocks the furthest one.

Helena Corday is chained to the wall by her hands and feet. Her hair is just as dark, her face just as delicate as it is in real life. Yet something is different. Then I see what it is. There is no fear or concern in her expression.

'Hello, Ellen,' Lord Allenby says.

'Lionel.' She smiles thinly.

'I thought you were dead.'

'You were meant to.'

'What did you do with Clement's body, Ellen?'

'I threw it into the Thames.'

Lord Allenby stares at her in disgust. 'He was your friend.'

Ellen stares at me, but says nothing. It's me who breaks the silence. 'I think I understand why,' I say.

She raises an eyebrow, permitting me to speak. 'You didn't belong in the knights. You were scared all the time. And Mum promised you that she'd find a way to help you, so you'd fit in.'

Ellen nods. I'm now entering shaky territory, feeling my way as I go.

'She was researching morrigans. She wanted to see whether they could be used to remove whole emotions.' I look at Lord Allenby and Ollie. 'Samson thought about removing self-hatred, to combat a poisoner.' I turn back to Ellen. 'But what if Mum wanted to remove something else? What if she wanted to take away all of your fear?'

'Go on,' Ellen says.

'I don't know exactly what happened next, except it went really wrong. Mum was upset about it but she didn't say exactly what happened in her diaries.'

Ollie chimes in, '*Too much fear turns us to stone, but not enough and we are no longer human*.'

I nod. '*It's all going wrong*, she wrote. You weren't the same person afterwards, were you?'

Ellen smiles at Lord Allenby. 'Shall I show them?'

'No,' Lord Allenby says, stepping forward.

'I can't hurt them now. The boy has the power, doesn't he?'

Ollie tentatively takes Ellen's hand. I grasp his wrist and am immediately thrown into an anonymous London street.

The first shock is seeing my mother alive, younger than she'd been in the memory of her murder. The portrait from the archives didn't do her justice. She is beautiful, yes, but there's an intriguing hardness to her as well. She's spiky, I realise, like her handwriting. With a rush of affection I suddenly, strangely understand exactly why she fell in love with my soft, devoted Dad.

She's watching me – Ellen – eagerly. Next to her are two men. One I recognise as a younger, clean-shaven Lord Allenby. It's so strange seeing them together. In my head Mum has been frozen at twenty-seven years old. Eternally young. But Lord Allenby looks so much younger than he does now. I don't recognise their companion – a stocky, brown-haired man – but I guess that this is Clement Rigby.

A morrigan is feeding on Ellen – on me – piercing the skin just beneath the collarbone. I can't feel that needle-like beak, but a sense of bliss washes over me. Then the morrigan finishes, sated, withdraws from my skin and takes flight. Ellen turns to my mother.

'How do you feel?' Mum says.

'Incredible,' Ellen replies. She looks down, almost without thinking, at the fang tucked into her belt. She removes it. 'Shall we go hunting?'

My mother smiles, and Allenby and Clement cheer and clap her on the back. Ellen doesn't want their congratulations, though. She wants to ride this feeling of control. She begins to run, outstripping the others, even Mum. It doesn't take them long to find some targets – werewolves attacking a young dreamer. The others ready their weapons but Ellen stops them. 'Let me try.'

Ellen throws herself into the fray. I know she's being reckless, but seeing all this from inside her body gives me an inkling of how she feels. She doesn't care. She is totally fearless. She's enjoying her work.

Her fang slashes left and right as she whirls between the werewolves, not caring about the flesh they rip from her moving form when they catch her. At first I think, *Good for her*. It reminds me of the adrenalin rush I got after saving that little girl from the wolf-children. But then Ellen's movements take on a more worrying edge. It's like being in the passenger seat of a car going too fast. She starts to prolong the deaths, getting so caught up in her newfound bravery that she's forgetting what's important. The dreamer, the young man, is still fighting one last werewolf.

Ellen stabs the werewolf in the back and hauls it off the

boy. Clement cheers, but Mum sees what's about to happen.

'No, Ellen!' she shouts. 'Not him!'

But it's too late. Ellen raises that long fang and stabs down, again and again, into the boy's stomach, his chest, his neck, until he's nothing but a pincushion of blood. Mum is screaming, grabbing Ellen round the waist, trying to pull her back, shouting, '*Not him*!' over and over. Lord Allenby is trying to wrestle the weapon from her grasp. Clement just sinks to the ground in shock.

Gradually, Ellen comes back to herself, panting fiercely, eyes wide, already looking for her next target. 'Did I get them all?' she keeps saying. 'I got them all, I did it, I did it, I did it, did you see me do it?' As her breathing slows, she looks down and sees the dreamer lying in his own blood. She looks at the fang in Lionel's hand, comprehension dawning. The only sounds are of the man's ragged final breaths, and of Mum sobbing as she grasps her friend round the waist, half hugging, half imprisoning her.

I pull out of the memory at the same time as Ollie. We look in horror at Lord Allenby. He avoids our stares, but says, 'No one ever found out what we did. They just learned that a dreamer had died on our watch. We were all called into Lady Caradoc's office to answer for what happened. Una took the blame for it. She said she'd distracted everyone. She accepted the punishment for all of us.'

'She made you pay for it, though, didn't she?' I say. 'She demanded a debt.'

'You were wrong about one thing, Lionel,' Ellen says. 'Sebastien found out what happened that night.'

'He read your memories?' I ask.

'Yes. Una warned me about that, but I didn't care. That's the problem with not feeling fear any more.' She looks at Lord Allenby. 'I think you all knew what you'd done to me. You started distancing yourselves from me after that night, apart from Una.'

'I didn't mean to –' Lord Allenby starts, but Ellen interrupts him. Her features are twisted into a smile, but I can't see any emotion behind it.

'I didn't think I belonged before and after that night I definitely didn't. I couldn't feel fear any more. I couldn't doubt myself. I was halfway a treitre before Sebastien ever learned what I'd done and offered to help me complete the transformation.'

'But why, Ellen?' Lord Allenby says. 'What happened with that dreamer was . . . You were never a murderer.'

'He offered me a second chance. He said that if I joined his cause he would give my life back to me.'

'What do you mean?' I ask.

When Ellen speaks it is with such quiet dignity that I almost feel sorry for her. 'You will never understand how lonely it is to have no fear. At the end, when all was done, after I'd killed for him in Annwn and spied for him in Ithr, Sebastien was going to return it to me. He was going to allow me to live as I used to –'

'But you know that's not possible,' I interrupt. 'You know what he's planning on doing to Annwn – you wouldn't be able to live like you used to. You'd just be one of his zombies like everyone else.'

Ellen turns her head away, like she doesn't want to hear it.

'Does it matter, as long as *she* believes it?' Lord Allenby parrots Medraut's line. And I see that he's right. Ellen had to believe that Medraut would make this happen for her. By the time she realised he was lying, she had done too much to turn back.

'That doesn't explain why you killed Mum,' Ollie says. 'She'd retired from the thanes. She wasn't a threat to Medraut any more.'

'She was,' Ellen says, and this time there's real pain behind her words. It's the first time she's shown any true emotion. 'She was more of a threat than ever. Why couldn't she have stayed out of it? Why did she have to go looking? She told me that she'd found something that would defeat Medraut forever. I thought she'd stop looking for it when she resigned, but she kept coming back to Annwn.'

'Looking? For what?' Lord Allenby says.

But Ellen doesn't reply. Lord Allenby goes to the door. 'I'm sorry, Ellen,' he says. 'I'm so sorry for what we did to you. I hope you know that we just wanted to help you. I'll try to help you again now, but in return you'll need to tell us what you know.'

Ollie and I follow Lord Allenby to the door. I look back before I leave.

'When you messaged me I thought you were being cruel. But you weren't, were you? You were asking for forgiveness.'

Ellen stares at me. 'I don't know any more. Nothing seems to have purpose when you can't be afraid of the consequences.'

I make to leave.

'Wait!'

She is standing now.

'If I'd known . . .' she falters.

'Known what?'

'Do you think you could have helped me? If I had waited . . . If I'd known you had Immral too?'

I shrug. 'What does it matter now?'

She smiles shakily. 'You're right. It's done. It's all done now.'

I should despise her, but all I can feel is pity.

Lord Allenby is waiting for me upstairs.

'What did she say?' he asks.

'Nothing that makes a difference.'

Lord Allenby signals Ollie and I to follow him to his office, but before we go far there's a shout from below, then the sound of crunching metal and wood. A reeve staggers up the stairs. His face is covered in scratch marks and his nose is broken. 'She's gone!' he gasps. 'Ellen Cassell's escaped. She's gone up to the eyrie.'

Allenby, Ollie and I look at each other in horror. We know what this means. I race ahead of the others, half flying, half leaping up steps. The eyrie door has been hauled open. I hear someone protesting, and then a shout of alarm. I round the final corner to see a veneur collapsed on the steps outside the eyrie.

'She's crazy!' he splutters. 'She's going to upset them all!'

'That's the point,' I say softly, walking to the door.

Inside, Ellen is twirling around and around, flinging the hoods from the morrigans and chasing them from their perches.

'Ellen!' Lord Allenby shouts. 'Please don't do this!'

But she doesn't answer him. The air inside the eyrie is a tornado of bat-like wings and sharp beaks. They whirl around her and she stretches out her arms, inviting them in. One by one, they land. On her shoulders, her chest, her hair. They stab their beaks into her legs, her arms, the soft flesh at her throat. They begin to feed.

I cannot look away. Her eyes are closed at first, but then they open and find mine. We stay like that for a long time. Veneurs gather behind me in the doorway, but there's nothing anyone can do for her now.

I can no longer see Ellen clearly beneath the flock of morrigans. Then I realise that I can't see her because she is fading away, blurring like a badly taken photograph.

Something brushes against my arm. Ollie's hand is there, open. He is offering it to me as a comfort. I take it.

Ellen is very faint now, translucent as a ghost. Then she disappears forever.

53

October 1993

Una trailed the other knights as they filed towards the portal that would take them from Stonehenge back to Tintagel. She played with her new weapon, not really looking where she was going. A sharp little knife. It was less elegant than she'd imagined any weapon of hers being. Still, it was beautifully crafted, whoever or whatever had crafted it – she still wanted to find out exactly how that worked. Was it wholly her imagination that had made those little grooves in one side of the blade? Or was some outside force, some judging god trying to tell her what kind of person she really was?

It was the first time she'd felt uneasy since the white light had called her from her bedroom to the platform outside Tintagel. When she'd seen it, she had felt only intrigue and excitement. It was obvious that the light wasn't trying to hurt her, so the logical alternative was that it was offering her an adventure, and Una never said no to an adventure. When the old woman, Lady Caradoc, had explained the truth and shown them some of what Annwn could do, she had felt like punching the air in triumph. Una loved a conspiracy, loved a secret society, and now she was inside one.

'Do you need a hand?' an eager-looking boy asked her. She took him in. She remembered seeing him recruited into the reeves. Not interesting, not interested.

'I'm fine, thanks.' He dallied next to her, so she had to pointedly say, 'You go ahead.'

This was the problem with groups of people her own age. They had a tendency to want to make friends indiscriminately, just so that they could be seen to have friends. It was as though they thought they were in a game of musical chairs and none of them wanted to be the person left standing when the music stopped. Una wasn't worried about that. She could click her fingers and conjure up as many friends as she pleased. No, she would choose the people she was interested in, and in her own time.

'Leave me alone,' she heard someone saying from a little further ahead. It was a timid voice but the words were strong. The girl who had spoken was crumpled on one side of the pathway, clutching something in her hands. The eager boy was hovering over her, wanting to be helpful. Idiot. Anyone could see the girl just wanted some space.

'Making a habit of pestering young women, are you?' Una said, more sharply than she'd intended. The boy scurried off.

Una watched the other girl from a distance. She didn't seem to want to engage with Una either, so Una stayed where she was.

'You're a knight, too, aren't you?' the girl said. She looked up from a tear-stained face and Una suddenly recognised her. She was a mousy little thing, with unremarkable shoulder-length hair and eyes that squinted in a way that told Una she wore glasses in Ithr. There was a desperation in her expression that almost made Una walk on.

'You were amazing, the way you just knew what to do when that man attacked you. And volunteering to go first? I couldn't ever be that brave.'

Una shrugged. A suck-up. Great. Now, how to get out of this before the girl assumed a friendship that Una no longer wanted?

Suddenly, Una became aware of someone behind her. She knew immediately who it was, without needing to turn around. When they'd been waiting to take the Tournament almost every eye had been dragged towards him. When he'd shaken her hand upon joining the knights, her whole body seemed to vibrate. She didn't like it. No one should be able to command that kind of control over anyone without their consent. It made him dangerous.

'Medraut.' She acknowledged the boy as he came to stand over the girl. His friends loitered at a distance.

'Ellen, wasn't it?' he asked the girl. She nodded, as captivated by his violet eyes as everyone else.

'Better try to buck up,' he said. He indicated her weapon, which Una now saw was a huge fang, something that had once belonged to a dragon or an anaconda. 'You've got to try to live up to that, haven't you?'

Although his voice and expression were kind, Una bridled at the undercurrent of mockery. She wanted to say something, but for once her spirit deserted her.

But Una didn't need to say anything, because Ellen had

sensed Medraut's tone as well. Her eyes sparked. She opened her mouth in a thin grimace, and she hissed at him. A proper, melodramatic, snake hiss, to match the fang she was holding.

Medraut took an involuntary step back. Una laughed.

'See you back in Tintagel then,' he told her, walking on.

Una stepped forward and offered Ellen her hand.

'I've decided something,' Una said.

'What?' Ellen said, allowing Una to pull her up.

'You're going to be my friend,' Una replied. 'My best friend. Okay?'

And she led Ellen back to the portal, tucking the other girl's arm inside her elbow, like a gentleman leading a lady to a dance.

54

The next few nights are a series of bittersweet events. Natasha taking me out for a gallop, away from London's nightmares and out across vast meadows teeming with fairies, past ancient villages where thatched cottages sprout golden flowers, all the way to the coast where Lamb and Domino paddle in the mouth of the sea. Samson appointing Ollie and I joint second in commands of Bedevere. Dad going all out with the cooking to make some of my favourite dishes. He seems to have taken my collapse as a sign that I'm not eating well enough, and I'm not complaining.

But the best moment of all is when Ollie approaches me in the knights' chamber one night.

'I lied to you,' he says. 'That night when we found Mum's research? I said that the shelf in the wall was empty, but it wasn't. There was one thing on it.'

He hands me a sealed letter with my name scrawled on the front in Mum's handwriting.

'Why didn't you tell me?'

He shifts guiltily. 'I wanted to see if there was another one . . . I was going to use it to get you to come back if the messages from the others didn't work, but then you agreed and . . .'

He peters off. There it is. That particular type of jealousy that I thought only I really understood.

'You can be mad with me,' he says.

Once upon a time, not so long ago, I would have been.

'No,' I say. 'You've done a lot of shit, unforgivable things over the last few years. But this isn't one of them.'

I open the letter when I'm on my own.

Dearest Fern, it reads.

I am dead. I must be, for you to be reading this. To be truthful, I'm lucky to have survived this long.

My darling baby girl, I wanted so much to watch you grow up. But I have dangerous work to do. You will understand by now that sometimes we must put ourselves in harm's way for the sake of finding the truth.

I don't know if you know the extent of your abilities yet, but I want you to always, always be searching for ways to be strong. You may need to finish the work that I have begun. I have left a gift for you in Annwn. King Arthur's sword – Excalibur. I found it and have hidden it for you to use, when the time is right. If you have found this letter, you will have found the first clue and be on the path already.

I love you, my Fern, my beloved. I had always thought that your father was the love of my life, but then you arrived. Be strong, be dangerous, be curious, my daughter. Go after what you believe in with determination and ruthlessness. If you do that, you will always have me with you.

Mummy

* * *

I tell Ollie about Excalibur, and we spend many a morning walk talking about where we might find clues, what the sword might do if we find it. Most of all, we ask ourselves whether this is the item that had made Ellen and Medraut so worried; whether if Mum hadn't been so set on finding Excalibur she would have been allowed to live. That's something that I worry at, like a mouth ulcer. Was this gift, meant for me, the reason for her death?

I don't mention the rest of Mum's message to Ollie. It would only hurt him. I fold it up and keep it in my tunic, close to me whenever I start to think about how Rafe and Ramesh and Phoebe's deaths are my fault. It is another of my weapons, every bit as powerful as my scimitar or my diamond marbles. Once, a long time ago, I was the most beloved.

As school winds up for the year, I realise that Lottie has been spreading rumours about me. She doesn't say anything in front of me, but I spot her casting significant glances at her friends when I'm around. I can't be angry with her. I know it is her father making her do these things, and of course I feel that I deserve it, even though she does not know what I've done. Sometimes I think about the way Medraut was willing to hurt his own daughter just to entrap me, and I can't help but pity her.

'We've got a long battle ahead of us to bring him down,' Lord Allenby said one night as he addressed the surviving knights. 'He was caught off guard because he's never faced anyone with a modicum of his power before. He'd become complacent. But he won't make the same mistake again. We have to be ready for his next move, whatever it is.'

The thanes of Glastonbury report a sighting of Medraut near the Tor, not long after his treitres were defeated. So he found a new portal sooner than we'd hoped; illegal ones are even harder to come by than legal ones, but his kind of wealth and power can buy almost anything. At least he is keeping away from London for now. Even though we managed to stop the total slaughter that Medraut had planned for that night, the thousand deaths achieves something of the result he was looking for. In the wake of the national outpouring of grief, Sebastien Medraut is constantly there, a reassuring presence, promising answers and subtly laying the blame at the feet of those of us who don't fit in.

The sense of dread that he has been seeding over the last year is having a catastrophic effect on people's dreams. As he attacks their ability to imagine any world but the one he paints for them, their inspyre dwindles. Now, instead of walking through blue air wherever I go, inspyre lurks in frightened clumps, desperate for a dreamer who is still able to give it form. Annwn is crumbling. No angels now fly above Tintagel's towers. No great oak trees dig their roots deep into the castle's foundations.

Sometimes I spot Medraut picking up Lottie in the car park after school, playing the doting father. One afternoon he catches my eye as I head out, hoodie already on in the blazing heat. I pause, wondering what to do. Ramesh, Phoebe and the others flash through my mind, as they tend to do at least a dozen times every day. So too do the treitres I helped to kill.

I cannot quite shake the expression of the man whose little red-haired sister I slaughtered before his eyes. I made his worst nightmare come true in his final moments. Medraut made me do it, I keep telling myself. I had no other choice.

I take my anger and my grief in my hands and change direction to pass him as he opens the driver's door.

'Hello, Mr Medraut.' I smile, imagining how crazy Lottie must think I am as she sits in the passenger seat.

'Good afternoon – Fern, was it?' He does a good impression of looking as though he only vaguely recognises me.

'That's right. I'm surprised you remember, since you're so busy reassuring people about these deaths.'

'I'm surprised you're not more frightened about it. Isn't your age group the most at risk?'

'Oh, I am frightened,' I tell him, 'but a bit of fear's healthy, isn't it? It warns you not to underestimate people. That was Helena Corday's problem, I think. It's a problem you have too, isn't it?'

I don't wait to hear his answer. I've got somewhere to be.

I meet Dad and Ollie in Victoria Park, where they're waiting next to an ice-cream van. We wander past Mum's old flat again, and then Clemmie joins us and we meander slowly through the park and back towards Clemmie's house in Wanstead. She's cooking us her famous Moroccan chicken tonight. I'm not sure what makes it famous. Maybe she puts extra olives in it.

As Dad and Clemmie fall behind, Ollie and I walk side by side in silence.

'I can't help but feel sorry for Ellen – Helena – whatever

her name was,' Ollie says after a while, with a glance behind us to make sure Dad can't hear.

'I don't. Whatever happened back then, it doesn't make it okay for her to kill all those people.'

Helena's breakdown was second-rate news compared to all the deaths. She's been removed from her position and put in care. The morrigans took everything. All her imagination, her dreams, her ambitions – her ability to come back to Annwn. They took her soul.

'She wanted to be strong, like Mum,' Ollie says, 'but she didn't understand that having doubts about yourself doesn't make you weak. It makes you human. It's a mistake a lot of people make. It doesn't make what she did right. I'm just saying I can understand how she got that way.'

'Yeah, but just because she felt like she didn't belong doesn't mean it's okay for her to do what she did.'

We consider each other's words.

'Hang on, do you think you're Ellen in this scenario?' Ollie says.

'Well, *you're* not Ellen, are you?' I say.

'Yes, I am.'

'No, *I* am!'

We stop, register that we're both fighting to be compared to a serial killer, and walk on more companionably. So Ollie thought he was like Ellen too. That's what's inside his head: insecurity and inadequacy. All the things I've been feeling for years, he's been feeling too. We just had very different ways of dealing with it.

Wanstead Flats is up ahead. I can sense three pairs of eyes

watching me uneasily, gauging whether I'm going to have a meltdown at the prospect of passing the place where I almost died two years ago.

'I think it's time for an exorcism, don't you?' I say loudly, breaking from the road and striding towards the trees.

'Fern? Where are you going?' Dad calls as Ollie tramps after me.

I turn back to him and raise my arms triumphantly. 'I'm a witch, don'tcha know, Dad! With powers beyond your wildest dreams! Let's see what I can do with them.'

I run towards the trees, feeling the strength in my legs and the wind in my lungs. The nightmares held within the shadows are still there, but I run towards them anyway, because now I know I'm not facing them alone.

Acknowledgements

The other day I looked back over my computer files and realised that it's taken nearly a decade for Fern's story to reach this point. While that says rather a lot about my powers of procrastination, I know that the process would have taken a lot longer without the guidance and support of many kind, clever and generous people.

My first thanks must go to my agent, Anna Dixon at WME, who read the first few pages of an early draft and has been my cheerleader ever since. Thank you, Anna, for dealing with my neuroses with patience and humour, and for always having my back.

Thank you to Georgia Murray, my Head Thane, otherwise known as my editor at Hot Key Books. You have pushed me to explore Annwn and Fern's journey more thoroughly than I ever thought possible, and the book is so much stronger for it. I knew from our first meeting when you arrived armed with about a million questions that I would be in good hands.

To the rest of the team at Hot Key and Bonnier – Jane Harris, Emma Matthewson and Jenny Jacoby in editorial; Lizz Skelly, Amy Llambias and Molly Holt in marketing and PR – thank you for taking a chance on a new, green writer. And thanks too to Melissa Hyder and Jane Burnard for their copy editing and proofreading brilliance.

To Simon Trewin for seeing the book over the finish line, and to Helen Trewin for being the first person to bring Fern and Annwn to life.

To Gavin Reece, illustrator extraordinaire, and Sophie McDonnell at Bonnier, for creating the cover of my dreams.

To Hilary Zaitz-Michael, Melissa Myers, Janine Kamouh and Laura Bonner at WME for taking the book overseas and answering my endless questions with endless grace.

To Joanna Briscoe, my Faber tutor, who gave me the courage to pursue this beyond the first chapter and to Molly Ker Hawn, who gave me my first invaluable feedback on the book and told me to join a writing group – the best advice I've received by far! To Robert Thorogood for taking my shy mention of book writing seriously and introducing me to Molly – thank you.

Speaking of writing groups – there are not enough nice things to be said about my Faber Academy gang. Amberley, Annie, Charlotte, Clio, Chris, David, Ilaria, Jo, Nancy, Sabina, Smita, Tommy, Trayner and Wendy: your unwavering support over these last few years has been so appreciated. See you at the Heights?

To the Savvy Writers' Snug, thank you for the advice and thank you for the therapy.

To Helen Bartlett, thank you for your Agatha Christie eye and your history books!

To Shefali Malhoutra, the most brilliant boss a woman could wish for, and now a treasured friend.

I have never regretted being an only child, but there were

times when I was a little older than Fern that I felt extremely lonely. Then I found a group of friends who have become my brothers and sisters, whose quiet (and at times not so quiet) encouragement I couldn't do without. So thank you to all of you, lindy hoppers and techies, Cambridge-ites and Orielenses, TV scripties and theatre luvvies – you know who you are.

To the Brie Bunch – Chris, Simon and our ever-missed Ros – thank you for Paris and all the cheese.

To my parents, Louette and Bob: I didn't realise it growing up, but you gave me gifts that so few children are granted – encouragement to be creative, and unconditional support. Knowing that you'd back me in giving up a 'proper' career to write means the world. For that and for so many other things, thank you forever.

And finally to my husband Alex, who is my better half by far. Thank you, darling, for the coffees, the shoulders, the eggs Benedicts, the DIY, the late-night feeds, the lifts, the hugs, the debates, the dancing, the laughter. Thank you for our daughter. Thank you for the adventures. Thank you for your love.

Holly Race

Holly Race worked as a development executive in the film and TV industry until she became a writer, although she still dabbles in script editing. She is a Faber Academy graduate, and *Midnight's Twins* is her debut novel and the first in a trilogy. She used to live in Fern's neck of the woods, but now resides in Cambridge with her husband and daughter.